PRAISE FOR

"*Ristenoff* comes out of the gates on a mission, snarling right along with the best of the Werewolf horrors that returned in vogue recently. Billingsley weaves his tale beautifully, equally comfortable waxing through the subtle terrors of small town pandemic living as he is waning through his bouts of violence, bearing his fangs and going for your throat with his sickeningly wonderful splashes of full-mooned savagery."

— William Sterling, author of *String Them Up*
and *Latchkey Monsters*

"Jeremy Billingsley's *Ristenoff* is a toothsome, bloody werewolf tale that tears at the flesh and the heartstrings!"

— Jendia Gammon, Nebula and BSFA Award Finalist author
of *Doomflower* and *The Shadow Galaxy*

"Jeremy Billingsley's *Ristenoff* opens with snapping jaws and gore, pulling the reader in from the first page for a sweeping story covering generations and curses both ancient and contemporary, set against a backdrop of political unrest. An epic tale of love, loss, and werewolves, peopled by sympathetic and complex characters, *Ristenoff* takes its place among must-reads in the genre of shifters."

— Laurel Hightower, author of *Below*

ALSO BY

J.R. BILLINGSLEY

A Mind Full of Scorpions (Eyes Only, Book One)
Observations and Nightmares: The Short Fiction of J.R. Billingsley
Under the Churchyard in the Chamber of Bone

Content warnings are available at the end of this book. Please consult this list for any particular subject matter you may be sensitive to.

RISTENOFF

J.R. BILLINGSLEY

ISBN: 978-1-957941-10-3

Book cover and interior illustrations by Ranxvrus

Interior design by Dreadful Designs

Edited by Lillian Ehrhart

First Edition

2025

To Kerri, for believing in me.
To Shadow, for being the best good boi ever.
For C, we love you son.

I am not what I am.

—*Othello*, Shakespeare

⠴⠦

Oh! the opium-sweet attraction of death!

—*The Werewolf of Paris*, Guy Endore

CHAPTER ONE

*C*hristmas *Eve, ten years ago:*
      I checked the lock.

Sam could hear it stalking about upstairs. It would stop and sniff the air, then cross the wooden floorboards. He could hear a lot, actually. The pipe ringing from the steady drip of some spreading moisture across the subfloor. The whimpering of the younger children. The creak of the floorboards, shedding motes of dust as weight shifted above, redistributing mass towards its inevitable encounter with him. His wife tried with futility to silence her own cries. He shushed them over his shoulder but dared not take his eyes off the ceiling and the path of the sound.

The steps above stopped. There came a snort.

Bits of sawdust rained down over him. His skin was slick, so the sawdust stuck to him like powder. He wanted to wipe his palms of the sweat but it would mean letting loose the shotgun, and he wasn't prepared to do that.

Behind him, the sounds quieted. Like penitents, his wife and children all were waiting for a sign from above. Never a religious man, Sam stifled a maniacal laugh at this. Barbara was religious. She'd prayed for boys every Sunday in church back when they were trying, and she sure got her wish. Seven of them. Though, if he were to believe the stories about his family, this wasn't the first time the Ristens had been "blessed."

"Sam," she whispered loudly from behind. He removed his hand from the pump of the twelve-gauge just long enough to wave her off. She was more than just religious, he thought, and stepped over the gas tank and then the mower and positioned himself at the bottom of the stairs leading up. She was prescient. The door was locked, but it was cheaply built and wouldn't hold. If *it* discovered they were down here, that lock would not hold. When *it* had sprung, when the glass had exploded inward and it had burst into the kitchen, an answer to Barbara's question before he could even open his mouth— *"Are you sure you locked the chains?"* she had asked—he had discovered just how worthless locks were.

"I checked the lock," he mumbled, gripping the gun tightly.

"Sam," she said again from behind him. *It.* How could he refer to it so coldly? A growl from above answered. Reminded him that what stalked the floor over their heads in no way resembled this innocent boy he loved.

TJ—Timothy James—had been closest. So close he threw up a hand to shield himself from the glass shards, so he wasn't able to see, like the rest of them, what had crashed through into the kitchen. He couldn't see it, so he couldn't react. Couldn't even scream, as it were.

Just let out a grunt as it drove the claws of one hand into his stomach and out his back, spine in hand, its sharp-toothed muzzle latching around his throat and ripping away bits of cartilage, the jugular, some muscle. Blood sprayed everywhere. The rest of them stayed where they were, frozen by the horror. Barbara had been next closest, rinsing dishes at the sink. She'd just called the question over her shoulder as a matter of habit, like she did nearly every night, while she loaded the dishwasher, fending off a question by TJ about some drive to Little Rock he'd wanted to take with his friends that weekend, when all hell broke loose.

"My son," Sam had only managed to say, before their instincts activated and Barbara just barely missed being tackled by the thing as it crashed into the cabinets and sink, knocking doors loose, sending a spray of water against the wall, nearly tearing away the peninsula of cabinets and the uppers that mirrored them, and Sam snatched the shotgun off the mount over the fireplace mantle and they all retreated to the cellar.

They had never wanted to use the twelve-gauge, but it had hung there loaded, like an extinguisher behind a glass panel. *"Break in case of emergency."* Well, it was a fucking emergency.

Sam wetted his lips as the footsteps resumed through the rooms of the house, across molded carpet pads and failing plywood and subfloors. Living room. Hall. Den. Stop. He felt it. It was looking at the door. Looking at him *through* the door. There was no indication of this from above. Above it was silent. But he just knew.

"Sam," his wife whispered.

He dare not take a hand off the shotgun to wave her off. Just shook his head. *Please be quiet*, he willed. Sweat stung his eyes.

"You can't do it," she said.

"But it killed TJ," he managed. He dare not take his eyes off that door fifteen steps over him. God, how many times had he taken those steps mindlessly before all this? For a lot of years, he hadn't bothered to know how many steps led from the cellar to the first floor. Now, since all this started, he knew. Fifteen.

"It?" she questioned. He knew what she meant. *It* had a name, and he knew it. His eldest stepped forward, brandishing the one thing he'd grabbed before they'd all made a bee-line for the cellar: the fireplace poker.

Sam Jr. nodded in short, quick bursts, bobbing his head. His chin, the way his blonde hair bounced soft like down in response to the movement, reminded Sam of himself. The young man was a spitting image. "I'm here, Dad," he said, clenching the poker. He'd been away at advanced training, having graduated boot camp just a week earlier, on furlough for a bit and so had made his way home this weekend to see his family.

Stupid, stupid boy, Sam thought. *You could have been the one. After all this, you could have been the one.* Where that thought came from, Sam wasn't sure, but the thing above roared.

Silence for a beat, enough for Sam to snatch a deep breath, and then, as if in response, a growl rose. The door vibrated. A sound like thunder rolled through the house. *Here it comes*, Sam thought, his sweaty palms keeping the best hold they could on the shotgun which he was sure would slip out at any minute. And then, a question. Could he shoot? Really? Knowing what *it* was. Knowing even what *it* did to TJ. When *it* burst through the door, could he pull the trigger?

As it was, he'd never get the chance to answer, or even evaluate that idea. There came a sound like a great thud, and the door quivered then gave, popping off its hinges and sliding down the stairs, a melody of splitting wood and snapping metal screws rising to crescendo. Standing above in the frame, the thing black, its eyes yellow. Sam thought crazily that such horrors should be contained in the shadows, but here it was in bright light, staring down on them, wearing the mask of a wolf's head, but the fur-covered body was more misshapen. It crouched and snarled, taking them all in. From where it perched, Sam knew it could see him and Sam Jr., but maybe his wife and the other boys were hidden enough, he thought, a last grasp for hope that was, he realized quickly, futile. It bared its fangs. It was so large. It. It. No, it had a name. *My...*Sam thought, in that brief second where he could think.

The thing with a name leapt. Sam Jr. jammed the poker upward, missing the beast's torso as it twisted in the air before crashing into the laundry machines behind, crumpling them at impact. But the young man wasn't unhurt. His blood sprayed across Sam's cheeks, little droplets dotting his father's face. Sam turned, shotgun still in hand, watching the beast rise with a growl and bark and leap and rip into flesh, listening to his family scream.

I checked the lock?

More a question than an assurance. Because if he'd really checked the lock, this would not be happening. To his left, Sam Jr.'s body lay crumpled near the stairs. His head, severed almost completely at the throat, lay cockeyed from the body, looking up to the ceiling. More blood sprayed on him, like he was on the bridge overlooking the most nightmare plume ride ever. The screams were intermixed with pleading and bargaining, but they were growing fainter as more bodies were violently dissected.

Sam held the shotgun, staring at the scene unfolding before him. Young Joseph sprinted for him, reaching out a hand, screaming and crying. Sam bit a lip and retreated a step up the stairs. Joseph was yanked back into the smoldering dark mess of blood and screams and murder. His eyes were so wide with fear. As Christopher was yanked from his mother's blood-spattered arms, his throat ripped out with its teeth, Barb looked to her husband to do something, anything. But the gun was a lead weight in his hands. Useless. He'd placed too much faith in its power. She was right. He couldn't shoot this thing because he knew, under its mask, what it was. Who it was. And he knew for certain he hadn't checked the lock.

Peter and Joseph lay huddled together. The gash running up Joseph's cheek and scalp gaped wide like a canyon and Peter's left arm had been tossed into the shadows while his shoulder fountained blood, but they were both alive. For now. That thing would make short work of them, even as it ripped Barbara's tits off her torso and squeezed them like fruit juice bottles, shooting blood into its yawning maw. She collapsed, reaching for the monster, unable in her dying moments to salve her caring.

Sam took another step back up the stairs as his son Paul screamed. He was on the other side of the stairs, and though blood-covered, he was otherwise relatively unscathed. Paul, a great student and on the honor roll in high school, a terrific writer and on the swim team. Of the seven boys, he had definite promise. Concrete aspirations. "Daddy," he said, reaching up for Sam.

The thing's face turned, directing a snarl up at Sam. Peter and Joseph cried out. Paul's hand quivered. "Daddy, please," he said. Was it smiling? He thought so. Cradling the shotgun, Sam retreated another step, as he read the thing's smile. *Go on up*, it suggested. *I'll finish with them and join you momentarily.*

He remembered the births of each of the boys then. Sam Jr. had squalled. TJ had what sounded like a whooping cough, and it had scared him and Barbara until the nurses assured them it was normal. Paul kept reaching to the bassinet nearest him, some girl doused in pink.

Sam retreated up the rest of the stairs, pulled the door closed behind him, and walked to the living room. He couldn't hear the screams below only because he was lost in the memories of their births. Peter they were afraid was stillborn. Joseph, like Sam Jr., cried, but where Sam Jr. had just cried in general, Joseph cried only when people approached. Most notably, people dressed in gowns and masks. He didn't like masks. Christopher just squirmed. And Michael? Michael was quiet. He was studious. He looked around and seemed to be examining everything.

"Michael's different," Sam had told Barbara. He'd been born a bit premature, so they wanted to keep him in the NICU for a few weeks, and Barbara had been laying in the bed when she and Sam had discussed this.

"He's a wonderful boy," she'd said.

He remembered, sitting down now in his recliner and setting the shotgun on the floor next to him, that it ended up being a sunny day the morning after Michael was born. "I checked the locks," he said.

"Lucky number seven," she had said.

The screams issuing out from beneath his feet, muffled by the house's frame separating the two floors, played a melody for his memories. The boys playing in the yard. Helping in the field. That time Michael fell into the roll of barbed wire, slicing up his right calf. Would this thing, under its suit of fur, reveal those same scars? It had been Barbara who initiated the investigation, noting simultaneously that nothing like this had ever happened in her family and that his family had a history of producing so many boys. And it was his family, after all, that bore the mysteries of certain lineages proudly. In America, one whole strand of Ristens had vanished not long after they'd immigrated here. From Europe the stories of both their prolific reproductions and mysterious deaths were even greater. There the name had been Ristenoff. Ristenoff had been the name of counts and princes and merchants. The Ristenoffs of Eastern Europe had worn crests and had, on several occasions, produced numerous offspring. Those lines had been wiped out according to history, with little detail save for the violence and the bloodied, rumored narrative of their gruesome demises which had become the stuff of legend and myth.

Sam engaged the recliner and stared up at the ceiling as the screams died down. Heavy footsteps carried the thing up the stairs toward him. He tried, in these last few minutes, to focus on the outside. Winter produced little in the way of soothing natural sounds. Nothing, in fact, penetrated the walls of this house. He only hoped, as the thing with the wolf mask stalked toward him, that the horror here would not abscond the walls to infect the outside.

CRSO

Spring, the year the pandemic started:

Emma Jenkins snapped awake to a scream so piercing it could have cut the glass of her single-paned window. But it wasn't the screams or subsequent cries that spurred her into calling the cops. It was another sound and what she saw outside. All of the residents of The Loft Apartments were college students, so there were all manner of noises at all hours of the night. Since the campus announced that it was going online as the pandemic spread, students found this a license to party. It sounded as if all two hundred units in this sprawling complex had joined for one big party that first night, and had kept partying until it became apparent that they weren't going to be back to school for the rest of the semester. More parties, sure. But then the parents were calling. Students, most out of work when restaurants and stores closed down, their parents unwilling or unable to continue to help them with their apartment rent, went home.

Sitting in the Oxford, Mississippi police station in her pajamas, Emma Jenkins wished she'd have gone home.

The detective's office was little more than a glass cubicle with a door, visible to the rest of the precinct, his desk littered with files and papers and a closed laptop, a framed picture of who Emma assumed to be his wife, a coffee cup that read: World's Okayest Husband.

He was a thin man, this Detective Peters. He had a thin mustache and he couldn't be but just a few inches taller than she, and she clocked in at just under five-five. That his voice was so deep and monotone put her off a bit.

Detective Peters re-entered, pushing the thick plastic frames up the bridge of his nose as he did so.

"Okay," he said, shuffling some papers on his desk before sitting down. "Tell me what happened."

⚘

Christmas Eve, ten years ago:

The morning cast gilt light through the window, shifting the blood sprays from indigo smears to red—nearly brown—arcs and droplets. Sam still sat in his chair. His eyes were open, turned skyward. His throat had been torn out. Blood ran down his neck; a rivulet of crimson between the hairs of his forearms to his right middle finger that dangled off the arm of the recliner. As the sun rose, there was still just enough to drip off the finger and splatter in a viscous cordovan puddle on the hardwood floor. The sound of this constant drip woke Michael Risten. He lay naked on the floor behind his father. The tween wore only a drying sheen suit of burnt umber.

He was nearly halfway up when the smell hit him and he realized where he was.

"Oh no," he said, and lifted his head. He saw the back of his father's head, his father's hand, the blood dripping to a puddle beside the chair. Michael didn't need to see his father's face to know he was dead. "Oh…" he managed as the realization struck him, along with the smell, and he vomited red chunks of raw meat. When the ghosts came, they came in waves. In this moment he could see flashes of them all. The very second of their deaths was captured as a freeze frame. These were the first images he'd store for a personal haunting that would last the remainder of his life, and they would not be the last.

CRSO

Spring, the year the pandemic started:

Emma Jenkins couldn't really say what woke her up. The complex had actually grown quiet. Yeah, there were still a few students. Not all the units were empty, but the pandemic was already starting to wear on people.

"But you did hear something," Detective Peters said.

"I thought," she said quietly, biting her nails. "I thought someone was laughing. That's what I thought I heard."

But it wasn't laughing. She could tell rather quickly that what she heard was not laughter, though it sounded just as maniacal. No, what she'd heard was a scream.

Maybe, she had thought drowsily, one of her neighbors was watching a horror movie, but the sound wasn't muffled from the walls or floors or ceiling. It sounded like it was coming from outside.

Peeling apart the blinds in her bedroom window, she stared out into the night. Pine trees stood at the edge of the parking lot, and the lights revealed few cars left in the residence spaces. When the scream came again, she slipped on her house shoes and shuffled to the living room. There she twisted open the blinds and let her eyes settle on the courtyard below. Less light illuminated the green space; the sidewalks in a great X across the courtyard could just be made out under the moonlight. She saw a few scattered lights on and figured others must have heard the commotion.

Then movement to her right. A door on a bottom floor apartment, open. Flickers of shadow from inside.

"Help me!" came the voice through the darkness. Emma was able to pinpoint it by the gazebo in the far corner of the courtyard. She saw a shadow cowering. From the apartment with the open door, something large came bounding across the courtyard.

A dog? Emma thought, frowning with confusion and fatigue.

It, whatever it was, because it didn't move like a human, made a beeline straight for the gazebo. The voice screamed again, and then she could make out other noises. Tearing noises. Growls, snaps, and barks drowned out then completely replaced the screams. The shadows and curtain of night obscured a lot, saved her from the worst of the carnage below.

She opened her eyes and found herself back in the police detective's office. "But," she said, balling up as small as she could in the chair. The detective didn't press her; he waited patiently for her to continue.

But. What had she planned to say? That she could actually make it out? That even in the shadow she recognized its shape? Its dog-shaped head, like a German Shepherd or a Husky, its broad, fur-covered body that both moved like a canine and yet, at the gazebo, stood on its rear legs and loomed over its prey. Its claws and teeth tore into the boy, but she hadn't screamed. She hadn't the breath to scream. Only let out a little huff. A gut-punch *whoof* and that was enough. Because the thing, you see, it turned. It turned and looked across the courtyard and up to her bay window on the second floor. She hadn't turned any lights on in her living room. In fact, she'd made a point not to so she could see outside better. But that didn't matter. And the distance away didn't matter. It saw her now. It had heard her make a sound she herself had barely heard. It knew she was up there and that she saw it.

She stood frozen, locking eyes with the creature. Of course her door was locked. Her mother had brow-beat that into her upon leaving for college. Single young ladies don't leave their doors unlocked. But would it be enough? She'd seen how quickly that thing had bounded from the apartment to the gazebo. If it so chose, it could be on her in no time, and she didn't think a deadbolt and chain would be enough to keep it out.

Her lip quivered. It stepped into the moonlight on its hind legs, like a bear. No, it wasn't a bear. Yes, it stood on its hind legs. It raised its muzzle and parted its lips and sang an old song in supplication to the great white orb in the sky, the goddess of the hunt, a song sung by its numerous cousins, the wolves, echoed by certain dog breeds, a howl that carried up into the sky and through the night signaling a triumphant hunt. When it was done, it gave her a long, rueful look. Then, slowly, it turned, lowered itself to all fours, and sauntered into the shadows.

She realized she'd barely been breathing and hardly moving. But it still knew she was there. Perhaps it could hear the thud of her heart in her chest, could catch the slight hitches of air when her body forced herself to breathe. Perhaps.

In the detective's office, she broke down. Tears came freely, some snot dripped out of her nose, her face reddened. His gaze made her feel just as exposed as when the thing had looked at her.

"And then you called the cops," he said, to which she could only nod.

⚜

Christmas morning, ten years earlier:

Lynette Cabot didn't want to be out on Christmas morning, but as the gifts were already opened and the mid-morning lull had settled

over her house, she felt it the best time to run the family gift out to
Dr. Bellanger. How they'd forgotten to get it to him sooner, she'd
later tell anyone who would listen to her story, amazed her, though
privately she knew quite well how. The radio blaring a country
Christmas tune, she turned out of her drive, the wrapped gift in the
front seat, and had turned left to reach his house three blocks away
when she slammed on her brakes. Like a black snake, a live wire
jumped and sparked against the stretch of asphalt. She turned the
radio down and could hear the hiss and pop of the electricity. The
night's ice storm had been worse than they'd predicted, apparently.
Heavy icicles hung like crystal stalactites off the pines and oaks and
glistened in the dull morning light on the tips of the grass. The ice
had crunched underfoot as she made her way from her porch to her
car. She'd nearly slipped once on the drive, carrying the present, when
she overestimated the sureness of her footsteps. It would have been
bad if she'd dropped the gift. She'd found the old clock at a little
corner store while antiquing up in the northwest corner of the state
back in October, and her husband had agreed that Vance would love
it, and no, it wasn't too expensive, and yes, it was impressive that it
worked pristinely. They'd been friends with the doctor since forever,
and Lynette always told Phillip that she imagined such holidays had
to be lonely for their friend. He had always worked such days, as he
was a bachelor and had no other family in the area, his sister having
moved up to St. Louis a number of years ago. Sure, he'd have gotten
the package of gifts from her and her family, as Vance would have
surely sent them their gifts, and there had been years in the past when
he'd made that trek up to St. Louis to visit them for the holidays, but
more often than not, he preferred to tool around his old Victorian
until he worked his shift up at Drew Memorial. He was, Lynette
opined often enough, too fastidious to keep a woman, and now, in
his years, it was probably too late for him to start a family. Phillip had

known him longer, since they were kids in fact, but it was Lynette who'd suggested they very nearly adopt him into their home. Phillip had acquiesced to her request amicably and silently, as he was often known to do. Still, Lynette often explained her reasoning as if Phillip had protested, adding pithy bon mots to illustrate her wisdom. Just this morning as she prepared to leave, she told her husband, "He should have gone into pharmacy like you," as if this would have given Vance Bellanger the life she thought he should have.

Phillip's response was a quiet, "Yes, dear," as he supped at his steaming coffee. Their son was already on the phone with one of his college chums.

Looking at the popping, dancing live wire, Lynette thought, *Well this just won't do at all*, and reversed the car the other way. There was, in this small town, only one way to get to the doctor's house now. She'd have to cut back by the trailer park and take the road out by the old Risten farm, then double back on the main fairway to reach his cul-de-sac. Sighing at this delay, she began to mentally calculate when the thawed and stuffed goose and turkey would each have to go into the oven.

Her son's girlfriend was nice. Perhaps a well-timed phone call could get her to lend a hand, though to hear her son tell it, the girlfriend, while he was serious about her, did not know the difference between a Dutch oven and a crockpot, so Lynette wasn't exactly sure how much help she'd be. She fished her cell out of her purse, chancing only one hand to feel around the pocket so her eyes stayed focused on the road and her left hand gripped the wheel tightly. Her lips and tongue twisted in a frustrated dance as she felt for it, finally retrieving it, pushing the contact list, then scrolling until she came to the L's. She wondered if her friend Bess could help instead. She hit the button and put the phone to her ear as she braked easily and steered the SUV onto the road that ran by the Risten farm.

"Bess, oh good, you're up…Yes ma'am, Merry Christmas to you too…Oh, I'm in a bit of a pickle. That storm last night knocked a powerline down by our house…No, we're okay. Still have power, but I'm trying to run a gift over to Dr. Bellanger…Yes, I'm in the Suburban…oh, you silly goose, I'll be fine, but…"

Her voice trailed off, and she blinked to make sure she was seeing what, in fact, she was seeing. A youngish boy, probably early teens, shuffled shoulders-slumped down the side of the road. It was one of the Risten kids, to be sure, but which one was hard to tell. His back was to her, for one thing. He was covered in something thick and red, nearly head to foot, for another. She neared, slowing. His hair was matted, and it looked—*oh, dear Jesus, that can't be right*—like he was naked. His butt cheeks jiggled with each step, and she could see the muscles of his back working just under the red plasticine film. Here and there it was lighter, and she could see pale skin underneath, flesh horripilated from exposure to the cold. She pulled up alongside and peered out the passenger window. It was the youngest boy, Michael, she could tell now. He stared straight ahead, unblinking. He walked slowly, dully, like something from one of those monster movies Vance and Phillip went on and on about.

"Call you back," she mumbled into the phone, dropping it onto the seat as Bess's voice called and called worriedly through the speaker.

"Michael," she said, remembering the window, then hit the button to lower it. "Michael?"

He didn't stop walking and didn't look at her. She pulled ahead of him a few yards, shifted to park, and hopped out of the vehicle, nearly slipping to her ass on the slick pavement. Catching herself, she used the hood of the SUV as a brace to lead her around to the side. Michael never acknowledged her, but he stopped when she stood in front of him.

"Dear Lord Jesus, what happened to you, boy?" she asked, reaching up to his shoulder.

Michael didn't respond. Just stared straight ahead, lost somewhere that wasn't here. He'd stopped walking when she stepped in front of him, but other than that, he didn't seem to regard her.

"What are you covered…" She could see it was blood. She could also tell that he'd walked from the house without shoes or socks on his feet, much less a stitch of clothing. "Dear God," she muttered, and gripping his shoulders, turned him around, searching for any signs of injury. "Who did this to you?" she said, and on the heels of that, spinning him back around so he faced her, "Where're yo' parents?"

He blinked; he hadn't done that before either, but he blinked and a light flickered in his eyes, and he regarded her for the first time. His lips trembled, pulled downward into a morose frown, and his face screwed up and he let out a wail, a deep, lamenting sob that shook her very core. It was a sound that told her something was really wrong. Keeping a hand on his shoulder, she pulled him to the vehicle and fetched the blanket from the back seat she and her husband had used when they'd taken their daughter and her fiancé out for a picnic the week before. She wrapped the blanket around his shoulders and ushered him into the passenger seat. When he was secure, she fished her cell out of her pocket, flipped it open, and dialed the sheriff's office up in Monticello.

"Ya gotta come quick, Sheriff," she said when she got him on the phone. "Ah think something terrible has happened. Something truly terrible indeed."

She glanced back over at Michael, but he was lost again, staring at nothing, unblinking, the blanket wrapped tightly around him. What tears he'd just shed were already dry on his red-streaked cheeks.

CRSO

Spring, the year the pandemic started:

Interpol agents have ponytails? Emma thought, then turned around. It was easier to look at the detective's desk. There was a wall behind it, for one thing, that looked solid. The pale blue paint allowed the dimples and rivets of the concrete cinder blocks through. And now his seat was empty. Out there talking to the guy from Europe.

She glanced back, then faced forward in her chair.

That guy was tan. Old, his skin like leather. She heard the whiff of Latin in his pronunciation. His hair was dry and stringy and gray, his goatee gray also. He wore a suit, and it fit his slim figure and broad shoulders well, but he looked uncomfortable. He continually tugged at the collar like it was strangling him.

List. She'd heard him ask for that, and he glanced her way. His eyes were black and sunken, and she shivered. Kind of like that thing's eyes.

Oh God, she thought. And froze. She raised her hands to her face, pressing them against her nose and lips, her eyes wide with terror. What if? God, could she even…

That thing had looked at her. Across the courtyard and up to her darkened window. It stood on two legs and flexed and its eyes had met hers. It had a wolf's head. Wolves don't stand on their hind legs. Men do.

She looked back. The guy from Interpol glanced at her again while in deep conversation with the detective. He was asking about a Michael somebody. She thought about the grad student who lived on the third floor of building B. Two floors up from the apartment door that had been open. His name was Michael, she was sure. He was a nice guy. Quiet. She'd seen him around the pool once. He was pale and skinny. Anytime she saw him, he was clean-cut, but always acted a bit shy. Some guys waxed, but given his demeanor, she was sure this kid was naturally hairless. Didn't even look like he was ready to shave yet.

"I assure you I do," he'd said that day when he was out tanning by the rectangular pool. She hadn't believed he was a grad student. His jaw showed only a hint of peach fuzz.

"You do," Emma repeated her words from that day, staring blankly at the concrete wall. "Shave. Like men do," she said coyly.

Men do.

Men stand on their hind legs. Like the wolf did.

She glanced back, and the Interpol agent shot another look toward her.

And smiled.

Oh, God, she thought, and bit into her palms, squeezing her eyes shut.

Men do but wolves don't. Men do but wolves don't. Wolves don't. Jesus, Mary, and Joseph, wolves don't.

But that one did, and she'd recoiled and nearly screamed when that wolf had stood up. It had done a thing a man does, and now this Interpol agent was here, asking about the attack, and his eyes were just as yellow-black.

She whimpered a bit. Looked back. The agent and the detective looked at her. God fucking dammit, had they heard her? The fucking walls in this place. Like paper!

The detective walked back in and sat at his desk. He shuffled a few papers for dramatic effect, never taking his eyes off her. "So," he said, a word he dropped like a heaven stone off the shore of a deep pond.

CHAPTER TWO

The day was hot and humid, and the South Arkansas swamp clung to the flesh with all its stink. The date on his cell read that it was transitioning from August to September, for whatever that was worth. More importantly, it suggested that time was transitioning from summer to autumn, and Michael Risten vaguely remembered worrying about this in particular on the drive home from Ole Miss the day before. When he walked into his familial home, he felt sick and cold and—simultaneously—like he was burning up. The house was long since empty, silent save for the echoes and the ghosts that waited in the shadows, empty if not for the dusty furniture and the stains that had been cast on the walls. He was still sick when he woke up the following morning. Sitting up in bed, his stomach roiling, the nightmares he'd suffered that evening faded. He'd hoped that the first night back home in his own bed would ease the turmoil, but it had only elevated his unease, and he found that he was surrounded by eight shadows, each chanting. Three on each side and two at the foot of his bed. Their rhythmic susurrations had roused him from his troubled sleep.

In the morning light, they faded. Still, he was sweating profusely, and he felt like puking, so he rushed to the bathroom and dry-heaved into the sink. Gripping the cool porcelain edges of the sink, he stared at his reflection in the mirror, and noticed the tile around the shower was crumbly, another sign that the house had sat in neglect. Around the edges of the mirror, the grout was a dingy dengue yellow, and hairline cracks and chips scarred the glass. If he were to stay, he'd have to fix numerous other things. This strange thought was salted with an immutable memory of staying at a friend's house watching old black and white horror movies. "See," John Kelly had said to him after *Frankenstein Meets the Wolfman*. "Curses like that can't be stopped by death." If he were to stay, he thought again, letting that idea trail off wherever it needed to wander. He hoped John Kelly and the Wolfman were wrong about curses being unkillable.

He walked downstairs to the kitchen and poured a bowl of cereal. His mind was preoccupied in a lackadaisical sort of way on why he'd bothered to come back. Preoccupied with what the old Creole witch called potus, for one thing, and that was a major thing, because he truly believed it had worked. To see old friends? Perhaps. He did miss them. When he wasn't haunted by the past, he walked fondly in the happier memories. So, if either or both of these things were true, then why had it taken him so long to return? Because he'd run out of the potus this past spring, and by then it was safe, and he wasn't worried about things. But autumn was coming again, and no matter if he were here or somewhere else, he'd need the potus when autumn came.

Unless, he conjectured, it hadn't worked. Those kids weren't attacked last winter or last fall. They were killed last spring. The cops had questioned him quite extensively about it. Had questioned the whole complex, in fact, but they seemed particularly interested in him. Or at least that's what his mind, conditioned to paranoia by years of fearing what the bright autumn moon would bring on, told him. That's what his guilty conscience told him. His more rational mind countered that he'd never changed in the spring. The danger was in the fall. It had always been during the fall months, and nothing had changed now. So, what was it, he wondered, that attacked those kids? Was it him, evolving further, or another like him? These answers evaded him, so perhaps he'd returned to try and find them—and some more potus too, while he was at it. Not being able to leave Oxford while the cops were questioning everyone had kept him from returning until now. It sure hadn't been the ghosts. They visited him always, slinking through the shadows, haunting his day to day, reminding him of what he was and what he'd done. It wasn't as if returning home had reawakened them. They were always there. Sometimes shadow. Sometimes as detail. But always there.

That's right. The ghosts. The ghosts were there, but he didn't see any ghosts of those kids. Whoever did it, if they were like him, they would see the ghosts. This clicked for him in the kitchen as he ate his cereal, and that realization was as much a relief as the feeling that returning home now was the correct move.

For ticking off all those reasons why he returned home and why it had taken him this long reminded him of the number one reason: He was tired. In the den, the record spun, filling the sounds of the house with a vinyl recording of a violin concerto by Bach. To this he sighed. He was tired of life and tired of running and tired of fighting. He was tired of anticipating the autumnal moon, and tired of trying to keep this thing at bay. He was tired of searching for answers, because if he couldn't find those answers, then he couldn't get more potus, and if he couldn't find a solution, then he'd have to reconcile the utter fatigue that hung on him like a quilt.

It was then the shadows returned.

"We love you, son," the tallest shadow said.

"The barn is still set up for tonight," the other said.

Michael nodded and finished his cereal, then walked into the living room. The blood spatter had faded to a dull pink on the white walls. The flies buzzed loudest when the record needle skipped and scratched and fell quiet, so he spent an hour getting revenge, swatting at them maddeningly, leaving their black carcasses where they fell, until he could find no more. Every now and then, his gaze cut to the closed door leading to the basement, but he deliberately avoided it. He could hear the flies down there, and he could smell the blood still down there, though the bodies had long since been buried. No one had ever cleaned up. People had offered, and Maddy's father and mother had come and attempted some form of bleaching until they realized he'd never want to live here again. And yet, here he was.

No, he would not open the door to the basement yet. Maybe he never would.

He whiled away the hours looking at pictures still hung on the walls and at photo albums and ate lunch when it was time. The afternoon was spent staring at the floor in his father's study. Sam, not a studious man, had used the room to draw out plans for his woodworking business. Michael stayed there because the room still smelled like his father, like cedar and old cologne. And it was where his father kept the key. It was heavy and thick and iron and weighted down his right index finger when he twirled it like a hula hoop.

He walked upstairs to his bedroom. His acoustic guitar still lay in its hard-backed case. The strings were out of tune, but after such an easy fix, he strummed some chords on the upstairs balcony as the afternoon sank into the evening. He thought about the key and the ghosts and how sick he felt. As the sun set, he watched the sky dimming to indigo, tucked the key into his pants, and reunited the guitar neck with an old wall hook he'd screwed into a stud years ago.

The hay of the barn was brittle and gray, like the slats that made up the walls. Cobwebs adorned the darker corners and some had stretched across the passages. Dried corn feed in oil drum barrels and musty bermuda hay burned the air like acid. Not like the house, which, though wiped clean, still smelled sweetly of blood.

He ascended the ladder to the loft and the remaining rotten square bales, and there he saw the thick iron chains. The rising moon just revealed itself over the trees, a great orange blot against the infinite black sky. The shackles clicked in place complacently as he stared back at that horrible full orange thing that faded to white and shined over him. It might not be time yet, he thought, but time was near enough. The moon was nearly autumnal bright enough to necessitate the chains.

CRSO

Morning came with dew on the low foliage and a fog hugging the ground, but the air above was bright with sunlight. Madeline Jeansonne's Camry had recently had an alignment, so it could steer itself straight along the narrow two-lane highway between the barrow-pits and rows of long-leaf yellow pine acting as sentries against the South Arkansas swamp, but still she kept her hands at ten and two, out of habit, with the radio cranked too high to a podcast on the mystical in an effort to prevent sleep or road hypnosis during this drive.

From her apartment off the campus at Dillard, the drive had been long, the scenery changing little from New Orleans to the Arkansas border. Now, just fifteen miles from her hometown, it was only the familiar sites that assured her this trip was almost over. She passed Stuckey's gas station, not that Stuckey had owned it in forever despite the sign still suggesting so. She'd heard Sheriff Charley had bought it a while back and let his nephew run it, but then again it was her brother who'd told her that, and he'd done so conspiratorially, hinting at some agenda that Madeline didn't exactly subscribe to.

She passed Stuckey's and headed into the town proper from the east, first entering the county and then nearing the turnoff to the Risten farm. She hadn't planned to stop, but hearing that Michael had returned home a day or so earlier found her turning the wheel, cruising down the county road, then slowing and pulling into what was left of the gravel drive, itself losing ground to a tangle of high weeds and a few small thorn bushes that scraped at her car's exposed underbelly. Weeds had successfully breached the arch in a campaign to reclaim it as part of the yard. The house looked mangy in the sunlight, the whitewash faded and scraped away, revealing the gray and weathered siding in great spots. The steps leading up to the porch were tattered and worn. The yard and farm beyond were overgrown; in the field the fescue stood waist high and swayed in the southerly breeze, a safe haven for ticks. The gambrel barn in the distance, always old looking, seemed ancient now in this forgotten land.

The state of the home surprised her, though it shouldn't have. No one had been here in years to care for the property save her brother, who made sure the roof hadn't caved in and nothing human, animal, or otherwise had taken up residence. But she remembered playing here as a child, playing with Michael and his brothers, she and her brother. They raced around the house in games of tag and had water balloon fights behind the workshop where she'd had her very first kiss with TJ, only to date Michael later as they entered high school.

But it wasn't meant to last. When Michael lost his family, there was little room for anything else but his grief, and Madeline understood the importance of friendship for him, so quietly they transitioned back to what they'd always been: childhood friends.

Movement caught her eye. She'd been standing in the yard, letting ghosts repurpose it to a more familiar setting where she'd romped so many years ago, the bright sun beating down on her, when something fluttered above, and she looked up to see a curtain bristle in an upstairs window. *Michael's bedroom*, she thought, then mounted the steps and knocked on the door.

"Michael? Michael, is that you? You home? It's me, Maddy."

She stepped back into the yard and, shielding her eyes from the sun in a salute, looked up to the second floor again. Nothing moved up there. There were no sounds. The homestead stood still and quiet, and its state of disrepair made her feel the place was haunted. She thought then that it wasn't Michael who was spying on her, but the ghosts of this place, and a shiver raced up her spine. She looked around and didn't see Michael's car, and that feeling of complete aloneness, isolation, and vulnerability only heightened the fear that overcame her now. Her palms were sweating and she shivered from the chill and so turned quickly and climbed back in her car and pulled away.

CRINGE

The curtains were thin enough that Michael could see her from his bedroom window and wondered why he'd pulled them aside. He told himself it was for a better look, but he wondered now if it weren't to get her attention, that maybe she would enter and help him.

CRED

Madeline didn't head to her family home; instead, she drove to the commercial area of Blue Rock, the closest thing the small town had to a square. There was a local jail but no courthouse, as the county seat was Monticello, just northeast of the town proper. She was happy to see Duke's was still open, just across from the park, the outside seating now spaced at the required six feet apart, though no patrons were there. Even with his mask on, she could spot Duke easily enough. She sat at the picnic table under the old elm as Duke and his wife, Amelia, each gave her a wave and a nod, and soon the middle-aged woman was carrying out a pitcher of iced tea and a menu.

"Now chile, we ain't supposed to hug or nothing, but heavens if I don't want to squeeze you right now. Why you just getting back to town? I thought the schools all went online back in March."

"They did," Madeline said. The truth was, this little town depressed her. As much as she enjoyed reflecting on her childhood, this town was also all that was wrong with the world today. It was slow and she no longer felt she could move at that pace, nor entertain its complacencies or its beliefs. "I had work to do. Got a job at a nonprofit and it was easier to work there in New Orleans."

"Well, here's a menu, Maddy. Though seems like you always got the tuna melt."

"You know what I like, Miss Amelia."

The older woman laughed, playfully swatted her with the menu, and walked off. About then Maddy's brother sat down across from her.

"John Kelly, where yo' mask?"

"Hey sis," and he reached across to hug her. "Ain't got one," he added, offering up a superficial shrug.

Miss Amelia returned, pouring John Kelly some iced tea, asking if he still wanted the chicken fingers basket and he said no ma'am, he'd like Duke's catfish po'boy, and she raised eyebrows at the change and left the siblings to reconnect.

"I's getting worried about you down in N'Orleans," he said.

She nodded. "I went out by Michael's. You said he just got home too. You see him?"

"I's waiting for you. Did'ya?"

"No," she said, and sipped her tea. She let her gaze wander. On the surface, downtown Blue Rock, Arkansas, wasn't remarkable. Several businesses housed in flat-roofed concrete and brick buildings, little imagination in their architecture, surrounding a patch of green that was supposed to be a park named for the county progenitor and third governor of Arkansas, whose statue stood proudly in the center of the grassy grove, with a couple of elm and maple to shade the spot. Even from this distance, she could see where birds had perched in the trees to relieve themselves on the statue and the wrought iron bench beneath it, the white stains like teardrops scarring the dark bronze that made bite her lip for fear of laughter.

"All around they're tearing down those statues," she said, nodding toward it.

"They won't tear down ol' Drew," John Kelly said. "As he was governor and all."

She rolled her eyes. "Never mind that he owned some twenty slaves at his plantation."

"So, what's the word on grad school?" John Kelly asked, and she knew he was trying to change the subject. He was never one to rock the boat.

She shrugged as the waitress brought out their food. Madeline had gone to school with Vicky Arsenault, who'd been prom queen back in the day. The boys had fawned over her blonde hair and blue eyes. But now Vicky, who offered Maddy a weak smile from underneath her own mask, the corners of her eyes crinkling nearly closed, looked either as if she were in her forties or just strung out. She'd lost a lot of weight and there were dark circles around her eyes. Her hair, once luscious, fell in straight greasy strands around her shoulders. She shook a little, which wasn't evident until she'd set their plates down. Though she wore a mask and gloves, Madeline found her appetite in question. She watched Vicky walk away then turned back to her brother, who was already digging into the food.

"She looks awful, John," Madeline said.

"She didn't make the food," John Kelly replied, his teeth tearing into the sandwich ravenously.

"She looks like she on meth!"

He shrugged. "Probably is. She's been hanging out with Remy Doucet."

Madeline looked back to the little building. She could see Duke and Amelia talking, and then a darker shape behind them, wearing an apron, hovering over the grill. Remy Doucet had asked Madeline to go to her prom with him (he was five years older than her at the time but thought that since they were from the same town, she'd take him). Even then, he'd been getting heavy into drugs, though back then it was pot and some crack. Vicky fit the profile of someone on meth—poor, white, low education—but Remy was a bit of a surprise. Though he was poor and poorly educated, meth wasn't really a Black person's drug, so she assumed he must be getting something more out of it, and she was pretty sure he was getting Vicky.

Over John Kelly's shoulder, a Drew County police cruiser pulled into the parking space two over from her Camry, and a tall and broad-shouldered uniformed man climbed out from behind the wheel. He wore a deep tan and his hair was cropped to a buzzcut, much shorter than how he had worn it when he played football for the Monticello

Billies, but she knew Aaron Bailey anywhere, and wasn't surprised that he'd gone into law enforcement, as his father had been sheriff in neighboring Desha County for forever.

He spotted them instantly. Sauntering over, he removed the gold-rimmed aviators and tucked them into his breast pocket before clapping John Kelly on the shoulder.

"Where's the mask, boy?" Aaron asked, though he wasn't wearing one either and he was the same age as her brother, both of them having played football and baseball together.

Madeline saw John Kelly's jaw tighten as he recoiled from the touch, set his sandwich down, and picked up a napkin. "I ain't got one, Aaron," John Kelly said.

"It's Deputy Bailey when I'm on duty," Bailey said, then nodded with a grin to Madeline. "Welcome back, Maddy," he said, flashing his bright white teeth, and strolled off before she could answer.

She saw the disgust in her brother's eyes. He'd played nice with Aaron Bailey all these years, but they'd never considered each other friends.

"Well, that po'boy ol' John boy's munching on looks mighty fine, Miss Amelia, but I think I'll have one of Duke's famous double cheeseburgers."

"You want your strawberry milkshake?" Duke asked him.

"Gotta have something to stir the protein powder in." Maddy turned around in time to catch him flex a bicep. She rolled her eyes and scrunched up her face, sticking out her tongue. John Kelly laughed and squeezed the po'boy, squishing some mayo-soaked lettuce out the bottom.

"Glad to have you home, sis. It's been lonely."

She nodded. "Missed you."

They finished their meals, talking about the town and what had changed and what hadn't, an unhurried discussion that lasted for a while after their plates had cleared. After he got his food, Bailey returned to his car and ate behind the wheel, then pulled out of the spot and drove off to God only knows where. Truth was, she didn't care.

"Well," John Kelly said finally. "Come back over to the house and we'll get you unpacked. Then maybe we can go visit Michael."

She nodded, asked where his car was, and he said he'd hoofed it, so she offered him a ride and he graciously accepted.

CR&O

The house hadn't changed much; it was still a small single-family home on a small, well-shaded plot of land. What grass grew did so in patches. A full-grown Lab met them at the door, licking at John's palm and whimpering a bit while wagging his tail, the dog admonishing his father for being gone so long. He tousled the dog's fur and pointed Maddy to the spare room. John Kelly had recently painted the outside, making the house shine against the few others on the street. Inside she put her bags in the smaller of the two bedrooms as John Kelly had taken over their parents' old room. She washed up in the bathroom, wondering if it had always been so constricting, reapplied some makeup, and then they were out the door.

It took less than ten minutes to arrive back at the Risten farm. John Kelly didn't seem much surprised by its condition. He took a second to look around, then mounted the steps and knocked on the door and, in a deep, booming voice, called out Michael's name.

The door opened. Michael hung onto the door frame, forcing a smile at his old friends as if that could mask anything, but they were shocked at his appearance. He'd always been a waif of a thing, a scrawny white kid with a wisp of brown hair, but he appeared totally wasted away now, worse even than the waitress. Madeline didn't wait for him to invite them in, but pushed her way inside, surveying the surroundings.

The interior of the home was in a worse state of disrepair than the outside. Cobwebs and stains and smells with invisible sources and layers upon layers of dust now infested the house. Movement drew her glance to the stairs, where a large spider crawled under a riser.

"Michael," she said, looking at him. "Are you okay?"

He closed the door behind them, locking them into this nightmare. "I'm sick. It's why I had to leave school." He said this with a shake of his head, as though arguing with himself.

"Where you been since they shut the school down?" John Kelly asked. He wore a heavy frown looking at his old friend now.

"My apartment in Oxford," Michael said. Up until recently, he'd been a graduate student at Ole Miss. He made his way to the couch and plopped down, sending up a cloud of old dust that instantly elicited a litany of sneezes and coughs from him.

"It's not the virus?" John Kelly asked. Any fits of coughing lately worried most, Madeline knew, as the virus was still so new, and it was highly contagious. They all three were very familiar with the horror stories coming out of New York and Seattle as the virus had spread across the U.S. at an unfathomable speed.

Michael shook his head, closed his eyes, and leaned back. "No, it's the fucking dust. You know I'm basically allergic to everything this goddamn state has to throw at me."

They each sat on one side of their old friend. Madeline reached out and took Michael's hand.

"We gotta get this place cleaned up. You can't live here like this."

"It's a mess," Michael said, but he didn't say this in agreement. It was more like he was just realizing this for the first time.

"I made sure there were no squatters," John Kelly said. "Woulda done more if you'd've left me a key."

Michael reached up with his free hand and patted John Kelly's knee. "I should have asked you to take some gasoline and a match to this place."

John Kelly stood and walked around, surveying the interior. "Ain't too bad, really. Some new paint. Fix a few boards. I got my dad's table saw and circular saw, and I remember your dad had a whole mess of tools."

"It's all still there," Michael said.

"Well, why don't we do it, then? Fix this place up right."

Michael shrugged. He didn't appear energized by the prospect. Still, he smiled at his old friend. "Hey," he said, still lethargic. "Isn't it weird we gotta wear masks now?" A broad smile spread across his face, and he sighed. "Masks," he said. "Hiding who we are or who we're meant to be."

"Or shielding us from this virus," Madeline said. "Protecting us."

"What if we're carriers?" John said. "A lot of people are asymptomatic carriers, and they say the masks keep it in so they can't infect others."

Michael opened his eyes and squinted at his friend. "I like that. I really do. The masks help keep the infection from spreading. Too bad it isn't true."

Ignoring him, Madeline said, "Tonight we should go up to Monticello and get some dinner. Just the three of us."

"But not too late," Michael said. "If y'all are okay with it, I mean. My stomach ain't been right and I have some more work to do before I settle in before dark. Say, in a couple of hours? Give us enough time to be back before sundown?"

Maddy and John Kelly looked to each other for approval and agreement, and since neither found a counterargument worth raising, they both agreed. When Maddy asked if they could help, Michael just shook his head and nodded toward the basement. It would make the perfect excuse, he thought. "Don't want anyone else going down there. I got to do it," he said, and neither Maddy nor her brother pushed back on this.

CHAPTER THREE

Blue Rock isn't a large town. It exists as a few streets off a state highway, a few homes centered around a miniscule town center featuring a few red-brick buildings and a park with a statue of an Arkansas slave holder, and a trailer park near a few farms. Blue Rock is hot and flat and surrounded by pines. The industry that has flourished here most is logging, though the citizens have not. People here are poor. The richest people in town are the local doctor, his best friend and area pharmacist, and the pharmacist's wife, a schoolteacher. Still, each of their salaries fall below median standards for Arkansas for their respective careers. But because it is dirt cheap to live here, they live like royalty. Their respective occupations take them out of the town to nearby Monticello, the county seat just to the north of Blue Rock. Dr. Vance Bellanger, fifty, has privileges at the regional hospital there. Phillip Cabot can commute to his pharmacy practice there. Lynette Cabot teaches high school there. Some of her students, former and current, are from or still live in Blue Rock.

This particular morning, Dr. Bellanger read the paper over a cup of coffee on his wraparound porch, dressed still in his sleeping attire and robe and slippers, enjoying the coolness of the morning. The dew had gathered not just on the grass but on the car in the drive, on the banister and the floorboards of the porch, and on the seat of his porch rocker, which dampened his backside. The air was crisp now and gave no suggestion as to what would become of the day. So many years in South Arkansas, he knew the temperature could swing either way this morning on the cusp of switching seasons. The old Victorian he'd long since paid off and called home was perhaps, as others in town whispered, too big for him, but it was his and he'd taken seriously his role as its caretaker over the years. From the large oak in the front square of the yard he heard a duet between a mockingbird and a blue jay, the former plagiarizing the latter. Further off, the caw of an Arkansas raven called out to the peaceful morning. The weatherman out of El Dorado said early morning clouds would give way to afternoon sun, but Vance preferred the overcast sky, the muted shadows, the gray monochrome tint of the day that washed out the color. It reminded him of the television shows he could still catch on MeTV, black-and-white sitcoms and Westerns that brought him back to his youth.

At the Cabot house, the morning was just as silent (Vance would call it peaceful). Phillip and Lynette had been married so long any conversation worth having had already been had, so they moved in a touchless dance through the morning. Percolating and pouring coffee (half-n-half and two sugars for Phillip, black for Lynette with some artificial sweetener her husband had long since quit cautioning her about due to its cancer-causing effects), shaving and showering, toasting bagels or toast or muffins. The sun had yet to appear, but the day was lightening toward dawn and Lynette paused to kiss her husband's cheek before heading out, her satchel in hand. Save for the summers, which she never worked anymore, she always left before him. First period started in Monticello at 7:30, but students were arriving by 7:05, and he didn't have to open the pharmacy until 9. Technically, his staff opened the pharmacy's retail shop at 8am; he had a woman who'd worked as office manager for a decade who counted out the tills and daily deposits, so he had to be there to unlock the apothecary as no one could be in that part of the building by law without a licensed pharmacist. The days of rousing their son for school and busying about to ready him for the day were in the distant past. Well out of college and living in St. Louis with his own wife and kids, he never bothered with them this early in the morning. Same with their daughter, who had been working overseas in Europe since graduation.

Routine was easy to establish in small towns like Blue Rock. For the upper crust like Dr. Bellanger or the Cabots, or local literary dignitary Bess Louviere, mornings were slow and enjoyable. That they were also slow for the unemployed or underemployed only reinforced the distinction that for the more impoverished, slow and enjoyable weren't synonymous.

C33ƎO

The first part of September, the carnival comes to South Arkansas. There is a Ferris Wheel and a Tilt-a-Whirl, a Viking-shaped ship that rocks on a great pendulum, a funhouse with misshapen mirrors and jump-scares masked as horror, a merry-go-round, bumper cars, a centripetal spinning thing that glued its riders to its sides, an octopus with arms where the riders sit as it whirls them around. These rides are situated along a midway with tents featuring games of chance and refreshment areas. Popcorn, soda, candy, fried foods, hot dogs. The restrooms are just out of reach, and that's by design. The carnies who set this up are old hats at assembling these things out of the box.

But it isn't all farmed out to the Floridians accompanying the trailers of equipment. It is imperative that the locals take part. That's what makes each carnival unique.

A farmer's market sets up on the perimeter with the finest crafts and produce from the area farmers. Michael Risten's dad was once a regular on this autumn circuit. Now, he's just another ghost.

Other area farmers supply their livestock for showcasing. Ken Welsey's sheep are always a draw. Ron Berryman's gargantuan pumpkin also brings in a crowd. Duke Livingston is used to being roped in for catering. In truth, it's his most profitable weekend, and that's given he's the only local restaurant in town and the most profitable business in the county.

CRESO

Sarah Larsen knew, after twenty years, how Bob liked his eggs. You crack them in the greased skillet, then scramble with the spatula. No fuss. No muss. No dollop of sour cream in the pre-mixed scramble. Bob liked his slow. This meant she had to get up at 5:45 every morning, a whole fifteen minutes before he rose to shave and shower, to get the breakfast started. Bacon to grease the skillet, then crack the two eggs in the frying bacon grease and start a-stirring, turning it down to low. The toast, she knew, you couldn't start too soon. And he liked it oven-baked, not in a toaster. They didn't even own a toaster. You spread the pat of butter, then stick it in the oven on the baking sheet at 350. Two slices. And get the strawberry jam room temperature.

After twenty years, Sarah Larsen knew how to prepare her husband's breakfast.

This morning, she heard the faucet running, a sure sign that he was shaving. That told her she was ahead of schedule by five minutes. The oven beeped, signaling it was ready for the buttered slices. She popped them in, smiling. Breakfast would be just right, this morning.

She thought of texting their son, up at Arkansas Tech, after Bob went to work, but pushed the thought away. Idle thoughts. She didn't need those now. Now it was time to focus on breakfast.

The shower started. She looked to the skillet, the bacon nearly done. Shit, she thought, biting her upper lip. The eggs will scramble too easily and it'll be cold when he sits down. Gosh darn, how had she flubbed up this bad? Gosh darn it all. Breakfast would be cold, and he'd be unhappy. A spitting sound from behind her and the smell of arabica reminded her that the coffee would be hot. Yes, by gosh, there would be hot coffee and if it is hot enough, he might just forget that breakfast wasn't.

Still, inspecting the bacon, she trembled. What if it wasn't hot enough, she thought. Outside the blinds, the sun streamed in hot white, brightening the kitchen, but at this thought, the room darkened, like a cloud had passed overhead.

The shower shut off. She froze at the sound, not because it was unusual but because freezing and listening had become a habit of hers. She always froze when the shower turned off. She could almost hear him grabbing for the towel, raking its fabric across his pale, doughy skin. He wasn't fat, per se, but he had a gut. Hair grew in the strangest of places. His back was like a soft down of brown mimicking the flow of his spine from his head to his tailbone. He had nice thighs. Perhaps that's what she had fallen in love with. His thighs. They were warm and inviting and the hair all grew toward his knees. She often nestled between them, in the early days, when they were still dating. She would kiss his thighs as he wrapped them around her and draped his calves over her chest and he would laugh and smile as she reclined against his stomach, even then hairy and flab-covered. But it was him and it was her and they were, she thought at the time, happy.

The bacon she laid on a paper towel she'd folded in half and placed on the ceramic, gold-rimmed plate and covered it with another twice-folded paper towel to soak up as much grease as possible. He liked the bacon, but he didn't like the grease unless it was absorbed into his scrambled eggs or served as a flavor base for his gravy on the weekends when biscuits were on order.

The oven timer dinged. She sighed and donned an oven mitt and retrieved the toast from the oven. Just then, the coffee maker spit the last few drops into the carafe. She heaved a large breath, one worn through twenty years of breakfasts, both those she'd perfected and those she'd messed up.

The book club…

…a thought attempted to intrude, but now wasn't the time. Like texting her son, this was a distraction.

She slathered the toast in the strawberry preserves and stirred the eggs again, then turned off the burner. For added security, she moved the skillet to the cool burner behind.

The door to their bedroom opened. She knew it did because she knew the sound, because she'd memorized it over the past twenty years. From behind her, as the door closed, a slow cough. A grumble. Something like 'morning.' Not 'good morning' and nothing warm, nor was it hostile. Just ambivalent. Like one might greet a robot secretary or a hole punch. A ficus, perhaps.

Onto the ceramic plate she scraped the eggs next to the bacon and laid out the toast and poured his cup of coffee, then sat both dishes in front of him at the table. He was dressed in a polo and khakis, and though she couldn't see, she was sure he wore his brown leather wingtips on his feet. His middle-aged gut bloated out the base of the polo.

"Going to the office first today?" she asked. The smile was forced. Maybe in the beginning it hadn't been, but now it was. The equivalent of a dog displaying its belly.

He nodded and grunted again. Slurped his coffee. Bob Larsen always teased that he liked his coffee like he liked his women: strong and Black. He'd always laughed at his own joke even when others didn't. His own hair was black and curly and fell to his shoulders, and his eyes were black as well. His skin was olive, and she thought— herself a demure and petite redhead—she was attracted to this dark and handsome man. Though he wasn't tall. Troll-like, more like it, but not tall. In her heels, she was taller.

"Gotta," he said between bites. It was like watching a Labrador eat. He was led by his nose and his mouth. His eyes were nearly vacant, hollow points meant to focus her attention. Not his.

"Mayor stuff," he grunted.

These words tasted bitter, like day old coffee. Like she'd left the bacon to fry to hell 'til it was blackened. *Mayor stuff.* He'd been mayor forever. This town, this god-forsaken town kept electing him, because they saw only his mayor face. They saw the face of the smiling, slightly chubby man with receding hair they'd elected.

She lifted her left hand to her cheek absently. There had been a bruise there recently. But what if they saw his other face?

He raised his eyes to her. Squinted. Munched on already softened food. "What?"

She forced a smile. Shook her head. "Nothing, sweetie. How's breakfast?"

He grunted again and nodded. His focus returned back to his plate. The fork scooped up scrambled drippings and his chest swelled with a great sigh, and he said, "Dealing with this goddamn pandemic's gonna run me ragged."

She let her smile broaden, and she nodded. Of course, she'd heard him call it the "kung-flu" with all the sensitivity of a drill instructor, but she knew this virus wasn't going away anytime soon. Still, she wasn't stupid enough to verbalize her fear of the pandemic in front of him. He'd always seen this job as a small but necessary function, and that no one could do it quite like him. These hours allowed him time in front of the books for this little town. He'd never kept from her his pencil marks in these books—these ledgers. They helped pad the soft years of his dealership up in Monticello. More importantly, those manipulated ledgers helped send their son up to college. They hadn't paid taxes in how long, she couldn't remember.

So that was enough. Financial security was enough. It was enough to help her to force a smile and nod complacently toward her husband. Still, there was the coming carnival. They were setting up as they spoke.

"Pecans," she blurted, excited, her face alighting. "I got the pecans."

He raised his eyes from the scrambled eggs on his plate and frowned at her. His fork hovered just above the yellow smear on the ceramic of his plate, quivering. God, she hated the way his dominant hand quivered, like a rattler sprung to strike.

She swallowed hard. "Pecans," she squeaked out again. "For the carnival. The book club's all participating."

He rammed another forkload of scrambled egg into his mouth and grinned something horrible and yellow, highlighted by red lips. His eyes darkened. This was certainly a sign of pleasantry.

"Pies," he said. She could nearly see him salivate over the word. Saw his mouth as a mewl of dripping fangs and his eyes roll back in his head.

She nodded. Satiating the beast that lurked in her home. "Pecan pies," she said.

More unearned income they wouldn't have to report to the accountant—that's what he was thinking. Something silent they could keep to themselves, she knew. Another book or two they could buy for their son.

That he'd see this as a tick in the deposits column allowed her to relax a bit. They were beating the collegiate system. Her acquiescence at least meant they weren't indebted to the institution of higher education. Say what you will about her complacency. Her husband had his temper, but what man didn't? At least he cared for his wife and his son—his family. He supported them. So what if his support came with rules?

Life had rules. Don't cross the street, she'd learned as a kid, without looking both ways. Don't backtalk an adult. Jesus loves you and Paul said the man is the head of the household. Rules. Ingrained in her since day one. You don't question them. You just accept them. And when you break them, you pay.

That's what he'd said to her, way back when. The first time. "You pay the piper." She'd forgotten the rules then. They had just been married and their son wasn't even yet born. She'd sat on the couch, mewling, biting her upper lip, bowing her head. He was caressing her back in a circular motion, whispering to her.

"Shhhh," he said, as if to soothe her. Jekyll and Hyde, she thought then, with her tears. She tried to smile at him. Tried to nod.

'Okay,' she mouthed. Everything would be okay if she just acquiesced. "Okay," she had forced out.

She had forgotten the rules, then.

And maybe there was one or two more times he'd reminded her. One or two more times his fist had driven against her jaw, and always he was there with an arm around her shoulder, comforting. Whispering. *You did this. You caused this. It didn't have to be this way.* The piper doesn't have to be paid, she thought, and blinked.

"Pecan pies," she said, beaming. "I got all the ingredients. Don't worry. We're covered." To solidify this, she reached out an arm and patted his shoulder, a squeamish gesture he, thankfully, didn't react to.

෬ഏ

Amelia Livingston did not look at her husband the same way Sarah Larsen looked at hers. For one, there was love there. Love for Duke, and for their dogs, and for their daughter attending Monticello Prep and living with Amelia's sister. It was a good school, and it was too much to commute daily, so her sister had agreed to let the girl stay with her through the week to help them out. And there was love for their son who lay up at Hillcrest cemetery, never getting older than the tiny infant they held and cried over after she delivered him stillborn.

For another, while there were things to be afraid of, especially as she was a natural worrier, she did not fear her husband. It was common, around Blue Rock and the larger town of Monticello, to compare the two most prominent figures of the town. Everyone in the surrounding counties and almost all of southeast Arkansas knew of Duke Livingston's restaurant. While she worried about the lean years, or about business drying up, that had never happened, and much of Duke's traffic came to experience his food and shop at a couple of the local curio shops downtown, all of which, suspiciously feeding the constant rumor mill that flowed like the Ouachita River through the small town, were owned and run by out-of-towners. No, her worry was based on prevention. Rather than follow the old adage of *ignorance is bliss*, she preferred to think of all the possibilities, especially the bad ones. She'd found, in her thirty-six years, that when she thought of the worst possibilities, they hardly if ever came true. It was like a wish in that way. She could will it away just by conjuring it in her mind. I've thought of you before you could happen, so now you can't happen.

So, breakfast, unlike at the Larsen house, was full of smiles and love. And pride. She knew what people really thought of Bob Larsen. Just like she knew what they thought about her husband. Duke was a better man. A strong man. Tall and proud. She'd often told him that if he ran against Bob for the position of mayor, there'd be a lot of folk, even white folk, that'd vote for him. He didn't think so. "They like me well enough in my place at the restaurant," he said, leveling his eyes at her and drawing the corners of his mouth down as an exaggerated frown the last time they'd discussed this seriously, nearly four years earlier. "But I don't think they'd go so far as to put me in office."

Though, truth be told, it wasn't much of an office, in name or location. But plenty of people were positive Bob Larsen was skimming off the top. Now, it wasn't like anyone was seriously investigating, but still, he didn't deserve their money. That money was for the town. The roads. The people of Blue Rock. Duke would be more honest. Plenty of white folk knew that. Saw the way he run his business and knew his reputation. He was generous and kind and a hard worker. No, she was sure, as much as she loved her husband and knew he was right about a great many things, he was wrong about this. He'd beat old Bob Larsen in a landslide if he ever decided to run.

But until then, she thought, supping on her bowl still half full of oatmeal even as he was sopping up the last of his with a piece of buttered toast, she prided herself in knowing. She had a good man, and they had a solid business and a pretty, bright little girl, and on plenty of mornings, that was more than enough. On mornings such as this, however, there were those susurrations picking at her, asking her how much longer. She never repeated these internal whispers to him, choosing instead to keep them all inside, but truth was, on mornings like this, she was tired. If he said they could pack it all up and move to Monticello or West Memphis or hell, even Jonesboro, and just retire and live out their days on their savings, she'd be right as rain with that.

CR&SO

Bess Louviere braked the Escalade so that it crawled over the gravel drive, passed the flora that she'd handpicked to provide sentry to the yard, inspecting the quality of lawncare as she pulled in. The hydrangea blooms were a bit droopy, and she wondered how much water they'd been getting. The colors were muted despite the fact that the oak provided the necessary partial shade. The azaleas looked a tad better, but even the lawn was a bit yellow. The spirea had, of course, lost their color by now, but the stems looked healthy enough. The viburnum shrubs were also colorful and showing their hardiness. She pulled through the circle drive and parked, careful not to consider the house. Not yet. It hurt her heart, to tell the truth. Rather, when she shut off the engine and exited, she concentrated on the smell of the honeysuckle this fine, late-summer morning.

The property was sectioned off by juniper on either side and long-leaf yellow pine behind the house, with a small squad of lilacs in the far corner of the front yard. This she took in with much pride even as she criticized the weaker areas. Thankfully the sun was shielded by the overcast day, but even now (and much to Dr. Vance Bellanger's chagrin), the clouds were dispersing and there was a hint that summer wasn't quite ready to cede to autumn.

Bess faced the house. When she was a little girl (*don't count the decades, dear*), this house sparkled in the sun with its whitewashed siding. The oak still seemed large, then, to her small stature, but old pictures she still kept in frames that robbed her memories of color showed that while she had been very small, the oak was nowhere near the size it stood now.

There was, tucked away under the surface, a remembrance of who she had been back when. How the sun felt on her forearms before they freckled and wrinkled. How she tanned once. She took a deep breath, taking in the house. Finally.

The memories it offered her were pleasant enough at first. She in a knee-high sundress, hunting for Easter eggs, barely approaching her father's belt. Christmas in the parlor with the live fir nearly touching the ten-foot ceiling, just enough room for the star on top. Cradling her daughter in the front room or reading to her in the library. Her washed-out memories grew darker as her daughter aged. The edges blurred and filled with shadow that slowly crept inward, narrowing the vision, until she could not visit this house without descending into dark ruminations.

But woolgathering on the positive and negative was her business and culling out the semantic from the episodic and echoic, and cataloging each into stories had put food on her table, afforded her a nice home not far from the area doctors, and allowed her to keep this home in family hands. It had all started here. Back then, she'd been given carte blanche to write in the bay window of the study, to pound on the typewriter on the roll top desk, to read in the library. Those memories were golden and pure and framed in brass in her mind. But nothing golden, framed in brass, can survive. Brass tarnishes, and gold fades to a sepia-toned yellow. Like the hydrangeas. Like daffodils in spring, yellow weeds threatening to overtake everything by autumn.

Her daughter had been at once the joy of her life and a weed. Eventually the weed had been pruned, leaving only a stem in the way of another child for Bess, a granddaughter who, it turned out, was cursed to follow in her mother's footsteps. Bess had spent hours cultivating the hedges that lined her thoughts, trimming back the thorn and brambles to expose the deeper threads in an attempt to trace them back to the root. What she found were roots, plural. Some of them hers and those joined with others her daughter, then her daughter's daughter, had established. Trauma was not an oak but a wisteria bush, Bess had come to realize, and she was just as much to blame for her own darkness as she was her offspring.

In the parlor, she paused to lock the door behind her and take another breath. The light as a prism through the windows snagged the dust motes floating freely above the hardwood floor. Arsenault had been a savage. She'd noted that from the start. He'd looked at her with dark, Creole eyes, blackened by hate. Passing. Pietro Arsenault hadn't passed her muster, though he'd wanted to hypnotize her like he'd hypnotized her daughter.

How many times would she replay this? Perhaps until the day she died.

"Vick!" she called. She took the stairs, one by one. "Remy," she called next. "Rayburn?"

The sum total of residents in the halfway house. There was room for at least six more. Filling this home wasn't the point, though.

Salvation wasn't the point. Providing a sanctuary for these three was more a matter of atonement for how she'd failed her daughter. Rayburn was a drunk. As successful as his brother, Duke, was with a spatula, Rayburn was just as talented with a hammer and the guitar. Vicky had promised at once to be a talented pianist and flutist, before falling into the harder drugs. Meth and crack had crept in like invasive species and smothered her talent. Overhead, an alarm clock blared. There was a thud, then another. Bess approached the landing, pausing in front of a stained-glass window that depicted a woman in red kneeling to stroke the fur of a wolf, whose eyes softened as it looked up at the maiden.

"Vick," she called again. Her voice wavered a bit.

It might be Remy. He was gap-toothed and googly-eyed and useless. She didn't know what her granddaughter saw in him. Probably not much more than Vicky's own mother had seen in her father. Unlike Vicky's father to her mother, Remy hadn't been a primary source of her ruin. He hadn't introduced her to the drugs that now wasted her. But he'd been the latest, and he was an enabler. Still, she could not save her granddaughter without him tagging along, and if the choice was saving Vick and Remy too, or chancing her running away with him because Bess hadn't approved and thus risking history repeating itself, Bess was willing to let him stay.

Bess steeled herself. She was going to march in the local Black Lives Matter event. She had not written a prejudiced thought in her six published short story collections. She was a literary dignitary. This she breathed in and smiled and took a few more steps, as this realization provided her the much-needed courage. Her vitriolic response to Remy Doucet and Pietro Arsenault was not thinly veiled racism because she, in her eyes, had not a racist bone in her body.

"Vick? Remy? Rayburn?"

A door above opened. Vicky walked out. She wore a tee that showed her breasts and nipples through the fabric, and a pair of panties. She scratched at her curly hair, blinking reality into existence. She was pale and skinny, her flesh the color of dull marble.

"What?" the girl called out.

"You up?" Bess managed. It was hard for her to not get caught up in the house's memories.

"What fucking time is it?" Vicky called down.

"The lawn needs watering," Bess said. She turned then, as the other two doors opened, refusing to look at the other tenants.

Vicky was mumbling something under breath, and Bess was sure she heard Remy offer a laugh. Rayburn said, "Mine y'all manners. That's yo' grandmother." They quieted, and the house quieted, which allowed Bess Louviere to turn on a heel and exit the house and drive away. It was all the time she could stand to spend in the halfway house, but it was just enough to reassure her that Vicky was alive and at least making an attempt to go to work.

⊂⊃⊂⊃

Blue Rock was Black and white, divided amongst the races. Five miles outside of town existed a Confederate cemetery, memorializing all those who "fought for state's rights." Black people were outwardly mute on this place, acting like it didn't exist, while any white folk asked would claim it's a celebration of heritage.

⊂⊃⊂⊃

A more contemporary cemetery lay just a bit closer, in the backyard of Tom Larsen's Methodist church, though not everyone buried there was a Methodist, or even religious, for that matter. Here there existed an integration of the town. Blacks and whites buried together, rotting together under the soil.

Blue Rock was easily bypassed thanks to the highway. A blip on the map existing as a single exit that many travelers ignored. In that regard, it was like any other small, southern town. The people here liked it that way. Monticello had what they needed when they had to venture out, and Little Rock might as well have been New York or Paris for all they cared. It was another world and one the majority of Blue Rock's folk cared not to visit.

⊂Rℰↄ

Everyone called Emily Evans "Grandma." Despite her meager settings, she was as rich as the white folk of Blue Rock, if not richer. She rented out trailers to the Davidsons, the Calhouns, to the Bailey girl, and to Chet Kelly Ludlow, John Kelly's and Madeline's cousin. Even in this small town, the trailer park was a scene unto itself, separate from the disparity of the town, reflected in its own poverty.

Grandma didn't let that worry her. No one expected her to keep up with the maintenance of the park. She was well into her seventies and stooped, hobbling along slowly with an old wooden cane with a silver head: a wolf's head. Sure, she could keep up with her own place and sure as shit polished that cane every day, but she'd never been one to oversee anything more than the rent checks there at the park.

Her husband, on the other hand, had built this mini empire for her. He was a carpenter by trade, a plumber by necessity, and an electrician by hobby, so when he came to her in their third year of marriage and said he wanted to buy a single-wide when they already owned a double-wide, and he showed her the picture of this rundown piece with rusted siding and the skirting missing, Emily Evans was a bit surprised. It wasn't so expensive that it would tamper with their livelihoods, so she acquiesced silently with a nod and let him have his plaything.

She was pregnant with their first child back then. First of three, though only two were still living, and one of them had spent more time in prison than getting to know his only boy, and God knows Emily Evans and her husband did their best to raise *that* child. Her husband would come home from work and walk out to that trailer which the semi had dropped off on their property and work until after dark hammering and sweating and sawing. She heard it all but rarely joined him out there. It was a mess of a thing and it had smelled something rotten the one time she inspected it with him right after it was dropped off, and in her state such noxious fumes sent her stomach churning. It was bad enough she could barely eat without blowing chunks, but that smell…

She couldn't quite remember how long he worked on it. Taking her coffee this morning, she knew which trailer it was. Casey Davidson and her father lived there now. Sitting on her front porch under the shade of a pine, sipping her coffee with two creams and one lump of sugar, Emily Evans stared at the trailer but saw little, lost in memory as she was.

"Come on, Emily," her husband had prodded one evening.

"Dear Jesus, you know I can't take that smell," she argued, but he insisted, and she followed, begrudgingly, as he led her across the lot and up the newly built steps and newly built porch and into the renovated trailer. It didn't smell. It was clean. The appliances looked new though she knew they weren't, because she'd gone to the auction with him when he bid on them.

"What's say we rent it out for $150 a month," he said. In 1975, this was a fair price, and she'd nodded, working out the figures.

"What about the water an' 'lectricity?" she asked.

He was already wearing a smile, and it just grew. "Got 'um coming out tomorrow. Lay enough line we could put another five or ten trailers on this bit of land."

Just over two acres. They'd never get ten trailers, but the three more trailers they'd eventually acquire would still serve them nicely. They'd have a nice nest egg, even after the big C took him in '93. Asbestos in his lungs. By then, they had their three kids, but they never lacked for tenants, and while she missed him like the dickens, she never worried for money.

Her eyes shifted to the next trailer. The Davidson girl sat on her porch and Emily didn't want her to think she was staring. Besides, she wanted to see if Chet was up yet. He was the only tenant to have reduced rent, and it weren't 'cause she was showing preference to a fellow Black person, 'cause so was Mrs. Calhoun and her son and they paid full price, dammit. It's 'cause Chet was supposed to do a bit of groundskeeping for her in return, though he more often than not skirted his duties, and the weeds were getting mighty high. Mighty high.

CR80

Casey Davidson struggled with duality. The same girl who had gone to prom with Michael Risten now wasted away under the pines that shaded her home, vaping and playing games on her cellphone, while her father, Skeet, wasted away inside, drinking his scotch from sunup to sundown. In high school she'd been popular. Now she played nursemaid to her alcoholic father, trapped in this listless life with him. The only time he didn't drink was when he was asleep. Casey thought about college, had entertained the idea of being a park ranger, but money wasn't there, and her grades weren't great. She'd been waitressing down at the dive Chantal Bailey danced at for some extra cash, but she'd always dreamed of watching over a state park. The waitressing gig wasn't a career choice. With no transportation of her own, she had to rely on rides and those weren't always available. While Chantal never refused her, they didn't always work the same shifts. As far as college went, the loans would be too much, so Casey spent a lot of time vaping, wondering if she shouldn't start stripping to help out her dad who was collecting unemployment and social security for throwing out his back when he was with the lumber yard.

Her father had worked as a farmer and logger for all his life until his back went out. He'd been raised in South Arkansas, had grown up on the cotton and rice fields of the Mississippi Delta, had buried his wife in the cemetery up the road just outside of town, halfway between their single-wide and Monticello. When a logging company came to town promising better benefits, Skeet was one of the first to jump on it. Life wasn't cheap for a single dad with a little girl whose mother had racked up the medical bills, and picking rice for a local landowner wasn't cutting it. But Skeet had little experience felling trees, and the work was harder. Sweatier. He found himself drinking more in the evenings to deal with the muscle pain, then taking Oxy's. But it was his accident on the job one morning after waking up from a night of drinking and popping pills that delivered him to this state: staring at the television, beer or something stiffer in hand, paying his bills with his workman's comp and disability checks. The rest he told Casey he was saving for her college, but there was never much left. He spent it on the Oxy his dealer out of Monticello got him and on the beer that left him red-rimmed and soulless by late at night, a zombie staring at the television, numb to everything around him. A house might be cheap for people who could afford it, but the monthly rent at the Evans Adult Trailer Park was only fair to the owner.

CRSO

Chantal Bailey plopped down in the hard wooden chair of her breakfast table, one of the few things she'd inherited from her parents, coughing again this dry, raspy cough. She pulled the cotton swab from the cardboard box and jammed the tip into her nose, shivering as the soft tip tickled the inner lining of her nasal passage. She counted each swirl, and after she was done, repeated the process in the other nostril. This time, there came more than a shiver, as the very act of testing forced her into a fit of coughing that tightened her abs and nearly made her hit her head on the table. *Christ, please be negative*, she thought. A futile prayer, though, as she had awakened with a fever and her mouth felt cottony. She'd tried to gargle with mouthwash, but the mint flavor was lost to her. *Jesus*, she thought again, resting her throbbing head on the kitchen table as she waited for the swab to react in the kit and confirm what she already knew.

The trailer was silent and cool, the only sound the A/C from the window unit in the living room cranked to full blast. The wood paneling enhanced the shadows and kept her in pleasant darkness. She'd have to miss work, and as the owner of the club was of the same mindset as many conservatives in this part of the state, her absence would not be excused.

Her brother had told her that the coverage was doctored to frighten people, and since this was also the belief of her coworkers, she chose to believe it, but that image haunted her now. Every cough erupting from her lips allowed those images of the sick and dying to brighten like a camera flash in her mind's eye. She could not afford to miss work. Rent was due, and while Grandma might be a bit more sympathetic to the reality of the disease, it didn't mean she'd offer Chantal much of an extension. Her brother had helped in the past and would again before he'd allow her to be homeless, but he would not let her forget his help. He'd hold his generosity over her head, forcing her to pay him back in whatever way he saw fit. Usually, this translated into free dances with her friends at the club, but the thought of missing work meant that she might not even have that. Not to mention, Aaron himself wouldn't acknowledge her sickness. He'd tell her it was allergies or a cold or something and to get off her ass and go to work. The club owner would sing the same song as her brother, of course, until she got one of the patrons sick, and then he'd change his tune. That's what happened with her friend Denise. Supposing she could go to work and perform, if they could tie a patron's illness back to her, she'd be out of a job, just like Denise was now. Fired for getting someone sick with a virus they didn't want to believe existed. It didn't matter anyway. Her head felt like an iron weight she'd need a forklift to raise. Another fit of coughing. Something spewed from her mouth, but the mere thought of reaching up to wipe it away exhausted her. It would take two hours for her to find the energy to find her phone. Another hour and a half to call her brother and then her club manager. Neither received the news well, but thankfully the dry coughs and weakness in her voice kept them from saying what she knew they were thinking. After that came bed and a dreamless sleep where even the fits of coughing didn't wake her but meshed naturally into her own circadian rhythm of breathing.

CRSO

Byron Calhoun noticed Casey the way one might notice a blue jay. He found her pretty, but she was older than he; he was still in high school. He watched her often as she vaped out on her porch, fascinated by her. Oftentimes he imagined conversations with her, engaging in subjects more menial than illuminating. This wasn't, however, some sexual fantasy. He found this white girl complex, and he wanted to get to know her better.

He'd grown up with his mother and with the trailer park owner, Miss Emily, as a kind of surrogate grandmother, but Byron had never known a father figure. He had no one to teach him the ways of being a man. He looked at Casey with a kind of fascination of the fairer sex, and so with a bit of innocence. Byron knew full well she regarded him, in their real conversations, few and superficial as they'd been over the years, as a little brother. Byron leaned more toward the Monticello high school wrestling team, not that his mother Astrid knew. He couldn't tell her. She pinned so much of her hopes on him. He couldn't let her down. His mother had been a waitress and cook at Duke Livingston's restaurant since forever, since they closed down the town's Walmart back when Byron was in pre-K.

ᑲᎦᏚᎣ

Chet Kelly Ludlow carried the ladder from the shed first, setting it up beside the Davidsons' trailer before returning to the shed. His next trip produced the tar he had to dig for and a thick broom and shovel. He carried each of these items up the ladder to the roof, his mind anywhere but here on this numbing work. Slather and paint, rinse and repeat. He wondered not for the first time how his cousins were getting along since Madeline's return. They were family, so he loved them, though privately he'd questioned Madeline's decision to leave town knowing full well John Kelly would always (and did always) defend his sister. Chet accused her of betraying her family while John defended her vocally, though Chet knew John thought he was right some of the time. You didn't have to leave to get an education, or to work. Chet and John Kelly knew that. Why Madeline thought this was okay was beyond him.

Chet had spent some time in the trenches. He'd worked at Duke Livingston's for a time in high school and worked alongside Skeet Davidson for a summer in the rice fields and then worked for the lumber company before they moved away, not long after Davidson's accident. But he wasn't out of work for long when he got his new job. It was less than a week, actually, when Bob Larsen had spotted him eating lunch outdoors at Duke's place and approached him.

"You that Ludlow boy, ain't ya?"

Chet had looked up. The day had been bright, and the pandemic was only a far-off Chinese prophecy. "Yessir," he said.

"You out of work, now, ain't ya?" Larsen asked.

Bob Larsen was a greasy-looking man, dressed that day in a striped French-cuff shirt with a loose tie and no cufflinks, so that the cuffs flared at the end, his dyed dark hair slicked back, so that his widow's peak looked all the more prevalent and made him look all the balder.

Bob offered Chet a job on the spot, well aware of his marks in school, especially in typing and English.

"You smart for a colored boy," Larsen said, and the only thing that helped Chet keep his mouth shut was that he knew he was smarter than Larsen.

"Rumor is state's getting more stimulus," Larsen said one day not too long before Michael and Madeline returned.

By then, Chet had come to wear the best of business attire he could afford—well, his boss could afford. Bob Larsen had driven him up to the mall at Monticello and used his corporate card to buy Chet khakis and dress shirts and ties and socks and a new pair of loafers. The money could have lifted Chet out of the trailer park (because God knows the salary he got as an assistant wasn't going to do that any time soon), but he took the clothes with a smile and felt glad he hadn't ended up perpetually stoned like Skeet Davidson. The discounted price at the park was also a blessing, despite the menial chores he had to perform for the old bat.

"You lookin' at another PPP loan?" Chet asked. Rumor was all loans might get forgiven depending on how the election was shaking out.

"I don't trust 'em for all that," Bob Larsen said, like he was confiding some dark secret, but the truth was, he went on this rant at least twice a week about the state folk up in Little Rock. Chet didn't know them except by reputation. His boss, he knew better. Bob Larsen was a smart man who'd figured out how to finagle some of the funds for personal use. But lately there'd been whispers from Little Rock. State auditors had called his dealership and rumor was they were going to send accountants down to look at the municipality's books.

Chet had become Larsen's whipping boy. The latter often called the former to bitch about the state of the world, and there was always something wrong. He weren't no punching bag, though, not that that pudgy sonvabitch hadn't tried. Save that for his long-suffering wife. No, he'd tried one day when he was carrying on about the Fontenot siblings who'd been camped out by the Risten farm for forever, and Chet Kelly knew cause Larsen had all but admitted it, that he hated them because they was poor and dirty and Black, and he'd spoken up. Well, ol' Bob Larsen went to wallop him and Chet Kelly caught his hand and said, in a low, even voice, that if he tried it again, he'd kill him.

That had stopped Larsen cold, and he could see it in Chet's eyes. Both men knew that, while bad, it wasn't like the old days. In the old days, Chet Kelly might have signed his death warrant. Nowadays, someone like Bob Larsen might not be able to out and out threaten him physically, but there were other ways he could put the screws to him. Cutting his pay, for one. Larsen liked to remind his assistant that theirs were state salaries, all dependent on budget, and while Chet was smart about some things, he wasn't up on numbers like old Bob Larsen who ran his own business, so when Larsen flashed him a sheet full of numbers that made his head spin before taking away half his salary, Chet had no choice but to accept it. Sure, he contemplated finding another job, and even vocalized as much, until Larsen used a ten-dollar word to hook a leash around his neck. "Complicit," Larsen had said, in the context of, "You complicit in some of our municipal dealings, and if the state auditors come down here and see what we been up to, and see those new suits you been wearing, then they'll lock you up right with me." And just like that, the trap had been set. Chet Kelly hadn't as much money as he had suits and a few other things, and things didn't last in the long run. Not like money. So, he saw Larsen's statement for what it was: a threat. One he couldn't shake off. Chet was smart enough to know that Larsen had delivered to him a wallop of another kind, not physical but one that could hurt just as badly, so he continued in his dealings with the town's mayor begrudgingly and was careful what he said around Bob Larsen or anyone who might report back to him. He internalized his thoughts and fears and growled inwardly. This became a regular pastime. Like this particular morning, summing up his life as he was wont to do while tarring the Davidsons' trailer roof for their most recent cracks. He'd promised the old woman he'd do it a month ago, and knew she was looking for him this morning with another list of chores, so he figured he'd best get this one taken care of before Skeet Davidson sobered up long enough to see his roof was still leaking and rat him out.

CRBO

The most prosperous business in town was Duke's Place, the local eatery situated at the southwest corner of the downtown square, straight across from the park. Outside of town, abutting the Phillip's farm, Duke Livingston owned some land where he'd grown cotton and corn, but his pride and joy was his restaurant. It was the only restaurant in this town of a few scattered souls, and everyone from all around ate there. They didn't care that Duke was Black or that he employed whites and Blacks, they gobbled up his grease-laden Southern comfort food delivered in checkered paper boats: cheeseburgers and fried chicken and fried chicken patties and po'boys and fish and chips and coleslaw and mustard potato salad. That the seating consisted of picnic tables outdoors with the whole of the red brick building dedicated to the kitchen and a little office where Duke kept a safe and worked his books was especially beneficial when the virus came to Arkansas. People could social distance without fear of catching anything but a full belly.

The town municipal building was a converted brick home, a double story where Bob Larsen worked the town's affairs three days a week. There existed an elementary school and two churches: one Baptist for the Black folk and a Methodist church for the whites, but neither congregation was large enough to fill either sanctuary because there just weren't enough people in the area. There was a bank and a branch of the post office, and that was it. You had to go up the highway another exit to get gas.

The land was flat, the roads that scarred up the town were a patchwork of neglected asphalt that had cracked and split under the hot delta sun, narrow things barely wide enough for two cars, any markings long since faded, with no shoulders. All around stood pastureland. The grass greened briefly in the spring then quickly dried to a tawny color for the rest of the year. Two roads led into Blue Rock from the state highway, and two more led out, turning into county roads that delivered travelers into the county proper, past a few farms. Out this way stood an airport, that is, a flat patch of ground with a wider than normal blacktop that had seen better days, stretching out to a dead end in the middle of what looked like a dried up field. A canary yellow Cessna seemed forever perched under a steel girded hangar, the terminal and tower a renovated, white-washed house with a three-story turret.

Logging, rice, and cotton were the industries here, the people excessively poor with no mobility, upward or sideways. The winters were mild, and if they got any precipitation it came in the form of ice. Tornadoes hopped across the delta regularly in the spring; when it rained the flat land would puddle up to form small ponds that perpetually saturated the ground until the summer sun evaporated it all and left the soil cracked and hard as granite. Red clay carpeted the whole region and was the primary material for the labyrinth of dirt roads that serviced more vehicles than their paved counterparts.

Deep in the pine woods some twenty minutes outside of the town proper, accessible by ever-narrowing roads that eventually gave way to a dirt and gravel path, a sawmill provided the headquarters for the loggers. While saws were portable to the job site, the pine timber was still brought here to be divvied up between logs and dimensional lumber. A belt fed a large bandsaw that could make short work of the wood. A chipper ground up the smaller limbs and brush. All this was tucked neatly under a wood roofed building with no sides. This was where John Kelly worked, and he enjoyed the work. Out here, he could relax.

CHAPTER FOUR

A high peal rises from the ground. It crawls over the hills and through the trees and can't be contained by the things that would pen it in. This wolfsong rises and must rise 'til it flies toward the moon, never reaching, but always pushing, climbing, barking up that tree, over hill and dale, louder and drawn out by the wind. Oh, calling mournfully and proudly, hauntingly somber but not sad, not yet, and it sends a chill up human spines, the sound so haunting. Such is the song of the child of the night. Mournful, maybe, because it is alone…for now.

ᘓᘔᘓ

The Pumpkin Patch Carnival drew an audience from the entire county and several surrounding. While Monticello was the county seat, the townsfolk had been generous for years in allowing the surrounding small communities to host the carnival. As it was, and much to Blue Rock's benefit, the area most accommodating to the space the carnival needed was just outside the little town's incorporation limits, and so the community saw the biggest benefit from hosting the annual pre-autumn affair. Many assumed, not incorrectly, that Bob Larsen had also managed to benefit from this arrangement, but no one, not even his wife, Sarah, knew for sure.

The day of the carnival was cool and overcast. Michael rode with Maddy and John Kelly in Maddy's car, John Kelly's dog Dart in the back with him, his new best friend. Michael stroked the animal's fur, experiencing for the first time just how therapeutic it was. While his stress hadn't vanished completely, it had lessened some. Still, he was nervous about being seen around town. He'd counted himself fortunate that they ran into no one they knew when they went to dinner the other day up in Monticello, but Michael knew he would not be as lucky here. Still, he knew this was the quickest way to see the old Creole woman this time of year, as she was a star attraction at the carnival.

It was as if the carnival had been frozen in time. The same gravel lot with a single rope tied to stakes around the perimeter, multi-colored flags waving in the slight breeze, whipping the tied-off rope about. The field beyond, people crawling over the dried and yellowed fescue, tamping it down. Tents set up, makeshift booths of the most rudimentary boxes, displaying games of chance and the rides straddling the fairway. Pumpkins and haystacks everywhere. To the other end, a corn maze. Food trucks offered up the standard carnival fair, and there, toward the back of the lot, playing into the clichéd role the town had pigeonholed for them, the three siblings who lived out in the swampier backwoods of the community, the sister serving as a fortune teller and the two brothers running the axe-throwing contest.

As they exited the car, Michael's eyes settled on the far-off trailer. The sister must be inside. The brothers he recognized. But there was a man with them. Older. His white hair long, tied back in a ponytail. He was dressed in dark clothing, broad shoulders, boots. As Dart scrambled for the new sniffs and a place to mark his territory, lifting his leg, the man raised his eyes. Was he looking directly at Michael? *Surely not*, he thought. Still, the older man's face turned toward him across the expanse of the fair built on this slow rise of a hill and former pasture, as though he sensed Michael.

"You're just being paranoid," Michael told himself.

"What?" Maddy patted his shoulder. To respond, he smiled and shook his head. The smile felt forced. All of a sudden, he felt too sick. Too exposed. This was not a good place for him. This was not a good idea.

It was Maddy's hand on his shoulder, and her smile, that relaxed him. Her brown eyes, deep like bottomless wells, promising more than the gold flecks they reflected, promising hope. Michael found himself smiling. Nodding. "Okay," he said. He was reassured by her touch. Reminded then that he'd always been reassured by her touch. A memory flashed of them as kids, her hand on his shoulder, or his forearm, and the day flashed golden.

John Kelly took hold of the leash and directed Dart down the fairway. Maddy tugged Michael's hand and pointed toward the corn maze. Michael nodded, accepting her excitement, welcoming it, even as he looked back downhill toward the fortune teller and her ilk. He didn't want to leave Maddy, but to talk to the Creole woman, he'd have to.

"Go ahead," he said to Maddy, nodding and smiling. He hoped she accepted these feeble offerings for what they were. A nod and a smile were just masks to placate the moment.

She tugged his hand with both her own, pouting her poutiest lips and batting her eyes. Michael could never hide a smile from her. She let go one hand just to triumphantly clench a fist and jam her elbow down. "The last time you wormed your way out of the Scrambler, so today…"

"That was at least five years ago," he said.

"So?" She shook a finger at him, one hand on her hips, but the playful smile told him this was all an act. "There's no time limit on worming out."

He nodded, but a glance back told him he hadn't much time to beat a line. If he were going to see her, he needed to go now. "Five minutes," he said, holding up a hand and fingers, and did his best pitiful look. "I promise. No worm today."

Reluctantly she nodded, but rather than join her brother, she stayed as Michael turned away and jogged to the fortune teller's trailer. He could feel her eyes on him. In fact, even as he reached the trailer, he turned around and saw her staring at him from the same spot.

The brothers were out leading the axe-throwing, but the trailer housed the old witch and her tarot cards, and he was hoping she'd be alone. So, he opened the door at the top of the steps and pushed through the beads, finding the interior cramped and dark, shelves on the walls filled with all manner of magical trinkets.

"You have de mark on yo' palm," she said. She was sitting at the table, her deck of cards beside her. She was dressed in rags that smelled of the swamp, a scent he could detect easily despite the mask of lavender and incense she put up. It might fool others, but others didn't have his nose.

He sat across from her. "I lost the potus. I need more." She was older, her face worn by time and poverty, gray in the dim shadows. She took his left hand and turned it palm side up; one crusted, yellowed nail, bent like a claw, traced a pentagram on the thin pink flesh.

"What happened to what I gave you?"

"Stolen," was all he said, dropping his eyes. How could he admit that it had been stolen out of his apartment, on one of the last nights of the bright spring moon? On a night when some of his neighbors had been attacked? "I just, I wanna get rid of it," he spat, his lips curling as though he'd tasted something bitter.

The old woman smiled, her teeth and gums as gray-black as her flesh, devoid of warmth or joy, but filled with malice and hate. "Oh, dear Master Risten. You cain't git rid of sometin' you was born wit. You ah de rougarou, young man, and it is you. Dis mask you wear, right now, you tink it's permanen. But masks gotta come off, for dey ahn't to be worn all de time."

"But I want it to be me. I don't want to be the other thing. I can't stand the dreams, the visions. I can't stand the things I've done!"

As he said this last sentence, he slammed his fists down on the table. She jumped back.

"Dear boy," she said, after a minute. "You got de visions too. Of dose you…of de victims?"

Tear-filled eyes returned her gaze, and his voice was weak. "Yes."

Her sighs were something rancid and it was his turn to recoil.

"I'll come to you, mon boi. To yo' home. I have tings to repel dem haints."

"How much?" He tried to recall what she'd charged him last time.

"No," she said. "I'll give. You sufferin' 'nuff. I cain't take it all away, but I can lessen i'some." That's right, he remembered. Nothing. Because that's exactly what she said to him the last time she offered to help. And the potus, and the charms, and all of it had been enough. The things had allowed him to sleep peacefully, to keep the other thing at rest, so he could finish his undergraduate and nearly finish his graduate work.

Between them there lay a stillness for some minutes before a knock at her trailer door forced him to jump. She yelled for the caller to wait as Michael stood by awkwardly.

"You cain't hide from yo'self forever, Master Risten," she said.

Outside, Michael tried not to react to what he had just experienced. Casey headed a short line of people anxious to have their fortunes read, so Michael ducked his head and tried not to acknowledge any of them. He looked away, which seemed enough to keep Casey from noticing him and took off up the hill, catching up with Maddy and John Kelly and Dart, who jumped up and licked at Michael.

"Find what you were looking for?" Maddy asked. She knew full well which trailer he'd run into. She had sat up there and watched him.

Michael, for his part, certainly hoped so. God, he hoped so.

"Come on," he said, tugging at her arm as he looked up at the overcast sky and around at the afternoon shadows. There might be time for a ride or two before he had to get back to the loft. "Let's go get scrambled."

CHAPTER FIVE

ichael awoke early to sunshine pouring in through the loft window. He unchained himself and slinked down the ladder, making his way across the short field to his back door, which led into the kitchen.

He felt good. He'd slept well, the lump of hay he'd circled and padded down and finally crouched upon with a huff cushioned his body well. The dreams had been peaceful enough. Nothing died in his dreams. He just ran. Felt the wind through his fur and breathed in the nighttime smells and felt the brush scratch at all the itchy places that fur brought on, like a stiff comb raking against him, against his skin. Was it a dream or a memory he recalled, backing up on all fours to stiff pine, itching his hindquarters against the bark 'til some of it peeled away, that immeasurably pleasurable feeling of satisfying an itch? Like an orgasm, he thought.

Reliving the dream (or memory, he wasn't sure, or maybe it was the true hope of the thing inside him, to be uncaged, to be let loose, unleashed and unmasked), he started the coffee. The tile was cold on his bare feet. This brought the memory of him peeing on all fours, lifting his leg. Next came the gratification of making water on a bush, that process which screamed to the rest of the world *This shrub is mine* and then he kicked his back legs aggressively. He dug the pads into the soil so they worked with the nails to till the dirt and spray up soft ground and sod. He'd sniffed indignantly at the air.

As the coffee percolated, he rubbed absently at his wrists. The key felt like an iron weight in his pocket. *What if*, the idea came to him on a whim, *you didn't chain yourself up every night?*

He didn't need to feel the ghosts behind him to know this was a bad idea. What he didn't know was where this idea had come from. The idea itself indicated a desire to work in communion with the other form. Like he could control it. Michael knew he could not control it.

Still, the idea pulled at him. It would be nice if the beast could be leashed. If he could walk out under a bright, autumnal full moon and smile his pearly whites at some pretty girl (Casey? Madeline?) and lead her through the darkness. Through the night.

Jesus, dude, he admonished himself, pouring his first cup of coffee. *They call that "delusions of grandeur."*

He padded into the living room and saw the remains of his own father sitting in his recliner, looking at him. Michael opted for the couch. The side furthest from the visitant.

"I'm not going to do it, okay?" he snapped. Before setting the cup on the coaster, he took a large drink. No amount of caffeine could take away the ghosts.

Nothing, he thought, would pull him out of his chains at night. He could not take that risk.

CRSO

Madeline stumbled from her childhood bedroom to find her brother's door opened and the bed empty. A sound drew her down the short hall, snoring coming from the couch. John Kelly stretched out the length of the couch, and Dart lay sprawled out with him, stretching nearly as long as his dad. When they both snored at the same time, she couldn't help but laugh, which roused the dog first, then her brother, both blinking blindly in the dawn light.

"What's this?"

John Kelly smiled and stroked the dog's fur. "We just went for an hour walk. Crashed while the coffee was making."

"Brewing," Maddy said, leveling her eyes at her brother. "The coffee isn't making anything. It's being made."

Madeline smelled the brewing coffee, which completed her return to her parent's house. It felt like any Saturday morning growing up. She half-expected Saturday morning cartoons on the basic cable.

"Dart," John Kelly said, and the dog lifted his head toward his master. "Give kisses?"

The dog pushed his muzzle in toward John Kelly's face then lapped at him graciously with his tongue. John Kelly laughed.

"He's smart," Madeline said.

John sat up. "Wanna give sis a kiss?" he asked, and Dart bolted up right then drug himself off the couch and stretched. His tail began wagging and he produced a grin on his lips as he looked to his master and inched toward Maddy.

"He knows the word 'kiss,'" she said, and the dog looked up at her and grinned.

John Kelly rose and strapped on his worn sneakers and pulled the harness around the dog and then attached the retractable leash. "I love you, sis," he said, pecking Maddy on the cheek, and then he and Dart were out the door. "Dart's gotta water a bush."

Madeline got her bearings while her brother was out. It was easy to do in the kitchen as she poured the coffee. She stared out the window over the sink to the backyard, remembering them as kids. She smiled. She poured a cup and wondered where the dog had been, when her brother had adopted it.

Out back, she found the old deck furniture, once white-washed, now scraped to rust in some spots by time and the seasons. Still, it held firm when she sat. She stared up at the pines barricading the backyard from the rest of the world and sipped her coffee and imagined penetrating this barrier. Had she not done so already when she'd left for school in New Orleans?

Do you ever escape your hometown? The question came within the breeze swaying the pines, a whisper carried along the routes leading here to Blue Rock, where she had to return. A deep breath and a sip of coffee. But the nation wanted reparations and demanded blood. Didn't she, too? Yes, but she also wanted peace. The warmongering exhausted her. But she didn't want the retaliation either. She'd read about the riots in Wisconsin and the "police-free" zone in Seattle and the protesters on the Brooklyn Bridge and, as she wept for her brothers and sisters, she wished that something more peaceful could happen here. Arkansas: in Fayetteville, the cops knelt with the protesters; in Bentonville, just twenty miles north, the cops stood with Proud Boys and shot teargas at the peaceful protesters. *Jesus Christ, this state*, she thought, the breath kicked out of her.

John Kelly returned with Dart and joined her on the back patio. Pretty soon, Dart joined them too. He smiled up at John Kelly first, wagging his tail, and when he was satisfied with the head rub, he moved over to Madeline and relished in her pats and rubs.

"What if it goes bad tonight?" she asked her brother.

He took a deep sigh.

"Just what I thought," she said.

CRSO

Deputy Aaron Bailey unlocked the side door and kicked away an old Styrofoam coffee cup while juggling a fresh shot of juice in his steel-lined thermos, his keys, and his laptop. He left the keys dangling in the door and nudged it open with his boot, set the coffee and his computer on the side table just inside, removed the keys and locked the side door behind him all in a swift series of movements that proved him more graceful than one might imagine a man his size.

The interior of the building never failed to remind him of Andy Griffith's place of business on that old TV show. The bulk of the room was open with a few desks, with four cells lining the perimeter, each quartered off with iron bars, each empty today save for a steel cot bolted to the floor and wall, a little toilet, a little sink. The mattresses for the bunks had been here long before he'd been deputized, but this didn't bother him. He wasn't running no motel here.

Only after he pulled up his laptop and drank half his coffee did he regard the cells again. They might all be full after tonight. "Best case scenario," he mumbled to himself. He was prepared for the protest tonight, as much as one could be. Still, he knew before the gathering he'd clean his service pistol again and load the magazines, inventory his zip ties, and clean and load the scatter shot pump still strapped between the front seats of his patrol car. "Best" was a word he used because that helped the idiom ring true and not because he was especially hopeful or concerned. For himself, maybe. He'd made the sheriff state explicitly just when he had the authority to use lethal force. The sheriff, for his part, regularly denied Bailey's request for a partner or a ride along, choosing to come down himself whenever it was possible and Bailey needed help, which was almost never. A few times he'd sent one of the other deputies, and this Bailey didn't mind usually. Sure, there were a couple of useless men on the force, but every department had that.

What Bailey really wanted was to work in Little Rock or Memphis. He regularly checked their websites for open positions. He'd applied a few times already (once to North Little Rock and twice to Memphis suburbs Germantown and Midtown) but lost out to two coloreds and a Mexican. *Goddamn affirmative action*, Bailey had said to the sheriff when the bad news was delivered to him.

The sheriff would be present at Blue Rock's march. He'd told Aaron as much, even though they were having their own protest up in Monticello. Sheriff Charley was going to let his three men up there wrangle that one. Division of resources, he'd told Bailey, but the deputy knew the truth. He might have been blind to just how people saw through him (or, more to the point, he just didn't care), but he knew the sheriff preferred to keep special tabs on him. It wasn't like he'd hurt anyone. Not like that at all. But he knew everyone saw him as some kind of unlit powder keg, ready to go off at any minute. That was fine with him as well, just as he understood that tonight just might be the night the fuse was lit.

CRSO

Only the preacher of the Methodist church lived in Blue Rock. Tom Larsen liked the little town, especially since his brother ran things. Not that he, a pastor, and his brother crossed paths much in the way of business. Sure, Bob had given him a good deal on a Buick a few years back, but Bob had done more than that, hadn't he. He got his accountant to show Tom how to avoid paying taxes on his income, undercutting to the IRS what he was reporting while pocketing more of the tithe. This wasn't exactly illegal, as technically the tithe went to the church, as long as you understood that in little towns like this, the church wasn't an organization, but the man behind the pulpit. Yessir, Tom liked his little town just fine. He liked the quiet. He liked his trips to the titty bar in El Dorado where no one knew him. He liked the scotch he bought over in Desha County. Unlike Drew County, which restricted alcohol sales, Desha was "wet all over and twice on Sunday" he liked to say, usually to himself, on his weekly post-sermon afternoon drive across county lines. He'd said it once to Bob and he'd just looked at him like he shat his pants. "What the hell does that mean?" But Tom had ignored him (and had never explained himself) and went on cackling, then proceeded to regale his brother with the story of the stripper he'd met named Desha and how much fun he'd had with her name while she grinded and gyrated on his lap two nights prior.

This morning, Tom checked his stash and realized another trip to Desha (the county, not the stripper) was imminent, gauged whether or not he'd have time to go before the festivities, then decided he'd make time. He had promised himself and his parishioners that he'd prepare a sermon for the evening promoting brotherhood and unity. Despite his failings, he did care about his town and his neighbors, no matter their skin color, but he'd come up with bupkis so far beyond the usual (Christ had said something about sectarianism he thought he could twist up), so a drive and a pint might do him some good. He'd worked on a few note cards since awakening. Nothing too long. He hoped to keep the peace and not steal the stage, and most of all that the goddamn deputy might heed his words.

To varying degrees, these were the things that worked through Tom Larsen's head as he puttered about his home, climbed into his old car, and headed up to Desha, not realizing this would be the last trip he'd ever take, and the last pint he'd ever buy.

❦

Michael had wanted to attend the rally. He knew Maddy wanted him to go, and John Kelly would appreciate him standing beside them, but he felt it, upon awakening. The draw of the moon. Though the sun was up, and it was warm and sunny, he could feel it. Fall was coming early, and tonight's bright moon was tugging at him already. As the day pressed on, he grew more restless, and more than once caught himself pacing the downstairs. Nerves or something. Was it too early in the season? No, autumn was on her way, and Michael was more aware of this fact than even the most studied meteorologist. Autumn was coming, and the moon in all her bright phases was calling to him.

He crossed the backyard to his barn, checked the chains up in the loft, found they didn't need reinforcing and set about making preparations. Step One: Protein load. Eat until he was nearly puking. A full belly seemed to keep the beast from getting too hungry. Breakfast was six eggs, three rations of bacon, and some ham, and he fried up three chicken breasts for lunch. Not the little dinky breasts either. Plump, steroid-filled breasts that must have come off chickens nearly knee-high. Step Two: Lie. As the truth would sound absurd, he called Maddy and told her the simplest lie of all. He was sick. That was kind of true, anyway. He *was* sick. And, technically speaking, he might even be considered contagious. He certainly didn't want to risk hurting anyone. Her especially. Maddy offered to come over and sit with him, but he told her no, it was better he stay in bed, and apologized profusely about missing the evening. Earnestness rolled off his tongue because that was the truth. He was sorry. She thanked him. Told him she'd call him later that afternoon to check on him and again in the morning. *Call all you want,* he thought. *Just don't come over here.*

෬෧

Angelique Fontenot stooped over a pot stirring, stirring, methodically, slowly, the potus stinking and bubbling over the fire that heated it. She did not take her eyes from the iridescent liquid, ever-tumescent bubbles popping when they could swell no more, releasing something foul into the air. She didn't react. Nor did her brothers, who stood near enough by, toiling in the dirt or making themselves look busy, not wanting to leave their sister's side as long as the stranger was with them. The older man had invited himself in, seemed to know a lot about them, more than anyone should. Basil and Bela both wanted to run him off, but it was their sister who stopped them. "It's in his eyes, you see it," Angelique had said, spying something ancient in his gaze, like he'd seen it all.

He had arrived, looking for the loup garous, and knew to come to them. To her. "You know," he'd told her. His voice was gravelly, broken either from years of use or disuse, she wasn't sure. His voice and his eyes, and his white hair, were all there was to suggest he had years on him. Broad and standing pine-straight and strong, his strides confident, no step faltered or hitched, no cane or stick supported him, and no limp.

He was going to stay with them, and much to her brothers' disapproval, Angelique was going to allow it. But she wasn't going to disclose anything more. She knew why this man had come to town. He meant to destroy it. Angelique could not have that. Not yet.

"I've smelled that before," he said now, standing over her shoulder, the potus stench filling the air around their camp. "I think, madame, that the loup garous came to you at the festival."

This line of questioning was commonplace. He'd make statements and wait for her reaction. Angelique would not react. At least, not in the way he hoped.

"Mayhaps," she said. She tried to place his accent but couldn't. He was from the old country. Europe at least, but as to which country or region, she could not tell. Little inflection coated his words. 'Madame' and 'loup garous' came out with nearly perfect French, but the rest refused to be identified.

"Your potus, I think, is not right."

She continued to stir. Basil and Bela knew how they were going to distract him later so she could deliver it, but nothing kept him from looming over her now. "The town gathers tonight," she said, as if to no one.

"You think, madame, that you protect this thing? Maybe created it? You are so mistaken about its power. This potus will not keep it hidden from me forever."

"The loup garous run under an autumn moon, Monsieur von Slacher. Even you still feel the heat of summer this day."

He did not sweat. This bothered her. Instead of answering right away, he tilted his head skyward and his nostrils flared. "As with everything else, madame, you are wrong. Autumn is upon us."

Then, she thought silently, the potus will most certainly be delivered tonight, and the beast, leashed by the chains in the loft, will bow to her. It will allow her to unlock those chains. But even then, it won't hurt her. No, the potus will ensure it. Instead, it will run free and roam Drew County's pine covered forests, howl under the South Arkansas moon, and feast and feed on the blood it smells.

CHAPTER SIX

The evening came without obstruction. The clouds cleared and the humidity dropped and the temperature, while still warm, became more bearable. The town stretched out from their front porches. They gathered at the statue at the center of town. John Kelly led Dart on a leash up to the park with his sister at his side. Duke Livingston held a torch in his hand, his baritone voice ululating into the night. Around him stood some of the Black members of the community, all wearing masks. Bess Louviere, her mouth and nose covered in a thickly sewn mask with the letters BLM across the front, also stood with them. Duke was telling everyone about the history of the town statue. Across from them, a few white people stood, and further back still, Aaron Bailey, his massive arms crossed across his chest, and the sheriff, who'd come down from Monticello just to see the commotion, both leaning on the hood of the patrol car. Unlike Aaron and some of the white folk, the sheriff wore his mask, a triple layered and pleated covering that fit his face like a glove.

It was the pharmacist's wife, Lynette Cabot, who spoke up first, aiming her words not at the crowd but at her friend, Bess. "Now, Bess, all lives matter!" She said it during a break in Duke's storytelling when a couple within the crowd shouted the rallying cry.

"Lynette," Duke said, turning to her. "We ain't saying that ain't true. We know all lives matter. We know white folks's lives matter. But it ain't the white folks' houses that's burning down all across this nation. If it were, we'd demand they turn the water on that house to save it. But it's our houses that's burning down. And we need the water more than anyone right now."

Lynette wrinkled her nose at this. "Ain't no one's house burning, Duke Johnson. I thought we were talking about lives?"

Phillip patted his wife's shoulder. "It's a metaphor, dear," he whispered.

Rayburn Livingston spoke up. "'Member when you brought me in for that drunken disorderly," he shouted over to the deputy. "You rough up ol' Skeet Davidson when you brought him in for the same thing?"

"Shut the fuck up, Ray," Skeet called back, his words slurring together. "Just what are you accusing him of?"

"No one accusing him of anything," Ray shot back, "'cept being a racist cop."

This drew more noise from the facing crowds. Voices raised, people shouting at each other.

"This gets out of hand," Sheriff Charley said under breath to his deputy, "then you got to get control."

Bailey hitched a thumb over his shoulder as he nodded, never taking his eyes off Duke Livingston or the crowd around him even when he answered. "Riot gun loaded with rubber bullets. You just give the word."

Charley raised a hand and waved him off. "Not just yet. Let's see how it plays out."

Tom Larsen spoke up above the noise, pulling his mask down as he did so. "Remember, brothers and sisters, that God loves each and every one of us, and He does not see skin color."

"Bullshit," someone from beside Duke Livingston said.

"Why ain't a colored person been in your church," another asked. Behind the masks and in the growing darkness, it was getting harder and harder to identify the speakers.

"Saying you don't see color is just as bad as saying you aren't racist," Duke Livingston said. "Silence is complacency."

This was catchy, and the whole crowd on Duke's side started chanting it. "Silence is complacency! Silence is complacency!"

Maddy leaned back to put her mouth near her brother's ear. "It's about time to go."

"They making some good points," John Kelly said.

"I'm tired, John," Maddy said. In truth, she was afraid, but of what she couldn't say. The air around them was electric. Hairs stood on the flesh of the congregated. One might have thought a storm was brewing, but when Madeline looked up, she saw no evidence of this. Above all of southeast Arkansas spread a cloudless sky and a bright moon.

"John," Maddy said, and touched his arm. He looked at her and smiled and when she nodded toward their house, they returned home.

CRWD

Michael Risten locked the chains around his wrists and ankles. He settled back into the plume of hay that cushioned him and closed his eyes. He could feel the change coming. It was red and it was hot, what rose within him. His flesh burned. His vision whited out. He was thankful he wouldn't remember the pain that was to come, so he let his vision fade and the scream rising in his chest to vanish into oblivion.

CRSEO

The beast's eyes opened. It stretched its arms and legs. There were no restraints. Nothing inhibited its movements. It snapped its head up and saw the older Black woman, key in hand, sitting Indian style against the clapboards of the barn. The sound it emitted was as much a growl as a purr. Something guttural. The woman, who saw herself as a witch, just smiled.

The beast scratched its ear with a hind paw like a dog might. It flipped onto its back and lolled a tongue out to her. She smiled and scratched its belly easily. Finally it huffed and righted itself.

"Yo free," she said. "Go run. Go run tonight."

It hopped up on all fours, bowed to her, backed away. Only when she nodded did it climb down the ladder and bolt off into the darkness.

CRSEO

Tom Larsen liked his pre-drink nightly sojourns. He liked staring up at the stars, and even though tonight some were blotted out by a smattering of clouds, he still liked the peacefulness of it all. The wind shuffling through the trees like it hadn't a care in the world, the cicadas humming in the darkness, the crickets chirping.

His walks allowed him time to reflect. Getting lost in his thoughts was a favorite pastime, as relaxing as a Sunday afternoon baseball game, as rewardingly contemplative as meditation or nightly prayer. Wasn't this the same thing? What was meditation or prayer but silence and regulated breathing and the opportunity to unfocus thoughts? To let them wander freely and explore otherwise untethered connections and pathways. Too much noise interrupted free thought and discourse. Silence and listening were the posterns to truth.

So where did such evening sojourns take him? Away from the debacle that had become the protest, for one. It was when they started screaming for the statue to come down that the law had stepped in, and the deputy had brandished the riot gun like Tom's second grade teacher had held the paddle when the class got unruly. He even had the same look on his face. Like he was telling them he didn't want to use it, but he did want to use it, so he was really daring them to get out of line.

If this walk carried him from there, then it brought him to his childhood, for one place. The life they had been born into. Their father's rabid, drunken, nightly attacks and the boys tripping on eggshells. The fear he instilled in them. Tom had made his peace long ago with the demons his father belched daily that stank of whiskey, until the day he'd keeled over in his chair from a massive coronary. How mighty cold and distant you speak of such things, Preacher. That's what booze and porn will do for you, young parishioner; numb you so you can vocalize such mundane horrors that we as a society tend to shrug off. Who didn't come from such auspicious beginnings? Your white poverty story is cliché and derivative, even for a Southerner. But does that make it any less horrifying?

So, let's dig in, then. Dissect those images the booze and porn won't unfreeze in the mind, or couldn't he bear to put them to narration and recreate a coherent memory? After all these years and all these pints and all these lap dances, was he still afraid to link the cry from his mother, the leather *THWACK* of the belt spilling across his spine and thighs, the booming words from his father that carried more weight than if anyone else said them: "worthless," "loser," "waste," "stupid," and the cursing, all daily mantras singing through this house, praising hosanna to the god of misery and bitterness and entitlement.

Or what about the silence? The look his brother offered—abject terror as wide as his teary eyes would allow, and as round as his mouth (*God damn you, Pa*) or that look from your weeping and terrified mother.

For another, you might trace your evolution—

—(*heh, heh, see what I did there, preacher-self*)—

—to the events that led you and your brother down these divergent paths.

Or when, after years of conflict, you realized your paths weren't that different and commiserated your differences over boilermakers after your father's funeral.

Nature, by the way, was symphony to God. Some cicadas joining the crickets now, and the percussive crunch of his loafer soles on the clay dirt road.

On evening sojourns such as this, you marvel at the stars above without trying to mark the moment in your conscious memory.

The dirt road railed by pines bends left, but at the stone markers you shift right and your shins swish through thigh-high fescue—the shape ahead geometric and silhouetted against a sweet bright moon. Sure, you could have walked the rest of it, to the drive, to your drive, because let's face it, this wasn't Christ's little chapel. It's yours. You are the only one to chase it. Hell, you pleaded to the UMC board to open this chapter in Blue Rock.

Because you own the salvation of this town. You own the souls here, not Christ. Christ isn't racking his brains for sermon ideas for the smattering of people showing up on Sunday. You are the prayer warrior in these parts, holding vigil over the folk in this area. Because this is your hometown. Signed, sealed, and delivered, this town is yours and you, because you were born here, belong to it. You belong to the people who show on Sundays and holidays and to those who sleep in, and to those who attend the Black church.

The swish of the high grass reassures you like a mother's shushing whisper as the building grows in your view.

And still, you might check for ticks.

Tom stopped to fish out his keys as the dissonance of the people from the rally fell in line with the discordant sounds coming from the dark. His eyes snapped up as his ears perked. The swish of the high grass originated deeper in the night, off to his right. Something was moving through the weeds. He glanced that way but saw nothing. No, not true. Under the light of the moon, he saw the grass swaying as something cut through it towards him.

"Who's there?" he asked, his voice cracking, the keys jingling in his hand.

The only clue the darkness would reveal, even as the tall grass stilled, was the low buzz of a primal growl carried to his ears. Tom Larsen felt the skin on the back of his neck ripple, forcing the hairs to attention. His balls receded up into his stomach, and his hands, sweaty now, unclenched. The keys dropped to the ground with a dull plunk.

"Fuck," he muttered, then knelt, scanning the darkness and the ground for any glint of metal, even as, from behind, he heard soft padding footsteps approaching. Groping blindly, his fingers slapped on the keys, nearly driving them into the dirt. Whatever approached moved carefully, its chest-deep rumble like the idling engine of some old muscle car. Tom could feel it in his chest. He snatched the keys up, fingered through them, and inserted the church's door key into the lock.

He didn't turn the light on right away, standing in the back office. He just pressed himself against the door after he locked it behind him, afraid to move, sure whatever had been out there still lurked outside. In fact, he did hear it. It nudged at the door. Not enough to make it move, but as if it bumped into the door to see if it had any give.

When a few moments passed, he turned the light on, offered up another sigh. Perhaps he should have just walked around. The back door was always locked, and he almost never—

There is a distinct sound when the metal-framed glass front door pulls closed after being opened, and in the silence of the church, that sound echoed through the vestibule and small sanctuary, across the dais and to the back hall, offices, and finally, this little space. Tom's eyes went wide, and his heart nearly stopped in his chest. A great lump caught in his throat, stifling any hope for sound. He could not shake the fear that had settled over him.

Still, his mind rallied against this. Taking a deep breath, he pushed open the office door and stepped into the back hall. "Hello!" he called, pausing long enough for the word to ricochet off the walls and reverberate throughout the building. Once he was sure his presence was known, he moved forward, pushing open the double doors to the sanctuary.

The smell hit him first. There was the wood varnish the cleaning lady used on the pews, the potpourri-smelling vacuum powder she sprinkled nightly across the carpet, the smell of the burnt wax from used candles, the incense. A hint of grape juice, even, from the last communion. But what he smelled most, what overpowered all of that, was something different. Something raw and wild, skunk-like almost, the smell of fur and the outside and of dirt.

The recessed lighting lit the sanctuary dimly in warm gilt softness that could not pool but diffused throughout the room. Nothing stood out from the pews that he could see instantly, but he was sure he was not alone. The smell suggested some animal had made its way in. Perhaps a fox or a chipmunk or, yes, a skunk. He scanned the shadows and rows of pews for any sign, for any movement, all while under a blanket of impenetrably chilling silence.

He fished out his cell and dialed the number for dispatch. When the line was answered, his voice rang hollow, upsetting the peace and sanctity of the room. "I think I have an animal in my church…Yes'm, Tom Larsen, down here in Blue Rock…You got animal control— Oh, okay. Well, yes, send the deputy then…That ought to be fine… Yes'm, the Methodist church."

He hung up and shoved the phone back in his pocket, never taking his eyes off a shadow in the back of the room, just behind the rear left pew. He'd been focused on it since he dialed, all through the short conversation, and now he could not tear his eyes away. It seemed to be vibrating, or moving, or ruffling.

A sound. The A/C had kicked on. Yes, he'd set the thermostat at sixty-nine degrees before heading out to the rally, so yes, that made sense that it had kicked on. Chancing a glance up to the ceiling, he saw that the shadow lay just below a vent, and so the ruffling made a bit more sense. It was like hair blowing in the wind. Hair.

The growl rose up from behind the pew not as a converted parishioner ready to sing the praises of Jesus, but as if the devil himself had arrived to offer rebuke to the congregation's misplaced faith. The sound climbed over the pew and snaked down the aisle and reached Tom Larsen's ears and told him that what existed inside this building was not a holy thing or a thing created by God. What had found its way inside was death, and this was its carrion call.

And then it stood. Simply and clearly, it stood. No need to hide anymore. It knew, just as he knew, there was nowhere to run. So why play games? Why stick only to the shadows? It was so much easier to extend itself and really strike the terror in him.

He thought the wolf's head was a mask at first, and that someone wore a whole costume. But then the lips snarled and the eyes—which weren't deep set as though someone staring out through a mask—widened, the pupils adjusting in the soft light from bright black orbs to pinpricks, an action so apparent he could see it all the way on the other side of the small sanctuary.

The beast cocked its head back and let loose a howl that shook the walls of the building, the high, piercing sound like needles in his ears, stabbing at him. Tom Larsen, already feeling the piss run down his thighs, uttered the meekest of screams, a squeak not unlike a titmouse evading a hawk, clapped his hands over his ears in an effort to shield them, and ran back into the back hall.

His mind was empty save for the scream he wanted to let loose, blocking any and all rational thought. He tried doors much like a warbling zombie, even as he could process the sounds of the beast approaching. It did not stalk mutely. No sir. The pews were upturned violently, wood colliding on wood, wood splintering, and all the while the thing spit and growled and snarled and barked, its sounds closing in and closing in and he was running out of safe places. Until he saw the front doors. The doors he'd neglected to lock before leaving earlier that night. A glimmer of hope touched him. Perhaps the deputy was on his way. Perhaps, if he got out in the open, he could better gauge this creature's progress and he could meet the deputy. In the coming minutes, he would realize the folly of this logic, and that it would have been better to lock himself away somewhere and hide. But his terror had paralyzed any rational thought, and so in one last great attempt at survival, Tom Larsen bolted for the glass front doors, slamming them open, his left foot coming down wrong on the concrete porch and his hip twisting so that he settled instantly into a shuffling limp. He saw headlights in the distance. His arms frantically waved, and he found his voice, calling out, as from behind the growls and snarls grew, and joining them the sound of pads thudding on the pavement and claws clicking on the asphalt. When it sank its multitudinous canines into the flesh of his neck, dragging him down onto the pavement of the parking lot, Tom Larsen could only look up to the big bright moon and think of that one thing Christ had said. "I send you out as sheep amidst the wolves." So even Christ knew the wolves would eventually get them. Every last one of those pathetic, damned sheep.

C3&80

Because the radio silence was unrelenting, Aaron Bailey often blared the outlaw country station out of El Dorado through the cruiser's speakers as he patrolled the streets of the meager town of Blue Rock. At the moment he found the bloody mess in the parking lot of the Methodist church, an Arkansas native was crooning his own requiem while fumbling an acoustic guitar.

The car shut off and all but the cicadas silenced. Aaron approached the mass, squatted, recognized legs, arms, a head, a torso. The mass had clothes, and the clothes were familiar. As in…he'd just seen them. Worn by the local preacher at that rally. And all at once Deputy Bailey, constable of this little burg, understood the mystery of what lay in front of him and who brought it here.

Tom Larsen lay dead and mutilated by one of those Black Lives Matter supporters at that rally. Goddamn, he should have turned the shotgun on them. Tom Larsen was a good man. A peaceful man. A God-fearing man. What did this didn't fear God or nothing else.

Bailey fished his cell from his pocket as he scanned the road, dialing the operator up in Monticello, a dimwitted twit too old to even use the equipment.

"I need the sheriff," Bailey said.

"Who is this?"

"Fuck," he muttered to himself. "Bailey. Aaron Bailey. Deputy…Constable of Blue Rock." Not an official title, but one he'd awarded himself, not that the original title would have mattered to her.

"Who?"

"Jesus fucking Christ, I'm…"

The field next to the parking lot stood overgrown with thorn bushes and weeds and a few saplings stretching up before the pine forest took over at its other end. The blades of grass now trembled from a growl erupting in the shadows. Bailey's hand holding his cell fell limply to his side, the phone tumbling from his fingers to the asphalt, and he stared at the brush, shuddering from the growl. Were there stars overhead, or a full moon, beating down on him, giving light? He couldn't see this for what crouched in the darkness, singing praises to Helena in its guttural transmissions that vibrated his chest like an old 8-block roaring to life.

He drew his gun. "You come out now, ya hear?"

The cicadas quieted, and he smelled sweet honeysuckle mixed with the blood of the dead preacher. What he heard came as a bass line and sounded angry but almost tired by his presence. The brush swayed again. A cool wind tried to blow, but it only irritated the sweat and hairs on the back of his neck. For Aaron Bailey, all rational thought muted, and he swept his gun from side to side as he scanned the underbrush.

The brush stopped. Only silence and darkness met him. For seconds that felt like hours, nothing moved, and Bailey had just begun to feel he was alone when another growl erupted and the foliage parted, and from the underbrush the beast revealed itself.

The shadows tried their best to conceal the creature from the moonlight and Deputy Bailey's eyes. The head suggested a wolf, but it stood on two strong legs and its front paws more resembled arms with long claws that still dripped Tom Larsen's blood and innards. Its muscular body was covered with dark hair. It lifted its head toward the moon and cracked its jaw wide, loosing a howl that set off the patrol car's alarm and shook the flora behind it. Bailey ducked and shielded his ear with his free hand, but while he tried to keep the handgun aimed at the creature, he couldn't help but wince his eyes shut to help guard against the sound. But in that quick second, in that briefest of seconds, as Bailey reacted involuntarily to the sound, the beast took notice and lunged. The deputy found himself on his back, struggling against the creature as it gnashed its jaws and thrashed at him with its claws. Luckily, he hadn't dropped his gun, but he could see his own blood spraying up as the snout of the thing dripped blood-stained saliva onto his neck and cheeks and mouth, and he knew he couldn't survive much longer, so he raised his gun and aimed and pulled the trigger several times successively into the torso of the monster. Its gut exploded into chunks of meat and blood, and it yowled in pain, leaping off him, retreating back to the brush line, looking at him hurtfully before skittering into the foliage and the shadow.

Bailey sat up and bent his legs, the gun and the hand that held it perched on his knees, ready to fire should the thing come back, as his free hand clutched his own stomach. The blood flowed out of him freely; with each pump of his heart his vision blurred then darkened. Soon, he wouldn't even see his life leave him. Yes, he was dying, and the process was cold and dark and lonely. His mind was on fire and his senses stood at attention, alert to anything subtle, anything minor. A crawdad scurried toward him from the ditch, and his finger twitched. An aura stood around the brush, cast by the moonlight, and he watched the individual blades of grass dance. His attack was a dream already, something ephemeral, silent like the old movies at the cineplex in Chittester, spurned on by music but no real sound. Real sound had stopped. The landscape felt abandoned. Cold.

Though his cell lay out of reach, Bailey stretched across the asphalt to snag the instrument and, struggling for breath, called for help. He was pretty sure he got the words out before blackness encompassed him and his world went silent.

∽∽

Michael awoke with a fire tearing through his gut, his back and stomach covered in blood. He screamed out, startling a coupling of kestrels who fluttered away noisily. He twisted himself into the fetal position, clutching at his gut, sure they'd spill out. He inhaled greatly, felt something in his throat shift, the air cut off. Then, he began gagging. Something had lodged in his esophagus. He crawled to his hands and knees and contracted his stomach, attempting to force a cough, something. No air came. A great creaking sound came from the blockage in his throat. He stared at his hands and counted his appendages as his vision blurred, first two then four then six, felt the tears, made a creaky aspirated sound again, and coughed. Projectiles exploded from between his lips. He tasted, or thought he tasted, brass. He saw them shine against the dull straw and dusty shadows of the barn wood slats. Three shells. Bullets. He touched his stomach and looked down. Three craters not there the day before tattooed his stomach. But if he'd been shot, why wasn't he dead? This was something new and uncomfortable for him, and he didn't know where to turn for answers.

CHAPTER SEVEN

Blue Rock crawled begrudgingly toward autumn, choosing to hang on to summer for as long as she could. Anymore it wasn't unusual to find a run of days in the upper seventies or lower eighties, even into late September or October. First frost didn't occur until mid to late October, and generally after that came what the old timers called "Indian Summer," though that term didn't fly with the younger generation. A month had passed since the Black Lives Matter gathering, but even with the death of Reverend Larsen, the heated rhetoric had diminished little. Duke Johnson and his allies wanted the Drew statue removed. Bob Larsen, the sheriff, and their sympathizers opposed such a drastic change.

The morning started for Madeline when she rolled on her side and felt a wet tongue lap across her face. She opened her eyes and waited for them to focus. A large, rectangular shape filled her vision. Brown oval eyes came into view as sleep abandoned her. The eyes were soft, training on her with a pitiable look. Hot breath reeking of dried dog food and stale treats wafted into her face.

"Dart," Madeline said, wishing she could sink deeper into her own pillow and mattress. The dog huffed. Spun in place as if chasing his own tail, then wagged his butt and pulled his lips back into his best impression of a human grin, his eyes softening.

"John!" Madeline called out. Dart adjusted himself, but other than the swish of the dog's tail across the hardwood floor, the house was silent. Madeline lifted her head a bit. "John Kelly!" she called. Dart stepped to position himself in front of her, and raised his head. His tail swept the floor underneath bare of all dust. Madeline raised herself onto her elbow and dragged her phone off the side table. That was when she saw the text.

Hey sis, left for my 6 wk shift at the lumbermill, they gots us clearing another tract so time to make a bit more $$, love ya, see to Dart will ya, 4 the nex few wks see how Michael feeling yeah JKJ

JKJ. Madeline sighed. Her brother was just as daft at texting as Boomers. She ran a hand through her hair and dropped the phone on her mattress and the plush blanket that cushioned her. And his abysmal grammar. She shook her head, imagining both parents rolling over in their graves. There was a time when John Kelly knew better.

She thought back to their argument the night before. John Kelly had come inside from the backyard, soured from a phone call. "Leave's over," he said, a bit terse. "Gotta go back to making the Benjamins."

"We still haven't been able to reach Michael," she had said. This hadn't been meant as anything other than a fact, her voicing her own concerns, but it set her brother off.

"Man, fuck Michael. He wanna diss us like this, then fuck him. I got bills, Maddy. Mom and Dad left us a mortgage. This house ain't gonna pay for itself."

"I know," she said, a bit taken aback. She'd been sitting on the couch, loving on Dart, when John Kelly had entered, but now she stood and faced him.

"And all your schoolin' ain't gonna pay the goddamn bills either," he continued. He was rummaging through the cabinets in the kitchen, found a glass and turned on the tap, then moved to the fridge and pulled an ice tray out of the freezer, popping a few cubes out and into the plastic cup before filling the rest with water.

"You can't run away," she said. "Equivocating will only keep you on the sidelines for so long."

"What you say?" he asked, turning toward her. "What the fuck you just say? I'm paying bills, Maddy. Call me 'equivocating.' What the fuck that even mean. Shit. You the one running. Who stayed behind, taking care of Mom and Dad and our home—"

"You didn't have to," she interrupted, rounding the couch to confront him in the kitchen. Dart's eyes shifted between the two. "We could have called in hospice. Christ, we can even sell the fucking house."

"No white folk from Monticello gone come in and overcharge us to sit nursemaid for our parents when we cain't even afford that shit."

"Insurance would have—"

He pointed to the stack of envelopes on the table. "That's all what insurance din't pay, Maddy. Didn't pay shit. And we stuck with it. Well, I am anyway."

"I'll help you pay—"

"With what? Your goddamn student loan? A Pell grant? You ain't got no job, Maddy. You just got words like 'anodyne' that ain't gone cover no bills."

"Do you know how much people with a Master's in my field make?" she asked.

"But you ain't got no Master's, yet, Maddy. And how long will it take? Two years? Three or four? We ain't got that kinda time. Bills due now, Maddy."

"You're scared," she said then, her eyes narrowing. When he turned his back on her, she grabbed his shoulder and made him face her. "You're scared, John Kelly. You're pissed that I've gone out and pursued my own dreams and you're too scared to pursue your own dreams, so you stay here like it's some kind of duty. When all it is, is you scared."

He was breathing hard, looming over her, his chest heaving. He was a good head taller than she, and he wore a look now that anyone else might've misinterpreted for vehement hate or a longing for violence. She knew her brother, however, and knew he wasn't capable. He was all bark and no bite.

"Not everyone has the luxury of pursuing dreams when…" His voice trailed off, and he resumed staring at her.

"What?" she asked, all the fight gone out of her own voice.

"Nothing," he said, and downed the glass of water. "I'm going to bed. Gotta be up early tomorrow. Ride's coming before dawn."

❧

She sat up in bed and ruffled the top of the dog's head. That was how they'd left things, and now he was back at the logging camp. The dog huffed at her expectantly.

"Your daddy's gone out to make a buck," she said to the dog, and regarded him. Dart seemed to already be aware of this and had appointed her *master au lieu de*. "And you need breakfast."

This word sent the Lab into another tailspin, and drool formed at his maw. Maddy rose and padded into the kitchen, scratching an itch where her underwear had ridden at her thighs, checked the dog's water and, seeing it sufficiently filled, seized a cup of dry food out of the bag in the pantry so the pup could scarf it down. She'd just turned to the coffee maker when she muttered, "Fuck," and returned to the pantry, this time fishing out a gummy-like pellet from a bag promoting joint health, remembering at the last minute that Dart took this supplement with breakfast every morning. Dart eagerly took the treat then raced to the back door.

"Creature of habit," Maddy said, grinning despite herself, opening the door so the dog could live up to his namesake and bolt out to relieve his bladder.

It was over coffee that Maddy got her bearings and knew she wanted to see how Michael was. Dart returned and curled up at her feet, close enough that she could just bend down and stroke the fur while not disrupting her imbibing, so that both petting the dog and drinking her coffee became nearly mindless activities, freeing her brain for more introspection.

He'd darted out of the gypsy tent so quickly that day. He was so adamant about them going home not long after. For the two week's since, he'd been sick, and while at first he took her calls or responded to her texts, for the past few days there had been no word from him. *Oh, Michael*, she thought. *What's wrong?* Something like a shadow flitted over the kitchen window, darkening the room, the table. Dart let just the briefest of whimpers.

CRⱭ

Evening walks proved peaceful and effective in reducing Maddy's anxiety. A few nights later, Madeline allowed Dart to lead her on one of those walks, guiding them by his nose, and decide when it was time to lead her home. The walks helped her push away thoughts of grad school and even of Michael, both still there, but they weren't present on the walks. She let her senses take over, focusing on the smells and sounds and autumn air of the outside. Crickets chirped and while it was hot and humid, her shirt clinging to her form, she was sure she smelled rain. Flashes of summer thunder convinced her to end the walk early and return home. As they walked back into the living room, she removed Dart's leash, and he jumped up to offer her a peck, his ears back, a grin on his lips. His tail swished across the floor, his doe-eyes focused on her. She squatted and ran her fingers over the bridge of his nose, his brow, down the back of his skull and his spine, caressing the fluffed fur of his coat. To respond, his tail thumped on the carpet and his tongue lashed out again, catching her lips.

He deserved a treat, so she followed him into the kitchen and fetched one from the pantry. She also grabbed the hot chocolate and made herself a cup. The dog, finished with his treat before she added the marshmallows to her mug, curled up on the couch, ready for snuggling. From the wood box, she threw in a few twigs, added a wax starter, lit it, and watched the flames. When they rose high enough, she added a thicker log. Then another. The fire was warm and comforting. They had been assailed recently by storms from the gulf. The national weather service had resorted to the names of the Greek alphabet in an effort to name the invading storms, something that had never happened before.

When she sat, she ran her fingers through his fur. It was pliable, his skin underneath giving, his muscles relaxed.

Michael was alone in that house. Isolated, alone, and cold, and perhaps haunted. Of course, he was haunted. Why else would he stay there? The only rational reason she could fathom was survivor's guilt. Not only had not enough years passed, enough would never pass to relieve him of the loss of his family. She realized he'd chosen to live with their ghosts, to wallow in the past, to flagellate himself on the daily for preconceived wrongs or sins or whatever the fuck he chained himself to. She didn't want this to be her problem. It wasn't, truthfully, except that he was her friend and had been her friend and that meant something to her. Their shared childhood, growing up together like extended family, could not be ignored. And he hadn't done anything to her personally. He hadn't raised a voice to her, or told her to get lost, or even try to manipulate or gaslight her with his guilt. He had withdrawn into that house, into himself, and let the torrent of his depression and grief vanish him. She could not, in good conscience, allow him to remain a castaway to his troubled mind.

Another storm was blowing in. Today the temperature dropped some thirty degrees from the day before, such was the climate in Arkansas. The wind assaulted the siding in screams and howled around the gutters, and the rain began with its steady, rhythmic drum beats on the tin roof, echoing around them. The shadows hung coolly over the house and its rooms, the light through the windows dim and illuminating little. With no A/C or heat on, with only the fire in the fireplace to break the chill, the house maintained an even temperature and stayed silent to boot. She slept well in storms as long as no dangerous weather was expected, so tonight, she figured, she would sleep like the dead.

Maddy approached the bed, slipping into her pajamas, brushing her teeth, using the dental wipes on Dart, who reluctantly agreed as she cradled his head. Lightning flashed through the closed blinds.

Another howl, but Dart raised his head and perked his ears, a low growl in his chest, and she thought, *That wasn't the wind.*

She sank onto the mattress in the second bedroom, sure Dart would curl up next to her as he had in the past, as he had with John Kelly in the master, but the Lab stood and moved into the hall, staring into the darkened house, conversing with just a few huffs.

She sat up and wondered if she heard something at the window even as Dart stood at attention. Madeline pulled the covers back and slapped the mattress and offered a smile, to which the dog turned tail and entered the master bedroom.

Madeline glanced back at the window, listening to the storm, seeing the flashes. Was there something, just outside the thin pane of glass, itching to get in? Only her imagination, perhaps. She left her bed and walked into her parents' room. The dog lay curled on the mattress, staring at her longingly, brow furrowed, willing her to join him.

The dog saw this room as John Kelly's, not her parents'. Maddy found herself a bit upset by this. It was as though her parents' memories were being erased. There was little room for her and nearly none for them, now. This space felt confined, claustrophobic, alien. She was invading this room, a long-sealed tomb her caravan just penetrated, and Dart was prodding her to do so. From outside came a sound, like someone had taken a rake against the siding and huffed and snorted as it circled them.

Maybe this was where she belonged. What could it hurt, she thought, sleeping here one night. At least. Perhaps it would keep whatever was outside at bay.

She pulled the covers back and climbed in bed. It smelled of the ghosts of her father's Drakkur and her mother's Dream Angels Heavenly, or at least she wanted that to be true. Her brother had imprinted no scent, not yet, or none that she could detect. The dog pressed his spine against her thighs and rolled over, and Madeline switched off the lamp. With the darkness came a peace and a silence that she wasn't prepared for. While the house was still cold, she wasn't, for the snuggling of Dart. Whatever raked against the siding had subsided. However temporary, peace had come to her.

CRSO

The only way Michael could survive, assuming that was his goal, was to fall into a routine. A routine would keep him safe. At least from himself, if not from others. It was a blessing that the deputy wasn't killed. As summer faded to fall and he grew used to the chains in the barn, Michael felt the ritual spread out in front of him.

The willpower to chain himself up at night came easily, for fear of hurting others, but it didn't relinquish the dreams. He dreamed nightly of running, trancing through the brush, feeling the prickly blades of pampas grass ruffle the fur down his spine. He dreamed of catching squirrel or deer even, or one time an honest-to-god wild razorback, and sinking his teeth into the buttery meat, the taste of salt and copper touching his lips first, followed by the flesh and muscle, sinewy but tearing easily with his canines.

The daylight was the hardest of times. He longed to see Maddy again, to talk to people. He began pacing his home, hoping to avoid the ghosts, watching the world pass by outside the windows. One day, to pass the time, he began cleaning. It surprised him how much time passed. When evening finally came, the entire living room was spic and span. Still, it needed something more, after the dirt was swept and the windows were cleaned and the baseboards were scrubbed, the furniture dusted. He decided, noting the hour, it needed a paint job.

Returning to the barn that night, Michael took the time to find some brushes and a few gallons of paint that hadn't been all used up. These he set by the locked door to pick up in the morning, and started for the ladder up to the loft, when he noticed, tucked in the corner, a large gray canopy covering a massive heap. The canopy he removed, as it got cold up in the loft, and as the year progressed on, it would only get colder still at night. What he found underneath surprised him. Stacks of dimensional lumber and plywood, all ready to be cut. There on top, a number of pieces of crown molding. The living room could be dressed up with some trim, painted also. At his father's old work bench, he found that while dusty, the tools he'd need were all there. He plugged in the miter saw and squeezed the handle just long enough to see the blade spin to life. The pneumatic nail gun with a working electric air compressor still fired. The outlets worked. Michael had never allowed the electricity to be cut to the property, but given the age of the home and the barn, he was surprised the wiring still held up.

He'd wadded up the canopy as best he could, and tucking it under one arm, carried it up the ladder with him. He laid it close by should he need it. After he kicked off his shoes and peeled away his socks, he snapped the bracelets first around his ankles, and then around each wrist, and, laying back, stared out the west-facing window to watch the light fade. His last pure thought before he felt the draw of the moon was that fixing up his father's house, his family home, was at least a good first act of atonement.

CR€O

The next day, the walk took her and Dart by the silent and still Risten farm, but the emptiness wasn't what unnerved Maddy. Dart tugged at the leash, to the point of nearly coughing, but Madeline held firm, restraining the dog from exploring so she could fully take in the old homestead.

"Michael," she called. She mounted the porch steps and tried the door, but no sounds indicated anyone was inside. Had he left again? The quiet suggested so.

That Christmas morning ten years earlier returned to her clear as day. There had been bunk beds then. She had the bottom bunk. John Kelly the upper. It was her mother who'd entered. She could hear her father on the phone out in the living room. His voice was hurried and near panicked. She'd never heard her father like that. As sleep abandoned her, she had caught snippets of words that had stuck with her since. "Massacre." "Survivor." "Homeless."

She'd felt it. They—her father and whoever he was speaking to— were referring to Michael. Michael had been her friend since forever. She'd grown up with him. With his brothers. She lay there, her mother cradling her, shushing her and John Kelly though neither had really acted upset.

"Mama," Madeline had said.

"Shush, chile," her mother said, and tried to rock her, though with the way Maddy was laying, rocking her only hurt her neck. She coughed because her airway was restricted.

Had she been inside since that day? As Dart pushed the limits of the leash, anxious to sniff at the boundaries, she struggled to remember. Perhaps not. Probably? She knew the interior of the house like the back of her hand. But had she seen it? Not since that day.

That day Michael moved in with them. Looking like nothing you could say would help him, because he'd lost his whole family, and she couldn't understand such loss even though she, too, had been close to them.

She knew she should not measure in gradations the levels of loss. She could not, nor should she, dismiss her sadness at losing a whole family she had been close to. She had laughed with them and had shared with them and the Ristens had been a part of her life since time immemorial. Their funeral (one massive requiem for the entire family, a collection of closed caskets like a funeral parlor sales event) left her weeping uncontrollably and neither she nor Michael could console each other during the services.

But Michael was distressed, and Madeline was distressed for him. How many nights after the funerals had she cradled him? Consoled him? How many...

Not right after. She pursed her lips and stared up at the blinds. Had they shifted? With the gleam of the light she couldn't be sure. Dart, desperate to run, whined. Maddy nodded and shushed him. He sat obediently and waited for her next command.

"Spring," she said. The tall stalks of fescue quivered in the breeze at the whisper of this word. His parents had died that Christmas, but she didn't see him again until the next spring.

But that wasn't true, either. She saw him during the day. All the time, in fact. But she didn't see him at night. She saw...

And froze in thought. Some image was there, trapped in time. It involved her father. It involved her mother coming to them. Her mother had prayed a lot in those days.

But there was prom. She saw him at prom. She knew he was there at prom. And he had been. But prom was in the spring.

And the farm was abandoned then, and it is abandoned now. Except, he should be here.

"Michael!" she called.

No answer. The house was still and cold and the fescue whispered in the wind, but not to address her. It was as though the earth found her plea trivial.

Dart whimpered, rushed back to her side, pressed against her shins. Absently, Madeline bent and stroked the dog's spine.

CRSO

When she opened the door that afternoon, she was startled to see the sheriff. He stood alone but just as imposing as if he'd been surrounded by a cadre of deputies. He removed his cowboy hat and dipped his head as if nodding before asking to enter. Dart approached long enough to sniff him out and let the sheriff ruffle the top of his head.

"Miss," he said, rising only to bow his head. The bleached white cowboy hat contrasted his pudgy ruddy cheeks, his greasy gray hair, his gray eyes. He stood a hair shorter than she. His lips were cracked and pale. Maddy nodded and stepped aside so he could make his way. Dart hugged her, glaring at the intruder while pressing up against her so hard she nearly toppled over.

"Got any coffee?" he asked. He removed his hat and sat on the loveseat.

"I can make some," she said, frowning at the intrusiveness.

"That'd be mighty fine," he nodded. She'd not felt so powerless in her home in a long while.

As the coffee brewed, she gripped at the kitchen counter and called out, "What's to your visit, Sheriff?"

"Naw," he called back. "Best let me get a sip of the java first."

"How you take it?"

"Black," he responded, something proud in his voice like it ought to ease her or something. The word off his lips forced a shiver.

She sat the cup in front of him, a saucer underneath, and sat back on the couch as Dart jumped up and curled next to her.

"Purty dog," he said, raising the cup to his lips and sipping.

"How's Deputy Bailey?" she asked.

He dropped his eyes and nodded, but his countenance revealed little.

"Little better ever' day," he said. There was a bit of the grave in his voice. The whole town knew Aaron Bailey had been in surgery for thirty-six hours after the attack.

"I'm sorry," Maddy said, but didn't feel it, and wasn't surprised to realize she didn't mean it.

Dart huffed. Maddy stroked his fur.

"You been in town about as long as that Risten boy," the sheriff said.

"Michael?"

The sheriff curlicued his mouth and nodded. Raised his eyes as he took another sip then dropped them quickly. "Yeah, forgot y'all knew each other."

"A long time," Madeline volunteered, but she didn't want to reveal much else. Even still, she was sure the sheriff had done his homework.

"Sure," he said, nearly winking at her. He took another sip. It was like he was just tasting the coffee, not really drinking it.

"What can I help you with, Sheriff?"

He smiled. "You know Ole McDermott over just outside of Dumas?"

Madeline shook her head. She'd never heard the name.

"Well," the sheriff continued, sipping again at his coffee, "he got a chicken farm."

E-I-E-I-O, Madeline thought.

"And that chicken farm got raided a week or so ago," the sheriff said.

"What do you mean, raided?" Madeline asked.

The sheriff shrugged. "His chickens are dead. You know, Miss Jeansonne, who the biggest turkey farmer in the state of Arkansas is?"

Dart stretched, pressing his front paws against her thigh. She ran her fingers through the fur on his spine.

"I don't care," she said. "What is your purpose here, Sheriff?"

He smiled, took a final, long sip, then dropped the cup on its saucer. He leaned back on the loveseat and folded his arms and winked at her.

"You and Michael Risten are both new in town. Since you've been back, we've had chickens attacked and steers killed and that turkey farm incident, not to mention Tom Larsen's death and Deputy Bailey being hospitalized."

Maddy shifted in her seat. She dropped her eyes a little.

"Now," the sheriff continued. "If that were all, we might say it's all coincidental. But we got to factor in that big murder of the Risten family way back when."

"Okay." Maddy kept her voice even. "So. If you're accusing me or my brother, or Michael, even—"

The sheriff smiled and waved his hand. "No, ma'am," he said. "I'm just talking is all. And your brother is a fine member of this community. But I got to look at the trail that's formed, and it all seems to lead back here."

"I don't think I can help you, Sheriff."

She pet the dog, curled up beside her on the couch, and dropped her eyes. Did he know that the power he wielded could make people feel guilty even when they did nothing wrong? She imagined so. He'd been in law enforcement a long time here in South Arkansas.

"Michael ain't here, I guessed. Must be back at his folk's home. I might just mosey on out there and talk to him a spell."

"Michael…" she muttered again. Had the sheriff been watching her? Did he know she was just out there looking for him? He had to have. It was too coincidental.

The old man winked. "Awful lot of death surrounding you kids. Especially when you factor in what happened at Ole Miss last spring."

Michael had been attending Ole Miss last spring. Maddy frowned. "What…"

The sheriff stood, brushed off his pants like it was a matter of habit, frowned at her and turned to the door. "Awful business really," he said, and reached for the doorknob. "That murder at his apartment complex."

"Murder," she repeated. Her lips pressed together in a straight, flat, thin line that robbed them of color and her of her voice. The sheriff nodded and excused himself. Madeline stood frozen, arms by her side, her lips quivering. Dart looked up at her expectantly. Only when she heard the engine start did she sit and stroke the dog's fur, and Dart reclined, content. If only Maddy felt the same.

CRS8O

In the weeks since Aaron Bailey had been attacked, a lot had happened. Ole McDermott's chicken coup was raided, for one. Then there was that turkey farm not too much further off. Then Daly Pond: that incident. And don't forget the deer. Where to start?

The deer were in the news. The Democrat Gazette reported the story just because it was so strange. It wasn't just one dead animal. State troopers had responded to calls from excited motorists who, commuting to and from jobs along the highway abutting Blue Rock, reported seeing a multitude of deer carcasses along the shoulder of the divided state highway. There were even a few scattered bodies in the median.

They weren't roadkill. Sure, some of the motorists saw this, but this fact wasn't truly discovered until the state troopers arrived on scene. They'd never seen anything like this, and they bet no other peace officer anywhere in the continental United States had seen anything like this either. If it had been an actual bet, these troopers would have won.

The carcasses didn't line up with standard deer who'd met the business end of a metal automobile traveling seventy miles per hour. The trauma wasn't blunt. More, something had pulled their rib cages apart. Something had used what looked like a razor to slice open their flesh, and upon closer inspection, teeth marks could be seen on their internal organs.

Aaron Bailey dreamed of the deer. He thrashed in his bed so violently that the staff had to restrain him. Not all the time. Just when he dreamed about them. Not every night, but some nights. Nights when the moon shone bright through his hospital window. Once things got so bad, they administered Haldol. Still, when the autumn moon was bright, this barely restrained the deputy.

CRSO

Michael's projects carried him well into the fall, but it was only a day or so into the isolation that he realized he had a problem. Food was running out, and he had to find a way to restock his pantry and fridge without alerting the town to his presence. So, one particularly windy day he pulled on his jean jacket and a skull cap, a cloth mask and some sunglasses and took to the backroads and through the backyards of their neighbors, skirting any of the main thoroughfares, until he approached the old familiar Jeansonne homestead through the thin tree line that abutted the yards of the houses on that street. He clung to the bark of a pine as he watched, in the distance, Maddy outside, playing with John Kelly's dog. He could have stood there all day watching her, if not for the shift of the wind and the dog, sniffing the air, alerting to his presence.

"What is it, boy?" Maddy asked, facing the tree line as the dog barked.

Michael left, dejected. He couldn't let her know he was still here. What must she think of him? No, it was better to hide from her, let her think he had left town.

Skirting the town, he passed the old trailer park, and thought about reaching out to Casey before realizing she wouldn't be much better. The Calhoun kid saw Michael but didn't seem to recognize him. Byron had noticed the strange white guy walk around the park. The kid was loitering around the gravel drive in front of his trailer, playing on his cell.

Michael approached slowly, checking to see if anyone else was around.

"Hey," he said. Byron Calhoun ignored him.

"Hey, kid. Byron, right?."

Byron finally raised his eyes and studied what features he could see, a white nose and some tuffs of brown hair, white ears.

"What you want?" Byron asked.

"You wanna make a hundred bucks?"

Calhoun didn't back away, but looked Michael up and down, inspecting the goods.

"It ain't like that, kid. Can you keep a secret? It's me."

He removed the sunglasses and lowered the mask to better show his face.

"Michael Risten! Damn, I heard you was back, but I heard—"

"Keep your voice down!" He looked around to see if anyone had noticed them, then squatted to meet the kid eye to eye.

"I don't want anyone to know I'm here, okay. I just want to be left alone."

"Even Casey?" Byron asked.

Michael nodded. "Not Casey, not Maddy, not your Ma, not no one."

"So, what are you doing here?" Byron asked. A fair enough question.

"I'm going to order some groceries for delivery, for here, while your ma's at work. When it comes, you text me, and I'll come get it. Or else you can run them out to my house just as long as no one sees you. But for watching my groceries every couple of weeks, I'll give you a hundred bucks."

"That's it? Just watch to make sure your food gets delivered, and bring it out to you or else tell you it's here?"

"That's it, and in exchange I'll give you a hundred bucks." From his wallet, Michael pulled a crisp C-note and waved it in front of Byron.

"I can do that," Byron said, snatching the note out of the air.

"Now remember," Michael cautioned. "I'll text you to let you know I'm placing the order, and you'll text me when it gets here or when you're bringing it out. But I'm also paying you to keep quiet about seeing me."

Byron nodded, and they exchanged cell numbers.

With that little chore out of the way, Michael returned home, and as the weeks passed he found it surprisingly easy to fulfill his food orders that way. Most of the time, Byron carried the groceries to him, bored as he must have been at his home. He'd text Michael when he sat them on the back porch, and Michael would come out and hand him his money. Only once, when he thought his mother might have the virus but it turned out to be a cold, but as she was at home he couldn't get away, and she nearly caught the delivery guy dropping off the bags, did he text Michael and ask him to come get them.

It wasn't ever so much that he couldn't manage in one trip, either, especially if he repacked the groceries in fewer bags. Salad stuff, a half-gallon of milk, frozen fish and some boneless chicken breasts and some hamburger meat, some bread. Occasionally there might be some mustard or mayonnaise or even some ranch dressing, and once there was a big package of toilet paper that he had to tuck under his arm because it wouldn't fit in those flimsy plastic bags. But most of the time it wasn't bad, and he could take the backroads and cut through the trees to the Risten farm easily enough without being seen.

Michael spent the time working on the house. He painted the living room then taught himself how to cut crown molding corners, practicing first with the miter saw and some scrap pieces of 2x4's before moving on to the trim. When he finished the living room, he moved upstairs, patching holes, painting walls, adding trim and repairing the areas that needed it. it where it had fallen into disrepair. He found a quiet kind of existence in the isolation, upturned only by the violence of his dreams as he lay shackled in the barn loft.

One particular night, the dreams came stranger than any he could remember. Surrounded by howls, he dreamt he was pinned down by the old witch's brothers, thrashing with futility in their grasp as she leaned over him, whispering chants in Creole, before placing something over his head. After that, nothing. Just peace. And then he awoke.

Morning had come quickly, and Michael stretched, already feeling more refreshed than he had in years. But it was as he stretched that he noticed something. Neither his ankles nor his wrists bore the weight of the shackles he usually woke to. In fact, his reach was greater, not restricted by the chain length. Sure enough, as his eyes opened, he found that his shackles hadn't held. Panic set in quickly. Michael ignored it, ignoring just how good he felt, how rested he felt this morning, unlike a thousand mornings before. His mind raced. How could he find out if anyone got hurt? And then it hit him. It was grocery day.

He raced down the barn ladder and jolted across the yard to his house. In the kitchen he slammed his palms on the table. His phone was gone. He always left it on the table, every night, before locking the house and going out to the barn. What if someone had gotten into his house? What if Maddy had come, or Casey? What if they found his phone? What if they alerted the sheriff? *Oh, god.* His heart was racing. He could feel it thumping in his chest. Sweat beaded on his forehead. His cheeks flushed. Pacing, Michael began to try and calculate how much he had in his account, and where he could go. Mexico? South America? Jesus, most borders were closed to the US because of the pandemic. His thoughts swirled around him and he clutched at his chest, felt something hot in his fingers, heavy and jagged.

Jagged? His fingers probed to the object just under his shirt, and now he detected something like a chain or rope against the flesh of his neck. In the bathroom he turned on the light and unbuttoned his shirt and examined the silver pentagram hanging around his neck, a piece of jewelry he'd never seen before.

The dream came back to him, unlike anything he'd ever dreamed before. And then the peace. How good he had felt upon awakening. He'd slept like the dead.

Swallowing hard, digesting all of this, he returned to the living room. His cellphone lay on the coffee table. *Stupid!* How could he have missed it? Snatching it up, he quickly texted Byron Calhoun:

"Is everything okay in the town this morning? Do you know? Have you heard?"

Michael didn't like text speak. Didn't subscribe to it.

Minutes ticked by, then. "Fine. Wat up?"

"Nothing. See you soon."

Michael sighed. He thought of the most recent man haunting him, the mayor's brother. Michael still could remember the dream where he'd seen that man's murder. In the bathroom, he splashed water on his face, then went upstairs and changed his underwear and socks before redressing in the clothes from the day before. He visited the upstairs bathroom, splashing more water, catching only a glimpse of a sibling staring at him through the mirror's reflection. It didn't matter which one anymore. Eyeless, motionless, mute, they all looked the same.

The spring of the back door grabbed his attention, so he moved cautiously down the hall, looking over the banister to the first floor. It was too soon for Byron with the groceries, and Michael dared not alert anyone to his presence. He cursed himself for not locking the back door behind him.

"Master Risten!" the voice came, as if the old witch knew exactly where he was.

He plodded downstairs to find her alone, sitting at his kitchen table.

"You came."

"Came to see how you like your gift," she answered, motioning toward the amulet around his neck.

Michael took it in hand and looked at the pentagram again, his view from above caught the piece upside down, the kitchen light glinting off the sheen of the metallic surface.

"Saw one upstairs just now, didn't work."

Her laugh fit her: a high-pitched cackle, like a squeal. "'Dat ain't for dat, Master Risten. 'Dis is!"

She placed a black bladder shaped like a kidney, the narrow end corked, on the kitchen table with a plop and the base flattened some.

"Drink," she ordered, standing and backing away from the table, as though it were about to explode.

"What's this for, then?" Michael asked, motioning to the necklace, inching toward the black bladder.

"I tell you in a minute. Drink first. If you want rid of de visions."

The liquid filling the bladder shifted as he held it in his hands. It wasn't easy holding the pouch steady as he uncorked it, and some of the liquid spilled out. Rank putrescence greeted him, and the Creole witch turned her head away.

As bad as the smell was, the taste was worse. The liquid that had spilled was a tepid brown, something thick like gelatin, that coated his throat and slid down it like ink. He imagined he tasted feces and blood and other unpleasant things, and finally thrust the half-empty bladder toward her as he doubled over gagging, florid cords of drool dangling from his mouth.

"Take it," he managed.

"No," she said. "You must finish it fo' it tuh work."

A long moment passed as he struggled to regulate his breathing and squash the reflex to gag, then, his breathing regular, he wiped his mouth with his sleeve and straightened, glaring at her. He felt he might die if he finished this, but death would be better than seeing these damn ghosts. So, after a few deep breaths, Michael pushed the opening to his lips again and, squeezing wincing his eyes shut tight, tilted the bladder up and his head back, opening his throat.

When he was done, he collapsed at the kitchen table as she took the empty pouch and its cork and returned them to her burlap bag with the leather strap, the witch's purse. She then set about fixing him a cup of coffee, which he sipped gratefully, eager to remove the taste from his mouth.

"The medallion will hep you sleep at night. I slip it 'round yo' neck las night while you up in de chains."

"You took them off me."

She nodded. "You don't need 'em most nights, with dat. Only when da pull is strongest. When you can't resist, not even de amulet will hep you. Not even chains will help. The Rougarou will run free because it want to."

"What was that shit I just drank?"

A smile crept up to the old woman's lips, and a hint of that cackle returned before she spoke. "Yes, and other tings."

Michael shivered and gagged. His head swooned. He was sure he was about to vomit it all back up.

"Don't do dat, Master Risten. Not 'dat. You just get 'hold yo'self and breathe. No, not through yo' nose. Yo mouth. Like dat. Slow and easy."

Following her direction, the nausea passed slowly.

"What was that? That's not what I've taken in the past."

She wagged a finger at him. "Oh yes t'is, just mo' concentrate. A bit of wolfsbane, just de right amount, and a few other tings. I declare. Too much o' tha wolfsbane at de wrong time bring out de rougarou, and too much at de wrong time kill you. But just enough, with de right ingredients, along with de amulet, heps de animal sleep. You see no visions. You smell no weird tings or hear no weird tings normal people can't hear. You are at peace and so is de beast."

A few more breaths. His mind calmed. Rational thought slowly returned to him. Byron would be here soon with the groceries. "Thank you," he said. "Why'd you do this for me?" he asked.

"Phew!" the witch called out. "I didn't do dis for you! I did dis fo' Angelique Fontenot and her brothers Basil and Bela, and I did it for all de townsfolk who don't wanna end up dinner for de rougarou."

"I understand," he answered.

"I don't need no beast traipsing tru my home, eatin' me alive. Whew we, lahds no. I should o'come to you sooner, truf be told, but de bones were all reading wrong, and I couldn't find de time, what with dat man staying wit us."

"Who is he?" Michael asked. "He was with your brothers at the carnival, wasn't he?

She made an effort to nod but stared off as if deep in thought about the question. "He from de old country. Not France, where some my people hail from, and not from where my other people were stolen, but in Europe. He came to us several months ago and now he won't leave." She shook her head and looked away, and Michael could see worry on the old woman's face.

"What's wrong?" Michael asked.

She reached across the table and took hold of both his wrists, her dark, cataract-covered eyes staring into his own. "He here for you, Michael Risten. He here for de rougarou, and he ain't leavin' 'til he got you in da ground but for good. And Michael, dear, I cain't help you wit him. I cain't stop him."

"What should I do?" Michael asked.

"You run, child, and he follow you. You stay and he'll find you. Maybe you hope he finds the rougarou instead and it tougher dan he. Do' I warn you, child, he faced many a rougarou before and he still alive."

The panic attack started with a quivering lip, and soundlessly Michael sank his head to the table, wrapping his arms around to conceal his face. His breaths came shallow as the thoughts of his own mortality overwhelmed him. But why shouldn't they, with the pain and hurt he'd caused? Maybe he *should* just die. Maybe he should take his father's shotgun and just load it up with buckshot and put both barrels in his mouth.

"Why is all this happening? I didn't ask to be like this. I didn't want any of this."

Her hands were crusted over and dry and her palms were cool. One patted his forearm in what was meant to be, he was sure, solace.

"We play de hand we dealt, child, and you weren't dealt a good'un. Your family has secrets. I know some, not all. I know rumor, but tere are dose dat know de truf, and de truf is buried somewhere in dis house, if you got de stomach fo' it. But deah boy, it more bitter dan dat drink you just drunk, and you may not like de way it taste when all said and done."

And that was it. The weight of the world now rested on Michael's fragile frame. Tears pooled on the table below his cheeks. He didn't whimper or whine or call out; it was as though the burden that had become his life had settled on his shoulders and squeezed the tears out of him. When he looked up, finally, his cheeks streaked, he found that the witch was gone and that Byron Calhoun stood at his back step, bags in hand, and from the way he looked, he'd been there a while.

CRRO

Madeline found stories and pictures on Facebook, short testimonials on Twitter, pics on Instagram. She saw the deer carcasses and the bloodied chicken coop doused in red-stained feathers and enough turkey guts to swear her off Thanksgiving for the rest of her life. She knew where to look more closely. Aside from the proximity to the Mississippi River, there weren't a lot of natural bodies of water. In fact, most in these counties were self-contained within this land-locked state. Such was the case of Daly Pond. Daly

Pond had once been a gravel quarry, before rain and a deep-struck well changed its fate. Recognizing that ecological shift, state authorities began to accommodate. The quarry was opened for swimming, and every season—as the lake grew—the Fish and Wildlife Service replenished the aquatic life so that fishermen could enjoy the lake along with the swimmers. Catfish and bass and trout were populated. Parents and their kids stood on the shore or paddled out in boats to mine the treasure-trove of lake fauna.

It isn't important the name of one such parent or his child. Just that they'd arrived this early autumn morning, while Deputy Bailey healed up in his hospital bed. The father and his son had risen early. Prepared their bait. Their lines and lures. As dawn broke in the east, they'd hiked their gear, skidding down the gravel to the shore, pausing only for the gruesome scene in front of them.

They lay there lifeless. Countless silver eyes fixed on the sky above. Perch. Bass. Catfish. A smattering of trout. The scales were recognizable. That is, the bodies were identifiable. But something had torn into them.

This was the first place Maddy and Dart visited in person. It was accessible and didn't need the permission the chicken coop or turkey farm required. The dog was very interested in the rotting fish, so she had to tug back on his leash. Luckily, it was attached to a body harness, so he didn't choke or cough, just looked at her forlornly.

Maddy knelt at the water's edge. Her breath caught in her throat as the dead and rotting smell dripped through her nose and down to her stomach. Dart could barely contain himself. The Fish and Wildlife Service had done little to clean up the scene. Her fingers traced the current lapping at the gravel shore. The water was cool. The air was poisoned by the rotting and slaughtered carcasses of the fish scattered over the beach.

Dart pulled to the lapping waves, eagerly sniffing at a catfish carcass. Maddy yanked the leash then stroked the dog's fur when he looked at her with sad eyes that suggested, "I love you, Mommy."

"I love you too," she said.

But there they were. Countless eviscerated fish bodies, no longer flopping, on the shore. The blood had been washed away, but still the carcasses remained.

Maddy sighed. Dart curled up by her, feeling her warmth. Maddy nodded. "Something was hungry here," she said.

CRSO

When Deputy Aaron Bailey awoke to the sunlight streaming in through the hospital blinds, he screamed out. He'd dreamed of deer and dogs and cold. But these dreams, so vivid they roused him from a sound sleep to find his sheets soaked in sweat, his heart thudding, played in his mind even after his eyes opened. He could see the fish flopping on the shore, could smell their entrails, could taste the iron in the chicken blood. Deputy Aaron Bailey looked out the hospital window to a waxing moon drowning at the horizon, the blue of dawn, and his senses alive. Somehow, he knew, whatever had attacked him, he was now connected to it. What it saw, he saw. What it smelled and tracked, he smelled also. And when it killed, he could taste it, and he liked what he tasted.

CRSO

It was a short drive. The turkey farm smelled of shit worse than the chicken coop. She smelled it even before she exited the vehicle, even before she could see it. A row of oak and pine fenced in one side of the property. The yard was flat and uninspiring. Its most exciting decoration, a red, white, and blue campaign flag promising four more years of the current presidency, lay limply and weather worn against the single-story prefab house. Her anxiety increased. She retrieved Dart from the car and held tight to the leash attached to his harness, the dog eager to run and sniff and explore. To her left, the lazy majesty of the Ozarks stretched out. This was the furthest north she'd been in her life.

She had skirted Monticello and steered northeast, entering into the delta region of the state. Here, rice was the main cash crop, but that hadn't stopped a few intrepid farmers. The turkey farm was surrounded on three sides by flatlands that grew rice and corn and beans most of the time. Only to the north and west could she make out the first foothills of the Ozark hills beyond the copse of trees.

The wind blew south from that direction, dragging with it a bitterly cold sting to the flesh, burning her cheeks. Dart even winced, standing beside her. Clouds were amassing on the western horizon, pressing ever eastward. When the voice called out from behind, she didn't hear it at first. It was Dart, letting out a brief bark, turning in place, that alerted her that someone had stepped up to greet her.

She turned to find a meek elderly woman in a flower-patterned dress and apron, her hands working a towel into knots as she inched forward.

"Can I help you, miss?" the older woman asked.

"I'm sorry to bother you, ma'am," Madeline said, "but I heard you had an attack here recently. Your turkeys?"

The woman inched closer and squinted, studying her up and down. "You a Mexican, dear," the old woman said. Neither a statement nor a question, not an observation nor a judgment. That was how casual racism ran in the Ozarks. A woman such as this could not understand just how offensive her comment was.

"And what does that matter?" Madeline asked. "Would you not speak to me if I said I were, or would you prefer me to tell you that I'm African American…Black, and maybe what your grandparents would have considered as passing? The fact is, ma'am, I am worried about a friend of mine, and before you ask, no, he is not 'colored,' but a young white man, and he is in trouble, and it could be tied to what happened to your turkeys."

The woman frowned at this. That frown suggested that the meat of Madeline's point had completely gone over her head. "Well," the woman said, "I don't see how, unless he's the one what sicced the dog or whatever on my farm. Was your friend responsible?"

Maddy shook her head. "No, ma'am. What dog?"

"That's what our sheriff said. What he told the other'n. Several days ago. Said that it must've been a big dog or even a pack of 'um, or even some coyotes, though we only found one set of tracks in the mud lot leading up to the turkey house, so I don't see how it could have been coyotes."

"The other? Another cop?"

The woman nodded. "Sheriff from down yonder. But it weren't no coyotes—" she pronounced this *Kie-Yoats* "—neither. Tracks too big."

"I'm sorry for your loss," Madeline said. That sounded hollow and she knew it as she said it.

The woman shrugged. "Insurance'll cover it, I suppose. Force major or some such thing the insurance man said. Just lucky it weren't my grandbaby out in the lot at that time. Hate to think about that thing getting after a toddler."

"I'm sorry to bother you," Madeline said, and turned to her vehicle. "I truly hope this didn't set your family back."

She had just opened the rear door so Dart could jump back into the seat when the woman spoke up. "Young miss," she called out as

Dart looked expectantly out the window. "We ain't had wolves in this part of the country in decades. Maybe your friend owns a wolf?"

Something ticked across Maddy's brain, and she shook her head. "No, ma'am. He doesn't own any wolf."

She waved and thanked the lady again, sank behind the driver's seat, and drove off. She was hungry, and was sure Dart was as well, but there were only fast-food places to stop in this area of the state and Maddy really tried to not frequent such establishments. High blood pressure already ran in her family. She stopped at a gas station and found some low-sodium protein bars and a bottle of water. Snagged a paper cup and poured some water for the dog as she sat behind the wheel, processing all she learned.

A wolf. The lady at the turkey farm said wolf. The tracks were too big for a coyote.

If not a wild dog, then there was a wolf in the area. It wasn't until later that evening, curled up under a throw on the couch after a shower, Dart at her feet, that Madeline got the desire to pull up her laptop. She'd been trying to read, but the book wasn't holding her interest and she couldn't escape the idea that a wolf was prowling Arkansas.

First and foremost, she went to the Drew County Sheriff's website, but finding nothing of value there, she logged into Dillard Library's database system. Finding the right database took a little time, but ultimately she was able to uncover information about the Risten family murder a decade earlier.

Truth was, before today, she'd never really tried. After Michael moved in with them, her parents rarely talked about what he'd been through, and Michael never showed a willingness to talk about it either, even with her. The attack had been so violent, so traumatic, she wasn't even ready to talk about it herself, and found herself fiercely protecting Michael as they finished out their high school years whenever other kids (or the occasional crass adult) wanted to bring it up. She'd assumed, therefore, that since there was never an arrest, the responsible party had never been caught. That would mean that the case file would be open and so unavailable to the public. Imagine her surprise then when, working off a hunch that evening, she found the actual police file during her search, along with a few articles in papers at the time. The articles only embellished what the police report had verified. Animal attack. Something vicious got loose inside the family's home. A large animal with claws. A bear or a large cat would fit that criteria, though the police report ruled them out given the tracks and saliva and blood found. Arkansas had plenty of bears, and panthers used to be native to the northernmost regions of the state. There was even a big cat preserve up in the northwest corner of Arkansas home to lions and tigers and panthers and other large predators. All of them had been rescued from other shelters or zoos or dumbass people who thought a lion or tiger cub would make a cute pet and not realizing just how big the animals got or how illegal it was to own one. But no, the police report, signed by Sheriff Charley himself, had ruled out those possibilities. It had been a wolf.

Maddy sat back and bit her lip.

⋘∞⋙

As the fall pressed on, as the weather cooled, the undercurrent of meanness that followed the reddest of wasps and the orneriest of townsfolk through August washed away. Day by day, the temperature dropped in steps. 88. 85. 85. 84. Then perhaps a cold front would wash in. Temps would drop another ten degrees, hover for a bit. Maybe rise a day or two, then fall again. The nights were cool and growing colder.

The day Maddy heard Deputy Aaron Bailey was released from the hospital, she'd stocked up on wood for the firepit out back. John Kelly would kill her if he'd known she'd paid for a bundle of firewood, especially if he'd known that it cost her five bucks at a local gas station and probably wouldn't produce a fire that would warm a mosquito. But she'd invited Casey Davidson over and planned for them to sit out on the back porch. Temperatures dropped quickly once the sun set this time of year. On the way back from getting the wood, she had tried the Risten farm once more to see if Michael was home, and when she couldn't reach him, she returned to get ready for Casey's visit. Her worry for him, not hearing from him in so long, and given how he seemed when she did last see him, had plateaued at a great height. Her emotions weren't a roller-coaster and weren't all-consuming but had piqued so that whenever she thought of him, which was often since returning to this town, she found her anxiety nearly unchecked. Still, she carried on with her daily life as best she could. She chilled a six pack of wine coolers and drove to Monticello to pick up a pizza well before Casey was to show.

Back in the day, Casey and Michael had been sweet on each other. Michael had even taken her to prom. The thought had come to Maddy early on whether she ought to clue Casey in on what she'd learned, but what that was, she wasn't sure. She inventoried the facts stored in her mind over and over again, but she still couldn't see the connection between Michael and these latest attacks, other than proximity. That, and Michael was one of the victims.

There were wolf attacks in a location where wolves hadn't lived for decades. Not just other animals both wild and farmed, but also people. Michael's family, for one, but then those guys in the apartment complex Michael lived in back at Oxford. And while the attack at Ole Miss occurred in the spring, all the others were during the fall.

Just as Casey was set to arrive, Madeline found herself on her laptop once more, scrolling through what would have appeared to be the most random of sites to anyone else. The site was the US meteorological site that cataloged, among other things, weather conditions and temperatures around the US. All of the recent attacks in southeast Arkansas had occurred under clear conditions, the moon full or nearly full, and all as autumn pressed in. When the knock at the door came, Madeline didn't get up, though Dart barked and rose to greet the visitor. At Madeline's call, Casey entered, though Madeline couldn't pry herself away from her laptop just yet. She'd just typed in the date and location of the Risten family attack and found the same: late autumn / early winter, Christmas to be accurate, clear skies, gibbous moon. A fat, plump moon. Not full, per se, but still enough to give off a bright light over the night sky. Madeline quickly typed in a new location and date: Ole Miss and the attack at the apartment complex the sheriff had mentioned to her.

"Whatcha looking at?" Casey asked, grabbing her shoulders from behind and bending over her to peer at the laptop.

Madeline snapped the screen shut and forced a smile up to her friend. "Nothing. Bored with Reddit, is all."

Casey studied her like one studying an image for subtle changes. Her own smile faltered, and she nodded. "Okay. Say, thanks for inviting me over."

Madeline stood and dropped her laptop on the couch cushion, then led her friend into the kitchen to the pizza on the counter. Casey was talking about something, and Madeline nodded along and smiled and did her best to pretend to listen, even as she realized that she still couldn't understand this new bit of information or why the conditions at Ole Miss unsettled her. Then it dawned on her. The attack at Ole Miss had occurred during the spring, but all other attacks were reported during the fall.

Despite her fears and her brother's voice in her head, she got the fire pit going, and found conversation easily enough as the temperature dropped. When the high flames weren't enough—or when enough of the wine coolers had impacted their heads and eyes—each girl snagged a blanket and settled into a comfortable silence, Madeline in the chair with Dart at her side, and Casey in the chaise.

Madeline filled the silence by mentally reviewing the facts, almost forgetting her friend sat with her, before Casey piped up.

"I saw Michael," she said.

Madeline shot forward, looking at her sharply. "What?"

Casey shrugged and looked away. "I mean, he didn't see me. Twice now. Once back during the fair. He was there with you. I saw him coming out of that fortune teller trailer. But then just a few days ago."

Madeline hadn't seen him in weeks. She had almost convinced herself that Michael had left town. After all, even the sheriff had stopped by not long ago to update her, saying he and a few deputies had all been out to the Risten farm on a few occasions and each time, it appeared abandoned and empty.

"What...?" Maddy started, but was unable to direct the question down any one particular path.

Casey took a sip of her wine cooler. "So, I noticed a few weeks ago that that kid who lives next to me, Byron, well, once or twice a week he'd go sneaking off, and then he'd come back some time later. It seemed pretty regular, and he was evasive when I asked him about it. You know, he's hiding from his mom, doesn't know that nearly everyone at the trailer park knows, so I thought he had a boyfriend or something, but one day his wallet was open and I caught a wad of cash, so then I got to thinking about how he might be doing something dangerous and still wouldn't tell me, so I decided to follow him. Well, turns out he was doing a grocery pickup with a driver from Monticello and carrying the groceries out to the Risten farm. I followed him right there and saw Michael open up the back door leading up to the kitchen and let him in."

"You sure Michael didn't see you?"

Casey's face screwed up in a bewildered expression. She bit at her lips, deep in thought. Maddy thought it was a simple enough question, and was surprised it had perplexed her old friend. Slowly, Casey finally shook her head and added, as a punctuation, a "no" drawn out not excessively long, but longer than the one syllable required. The end of the word intoned upward as if she were asking a question. For the moment, she seemed to lose sight of Maddy, lost in her own thoughts, and it wasn't until she realized where she was that she straightened again and forced a smile.

"What's wrong with him?" Casey asked.

Maddy could have played the fool, acted like she didn't know what her friend was talking about, but that didn't seem proper or fair to Casey, to Michael, or to herself. So instead she shook her head and answered as honestly as she could. "I don't know."

CHAPTER EIGHT

South Arkansas thunderstorms are violent, cataclysmic events that shake the ground and the pines rooted there, flood the barrow pits, and muddy the dry, flat, thin soil. Lightning and thunder and wind thrash across the delta, driven in either by the remnants of a tropical storm that had swirled through the Gulf of Mexico or from the pressure system driving in from the west. The storm that Madeline watched now revealed with each flash of lightning how the pine trees swayed, the rain sounding like gunfire on the roof of the house.

Madeline watched the storm from the porch until the wind got too violent and the lightning too close, and then she moved inside and opened the blinds. Dart sat curled on the couch, his brow wrinkled into a worried look and his nose tucked down. Madeline sipped on some iced tea. She'd made a pitcher of sun tea on the back deck that afternoon before the clouds rolled in.

Madeline enjoyed watching storms. The way lightning brightened the pine trees and the surrounding land for but an instant before all returned to darkness. The sounds of the storm provided a kind of catharsis. She used to watch storms with their father. Their father always said storms were chaos and watching them from the safety of their home was like giving into the chaos just a bit, just enough. You give into the storm, he told his kids, and you give it your worries and your troubles, and the storm just blows out and your worries blow out with it.

On this particular night, she thought about what all she'd learned and what all she'd witnessed. Could this storm carry away this much worry? Haul off this much trouble? For Michael's sake, she hoped so.

CR&SO

The cops up at Ole Miss had only confirmed what she already knew, which meant they were of little help. More help was the girl she'd found when she and Dart had poked around the apartment complex where the attack had happened.

Just two days earlier she'd made the four-hour drive to Oxford. Of the two cops working that day, one was an old veteran. Kept calling Dart "Scooby" and asking her if the Scooby gang were investigating while the other, much younger officer, only looked at her lasciviously.

From the police station, she drove to the apartment where the attack had occurred. Gray skies dipped low as she parked and a cool breeze greeted her as she exited and escorted Dart from the backseat.

He sniffed indignantly at the coming westerly storm. Maddy sighed and looked around. There was something off here. The air was all wrong. Like, this place was cursed.

She walked Dart between two concrete buildings and entered an expansive center courtyard. The sidewalks met in the center from diagonal outlets to the parking lot. A gazebo, pool, hottub, and tennis court met in the center, and around them all, green grass trimmed like crewcuts. Maddie gave Dart free reign to sniff and explore, but she saw nothing. Even the concrete had been scrubbed clean. As Dart sniffed and pulled from spot to spot, Maddie noticed a girl descend the stairs to the north of the yard and approach. She wore grungy sweats, her hair pulled loosely in a ponytail, her glasses sitting atop her makeup-free face.

"I heard you were asking about the attack," the girl said.

Madeline nodded.

"You shouldn't stick around. I don't know how long you plan to be here, but the sooner you leave, the better."

"I just want some idea what happened," Maddy said. "I think a friend of mine was here at the time, and I want to make sure…" she faltered at this. What could she say that wouldn't cast more suspicion on Michael? "I'd just like to know what happened."

The girl introduced herself and said she was the one who'd called the cops.

"Then you saw it?" Maddy asked.

The girl, Emma, shook her head and hugged herself. She looked anywhere but at Madeline. She seemed to watch Dart suspiciously, though he was in a happy, nearly playful mood.

"I can take him back to the car if you want," Maddy said, suspecting he was making the girl nervous.

Emma shook her head again, kneeling. Her hand shaking, she reached out and let the dog sniff her. Dart nuzzled her and she jerked back a second, then reached out and pet him slowly.

"I have a dog at home," Emma said. "Weimaraner. Douglas."

"Douglas?" Maddy said.

"Got him when I was ten. I wasn't very creative. I love dogs. Always have. Just that, since that night, it's taken me so long to…" She pulled her hand away, hugged herself. "Jesus," she whimpered.

"What did you see?" Maddy asked, kneeling, pulling Dart's leash tighter 'til the dog pressed against her in a canine hug.

Emma had been kneeling also to pet Dart, but now plopped down completely on the concrete stoop in front of the complex where they spoke.

"I keep telling myself, I couldn't have seen what I saw," Emma said. "Cops said it too, but I did see it. I can't unsee it, in fact."

"What did you see?" Maddy asked calmly.

Emma's eyes were wide and glazed with tears. Her lips quivered both before she spoke and as the words trickled out. "A dog. A wolf. I don't know. But bigger. Go ahead and laugh at me. I know I sound insane."

"I'm not laughing," Maddy said.

Emma shook her head. "Cops sure were. Acted like I was ready for the nuthouse. I didn't even bother to tell them the real crazy thing."

Maddy had waited for Emma to go on. The girl sat trembling, averting her gaze. All the while, a fear grew in Maddy that what Emma was about to say would confirm her worst fears.

"It was walking upright, on its hind legs, and reaching out like it had arms."

Outside, a double-tap of lightning made her jump, and in the tree line Maddy saw it for the first time, in the first flash. A wolf's head atop a fur-covered, humanoid body, standing upright, staring right at her house. With the second flash, it was gone. She had never been a big partier and had never liked the way alcohol made her feel, so drinking wasn't a priority like it was for some of her peers at Dillard, but as the ideas coalesced in her imagination to paint a picture of what was going on, she realized for the first time in her life that she wanted—no, she needed—a drink.

CRSO

With the coming of the storm, the saws had been shut down. They'd been warned by the blast of cool from the northwest that preceded the storm cloud, chilling the loggers as the pressing clouds roiled and bubbled like a dust cloud kicked up by a stampede. By the time they could hear the thunder, it was already lightning fulgently. There came little, if any, silence between the strikes and claps of thunder, and the men retreated from the camp to their cabins looking nervously about. Most men were too skittish to shower in this weather, and John Kelly counted himself firmly among them, so he stripped down and used a wet washcloth to get the bulk of the sawdust off his naked form, used another to sop up the sweat off his body, put on more deodorant and dressed into the sweats and t-shirt he liked to sleep in. He poured himself a coffee cup of bourbon and watched the storm for as long as he could stomach it. Madeline was the storm watcher. Still, having lived here all his life, John Kelly knew what a storm like this meant, this late in the year. Logging season was just about done. He'd worked all spring and most of the summer, taking time off for a furlough to see his sister return home, but now they were most likely finished until next spring. After this, the temperature would drop again. The mornings would come with more and more frost, and the saws would run the risk of seizing up. Just the thinnest layer of frost would turn the sawdust-covered floor into an ice rink. John Kelly had seen one too many men slip and bust their heads on frost-covered sawdust. As the wood froze, sap would freeze, and cutting through some of these logs with frozen sap would be like trying to slice through stone or concrete. Saws didn't last long against that.

Before the full force of the storm had hit them, just as John was returning to his room, he'd spied a small family of deer grazing in an open meadow. He wondered if these animals sensed safety here. Loggers were banned from bringing guns, and it was illegal for hunters to trespass on the lands marked by the logging company. So even though the makeshift cabins had been set up a stone's throw from the sawmill in a clearing so that men working wouldn't have to commute home every night, the deer seemed to know that this proximity to people was actually safe. This wasn't the first family of deer he'd seen here, and he knew it wouldn't be the last. Until this moment, he hadn't given them much thought. In fact, as the storm raged, if he'd thought about them at all, he'd assumed they'd moved far away, back into the safety of the pine forest.

He could see little. The rain came down as a continuous paradiddle on the tin roof, a sound that, with the whiskey and dinner of camp-cooked barbecue in his belly, forced a yawn. It was early enough in the evening, but before they'd shut down, it had been a full workday.

Lightning flashed. It was violent, the storm this evening, and its violence suddenly unsettled him. Perhaps it was the electric air, or some faint smell, but as the thunder shook the buildings of the camp, he stepped back inside from the porch, shut and locked his door, shut the windows, and turned out the lights.

Another sip of bourbon, and he began to consider if the previous encounters with the hard drink had made him paranoid. Before he stepped too far down that path, several sounds, far too close for comfort, wrenched him back into the moment.

Lightning snapped across the sky in an explosion that penetrated the veil of rain, and John Kelly heard the bleating scream of a doe or a fawn. This was when he thought again of that family of deer. He heard the sound of tearing, like leather being rent, and heard an organic rumble. This sound quaked his chest and forced his heart to shiver. That something existed that could make such a sound terrified him at the primitive level.

CRSO

The wolf doesn't think. It doesn't reason, not in the sense that it is controlled by some internal monologue. There is no bit of narration guiding its choices. The wolf just is. Even still, the wolf understands ideas. It understands, for example, the thrill of the hunt. It understands fear. It tears first into the gullet of the buck that led the family of deer John Kelly had seen. It went for the more powerful deer first, the father, the protector, and ripped its rack from its skull when the animal tried to defend its family. It lapped at the blood and chewed the lean muscle, savoring its kill. It howled again, wearing the blood of its kill, a siren call to the night and a warning and a threat, all in one. The doe ran with its fawn close at hand, and that was fine. If the wolf could rationalize, it would say that running was fine, because was the buck was dead and it could run faster than they. It would catch them, follow the scent of their fear in the air before the storm could wash it away.

CRSO

When it howled, its moment of bloody triumph realized finally, John Kelly sat straight up in bed. He was drenched in sweat and his flesh ran cold at the sound. He wondered if it could smell him in this little cabin. Wondered if he were to be next. Wondered if that was why he went for a walk upon returning to the camp every day, scouting for more wolfsbane growing here. There wasn't much, but he'd found a few sprigs of the plant among the natural meadows south of the Ozarks. A body really in search of the stuff would do better in the fields below the Rockies, the Appalachians, or even up under the Alaskan peaks, but beggars can't be choosers and men without cars or driver's licenses can't gallivant around the country all willy-nilly.

Still, he'd found some, and collected it here in the cabin. The Creole would pay another goodly amount for what he'd been able to harvest. She always had. On the heels of this, he thought, *What Maddy don't know won't hurt her*, and that brought on a whole lot of thoughts. Like that one night he followed his father and Michael out to the family barn. It had been that first fall after Michael moved in with them that the two started stealing away after sunset. He scolded Maddy and John Kelly about following them, said it was dangerous, and would say no more about it, leaving the siblings to speculate where Michael was spending the night, as he didn't return with their father those evenings and not until he fetched him the next morning. He'd also warn them never to go out at night. *Never you mind*, he'd say, like he was scolding them still, like they were wrong to be curious. *Never you mind, just don't be caught out after dark. You get your butts home before dark*, he'd say, and because they were good kids, they minded. Well, mostly. There came a night when curiosity got the better of John Kelly, and he thought about employing Maddy as a lookout for about a second until he remembered just how big a snitch she was. Little miss perfect. He told his ma he was going to listen to music and didn't tell Maddy shit and he locked his door and lifted his window and escaped into the night.

Later, Maddy caught him sneaking back in. "Where you been?" she asked and then saw his face. "What's wrong?

"Nothing," John Kelly said, and crawled up into his bunk and went to bed, curling up in the fetal position and pulling the covers up to his chin. He wouldn't get up again until he heard his father return and his parents go to bed, and was sure Maddy was asleep, and then he'd check the lock on every door and window he could get to without waking anyone up. That meant every door and window in every room save his parents' room. It quickly became a habit, and one he did not break so easily after Michael left. He did, eventually, stop, until word got to him that Michael had returned.

He crawled out of his bed now and checked the door and both windows of the small cabin. How easy old habits returned, he thought miserably as outside the storm continued to rage. Every so often, he'd check online for the latest information regarding silver. Consensus had held that it was something mystical, possibly tied to the moon, or possibly tied to Greek myth. At the end of the day, however, it seemed silver wasn't any more or less effective a weapon than any other, and as he didn't have any left anyway, it didn't matter much. What he did have was stored in a lockbox under his bed, and boy howdy, talk about another fight with Maddy. When she discovered that their grandmother's silverware collection was missing, she accused him of hawking it and he didn't argue. He refused to give her the name of the pawn shop where he'd sold it though, because he hadn't sold it to a pawnshop, but visited this old redneck blacksmith up in Heber Springs who could do just what he asked. Melted down and reformed, it came out to a dozen shells: six for the .30-06 and six for the Glock 9mm. That plus the ammo he had ought, to be enough to put anything down, he figured. But even with the silver casings, he wasn't sure it was necessary. The reason he had to travel so far north wasn't because there weren't any blacksmiths in the area. Arkansas was lousy with doomsday preppers and DIY'ers and blacksmiths and such, but most of them didn't have a kiln hot enough to melt silver, and most didn't have the proper die casts as silver is so much harder than lead, it would break the molds. But it was the blacksmith in Heber who told him that this was just the beginning.

"You see," the old blacksmith had said, his reddish-gray beard a frazzled, hillbilly thing that bushed out to his chest, "when the gun fires, it deforms the base of the casing so that the gasses are trapped and force the bullet out at a higher velocity. But silver, being harder, won't expand like this."

"What if you leave the casing brass and just make the head silver?" John Kelly had asked.

"That could work," the old man agreed, "but being that silver's so heavy, it'd be hard to keep the shell together. Not only that, but you got the risk of the shell not rifling correctly. No, what you really want is hollow points, and making that out of silver ain't easy."

In the end, the old man created a copper plated jacket and a silver/lead hollow point. Wasn't pure silver, but there was enough of the stuff in there that if there was any truth to the rumors, it ought to do the trick. It cost him a whole month's paycheck and it took the guy something like three months, enough time that John Kelly feared the old redneck had seen this South Arkansas Black as a rube and taken his money, but he eventually got the shells. When he was able to catch a ride to go fetch them, the old man had pulled him away from his driver and stared at him a long minute.

"You said you was in South Arkansas."

John Kelly had nodded. "Yessir. Blue Rock."

The old man nodded back. He was chewing tobacco and took a minute to spit into a Styrofoam cup that had seen its share of chew already. "Good deer hunting down there." He paused but didn't wait for John Kelly to respond. "Yessir, good deer hunting. But you ain't deer hunting, are ya, boy?"

John Kelly shook his head. They stood in the old man's tool shed where he kept his forms. There was a short walkway lined on either side with work benches and vice grips and molds and tools. A single bulb with a chain hung overhead, casting a limp gold glow over the interior. The air was thick with the same dust that covered the tools and kits and benches. The old man walked away for a minute and returned with a leather pouch which he shook in John Kelly's face, grinning a smile that showed several missing teeth. He inventoried the bag's contents, handed it to him, and then stepped away again. At the old man's request, John Kelly had also left him his deer rifle and his Glock. The old man returned with these a moment later, handing them in turn to John who, even in this dim light, could see the modifications.

"They ought to fire the shells right nicely now," the old man said. "Won't have any trouble with silver bullets. Rifling should hold."

"What about regular shells?"

"Those too. Nothing changed there. I can help you carry these out." John Kelly thanked him, but when he turned, holding the pouch and the Glock, the old man shouldered the rifle and touched John Kelly's shoulder with his free hand. "I ain't ever seen one," the old man said slowly. John Kelly's breath hitched in his chest. "My grandpappy did once. Years ago. Said it caused a hell of a ruckus in his town. He was from a small Appalachian town over in Kentucky, and said it troubled the folk something fierce. Went after chickens and cows and even a couple of dogs. But when it went after a person, that's when the townsfolk knew they had to do something. Now, grandpappy was just a young man apprenticing under the town's blacksmith, but he learned right quick what needed to be done. He's the one what showed me how to form these molds. He said they formed a posse and went after it one night, and it kilt several of them pretty damn violently before they got it. Once they did, it turned back. Human. Said he knew the man, too. Had been a friend of his. But when he changed, that thing … that wolf … weren't a friend to no one."

John Kelly nodded, frowning a little. "I imagine not many people believed your grandpappy when he told that story."

"He never told it to no one but me, and he got snockered on hooch before he could tell it. Even then, his voice trembled and his face went white. I'll never forget the way he sounded or the way he looked, telling me that story. I never knew him to be skeered of anything, but he was sure skeered that night. Next morning, he brought me down to the shed and showed me how to make these bullets, these forms."

John Kelly didn't know what to say, so he only nodded. He turned to leave the shed when the man spoke again. "I sure hope the one you're after ain't a friend of y'orn."

John Kelly nodded and cinched the shoulder strap up, then stepped out of the shed. The old blacksmith followed him, toting his weapons.

The storm outside the cabin raged on, and further off, he heard the howl again, distant like thunder. That was good, but he still wished he'd at least brought the Glock with him to camp. Even with the bullets at home, those guns were about useless with Maddy. She'd always hated them. Before he left, she'd accused him of not making decisions. Maybe he still wasn't. If she knew about the wolfsbane he'd collected or about the lengths he'd gone to get the silver bullets for two different firearms, would she still think he was e...quiv...ocate?

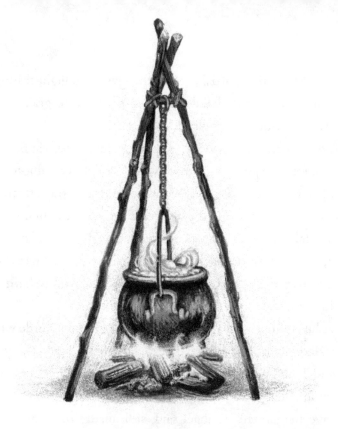

CHAPTER NINE

𝒶 t first, reconstruction on the house consumed his waking hours, so that along with the potus provided by Angelique Fontenot, Michael barely saw the ghosts. What he did see were passing shadows, flickers at the corner of his vision. But the closer it came to the next full moon, the more such distractions from his own torment proved futile. Well into October one morning, Michael woke to find the mangled and bloodied image of Tom Larsen sitting on a hay bale there in the loft.

Michael, naked, his clothes now a pile of shredded rags, kicked at the straw that served as his bedding, inching away from the visitant. His hands, as much as the chains would allow, searched for the key. At the edge of the loft, a doughy silhouette sat, legs dangling over the side. Its face turned in partial profile, the rays of sunlight through the slats illuminated certain details as though they were grains of sand spilled over an otherwise invisible feature.

The ghosts, he'd learned a long time ago, could pass at first glance as whole people, especially in shadow or low light conditions. But in the right light, as it was now, with the morning sun streaming in through the only window in the upper loft of the barn, their true form was unmistakable. Dust motes floated through the air, caught the sunlight, and passed through the ephemeral undead. In fact, Michael could see, from the angle of the sun, the slat walls of the barn on the other side of the figure who sat with his back to him.

That he could see through them, though, mattered little when no filter existed when they spoke. They came through as clearly as the living, and Tom Larsen, muttering now, was what allowed Michael to forget, momentarily, about the key.

"Leave me alone," Michael said, still unsure of what the ghost was saying.

"I can't," Tom said, turning toward him, exposing his mangled and bloodied face and chest, the flaccid flap of the torn jugular laying across the top of his chest and right collar bone. "As long as you live, I am trapped here. We all are."

Michael's right hand swept the straw laden floor, felt the iron of the key, snatched it up and unchained his left, then right hand, all without taking his eyes off the ghost.

"But I've been taking the potus!" Michael called out. Not only that, but he felt the weight of the medallion around his neck, and while he didn't think he'd gotten out the night before, something was pulling inside him. Even in the daylight he could feel it struggling to get out. Pulling against the leash of his flesh and consciousness, something animal ready to cast off the humanity and reason that was Michael Risten.

"No amount of potus," Tom Larsen's ghost said. "No charm will hold the true you. Your face now. That is the mask. You are the wolf, and it will not be satisfied until it can run free."

"I'm not it!" Michael screamed. "I'm not the monster. I never wanted to hurt you. I never wanted to hurt anyone!"

"But you have," Tom Larsen said. "And now you are trapped with us, as long as you live."

Michael bowed his head and found he was trembling. The words "as long as you live" hung like cobwebs in his mind. The other ghosts, the images of his family, had put forth this same resolution. There was, by their understanding, only one way out of this. Only one way for Michael to be free of the curse and for them to leave him alone. Michael had to die. Death clung to Michael. If he weren't the cause of it, then it was beckoning him to join.

"How you decide to go is your choice. I would prefer painfully, of course; given the pain you put me through in my death, yours should be no less unpleasant. But ultimately the say is yours. If I were you, I'd do it quickly and as mercilessly as you can stand, and well before the full moon."

The sun crept skyward, and more light streamed into the loft. Nude, exposed, Michael stood. The ghost was gone, but there were more. They appeared at their whim, not his, and he knew they would be waiting for him in the house. All with the same message Tom had delivered, and the same message he'd heard constantly since that Christmas morning ten years earlier, when he woke to find his family dead.

Michael found an old drop cloth at the base of the ladder in the stall below and wrapped it around his body. Perhaps they were right. But he knew he lacked the courage to do it himself. If only he could spring a trap for himself, for the wolf, and he thought about a rig in the loft. Setting the cloth aside, he climbed back up and stared. He could take his father's shotgun. Tweak a string and pulley, turn the barrel toward the chains, and load the counterweight, and set up a tripwire by the chain. As soon as he changed, he'd step and the trigger would pull.

Donning the cloth again, he scampered across the yard to his house, his plan formed. Perhaps the ghosts knew this and were satisfied, as they didn't greet him upon entry. A few minutes earlier without this delay, he would have heard a car pass by, and would have looked out to see Maddy driving down the road. As there was only one place she could go out here other than his house, he'd know her destination, and he would have gone after her, and that might have changed the course of this day.

But he heard and saw nothing, and that brought a modicum of relief. Still, he spoke out loud. "I know how to rig it. Watch me. After I shower and eat something, watch me out there. I can fix it."

He wouldn't know it was coming. When the wolf took over, it was like a dreamless sleep. There was no pain. No sound. No awareness of any kind. If he never woke up from such a state, that wouldn't be so bad.

CRXSO

Madeline knew the only road that would lead her close to the camp ran right by the Risten homestead. As the morning dew burned off the dry, yellow grass, and the fog evaporated in the sunlight, Maddy and Dart made their way down the road, stopping clear of the house. She exited and double-checked Dart's harness. Once she was satisfied that it would hold, she led Dart into the tree line.

It wasn't that the encampment was hard to find. Most everyone in the area knew where the Fontenot homestead was. Kids, hunters, and nature lovers alike had stumbled upon the ramshackle collection of buildings, smelled the stew cooking of whatever had been killed or the other alien odors wafting from the encampment. Most called it an *encampment*, and while that word stuck in Maddy's head, she didn't feel it was accurate, as an encampment had suggested something temporary and the Fontenots had been here longer than she'd been alive.

Most people knew—or knew thereabouts—the location of the Fontenot homestead, and most knew to steer clear. This family kept to themselves and embraced their reputation. There had been people who remembered them as youngsters, but those people could not recall them being enrolled in school, or so went the rumor. They were self-sufficient, and that scared folk. That they were known to carry a myriad of guns and made their own ammo didn't help matters. Nor did the stories about them running trespassers off their property with barrels in their backs, stories of fights started by one of the brothers at area drinking establishments, stories of feuds with neighbors where property was damaged or pets went missing. Funnily enough, the Risten family—geographically closest to the Fontenot siblings— never had any beef with them. Madeline could remember Mrs. Risten laughing at the children's boogeyman stories one day, even admonishing her and Michael and a few of his brothers. "You don't spread such talk about those people. They different, living out there, sure, but they nice enough, and they still humans, so you treat them as such."

Still, the rumors persisted about how dangerous it was to go out into the woods seeking the Fontenots. But Michael had gone to the carnival to see the old witch specifically, and that was enough for Maddy to believe that she might know what was happening with him.

Dart began sniffing about, his footsteps in tandem with Maddy's, crunching loudly over the dry ground and dead leaves and foliage. He unabashedly rammed his snout into holes and underbrush, even into the soft mounds of dirt. Maddy usually enjoyed watching his antics, how so much of this work sniffing out the world seemed important and necessary to him. Dart's frivolous *idée fixe* on smells while walking barely registered except as an annoyance. It had done the job of distracting her momentarily, however, when the first sounds came. Like they were being followed. She heard the snap of a twig from behind. Dart paused and stood upright, ears perked, nostrils flexing, eyes narrowed. His head cocked this way and that. At that moment, Maddy could not help but think about all the rumors. About mythological children who'd gone missing in these woods. Ghost stories meant to scare them as children, now spirited back into the forefront of her brain. She swallowed hard and felt the hairs on the back of her neck prickle. A bead of sweat slithered down her spine. She'd stopped, and now, mimicking the dog, she turned in place, searching for any sign that they were not alone. But the forest seemed preternaturally quiet and still this cool autumn day. No birds sang. No animals scurried. No bugs. Even the flora feared to move. If the stories were ever true, Maddy thought logically, then they'd be true now. They'd be true here.

The camp appeared faster than she'd anticipated. Rounding a short deadfall, the smell of something cooking hit her first, then something like the spray of a skunk, and finally the homestead itself came into view. There were the ruins of an old double-wide the Fontenot brothers had worked on to make livable, as well as a patched-up shed oddly crowned with a gambrel roof. A clothesline held an assortment of shirts and pants and socks on clothespins. She expected the ground to be littered with junk or trash, perhaps to find some blown engine on a crate or the skeleton of a car on cinder blocks, or the ground to be littered with all manner of detritus. The yard was surprisingly clean, and other than the pot (*cauldron*, she thought, wrinkling her nose) bubbling on the open fire and the clothes on the line swaying in the cool breeze, there was no sign of life.

Madeline listened. The whole of the forest was silent. No birds. No insects. Yes, it was getting late in the year, but should the forest be this silent? She expected at the least a scampering of small animals. Squirrels still out gathering nuts or something, but no. Nothing.

"Nuhting for a while, in fact," came the voice, like a rusted nail refusing to release a dry rot gray post, screaming when pulled free. Maddy jumped a little, as did Dart, and turned. Angelique Fontenot approached, smiling.

"How did you—"

The old woman waved her hand. "De same tought as crossed my mind time and again. De forest she afraid, so she has gone still and silent. Lest the rougarou find her."

The woman smelled of earth. She offered a smile; the teeth that remained were yellow-black. One of the front top incisors was cracked and appeared to have the texture of bark. Maddy took a step back.

"Miss Fontenot, I'm—"

"I know who you are, Miss Jeansonne. I'm surprised it taken you dis long to come see me. You here about yo' friend Michael Risten, ain't ya?" She turned away and hobbled back to the pot, picked up a wooden stick leaning against it and stirred again. "We haven't long to talk in safety. Might I offer you food or sometin' ta drink?"

Maddy looked at the pot. She needn't take another whiff to be sure she wasn't interested in ingesting anything from this place. Exchanging a glance with Dart, who whimpered, only reassured this decision. "No, thank you," she said.

"You have questions. I don't know if I can answer all of dem or give you de answers you want to hear." The old woman dragged a folded lawn chair from its place on the deck and sat in the yard near the pot, unfolded it, and then repeated the process, finally sitting in the chair closest to the pot and ushering Maddy toward the other. Hesitantly, Maddy took the seat, Dart right by her side.

"I don't even know the questions I could ask," Maddy said.

"Den why you come out here?"

Maddy sighed and swallowed. "Because I think you can connect the dots for me."

The woman stirred the pot, breathing it in, then stared off to the distance. "My brothers have him out, dis intruder to our community. You and your ilk don't realize, but dough we live outside the community, it is still ours and we, just like you, are a part of it. Perhaps, mind you, not a part you are proud of, but we are here, nonetheless."

She turned a mindful gaze to Maddy, one eye thick and milky white. "But you know what dat's like, don't you. You are too light for de Black folk, and too dark for de white folk. You are an outsider, like me. Sometin' mysterious. Wearing two faces at de same time."

"What do you mean?" Maddy asked, but the older woman only shook her head.

"Not your character, sweetie. You have a pure heart. No, your identity. How you see yourself and how others see you. Masks you can't take off, so you must wear dem both. Perhaps dat's why you love dear Michael so."

"What's wrong with him?" Maddy asked. This was the question that most drove her. The one thing she had to know.

"If I *connect the dots* for you, you won't believe. You must see dem connected for yourself."

Maddy stared at the fire, Dart at her feet, ticking off each piece of information aloud as if reciting lines for the old woman. "His parents attacked and his family killed. Then there was an attack at his school. And then Tom Larsen was killed and Deputy Bailey was hospitalized. Then all the strange animal attacks in the area…"

"School?" Angelique Fontenot sat forward, staring at her hard. "What attack at school?"

"Last spring," Maddy stammered. "I was just there. A girl witnessed it. Said a large dog killed some students in her apartment complex."

"Impossible!" Angelique said, waving this away as if it were a pestering fly. "De rougarou cannot arise in de warmer months. Just in autumn, as de weather cools, when de moon is bright, does that mask show."

Maddy frowned at this. "What the hell does that even mean?"

"It could not have been a rougarou," Angelique repeated.

"I don't know what that is!" Maddy snapped. She recognized it as Creole or Cajun, perhaps French, but she'd studied Spanish.

The old woman sighed. "When de autumn moon is bright, a man or woman might change. Don another mask. De face of a beast dat hunts and stalks and kills. Some call it a wolf. The Navajo have their own name for it—skin walker—and there are other names. *Lusus naturaes*. Lycanthrope. Changeling. Wolf. Loup garous. Or rougarou. They all mean the same thing."

"Wolf," Maddy echoed. A chill raced up her spine and gooseflesh broke across her arms. The word, the other word, lingered on the tip of her tongue, but she refused to speak it. It was absurd, of course, but it was more than that. Here in the dim forest, sitting at the camp with the old Creole woman some called a witch, Maddy was afraid to say the word.

"Dey were wolf attacks, were dey not?" Angelique Fontenot asked. "De witnesses reported seeing a wolf. Dat is de mask of the rougarou. De face de human wears under de shadow of de moon."

"That's impossible," Maddy muttered.

The old woman laughed. "You know it to be true. You were almost dere, to dat same place. You knew it at de edge of your mind, where reason and imagination meet in a realm dat some mistake for insanity and others shrug off as impossibility. Your friend, Michael Risten, is cursed."

The old woman focused on the distance. Maddy chanced a look, then down to Dart, who only looked up at her with a furrowed brow.

"We nearing de nex' full moon," the old woman continued. "As it draws closer, de rougarou's bloodlust will grow strongair, and young master Risten won't be able to contain it. When de full moon rises, dere will be no saving your friend."

The old woman, during all of this, kept her gaze steady. "You said we didn't have long," Maddy said. "You said your brothers have someone occupied. An intruder, you said. Who is it? Is he here for Michael?"

"Why do you continue to seek answers you already know, young girl? Yes, he is. He is a hunter from the old world. De name he gave us upon arriving is Kalos von Slacher, and he will not leave until he kill de rougarou and everyone it infect."

"Infects?" Maddy asked, but if there were more answers, the old woman would not give them. For just then the rustling underbrush and crunch of leaves revealed the Fontenot brothers and the older gentleman Maddy had seen at the carnival. He was tall and broad and his eyes were black. She felt naked when he looked at her. Dart offered up a low growl as the man approached, but Maddy held his leash tight.

"We have a visitor," von Slacher said, forcing a smile. "*Preentsesuh*," he said, his accent thick. "What brings you to our humble lodgings?" When Maddy didn't answer right away, he turned his lurid gaze to Angelique, who refused to meet his eyes. The old woman's lips trembled in the presence of this man, which offered

Maddy a new and unsettling insight into those surrounding her. Fear was not an emotion she'd have associated with the Fontenots, from the stories she'd heard, but it was apparent that whoever this von Slacher was, Angelique Fontenot and her brothers were afraid.

"If that is your final word," Maddy said, speaking up. "But as I said, I'm willing to pay well for a private reading." She turned to the old man and forced her own smile. "During the carnival, Miss Fontenot offers up fortune telling for our community. I thought maybe I could persuade her to give me a reading now. I'm worried about my prospects for grad school, you see, but she still says no."

"Steadfast in your refusal, eh," von Slacher said. "Surely you would consider bending for this beautiful young woman. At the request of your...*boyar.*"

Still, Angelique Fontenot refused to meet his gaze, and still her lips quivered. Maddy chanced a look to her brothers. The younger of the two stared defiantly between von Slacher and his sister. The other looked defeatedly to the ground. Both remained silent.

"I will not bend," Angelique said, enunciating each word, as though speaking them caused her great pain.

Von Slacher's smile broadened. "Well, there you have it, miss. I'm sorry to disappoint, but even I could not persuade her. Perhaps she and I will have further opportunity to discuss her impudence... after you have left."

Maddy swallowed, pulled Dart's leash tight, and stood. She looked to each of the Fontenots and nodded, unable to escape the feeling that abandoning them now meant leaving them at this stranger's mercy. But what could she do?

"Go with God, Madame Jeansonne," Angelique Fontenot said, and Maddy acquiesced.

CHAPTER TEN

The Ladies Auxiliary of Blue Rock met every morning for coffee at Duke's place and once a week for their book club. Amelia Livingston fished full cups from her husband and brought them to the table, handing one to each old lady, before taking her seat. The morning was probably too cool to sit outside, but there really wasn't indoor seating this autumn, what with the pandemic. Each lady, dressed warmly, only removed her mask just before the coffee neared her lips—save for Sarah Larsen and Lynette Cabot, neither of whom wore masks. Casey Davidson, like others, knew the habits and movements of the book club, and wasn't surprised to see them roosting around a single table as she approached.

Casey wondered what it would be like to sit with these ladies. Even though she had seen Bess Louviere around town for years, she still couldn't help but get starstruck. Bess got away and got her education and returned only when she could buy back a couple of homes just for writing some books people read. And Lynette Cabot and Sarah Larsen? They were married to rich, successful men. Hell, even Amelia Livingston, a Black woman married to a Black man, was one of the most successful entrepreneurs in the area.

"Two cups, black, no cream or sugar," Casey said to Duke through the window, her words muffled through her mask. It certainly was chilly this morning. And foggy.

"How's your pa?" Duke asked.

Casey could only nod. She felt the Auxiliary eyes on her. She took the cups and turned around to find them all staring up at her.

"Come sit a spell, dear," Bess Louviere said, patting the seat beside her. "We were about to talk about our next meeting. If you aren't doing anything. You can social-distance and join us."

"Thank you," Casey said. She was about to decline the offer but opted instead to accept. Why be in such a hurry to return to that trailer park, anyway.

"I'm surprised y'all are still meeting," Casey said, setting her father's cup aside and taking a sip from her own.

"Why is that, dear?" Bess asked, eyebrows raised impossibly high. They were painted black and arched, contrasting her white hair. She removed her own mask long enough to take a sip. "Because we're old?"

Sarah Larsen and Amelia Livingston exchanged glances and laughed. "We ain't old, honey," Amelia said.

Bess must have been smiling under her mask, because kindness returned to her eyes. "I'm only having a bit of fun, child."

Casey nodded in response. In a town this small, there are no strangers. She'd known each of these women since she was old enough to walk. Lynette Cabot had even been her teacher.

"So what is your plan?" Bess continued. "Do you wish to stay in this little town, or move on? Madeline Jeannsonne and Michael Risten went to college. It isn't too late for you."

"I wouldn't even know what to study," Casey said.

"Leave this town, dear," Lynette Cabot chimed in. "There ain't nothing here for a young woman like yourself."

"Yes, ma'am," Casey said. She bowed her head and averted her eyes, embarrassed and flustered. She didn't like being the center of attention. As if she could see this, Sarah Larsen spoke up.

"Let's leave the girl be," she said, and gave a knowing nod to Casey. If anyone understood, Casey assumed from the gossip about the town that Sarah Larsen would.

"Truth is, this town ain't good for no one," Amelia Livingston said. "That Aaron Bailey has always unnerved me, and now that he's got a badge…"

"We're sitting on a powder keg," Bess said, shaking her head in disapproval.

"I guess I just don't understand," Lynette started. "You two're sitting on the other side, but all lives should matter. Maybe Deputy Bailey has it safe here, but what about all those cops killed in the bigger cities? They put their lives on the line."

"Bailey ain't safe," Sarah interjected. "He was attacked not too long back."

"That was an animal, like a bear or something," Lynette said.

"The role of police has always been to serve racist policies," Bess said. "It's ingrained in the job and attracts like-minded individuals."

"Like Aaron," Amelia added. "I heard his pa was in the Klan."

"Lotsa folks were in the Klan down these parts," Sarah said.

"Still are," Bess said. Casey saw the sadness in the old woman's eyes, her whole mood darken, and felt as though she were trespassing on something deeply personal. "Nothin' changes," Bess said then. "Hate grows old and dies and is born again in the next generation. Sure, we've tried to hide it for a time, tried to sweep it under the rug, wear masks of civility and community while every few times a year we allow just a peek under. But for the past four years, those masks have come off. People ain't afraid to show the hate they wear. The evil."

She wasn't sure why, but Casey touched the old woman's shoulder, and stood and thanked them for allowing her to sit with them. Lynette and Amelia nodded to her. She bit her lip and nodded a few times for the awkward supplication, then picked up her father's coffee cup and—with a final smile—sauntered back home. Neither she nor the Ladies Auxiliary of Blue Rock was aware that this would be the last time they'd see her alive.

⚭

At home, her father still slept. His breaths came in halted stops and loud snores. She set his coffee in the microwave where he was sure to look. Their own coffee pot had failed a while back, hence her daily commutes to Duke's place. Some days there was money for breakfast, but those were few and far between.

A commotion drew her back to her father's room, where she saw he'd kicked away the covers then twisted in the night, so that his right leg was tangled up with the sheets.

"They coming for all of us. The pedophiles," her father mumbled.

"Sure, Dad," she said, and walked to the bed, adjusting the covers until they covered him better. One of these days, she knew she'd find him not breathing, having succumbed to the alcohol in the night. She kissed the fingertips of her right hand and placed them on his cheek, just as she'd done since she was five.

Her daddy subsisted on painkillers and alcohol to ease his discomfort. Relegated to the living room of a single-wide, he rested on the laurels of those depressants to soothe him.

She pulled the blanket up over his legs to his shoulders.

"Get some more rest, Daddy," she whispered.

In the living room, Casey looked out the window to spy on the circle of trailers. There was a strange car in front of Miss Emily's place, and the front door was open, the glass from the screen reflecting the day and keeping it dark just beyond, deterring Casey's prying eyes.

Byron stepped out on his porch, carrying some Walmart bags filled with, near as Casey could tell, some groceries. When he started walking away with the bags in hand, Casey considered following him again. What she couldn't understand was why Michael was holed up in that house alone, when he'd been so afraid of it for so long. He'd confided in her, during the after-prom in the high school gymnasium, that he would never return to that house. He kept telling her it was haunted. His mood that night had killed any hope of hers that they might move their relationship to the next level, that he could be her first. This had upset her at the time, but in the intervening years, she had barely thought about it. Remembering that night now, she felt embarrassed for such selfishness in light of what he was going through. Still, she thought, all the more reason to question why he was at that house now. Squirreled away inside as if to hibernate. Short of storming over there and asking him herself, she knew there was no way to answer this. When she saw Byron was already gone, she felt she'd missed her chance.

CRSO

The town itself was slow to wake this autumn morning. Perhaps the coolness had left it more relaxed than it was expecting, after the heat of summer and the pandemic and the fiery politics. The lumber mill fired up its saws a little after dawn, and the men crawled over the pine needles like wasps who've awakened to the cold and can only manage sluggishly. This would prove one of the last days the saws would fire this year. Just a few miles north, Madeline awoke long enough to let Dart out to the bathroom, but then snuggled with him on the couch as they both fell back asleep.

Sarah Larsen had left her house before her husband had awakened, thanking God for small favors. The night before had been especially bad. It'd be one thing if he were a drunk, like Skeet Davidson, but Bob Larsen was a sober heavy-handed man still enraged by the protests around the area and the nation and the death of his brother. It didn't take much to set him off. Last night, it was the mashed potatoes: They were too lumpy, not like his momma made them, though she'd followed the recipe to a tee as she had a thousand times before.

He never struck her face anymore, not since that one time when he had to explain her black eye to Chet and Deputy Bailey. Chet, of course, was too afraid to say anything and risk his job, and the deputy had probably done something similar himself to his trailer trash sister or that girl he was seeing up in Monticello. But there were others in town who wouldn't have cottoned to Bob's hand. Bess Louviere, for one, Sarah was sure. The Cabots. Dr. Bellanger. They could get together and cause a real problem for Bob. Sarah had made it clear to him she ran with their lot, so when he had blackened her eye, she explained to the deputy that she'd fallen. It would be so easy, Sarah thought, to steer the book club meeting from whatever they were reading, tell them how he treated her. She was pretty sure that the doctor and the pharmacist and even ol' Duke Livingston could run Bob right out of town, but pretty sure wasn't for certain, and Bob pulled a lot of weight both in Blue Rock and up in Monticello. She knew he was friendly with the sheriff, had helped to elect him, and it was because of this that she stayed quiet and did her best not to anger her husband any more than humanly possible.

Deputy Bailey and another deputy from Monticello pulled into the trailer park and knocked on the front door of the only double-wide on the property. Of course, Miss Emily Evans was already awake. Grandma stared at them through the screen door with a look she'd mastered over the years, wearing a mask of distrust and dislike and, worst of all, disapproval.

"What'choo wont?" she asked in a tone that reminded everyone she didn't like to be bothered unless one of her tenants were paying rent.

"We wanna talk to yo' grandson," Aaron Bailey said, not bothering even to wear a mask while out on official business.

"You remove yo' sun shades you wanna talk to me, Aaron Bailey!"

His cocky smile dropped a bit, and he snapped the Ray Ban Aviators off his face. Whatever his smile suggested, his eyes only reflected meanness.

"Ma'am," the other deputy started.

"Whach'y'all want with my Derek?"

"You know he's got outstanding warrants in at least three counties in South Arkansas, and we were told about another'n in Baton Rouge." For Aaron Bailey, no information was off limits, especially when he thought it could break an old lady's heart.

"I'll pay those fines," she said defiantly. But her lower lip quivered. And, Aaron noted, her chin was cocked just a bit too high. And look at how those eyelids fluttered with fear.

"Don't work like that," Aaron said. "There's some felonies."

"It's okay, Grandma. I'll go with them," a voice boomed from behind, a bit sluggish itself, as though roused from sleep. He appeared behind her, towering over her. He was tall and broad shouldered, muscular. Aaron's fingertips reached back and brushed the butt of his service weapon, still holstered.

"I'm calling that attorney up in Monticello," she said, even as Derek brushed past her and pushed the screen door open. Before either cop had reached for their cuffs, Derek's hands were already behind his back. Despite his cooperation, they still wrenched his shoulders while shackling his wrists and shoved him in the back seat, grazing his scalp on the doorframe of the patrol car. As he was being carted off, Emily Evans was busy working the phone.

This was the way of the town. Duke opened the restaurant at dawn, as languid as everyone else. He didn't even scold Remy Doucet or Vicky Arsenault when they came dragging in five minutes apart, the earliest of the two thirty minutes late. He'd already fired up the biscuits and started the sauce and counted out the till for the morning rush.

CRSO

Skeet Davidson had an amazing daughter; he just wished she wouldn't live her life around him. This was proven again when he awoke. She'd covered him with a blanket and left a sticky note telling him his coffee was in the microwave. She should have gone to college. Jesus knows he'd encouraged her, not sure how he'd pay for it. He knew full well it might even put her in debt. But he wanted her to have all the opportunities he never had, and none of the grief he still carried.

He missed her mother, despite her leaving them both so long ago. She was in Memphis now, he heard, or possibly Orlando. She'd never wanted to be a mother, but she'd sworn to Skeet that she'd try, dammit. For them. For their family. Casey often said that her mother didn't deserve the accolades he'd laid at her feet. She didn't deserve to be missed so much. But he and Casey's mother, who'd taken off when the girl was just entering the terrible two's, had lived a lifetime together before she was born. Had known each other some fifteen years, since they were kids, he from two towns over and she living just outside of Blue Rock, in a farmhouse now rented out by a different family, as her remaining relatives were long-since dead: cancer and alcohol and a hard living farming the dirt for scraps to subsist on.

Perhaps that's why she left, or perhaps it was her inability to take care of a child who, like most children at that age, tested the limits of her parents without realizing she was doing so. She felt alone, even with a husband, because he spent as much time as possible at the logging camp, angling for a job he'd never keep. If their lives reeked of karmic irony and justice for their misguided sins, then why was that impartial justice dolled out on their one and only kid.

He was thankful for one thing, even in the light of her leaving: She never got an abortion. They'd discussed the dreaded A-word, whispered well before anyone in town could suspect that two twenty-year-olds were with child, just driving up to Little Rock and finding a doctor who'd perform the surgery. To this day, he couldn't be sure what changed her mind, but he was thankful she did. If he didn't have Casey, he'd be totally alone. Yeah, he had his Ma in the assisted living home up in Monticello, but the dementia had taken her mind long ago, around the same time a heart attack took his Pa. No, without Casey, he'd be totally alone, and that thought terrified him.

Sipping the coffee his daughter had brought him, he fished out the old photo album with pictures of his ex and him in their younger days. In these pictures, Casey—when she appeared—was a tow-headed toddler with plump red cheeks. In his mind, she'd always be that little girl, just like he still saw himself as that young man he once was under the visage of ruddy, bloated middle aged alcoholic when he looked in the mirror. He realized that as much as he wanted better for his daughter, there was a part of him, selfish and immature and, yes, weak, that didn't want her to go anywhere. His rational mind couldn't assure him that such a move would be temporary, and there were more permanent moves that could happen, and that even if she weren't here in his presence, she would still be there in his life. No, he only thought about losing her, and if he lost her, he'd lose his whole reason for living. There would be nothing left.

So, he reclined in bed wanting better for her, and he said so in a quick prayer as he always did when he awoke. That she would grow and see better and more opportunities. But he followed that up with a plea that God would never allow him to lose his little girl. Up until today, God had answered that with silence that allowed for a continuance of the status quo, but that next morning, Skeet would get an answer finally: a resounding no to both requests.

The town as a whole was dreary to rise, willing enough to sleep away the morning and wile away the coming winter months as though they had the luxury to hibernate. This had been an exhausting year, after all, so they, like the rest of the country, were due a bit of rest. But what we think we're owed and what we're actually given are often two different things.

⊂⊇⊃

Rather than hanging out in the depressing semicircle of trailers, Casey made her way into town for an early lunch at Duke's place. She sat at the table in the middle of the others, all of them empty, and glanced around at her loneliness while she waited for service. Astrid Calhoun walked out to greet her.

"What you up to?" Astrid asked, plopping the menu down in front of her.

"Nothing, Miss Astrid," Casey said, a bit forlorn. She'd fished some change and a few crumbled bills from her pocket.

Astrid glanced back at the building, then said, "Put that away, girl. Duke ain't gone take yo' money. Now, what you want?"

Casey ordered her usual.

"Sorry, Miss Astrid," Casey said. She caught herself wanting to mention Byron, wanting to mention how he'd been skipping school and taking food to Michael Risten, and all the while Astrid waited on her, Casey felt like a prisoner in an interrogation. Surely Astrid knew, and she knew that Casey knew, and she'd catch Casey, just sure as shit, in a lie or something. But Astrid never said anything. She delivered the order to Duke and busied herself around the kitchen. Casey was thankful for the peace. She scrolled through the socials, but her mind wasn't on her phone or on tweets or threads or comments. Her life felt blank. It was like she couldn't see beyond today. A breeze cut through the pine trees and tousled her hair. She spent a few minutes watching the shadows shift and dance under leaves and broken clouds. The thought that this would be the sum total of her life from here on out depressed her. She didn't feel like eating, all of a sudden.

"How yo' daddy doin?" Astrid asked, setting the burger down in front of her and refilling her water.

"He good," Casey said. He was still breathing, so that wasn't a lie.

Casey picked at the food, pondering each bite with excessive mastication until there was only a soft mush to swallow. Only when Astrid returned and asked how it was did Casey give a thumbs up and took a big bite. She forced a smile. Astrid nodded, said, "Okay," and left again. Casey wiped off her hands and scrolled through the contacts on her cell until she came across the name of a friend she'd gone to school with up in Monticello. This number she dialed, glancing around for eavesdroppers. She'd purposely sat in the table furthest from the window out of fear of being overheard; she couldn't have word of this conversation getting back to her father.

"It's me, Casey. So, you said classes start in two weeks? What about the pandemic? Uh huh. That's good. Hang on a sec."

"Here ya go, hon," Astrid said, setting a paper bag down. Casey picked in and saw another burger wrapped in foil and another basket of fries. "No charge," the woman whispered.

While she mumbled a "thank you," Casey was tired of the gallantry of this town who knew her father hadn't a pot to piss in. No, she didn't want to leave him, for she was his world, but she couldn't live like this anymore.

"How much is tuition?" she asked. Her friend began to describe the various ways that beautician's school could be paid for without her coming up with money right now. "What about supplies, combs and scissors and such?"

"All covered," her friend said. "You just got to find a way to get up here for class and you'll be good to go."

"Oh," Casey said. Of course. A ride. How could she have been so stupid? She ran through the list of people who might be able to give her a lift. Plenty of folk at the Rock headed up to Monticello for work on the daily, so maybe she could hitch a ride with someone.

"Listen," her friend said. She also knew of Casey's predicament. Her words now carried the same pitying weight as the free meals at

Duke's place. "I can come get you a few days a week, but if you can find someone to hitch a ride up the other days, maybe scrounge for some gas money."

"Of course," Casey said. "Thank you."

As she hung up, a great weight lifted from her shoulders, exiting from between the pinched blades on her back like a great sigh that had loosened the vise of worry. Her shoulders relaxed and sagged. She would be okay. Her father would be okay.

In truth, she should have made this move years ago, and had thought about it then, but as she was her father's daughter, she allowed procrastination and second-guessing to control her. But fear couldn't hold her anymore. Her father's checks just weren't enough, and besides, she needed to be out on her own. She could have her own place, her own family even, and still be there for her father. But she couldn't kowtow to his neediness anymore.

She finished her fries and sandwich and water, dumped the stained wax paper and napkins in the receptacle, set the plastic basket on top, and walked away, still tasting the barbecue on her tongue, the aftertaste of the slices of red onion and pickle.

Walking away from the last meal she'd ever eat at Duke's place, Casey steered toward Madeline Jeansonne's home, excited to share her bit of news.

❧

Entering the one-room deputy's office near the square, holding onto the prisoner's cuffs, pushing him forward, Aaron Bailey thanked the other deputy when he opened the cell with a nod. "I got it from here, thanks," he said, and glanced back to the door.

The deputy, a scrawny little guy with a hooked nose like a buzzard's beak, was slow to take the hint, even pausing to look down at the cuffs Bailey should be removing before depositing the prisoner in the cell. When Bailey didn't move, however, the little man nodded and made his way to the door.

Bailey grabbed the cuffs and pushed Derek Evans into the cell. Truth was, and he was sure Derek knew this, he had no intention of taking the cuffs off yet. Yeah, Aaron was a big guy, over six feet and solid muscle, but Evans was big also, and perhaps a little broader in the shoulders, so uncuffing him would be a huge mistake. Right now.

Wasting no time with things like pleasantries or Miranda rights, Aaron instead removed his baton from his belt, and with a twirling of the knob, he swung the long end around to catch Derek in the gut, forcing him to double over. He yanked hard on the cuffs to straighten the prisoner again before delivering another blow, this one sending Derek to his knees. He'd hoped Derek would say something, plead for something, but he'd known Derek long enough to know he wouldn't.

"I don't care if your grandmother is on death's door, Derek. Isn't that what I told you?"

Grabbing the nightstick by the long end, he swung it like a baseball, so that the short end and knob connected with Derek's jaw, sure to leave an L-shaped bruise.

"What did I say, Derek?" Derek lay on the ground, the whole of his body weight crushing his cuffed arms under him.

"What did I say that last time you was in town, last year, was it? What did I say?"

Derek, still silent, glaring up at the deputy, funneling as much hate and anger into his gaze as he could muster. Bailey stepped back and delivered the front of his steel-toed boot to Derek's rib, forcing him to curl up on his side in the fetal position.

"What the fuck did I say to you, boy? I told you last year not to come back here. Not ever. I warned you, boy, didn't I?"

He crouched down right in front of his prisoner. How stupid had this boy been, going home like that? Didn't he realize the deputy's own sister lived at that trailer park? That Bailey would surely learn he was staying there, sure as shit sugars a fly? When Chantal had texted him, and Bailey called up to Monticello for backup, he worried some that his freshly healed shoulder would catch on him. This was a new wrinkle he wasn't happy with. He used to sleep like the dead after a day of patrolling and after getting a solid workout in, but anymore his sleep was fitful, full of nightmares and horrible images, and he awoke stiff and sore. Someone had told him once that comas were like dreamless sleeps for patients, but Aaron recalled everything he saw while sedated in the hospital. Since he'd awakened, he'd never been the same.

Lost in his own thoughts, ignoring the spite Derek shot his way, Aaron considered his own hand. The nails had grown again. Not much, but there definitely existed a white ridge just beyond the nail bed. And they were sharp. Damn, his nails were sharp. He'd checked his supplements for an increase in biotin not long after returning home, feeling like his hair was thicker, his nails stronger. But the formula hadn't changed, so he largely forgot it. Until other things started happening. And the dreams continued.

The fingers of his right hand dangled between his knees as he held his left hand at eye level, fingers splayed, watching it tremble, the digits twitch. Nearly hypnotized, he watched the fine hairs on the back of his hand stand on end. Footsteps crunched over leaves, a sound he realized that had to be coming from outside. He didn't recognize the pain in his right hand immediately, not until it came searing up his arm. Aaron looked down to see that Derek had two of his fingers in his teeth, chomping down as hard as he could, drawing blood.

Aaron screamed and yanked his hand away as the other swung down and the nails raked across Derek's cheek. He stood, recoiling back, delivering another kick to Derek's gut. He backed out of the cell, slammed it shut, and locked it. His left hand cradled his right. Blood gushed down his arm, and Aaron again yowled in pain. He found some paper towels at his desk and wrapped his hand with half the roll, as from behind Derek mumbled a mix of laughter and audible sighs of pain, and still, further away, the sound of shuffling through dead leaves.

Aaron took a few deep breaths and made his way to the front door, hoping the cool autumn breeze might do him some good. The town square was virtually empty, save for Casey Davidson on the other side of the square, turning down a side road that would lead her further away, her feet shuffling through the dead leaves that covered the sidewalk, right in time with the sound that filled Aaron's ears. Forgetting his hand for a moment, he wondered how he could have heard her walking from inside the jail, and he wondered, as she moved further and further away, and even turned the corner, how he could still continue to hear her footsteps.

As a test, he looked out towards Duke's place. He stared at it, willing his ears, until—*did they move?*—he heard the voices of Duke Livingston and Remy Doucet.

"…dinner rush… you be good for dinner rush… You late again…"

And Vicky Arsenault and Astrid Calhoun.

"…shit together, Vick… I know, I know… He ain't no good…"

Aaron shook his head and looked away, and the sounds faded. He realized then that there was no more pain in his hand. Unraveling the mess of blood-stained towels, he held it up to his line of sight. Yeah, some blood stained the fingers, but the skin didn't even look broken any more. *Fuck*, he thought. *Just what the fuck is going on?*

Casey hadn't intended to spend the afternoon with Maddy, but as both women seemed to welcome the company, and neither appeared to have any other obligations, that was how the rest of the day played out. She'd arrived after a five-minute walk from the square, not thinking of what she would say or what excuse she'd give as to why she was on her friend's doorstep, but Maddy had offered her a friendly smile and a warm hug and had invited her in quickly, shushing the Lab that huffed at the stranger at the door and offering her a drink.

Dart sat pretty in front of Casey, eager for pets and kisses, which she supplied before following Maddy into the home.

"John Kelly still at the logging camp?"

"There now 'til first frost," Maddy said, setting a tea kettle on the stove to boil, then drawing some cups out of the cabinet. "How's your pa doing?"

Casey parked herself at the kitchen table and scratched the dog's head absently as she mulled over the loaded question. "Drinking pretty regular. Not even trying to... hell, I don't know... he's given up." Her deep, soulful sigh brought Maddy to the table to sit and take her hand.

"What is it?" Maddy asked.

"All this damn pressure, Maddy. He says I'm all he's got and his life ain't worth living if his little girl is gone, but I can't live my life for my daddy anymore, can I, Maddy?"

She patted Casey's hand with a consolatory smile. "You can't live your life for any man, be he your dad, brother, friend, or lover." Maddy rose and retrieved tea cups and saucers, two tea bags, some lemon, and a crystal bowl of sugar just as the tea kettle whistle-hissed the water was ready.

"Got a chance to go to school," Casey said after a minute.

"That's great," Maddy said. Casey thought she meant it, though she was sure they both knew it wasn't college.

"Beauty school, up in Monticello. My friend, Patrice—you remember Patrice, don't you? Culpepper? Lives out in Theodosha about ten miles away? Well, she says I can get grants and such to pay for the schooling, and they'll provide all the scissors and stuff I'll need to get me started."

Maddy smiled warmly at her friend. "You were always into doing up our hair and makeup and stuff. You be good at it."

"'Member Prom?"

"Oh, God yes." The two young women set to laughing over the memories. Less than a decade old, yet a lifetime ago.

The next hour or so, they sipped their tea while seated in the living room.

Casey said, "Hot tea in the South, Maddy?"

Maddy smiled and ran her fingers down Dart's back. "I know, sacrilege, right, but it felt a bit too cool to offer you iced tea, and a little late for coffee, so I thought…"

"Say," Casey said excitedly. "'Member when Michael and John Kelly stole the teabags from the teacher's lounge and dumped them in the pool the night before the swim meet?"

Maddy let out a laugh that startled the dog, who was quite comfortable laying beside her on the couch. "Lord, yes," she said. "Jesus, I just knew they was gone get suspended."

"What was his name?" Casey asked. Maddy frowned at her. "Oh, you know. The swim team captain. That boy picking on Michael that year."

"Oh," Maddy said, raising a hand. "His folk own that accounting service up in Monticello—"

"Well, 'til that one chain moved in. Ran 'em right outta business."

"No way," said Maddy. "They was on the city council. Nielson Tax Service. Din't they hold a lot of accounts up there? Like Larsen's dealership?"

"And the Cabot Pharmacy, and the clinic, and some retail outlets. Yep," Casey said with a nod, and sipped her tea. "Ran 'em right outta business. Word is, he got in trouble with the feds. Really screwed some people over."

"Not Bob Larsen, though," Maddy said.

Casey shook her head. "Naw. He a snake. He can walk through a pigsty and still smell like a rose."

The girls shared a laugh and sipped their tea for some minutes in silence.

"I've missed this," Casey said, staring at her empty cup, the grounds of tea floating the bemired liquid at the bottom of her cup like some prophetic Rorschach shape.

Maddy said, "Michael kind of disappeared when he was with you."

"I meant, I miss having someone my age to talk to," she said. "Sure, there's Byron in the trailer park, but he's a few years younger, and everyone else here is so old."

"John Kelly said y'all hung out some about a year ago."

Casey smiled and blushed a little. "We dated a minute, but we better friends. 'Sides, I think it cramped his style running around with white trash."

"Hush up," Maddy said. "Don't ever talk that way about yourself."

"It's true," Casey said. "I'm surprised I ain't knocked up yet. I know Aaron Bailey would sure like a go, and don't think he didn't try, but I'd kill myself before being linked to him. Bad 'nuff I gotta live and work aside his sister."

"He was mean in school. Don't surprise me he's a cop now."

"Other than Michael, that seems like that's all the white boys down in these parts."

"So, don't limit yourself."

Casey raised her eyes, questioning.

"Well," Maddy went on, "my brother *was* sweet on you."

"And I was pretty sweet on him, too," Casey admitted. "But it felt weird, given how you and he are all tied in with Michael, and Michael and all he went through those last few years of school. Besides, and please don't take me to task for it, but my daddy wouldn't be too pleased if…"

Ashamed, she lowered her eyes and the blush on her cheeks turned another shade red.

"I ain't gone hold one person's beliefs against another, Casey Davidson, so don't you worry." With this, Maddy reached over and patted her friend's hand again. "Say, you hungry? I'm starving. How about I whip us up some dinner? Unless you got somewhere to be."

Casey glanced outside. It was still light out, though the shadows were growing longer. Dinner would put her getting home after dark, but by then her dad would be well on his way to getting drunk and she could probably just get to her bedroom unnoticed and unbothered for the rest of the night. She smiled and nodded as an answer to Maddy, and helped with dinner, loved on Dart, and teased John Kelly over Facetime when he called his sister.

Dinner was something simple to prepare, nutritious, but filling. Casey thought it was the most enriching experience she'd had in a long time. The greens of the salad weren't brown or wilted, the vegetables still snapped with freshness, the bread wasn't stale, and the chicken noodle soup was whisked together over the stove from a bag rather than a store brand can peeled open and popped in a microwave. But more than the nutritional value of the food, the company made the evening special. There came no shortage of conversation, and the two young women enjoyed themselves: laughing, reminiscing, opening up their deepest fears.

"I just," Casey said, slurping on a spoonful of broth, "I know Daddy want the best for me, but it'd break his heart if'n I left."

"That cain't be on you," Maddy said, sipping her tea. "Don't think John Kelly ain't try to guilt me into staying when Momma got sick, but it was graduate school, and there was nothing I could do here."

"It was a purty service," Casey said.

Maddy nodded contemplatively. "Now, I got this chance to get into this program…"

"Ain't you already done with schoolin'?" Casey asked.

"This is a different program. I'm looking at one up at Chicago."

"Whew," Casey said, rolling her eyes. "Big city now. You ain't never gone catch me in a big city. Hell. I ain't prob'ly ne'er gone leave Blue Rock."

Maddy reached across the table and took her hand. "You gone knock 'em dead at that salon, Casey, and you'll get outta here–"

Casey shook her head, so Maddy squeezed her hand and leveled her eyes at her friend.

" –and you gone meet a good man, maybe even give it another go with John Kelly, settle down and have a few young'uns, and yo daddy'll move in with you and you'll live happily ever after."

The thought made Casey smile. It was a pleasant enough idea, but suddenly she felt very strongly that it was wrong. Something nagged at her. Said this dream, as sure as it felt now with all the various kinks worked out, would never come true.

Shortly after sundown, Dart stepped into the backyard to pee, but something in the tree line caught his eye, and he rushed back in quickly, looking back only once. Maddy locked the door and he turned and stood by it, whimpering some. Casey, who'd gotten up to refill her glass with more water, watched the interaction with a bit of bemusement.

"You wanna go back out?" Maddy asked and reached to unlock the door again. At this Dart issued a growl, his eyes glued to the door.

Maddy shrugged. "Have it your way."

"What's wrong with him?" Casey asked as they sat.

"Who the hell knows," Maddy said. "Probably smells a squirrel or something."

The conversation continued, both casting side glances to the back door, where Dart stood resolute, staring, sometimes growling just loud enough for them to hear, a low rumble accompanying their conversation. They talked about television and movies and music and how it was all changing, about the town and about parents and how the older generation had let them down, about worry and, yes, even about Michael some more. All the while, something stirred deep down inside Casey, leaving her unsettled and perhaps even afraid, and she spoke as if she had to get out all the words she ever intended to say, because this was her last chance to say them to anyone who'd listen.

⚬⚬⚬⚬⚬

Bess Louviere's opulent living room in her old Victorian was where the Ladies Auxiliary of Blue Rock Literary Society and Book Club often met. Every object, whether it furniture or knickknack, reflected her wealth while staying true to the history of the home, from the claw foot antique seating furniture to the silver tea set to the Tiffany lighting. The Ladies Auxiliary of Blue Rock Literary Society sat in their chairs, each with a book on her lap, as a servant woman brought tea and a silver platter of snacks. Amelia Livingston sat next to Lynette Cabot on the sofa, Emily Evans was present, seated in one of the fireside chairs, the other occupied by Bess Louviere, and Sarah Larsen sprawled on the loveseat.

Bess said, "So I hope you all found Bouviere as fascinating this time as I did the first time I read it." She looked around and was met with nothing but silence. "Come now. Don't tell me I'm the only one to read the novel."

Emily tossed the book on the coffee table. "Oh, to hell with your damn books, Bess Louviere. Some of us have bigger issues to deal with. I told you I didn't want to come tonight." This last statement she directed at Amelia, with whom she'd ridden.

Amelia said, "Oh, Miss Emily, we was all sorry to hear about Derek."

Sarah, lost in her own worries, thought it best to pipe up. "Yes, so sorry." But her words rang hollow.

Emily turned a venomous gaze her way. "You can take yo' sorry and shove it up yo' ass, Sarah Larsen. Enablin' your racist husband and that deputy a his."

Sarah sat up, flustered. "I had no idea they'd—"

"What?" Emily interrupted. "Snatch him up like a dog? No. Course you din't."

Bess felt the meeting slipping away and was desperate to get it back. They all needed this fellowship, whether they realized it or not. "It's like I was saying this morning—"

It was Lynette who interrupted her. "'Scuse me, Miss High and Mighty, but I got family that's police. My brother Terrence and I got a cousin and an uncle, besides. And they all worked with some Black officers, so how you can say that cops are racists, I just can't cotton to."

Bess took a breath in an effort to maintain composure. "The modern police force evolved from communal groups of deputized individuals meant to keep slaves from revolting. This continued through segregation with the prison system, the voting laws and restrictions of felons, for-profit prisons, school resource officers which are pipelines to prisons, and the war on drugs. All of these policies are inherently skewed against people of color. I might concede that not every cop is a racist, but racists and militants are still drawn to the profession, and these policies and the blue wall stymie a lot of blacks in their respective communities."

This would not deter Lynette, however. "I just think their lives are just as important, going out and putting themselves on the line like that every night." And there it was, Bess thought. An opinion stated as such but meant to be taken as a valid fact.

Bess wondered if reason would work and tried for it anyway. She'd known for years that Lynette could not differentiate between biased opinion and fact. "But talking about that serves only as a distraction from the issue people in these marches are trying to get you to see. No one is saying their lives aren't important, or that our white lives don't matter. No one is disputing that."

Emily broke in. "That bastard of a deputy, his life don't matter." She spit, more a sound than anything actually spewed from her lips. "He's had it in for my Derek for as long as I can remember."

Now it was Amelia's attempt to be the voice of reason. Bess couldn't remember the last time their little group's meeting had devolved so. "To be fair, Miss Emily, yo' Derek ain't no angel, neither. Now, don't give me the evil eye. I know you did your best with that boy—we all do—but we are all aware of the trouble he's been in, also."

Emily waved a hand, dismissing her. "That deputy and that damn Sheriff Charley has had it out for my Derek since he was in school. You remember, Bess. Like you said: pipeline to prison."

Bess could see all the tempers flaring as if reddish-black auras hung around every woman's head. Rationality, she feared, was ready to skedaddle from this salon. "I think what hurt young Derek's chances was being caught with marijuana in the 8th grade, and while I do believe that the 'War on Drugs' campaign is an egregious abuse of policing in our communities; nonetheless, it was still something he could have avoided but chose to partake in."

Tears welled up in the old woman's eyes. "He had so much gone 'gainst him for so long," she lamented.

Lynette tried a comforting arm around Miss Emily. "The chile had the odds stacked against him, we all agree, but that don't absolve the man of his sins."

Emily had been crying, and now removed a handkerchief from her purse and dabbed at the wet spots under her eyes. "I got a bad feeling, y'all, him being locked up there with them."

Reflecting on the truth of this, all each woman could offer her was merely a nod of agreement, and silence hung over them like a shroud.

Finally, it was Bess who broke the silence. "I've got a bad feeling in general. We on a powder keg that's got a lit fuse, and any minute now, it's going to explode."

She'd stated the obvious, but looking around the room now, she could see each woman agreed with her. From the couch came a sheepish, "Oh!" Miss Emily gave her a pitiful look. "Oh Bess, I so sorry. Here you wanna talk 'bout this here book, an' I'm justa carryin' on."

"It's okay," Bess said. "If you want to talk about this, we can."

Emily shook her head. "No. I read the book. If you other'n did too, we can talk about it. Do me some good to get my mind off my troubles."

"Do us all some good," Bess said, and the others nodded and affirmed in their own ways. And just like that, they were back on topic. But as the discussion continued, Bess could not escape the truth of that statement. There was a lit fuse and it was only a matter of time. In fact, she thought maybe it had already started to detonate.

಄಄಄

The waxing crescent appeared just a little less than two weeks before Halloween, and it hovered over the cone-shaped pines that lined the town as a stiff polar wind gusted across the land. She hadn't worn a coat, because the day was warm, but the falling temperatures now forced Casey to regret that. Autumn had fallen upon the community and, in Arkansas, that meant the temperatures swung like the pendulum of a grandfather clock. Bodies dressed in layers. Shivering, Casey knew this, but there was nothing else she could do now but press on toward her home.

Her mind was preoccupied with her father's wellbeing. At least to a degree. A part of her was relishing in the wonderful afternoon she'd spent kindling a friendship, reminiscing about good times, expressing hope for the future where an education might promise her a better life, even as another part feared letting her father know of her intent to move on.

After her mother left, and she was so young, it was Skeet who taught her to use the potty, who taught her to ride a bike, who was there to catch her when they took the training wheels off. He taught her how to brush her teeth and how to kneel at the bedside to say her prayers. Yes, the smell of alcohol still wafted off his tongue, no matter how much Scope or Listerine he gargled with, but he always did his due diligence when it came to his daughter.

Underbrush lined either side of most narrow dirt roadways in the county. A body might feel boxed in, walking along the path back home, the glint of the moon just overhead, a cool breeze raising the fine hairs to attention. Should the leaves shiver, then, as if something were traipsing through and disturbing them? Casey stopped and listened but could hear no footsteps. Still, the unsettled foliage rustled.

Casey took a deep breath and pressed on.

Her dad would understand. Once she explained herself, Skeet would acclimate to this new life. He'd realize that though she wasn't dependent upon him, or living under his roof anymore, that this didn't mean she'd abandoned him. No, if anything, she was giving him a security blanket. He could come live with her and whatever family she had. Skeet would be taken care of.

From the underbrush came a low, guttural growl. The night seemed impossibly dark and the air too cold. Casey hugged herself and looked toward the sound. Something was following her. She could feel it in the shadows of the trees; she had felt it back at Maddy's house. That's what the dog had sensed, but it knew better than to go outside, for it was no match for whatever waited.

Blades of pampas grass parted to reveal blackness and two gilded slits, from which erupted a menacing growl that rattled her chest. Staring into those two narrow slices through the night, realizing they were in fact glowing eyes reflecting light much as a dog's might, Casey thought about beauty school and her father and watched those things fade like ash in the wind. The thing in the bushes pounced, and she thought of giving birth and of having her father watch the little ones while she and her husband went out on the town and of becoming a grandmother. Images flashed in her mind of all these scenes.

And then she was on her back, a rock jagged and large digging into her spine, as this wolf with yellow slits for eyes pinned her down, snarling, snapping, growling, barking, its dagger-like canines inches from her throat, and then they sank into her flesh, and all those dreams faded, and thoughts of her father faded, and the future faded…

...to black.

CHAPTER ELEVEN

*G*ravity worked like on the moon in his dreams, which was how he could always tell when he was dreaming. Sometimes his steps would carry him normally, and the landscape around him would be so vivid that he thought it a normal day, until he sprinted and jumped and then the earth would fall away from him, and people would shrink to the size of ants as he saw the treetops, and he'd be afraid of landing, of the crash, bracing himself as he came down, until the ground yielded again like the stretched canvas of a trampoline, and he'd be back up.

Other times he'd find himself in a car, driving along, only to come upon an impossible corner, usually banked against a hill, and he'd miss the turn and take the hill like a ramp, the car lifting into the air, and Michael, sure the crash would kill him, would still tell himself that this was a dream and that he'd either be okay or die in his sleep when the crash came, and so he'd force himself to wake up just as the car came careening down.

The buildup to these various scenarios always changed. This morning as he awoke he recalled that he was on his first date with Casey, and that they were back in high school, but they were walking across the Ole Miss campus, talking about classes, which made no sense as was the case with most dreams, when he took that first leap, and he felt himself bound across the campus. Most of the time, in such dreams, people around him carried on unaware of his ability to defy gravity, but in this dream they screamed and ran, like they did when he dreamed of tearing across the countryside. There he also defied the laws of gravity, gaining more air with every successive leap, until (all four?) both (paws?) legs were off the ground, and the people looked at him and screamed. The people were screaming last night as he flew around them. Casey was screaming.

And then she wasn't.

Michael sat up in bed, instantly aware of his surroundings, instantly sure they were wrong. He shouldn't be here. Why wasn't he chained up in the loft? Throwing back the covers, he saw the mud and dirt, felt it caked on his feet and hands before he saw them, the grit under the nails, grouting the various wrinkles and curves and close spaces: between the fingers, the toes, in the creases of his palms, built up on his heels. *The gun*, he thought then. He'd finished setting up before he'd chained himself. It should have gone off the second he tripped it. So why hadn't it?

Familiar with the sight, though, of waking up in this condition, Michael knew that not all of what caked his extremities was mud and dirt. He could taste the other, like copper, every time he exhaled. Instantly his heart rate spiked. Maybe it was a coincidence, his dream of Casey, of their first date. Maybe he tasted chicken blood on his tongue now. *Oh God, let that be the truth,* he thought.

The silent vigil of phantoms surrounded him as he reached the bottom of the stairs, his parents and his siblings and Tom Larsen and there, the newest addition, Casey, her left eye hanging by a thread out on her cheek, a chunk of her throat missing, that side of her body painted red, her right arm gone from the elbow down. She opened her mouth to say something, but her tongue was gone, so all she could produce was a silent scream that Michael gave sound to as he sank to his knees, tears streaming down his face. Perhaps the sound he made resembled the word, "No," but it was so filled with anguish and despair, any meaning was lost. Kneeling, weeping as the visitants pressed closer, surrounding him, closing in on him, not out of solace, but as a reminder. They would never let him forget.

He dressed in his jeans and a T-shirt, then darted barefoot across the backyard to the barn, scampering up the ladder. The key was in the lock and the chains lay like dead silver snakes on the straw floor. The trip wires, hard to see at first in the dawn light, soon came clear. They lay just as loose in strands amongst the hay, severed in the middle as though someone or something had cut them, and the shotgun hung as dangerous as a Christmas ornament. Michael ran a finger up the string still tied to the trigger. It, too, had been cut. Had the wolf done this? Had it anticipated his trap and used its claws to dismantle what surely should have been its demise and his release? How could it have known, when he didn't remember its escapades? He'd lived through countless autumnal full moons already, and in all those years, he'd yet to remember where the beast had tread or what it had hunted. Likewise, it had never exhibited knowledge, as far as he knew, as to his comings and goings. They were separate entities sharing the same body, reshaping it to their individual likings so that they may survive. But as to the character of the beast, as to its desires and wants, its prowess and abilities, he felt as alien to it as to a stranger he passed on the street. They were roommates who never saw each other, passing coldly to tend to a single house when the other was away, and renovating each room to suit them only for the other to return and rearrange their hard work like a physiological feng shui war. No, the beast didn't know him, and didn't know what he'd attempted. This realization only allowed for one other option. Someone had cut him free and disabled his own trap. Someone had found a way to get close to the wolf. The idea of some outsider invading his life, setting him free, terrified him just as badly as the thought that the wolf had figured out his actions. Both options sent a shiver up his spine and made him feel all the more powerless.

CRESO

John Kelly surprised his sister and Dart when he walked through the door that crisp, autumn morning. The rattle of the door as a key jangled into the lock alerted the dog first, who sat up and emitted a low growl, his eyes fixed on the door. He let loose a bark that, had she been unprepared, might have jolted Madeline to spill her coffee. She wrapped an arm around him and shushed him, watching the door with him. The only other person to have a key was her brother. When he walked through the door, Dart let out a howl and bark of delight and reached him first, running in circles and panting and jumping up on him, all while his tail whacked against everything. John Kelly stooped to pet the dog and receive his kisses, even as Madeline finally caught up to them.

"What are you doing home?" she asked with a smile, accepting his peck on the cheek as he squeezed her shoulders.

"Damn saw seized up this morning. Seems we had a bit of frost and Jenkins, that idiot, didn't shut it down properly last night or account for the drop in temperatures."

She looked out the front bay window but saw turning leaves, a few more bare trees, and yellow grass. While clouds crept in overhead, she'd assumed it was another mild morning like they'd been having.

"Is it cold out?"

"Like twenty-eight degrees," he said, laughing. He dropped his bag in his room before meeting her back in the kitchen, stopping only to examine the thermostat. "You run the heat at all?"

"A bit last night when Casey said she had a chill, but I turned it off before bed."

"How's she doing?"

Maddy shrugged even as she considered the flannel pajamas she was wearing, the fuzzy slippers on her feet. The thermostat read 68, suggesting the insulation still worked in this old house, but she also attributed her warmth to her sleeping attire.

"This town's made her antsy. Can't say as I blame her."

John Kelly helped himself to the pot of coffee. "I still don't see how you can sleep in all that. I'd be sweating my balls off."

"There's an image," she responded. He reached into the fridge and brought out the half n' half.

"Almost out," he announced, tipping the carton on end as a few drops splashed into his cup.

"Guess what?" Maddy said.

Dart sat between them, a grin on his lips, his tail offering a few sweeps of the floor when John Kelly reached down and scratched his head. "What's that?"

"Aaron picked up Derek at his grandmother's place."

"D!" John Kelly said. "Evans?"

"Yep."

"I didn't think he'd come back here."

"No one did, I guess, but Emily Evans was telling everyone about it, says she's worried Bailey will let their personal history get in the way of things. Rumor is Derek's sitting down in a cell right now sporting some pretty fresh cuts and bruises. Duke Livingston called me yesterday, asked if I'd go check on him."

"Why you?" John Kelly asked, downing his coffee in one big gulp and setting his cup in the sink.

"Thought I'd have the most luck getting in. He also thought I had some connection with the NAACP to get Derek a lawyer. I told him there weren't any love lost between me and Derek Evans other than he used to be an awful flirt back in high school, but Duke says he's liable to not get a fair shake given the way things are going down in this country right now."

"Still think if he's so riled up 'bout it, he ought to do it."

"He might be right, though. Might have the best luck if it's me. You and Dart wanna take a W-A-L-K?" Sure to spell that last word because Dart knew what "walk" meant, but not "patience," and would be ready to go right then. Even still, his ears perked, and she imagined for a moment that he had learned to spell.

To this John Kelly gave serious consideration, before saying, "Let me shower real quick and put on some fresh clothes, first.

CR&SO

They walked with the dog on the leash, Dart loving the weather while the siblings were all bundled up, all the while planning out what they'd say to Sheriff Charley or Aaron when they got there, surprised when they saw the patrol car gone but found the front door unlocked.

Maddy poked her head inside, waved, and hurried back to her brother.

"You mind waiting out here? Don't think you can bring the dog into the building."

"Prol'ly not. Who you waving at?"

She furrowed her brow. "Some deputy. Probably up from Monticello. Didn't see the sheriff or Aaron."

"You in there, you best refer to him as Deputy Bailey. Don't want to step on any egos, make the situation worse."

"Trust," she said, ruffled the dog's head, then walked inside.

The unfamiliar deputy, who'd been sitting at the desk when she first poked her head in the door, had risen and crossed the floor by the time she returned, so that she barely could step inside.

"Where's Deputy Bailey?" she asked, looking around. Derek, sitting alone in a cell on the other side of the room, looked up from the bench he sat on. From where she stood, she could see evidence of a beating. One eye was swollen, and he had several red marks down one cheek.

"Called me'an the sheriff down," the deputy said. "He and Sheriff gone to look at somebody."

"Somebody?"

"No ma'am. Some. Body. Some farmer found it just around dawn."

Maddy's stomach dropped and she shook off a shiver before asking, "Can I talk to Derek over there? Just for a minute?"

The deputy looked back toward the prisoner then to her. "I really ain't supposed to let visitors in, miss."

Maddy leaned close, lowering her voice. "His grandma's just sick over his arrest, and she ain't doing well. It'd be mighty Christian of you to let me tell him." This little lie wasn't very Christian, but she thought she'd play on this white boy's sensibilities a bit. Plus, she could tell he was being nice to her because he found her attractive. That was fine. She'd play that off too, just to get what she wanted.

He looked around again, checked his watch, then nodded. "You got two minutes."

"Thank you, Deputy," she said.

"What in hell happened to you?" she asked Derek after she was sure the deputy, who had returned to his desk but eyed them from across the room, was out of earshot. Still, she leaned toward the bars and dropped her voice to a gruff whisper.

Mimicking her, Derek said, "Goddamn Aaron Bailey's what happened. He's lucky I was cuffed at the time. I'd've snatched that baton out of his hand and bashed his skull in had I the chance."

"He also scratched your cheek?"

"Fucker's got nails like a lady. Prissy little bitch, claw at me like we was in a chick fight. Drew blood. Still, I got some licks in. Counting the minutes 'til I can get more in, too."

"You just need to cool your jets," she warned. "You shouldn't have come back here."

"My grannie's here," Derek said. "Ain't no way I'm going to leave her alone."

"You know the trouble going on here, D. Going on all over. This town can't afford to have you rock the boat."

Derek just smiled, something wicked and cold and, yeah, a bit like an animal. "Maybe that's exactly what this place needs: a good boat rocking."

"Look," Madeline said, ignoring that comment. "I'll check in on Miss Em. We'll help her call a lawyer."

"Man, what a lawyer gone do anyway?" Derek's voice was loud and his movements exaggerated, like he was swatting away a fly.

"Just be on your best behavior," she hissed.

"This white boy wanna kill me," he whispered, his eyes wide. She saw fear in them. Real fear that he couldn't hide behind bravado or muscles. "I ain't never done nothin' to him, Mads, and he wanna kill me. He gone kill me."

"I know," she got out. She thought about saying something like, that's why he shouldn't have come back, but that's not what he needed right now. Besides, he was probably thinking it already.

"This place been tryina burn me down all my life, so maybe I oughtta burn it down. You help me. Burn this muthafucka down and we can get away. Just you and me. Like I tole you back in tenth grade. 'Member?"

Madeline sat back in her chair and glanced back over her shoulder. The deputy was scrolling through his phone. "Just cause I wanna help you get outta here, D, don't mean we got anything between us. I think you need to pay for your crimes, but not like this. Every man deserves a fair shake."

He pressed his lips together and looked away, and with his left hand rubbed at the scratch on his face. "I ain't no man," he growled under breath.

"Just behave, D, and we'll get you outta here. Hear me?"

But she knew that anger well. Despite him nodding at her, she knew with that look in his eye that he'd made his mind up, and if he got out of here, he'd do just what he promised. He'd burn this whole town to the ground and laugh while he did it. Derek Evans would not care who was hurt, either. Black or white, it was all the same. What mattered to him was retribution, and if you weren't standing beside him, it didn't matter what your skin color was.

Once outside, Maddy shared all of this with her brother, both Derek's words and what she thought about what he said.

"Then hear me out," John Kelly said, when she was finished. "Maybe we don't go to Miss Emily. Maybe we don't call a lawyer.

Look, Maddy, I get your heart, and I know what Aaron is doing ain't right, but I don't know that the answer is getting that thug loose. He liable to wreck some shit. He been ready to blow for some years, and if you say he was looking like that, then maybe he ready now. I don't want my sister near that."

She looked away, up to the swaying pines, the thick puffs of clouds drifting lazily through the sky, felt the cool air rake across her cheeks. Madeline knew her brother made sense, and she hated that she felt torn. She'd never been indecisive. When she made up her mind to do something, she stuck with it. Most of the time, this worked out, but now, walking back to their house, she wondered if her decision to return to this town wasn't a mistake in and of itself.

∞

That they didn't speak on the drive out to the location of the body suggested that things were bad. Sheriff Charley could be loquacious, but it was in his chosen silences where the mood could truly be judged. As they rounded a bend in the road, they saw first a pickup and then the pickup's driver, a scrawny balding man in dusty coveralls holding his cap between his hands like a child recently scolded. Bailey caught a hint of the carnage as Sheriff Charley opened the door, well before they could see anything. Charley, for his part, didn't seem to notice, but there was no denying the smell, or the fact that it didn't particularly disturb the detective. He realized, in fact, that his mouth was watering as he gathered up the crime scene tape rolls from the glove compartment. Upon exiting the vehicle, he heard the distant roar of engines fast approaching. State patrol, he thought sourly.

The frigid temperatures the night before and the morning frost had preserved the body. If this were the middle of summer, the bugs would have already been at her.

"You think this the same thing that got after you and Tom Larsen?" the sheriff asked.

Silent, staring at the sheet that now covered her broken and bloodied form, Aaron Bailey nodded.

"I think, then, we best keep this to ourselves," the sheriff said.

"I agree. These state boys will just muck everything up."

After parking, one of the state troopers approached them, flipping a tiny spiral notebook closed and tucking a pen back in his shirt pocket as he did so. Two others stayed back, one questioning the poor driver, the others ready to deter any would-be onlookers like this was fucking Times Square. Bailey wondered just who they thought they were showboating for.

"You guys got some aggressive bears around these parts," the approaching trooper said. Was he trying to make a joke? Aaron thought he could take the guy's head off with one swipe of his hand. "Someone ought to notify the father."

As if on cue, Duke Livingston's pickup neared, Duke driving, but someone, Aaron pretty sure he knew who, rode shotgun, and didn't wait for the truck to park before he was out and sprinting towards them. Several troopers moved to intercept Skeet Davidson, who screamed his daughter's name.

This didn't surprise Aaron. She was still identifiable, so he was sure that after he'd placed the call to the cops, this farmer called Duke Livingston and probably Emily Evans cause he didn't think Skeet had an operating phone line, and once they roused him from his drunken stupor and told him what had happened, Duke had brought him out. It didn't take Sherlock Holmes to figure out just how Skeet had learned of it, but here he was now, bawling his eyes out, struggling against the troopers, reaching for her, as though any of that would pull her out from under that sheet. From where he stood, Aaron could smell the beer on the man's breath.

Jesus, Aaron thought. The wailing was enough to drive him mad. It was all he could do to keep from reaching out and ripping that drunk fucker's head right off, a thought that brought a bit of a smile to his lips.

These thoughts, similar to the ones racing through Derek Evans's head, weren't new to the deputy. Some argued that Aaron Bailey's natural aggressiveness meant he was as destined for law enforcement as Derek Evans was the thug life. No, what was new for the deputy was how visceral the thoughts were. How perfectly animated they were in his mind. He could see his hand, nails as long and sharp as a bear's claws, swiping horizontally through the air, arcing toward the drunk man's jugular, slicing through his flesh like butter, blood spraying in a crimson arc, the nails not slowing but slicing through vein, bone, cartilage, muscle. The force of the swing would send the head careening off the neck, a look of shock frozen on the face as the head spun end over end, spraying blood as it flew like a punted football to a destination yards away, landing on the ground at the same time as the body that had hovered frozen after the decapitation, not aware that gravity should pull it down, not sure, like the face, that it was now dead.

He smiled at this thought. Nearly giggled. The man's blubbering didn't help matters. He put a fist to his mouth and bit down. This quelled the laughter some. To quell it more, he allowed his thoughts to turn to another matter, something else plaguing him. He could nearly see it, what happened to Casey Davidson. He could just close his eyes and hear her scream, taste her fear, smell her sweat and blood. He'd never experienced anything like it. It was exciting, like an orgasm. No, this thought carried the laughter away, but not the emotion. Not the jubilation. Whatever he was feeling now was new in its power, and he liked it.

CRSO

The first needles of rain fell as the sun went down. Michael stood on the back porch, his right arm wrapped around the whitewashed wood column, staring out on the unprotected flatland beyond. The pasture was so vulnerable. The storm could rage across this land and tear up all his father had worked for. Sure, that row of trees in the distance had buffered some of the worst winds, but that was the thing, wasn't it? Cloud cover did not necessarily diminish the effects of a bright moon, for at any moment it could burst through a break and the change would come. That's what happened to that farmer's cat that one fall at Oxford. What most didn't realize was that once the change happened, it would last until sunup, even if the moon was obscured again. Michael—and his brother TJ—learned that lesson the hard way once several years earlier, only a year, in fact, before that fateful night.

The dark loft felt dank as he ascended the ladder. The rungs were slick with humidity. Perhaps it was the rain outside, the cooling temperatures bringing frost to his breath. The key was, as it always had been, in his pocket.

"If I'd grabbed it before, then my jeans would be ripped."

This rationale made sense. He'd never found torn jeans pockets before.

Michael had locked the door downstairs—as always—and now threw a pillow into the hay while he ensured that the one key that could ensure his freedom was tucked safely in his hip pocket Outside the night hummed under the sheen of a bright, autumn moon. The pillow was one his parents had given him back when his memories were forming, when he was a toddler. Its cloth was faded now, its stuffing flattened. Still, he clung to it. Smelling it. He could remember them, through the smells of the pillow. He wept into it, as he'd wept so many times before.

The shackles clamped around his wrists and ankles. But before that he'd secured the shotgun, aimed at his head, from some wires that were connected to other wires that should be tripped by the wolf. Why they weren't the previous night, he wasn't sure, but this was the setup once more.

The rain fell through the window, dampening the hay around him, and he, shackled like a good boy, could only look out and dream of his one pillow, and then of treats and running.

He awoke to birds singing.

He opened his eyes but found the light streaming in through the window a muddled gray. Bright. Hints of gold in the sunlight.

And there were the birds.

The key rested in his pocket still. In the untorn pocket of his un-shredded jeans. It lay there like a silver weight, like his treasure. It unlocked his shackles and allowed him to face the morning. He paid it a perfunctory salute before he inspected the chains. Solid. Links unbroken.

CR&O

Michael began to worry when morning passed into afternoon and Byron had yet to show up with his weekly groceries. This had been the third morning he'd awakened still chained in the loft, and with each passing day his mind began to calm some. He'd never be totally at peace, he knew, as long as he was afflicted with this condition. Not the real him, as long as he could keep that mindless beast at bay.

"You're feeling pretty good," his brother, Sam, said from behind him as he poured himself a cup of coffee. Sam stood straight despite missing his right leg below the knee, his left arm torn from the socket, and his chest split open. "Slept like a sober alcoholic with no access to a bottle?"

"Who was it, Uncle Brian? The alcoholic?"

"Yeah, Mom's brother," Sam said. "Dad and I had to go bail him out of jail, once. Drunk and disorderly up in Monticello."

"He came to stay with us after that," Michael said. He carried his coffee to a chair on the back porch. Sam materialized in the other. "On the condition that there was no alcohol in the house."

"What's your point?" Sam asked. Did the dead have the right to be impatient anymore?

"I woke up early one morning, a few days after he arrived. He was sitting out here, right where you're sitting, and I sat right here."

Sip.

"You must have been what, twelve?"

"Something like that," Michael said. "It was before the change. He told me, drying out from alcohol, he was having some of the best sleep of his life. Peaceful, restful, dreamless. He felt nestled. He awoke refreshed. Every morning, like he was a new man."

"And that's how you've been feeling these past few mornings? Like a recovering alcoholic who beat the DTs?"

Michael sipped his coffee and watched the tree line. Some limbs were already bare. More would follow soon. The day was just as gray as the previous three, the distance hazy with rain and a cool fog that had settled over the town. The slow pitter patter of rain beat the tin roof of the back porch in a harried rhythm that only made sense to mother nature, but it was the kind of white noise that brought peace. For Michael, though, this tranquility was false.

"You aren't recovering from anything," Sam said.

Michael lifted his cup for another sip but found his hand trembled and he had to set the coffee down on the table between the two chairs.

"You're chaining yourself up, and the moment, the very moment those chains don't hold, you'll—to expand on your own metaphor—fall off the wagon again."

"No," Michael said.

"Yes," Sam said. "Look at me. You did this, Michael. You did this to all of us."

"It wasn't me! I would never." He not only turned his gaze away, but he shut his eyes as well.

"You did!" his brother said. "You did this! You ripped my arm out of its socket and clubbed me with it, and when I tried to crawl away, you grabbed my foot and pulled my leg off at the knee. You ate my calf like a fucking turkey leg, Michael."

"No!" he screamed.

"Then who, Michael? Who did this? The wolf? It is in you. It *is* you. If you did not exist, it would not exist. You get it now?"

Michael opened his eyes and looked across to the empty chair, his brother's words fading as if a distant echo. Suddenly he felt sick to his stomach, so he snatched up the coffee cup and hurled it across the porch, where it shattered as the last of the coffee splashed all over the boards. It wasn't him, but it was. His brother was right. The wolf wouldn't exist if he didn't. But he'd already tried, hadn't he. Tried to rig up something to take out the wolf as soon as it appeared. But wolves are crafty and this wolf, his wolf, had an ally. No, to take out the wolf, he'd first have to remove whoever helped it.

CRESO

This thought consumed him as the hours stretched on, until he realized just how late the day was getting. While he'd texted Byron that morning as the coffee was brewing, and the boy had texted back, he'd heard neither hide nor hair from the boy since. He was debating masking and gloving up and walking to the trailer park to see if he could find Byron or his groceries, when he spotted the boy walking across the road and up his drive. Michael met him on the back porch, his worry spiked some when he saw the shiner Byron sported.

"What happened?" Michael asked as Byron sat the bags down.

"I don't wanna talk about it." Byron snapped, and started to walk away, but Michael grabbed his shoulder and spun him back around.

"Byron, who did this to you?"

Up close, it was more than just a black eye. Byron's lower lip was split and fattening up even as they spoke, a trickle of blood dried on his chin.

"The deputy," Byron muttered. "Don't know why you want to know. You can't do nothing about it."

"Bailey?" Michael asked. He'd always hated that racist fuck in school. He wasn't surprised things hadn't changed. "What happened?"

Byron shrugged and pulled away, but he didn't try and run. Instead, his shoulders sagged and he wore a helpless, defeated look, like he had resigned himself to this torment. "Came to the trailer park, asking us all about Casey. When we saw her last. Was she alone? Any strangers milling about. I didn't mention you. But he wouldn't let anyone leave 'til he questioned all of us each. When it came to me, he walked me off some ways. Told me I better 'fess up before he hauls me in. I say I din't do nothing, but he din't care. Took out that baton and whacked me across the face. Told me don't sass him. I…"

Michael waited for Byron to go on, but saw the boy was shivering now, his split lip quivering. Michael touched his shoulder.

"Take your time," he said.

"I started crying, lying there in the dirt, and he just laughed and called me a pussy. Michael," and now Byron was crying again, great sobs pouring out of him, his cheeks soaked and his eyes puffy. "Michael, he say I cry like a bitch, so I should get fucked like a bitch. He know about me, Michael. He gone tell my momma."

That his mother didn't know surprised Michael even more than the idea that Byron thought he was still closeted. Still, Michael didn't say anything, just led the boy to the seat where his dead brother had been sitting earlier, brought him some water, and let him cry it out. When the sobs had given way to sniffles, Byron spoke again.

"Your house ain't the only place I sneak to. I made a friend, you know, up in Monticello. Sometimes, my friend, he'd come down here and pick me up, and we'd go back to his parents' house or drive out someplace private where we could be alone."

"Have you thought about telling your mom?" Michael asked.

"Lordy, no," Byron said. "She'd kill me. Go on and on about Jesus and how I'm a sinner. It's how she talks about fags on the television."

Michael thought about saying it was different when it was your own kid, but then he caught sight of his mother standing in the kitchen window, her eyes blackened, half her face clawed off, and realized that wasn't always the case.

"You could have texted me."

"I hid, 'til I was sure he was gone, and everyone returned to their trailers, and my ma left for work. Then I bawled some 'cause I din't want you to see me a cryin', but you did anyway, so that din't help, and then I made sure he was gone again, and then I grabbed your groceries and made my way out here."

A thought hit Michael then, one that made him nervous. "You sure he was gone? He didn't see you? Follow you?"

"No. I kept checking. Stayed off the road as much as I could. Trees kept the rain off me for the most part, too," and with that statement, the boy sneezed. Michael noticed then that the trees hadn't done a great job, as Byron was still pretty wet, so he ran upstairs and fetched him a towel to dry off with, and found one of his brother's raincoats for Byron to wear back.

"Thank you," Byron said. "My momma'll wonder where I got this. She knows I don't own no raincoat."

"Hide it under your bed," Michael said. "Tuck it away where she won't find it."

Byron, trying it on, nodded, then wiped his nose with his sleeve. Michael realized it was probably too late to keep the boy from getting sick, but it would keep him dry on the walk home. Seeing as how he wanted to beat his mother home and avoid seeing the deputy again, Byron said goodbye and trudged off, freshly paid for his labor in cash and outerwear, even as the rain kicked up again. Michael, watching him from the front room window, wondered as the rain increased if that boy would ever catch a break. Would any of them, in this godforsaken town?

CRSO

Rather than going to the hospital in Monticello for rounds, Vance Bellanger spent the day cooking. He'd awakened at five that morning refreshed from a sound night of sleep, rose to his carafe filled with freshly brewed coffee, poured himself a cup and drank it on his front porch, mentally preparing for the evening's festivities.

With the second cup, he began to take action. He pulled several books from the shelves in his library which might provide him and his guests with some entertainment. There was a text on the poisonous plants of South Arkansas, and a book detailing the folklore of the region. There was an investigative journalist's study into life after death, and a treatise linking Aleister Crowley to Gnostic and apocryphal New Testament texts. For his wife, Vance only had to consider her limited palate, as she got her intellectual stimulation from the regular meeting of the literary society she'd founded. She'd maintained a slight figure by consuming copious amounts of vegetables, some fish, poultry as her main source of protein, pork occasionally, and no red meat. He opted then for salmon as the main course, a side salad with rich greens like kale and spinach rather than iceberg lettuce, a side of buttered Brussel sprouts, a side of homemade mashed potatoes, and some dinner rolls. For dessert he'd prepare an apple tart to sweeten their teeth and would serve it with a pot of imported decaf from Italy.

This would of course take a lot of preparation, so Vance set upon it instantly, ordering the ingredients he needed for pickup later, organizing the menu, pulling his sources from his library shelves. Set upon his tasks as he was, his mind couldn't help but wander.

Whispers said that boy, Calhoun, what lived out at the trailer park, could be spotted carrying bags of groceries out to the Risten farm. Vicky Arsenault even swore she saw Casey Davidson head out that way on the very day she was murdered.

Vicky Arsenault was not a body to be trusted. She was a known methhead, and she ran around with that Remy Doucet, and how Duke Livingston could employ such a nasty couple of degenerates was beyond him. Still, her story lined up with the one he'd heard from Bess Louviere, who said she heard from Chet Kelly Ludlow that he saw Calhoun carrying groceries out to the Risten farm. If Casey Davidson was trailing her neighbor Byron, then the question left was why was he delivering groceries out to that abandoned farm.

Unless it wasn't abandoned.

Michael was out there.

Already preparing his meal, Vance found himself in a quandary. He paced about the kitchen, snatching at ingredients, spilling carefully measured tablespoons of water or oil as he pondered the possibilities.

Did Michael need medical help? How alone he must feel. How cold it must be, out there on that farm. Did Maddy or John Kelly know Michael was still out there? Mind you, Dr. Vance Bellanger had no tangible proof, but had been led to this conclusion by his critical reasoning, and because of this, he was absolutely certain he'd arrived at the correct conclusion.

So, he should call the sheriff, he thought. Or the area's deputy. He should call the Jeansonnes. Perhaps take them out there to search the grounds. Maybe confront the Calhoun kid.

Problem was, he trusted none of them as much as he trusted his best friend. In just a few short hours, Phillip Cabot and his wife Lynette would be at his table, and he could present to them his evidence, and he could judicate their advice. They would know what to do.

CR&SO

Duke Livingston had come to feel the power as the sun went down. As the world darkened, it became theirs; everyone caked in shadow, everything chilled, like they were all on equal ground. He'd heard this sentiment from others in other parts of the country, as the marches went on, cops and civilians alike shielded by the darkness, by masks, empowered by their anonymity. Both sides were equal, and they hadn't been equal ever, before now.

It was Rayburn that had set Duke on this path. Just a couple of years ago, Deputy Bailey had rounded up Rayburn for a drunk and disorderly and shoved him into the drunk tank in the office there on the square. Duke, cleaning up the eatery that night, had watched the treatment of his older brother. He'd dropped his broom and marched across the square, past that goddamn statue, right on up to the deputy. Beyond the badge and the gray uniform, he saw the tow-headed little boy that had asked him for a milkshake, and later the pimply-faced teen just discovering the weight room who'd begun to act snarky. The boy especially, but even the teen, had still held some respect for the elder.

"Yeah," the deputy had said as Duke had walked up on him. The deputy was dead behind the eyes; any sign of the little boy or the teen was gone. The badge and the blue-line looked out through those eyes now, dull, stupid even. A moronic service to some ideal, some flimsy belief in a false definition of community, serving suppression and regulation.

"What was my brother doing?" Duke asked Deputy Bailey. The closed door to the office couldn't mute Rayburn's drunken wails.

"He just carrying on," Bailey had said.

Perhaps he was, Duke had thought. Rayburn was known for just carrying on. Dramatizing things. But the badge possessing the eyes of that little boy, that obnoxious teen, was known for so much worse.

"That ain't what I asked you," Duke said, and he noticed the deputy stand a bit more rigid, and raise a hand to his nightstick, and a part of him was thankful it wasn't the hand closest to the holstered service pistol just as that same part of him thought, *How dare he, this impudent child whom I watched grow up?*

"You need to step back, sir," Bailey had said. Sir sounded a whole lot like *boy*. *Sir* and *boy* were synonymous with *slave*. What cut worse than any of those connotations, though, and what spurred Duke on to the chats about Black Lives Matter and led him to organize the movement here, was the complete callousness with which Aaron Bailey looked at him that night. He'd watched that boy grow up, but now Aaron didn't even look at him like he was human. And while this phenomenon wasn't new to someone Duke's age, that didn't mean it didn't hurt any less when he was faced with it.

"I just want to know my brother's okay," Duke said.

"He'll sleep it off," Aaron Bailey said. "I don't see us pressing charges, if that helps any."

It didn't. Duke's original question had never been answered, but he was going to let it slide, for that badge looking out through them eyes.

"I'll be here to fetch him in the morning then," Duke said, and Aaron Bailey had nodded, and the next morning Rayburn was none the worse for wear as he staggered out of the police station.

Now, on the eve of the next Black Lives Matter protest, as the temperature was falling into the low fifties, and a steady slow drizzle pelted the rooftops and pavement, Duke shut the neon sign off at his place and lowered the plywood cover to the serving window, locking it in place, even as his brother, crouching on the curb just ten feet away and three sheets to the wind, strummed some chords on the old acoustic and belted out a disharmonious melody.

Duke sat next to Rayburn and put his arm around his brother. This didn't affect the guitar players strumming, nor interrupted his humming.

"Rain gonna warp the neck."

"Fixed that newel on Old Bellanger's porch," Rayburn sang. He was a handyman by trade, but as good as he was with a hammer and a saw, it was no match for his strumming.

"Good for you, brother," Duke said, and pulled Rayburn's head to him and kissed his temple.

"Aw," Rayburn slurred. He was right sauced up tonight, and in no shape for another movement. Truth be, he ought to sleep it off.

Duke stood and hoisted his brother under his arm. Rayburn found his feet cradling his guitar. He stroked the strings and caressed the wood and hummed in tune with the vibrations.

"What's she singing to you, Rayburn?" Duke asked. He hadn't his brother's gift for the creative; Duke's mind had been more geared toward business. But he'd always loved to hear him play. As kids, he could get lost in Rayburn's playing for hours. Rayburn had seemed set on his current path for as long as Duke could remember. Their parents had always been on Rayburn, and Duke seemed to remember him always drinking. His fondest memories, in fact, were of Rayburn sipping on a bottle of whiskey while playing the Dobro for his little brother, singing old Negro ballads and slave spirituals. Rayburn had inherited the guitar (and his love of the drink) from their grandfather, who'd been lynched back in the middle of the 20th century by the white folk of the area, all due to the insinuation that this faithful, god-fearing family man had defiled a white woman.

"Just the melodies of heaven," Rayburn said, clinging to the old acoustic, the only instrument he had anymore, the Dobro long-since traded in for money or hooch.

Duke pulled his brother down the sidewalk. With any luck, he'd have time to tuck Rayburn into bed and make it back in time for the movement to start. It was imperative he make it back in time for the march. Not only was he the instigator, but he also saw himself as the march's conductor.

"The wolf," Rayburn said, pulling against his brother. Though Duke was the sober one, and broad and healthy, Rayburn still had the strength to nearly pull him off his feet. He placed his arm back around his brother's shoulders and urged him on down the street. Few houses lined either side and the streetlamps, spaced just so their pools of light illuminated yards and sidewalk and pavement, left great swaths of darkness that concealed the unknown.

"Bed," Duke said. "Let's get you tucked in."

Rayburn howled, breaking the silence of the night, and when Duke tried to shush him, his elder brother just laughed.

"Rougarou," Rayburn said in a singsong kind of voice. "He coming for you!"

"You've had a lot to drink, brother. More than usual."

Rayburn's guitar was secured to his body by a strap over his shoulder, which left both his hands free to press the palms against Duke's cheeks, and he stared into his brother's eyes.

Rayburn tried to enunciate the word, "Seriously" but failed miserably, and he swayed some. "You hear it on the night air? Screeching? Howling? The darkness is bringing it. I can feel it. You can, too. Its breath is rancid and warm on these cool nights."

"You need a good night's sleep," Duke said.

Rayburn backed away, looked around, then nodded. Then, without saying anything else, he turned on a heel and marched right up to the front door of the halfway house where his room waited for him.

⚇

Oh, how Michael's hands clung to the rungs of the ladder leading up to the loft. His stringy forearms pulled his weight up. He gripped the rough-hewn rungs of the ladder, feeling every splinter, every ripple and divot of each rung. Though he knew the shotgun wasn't set up, he still ducked the barrel as he climbed into the loft, resting on some hay. That insignificant act proved, at least to himself, that he wasn't suicidal.

The shackles fit easily around his wrists, his ankles. Soon he was staring out at the waning moon, listlessly drifting into sleep. A dreamless sleep. His mind cooled while his body was warmed by the hay.

Angelique watched from the shadows.

She crept up the rungs of the ladder, avoided the tripwire, curled herself like a slinking cat away from the danger, all the while her eyes on the shackled man now just beginning to toss and turn.

He was purring. Such a soft, docile sound.

Right now, Basil and Bela were gigging the catfish lines down by the lake.

Digging into Michael's pocket proved especially dangerous as he tended to thrash and growl when the change began. Straw tossed every which way as he shook against the chains and rattled the barn. But she fetched the key and spoke to it like she was enchanting a sacred, ancient artifact.

"What we deserve, what your family deserved, my dearest boy, as the moon dictates, the whole town deserves."

It rose, replacing the young man. It was dark and covered in hair, its limbs now unshackled, and in the moonlight it turned an illuminated profile and howled. It revealed a snout and teeth and powerful, muscular thighs and calves and feet. The feet, as with the hands, were clawed.

The beast snarled and focused its yellow eyes on her.

"Not me," she said. He was more awake than other nights. Perhaps this was why she was more afraid.

The beast snorted and flexed its claws. Angelique merely pointed toward the night.

CR80

Rayburn Livingston heard the first howl just as he was drifting off. The wind carried it through the night, across the land. It sounded distant, but no less dangerous. He'd just about drifted off again when another howl came, this one closer. His eyes refused to close this time.

So, it was closer. So what. He'd heard the stories, of course. What happened to the deputy and that preacher. The attacks on the farms in the area. People were saying a wild pack of dogs. Maybe a bear. Remy Doucet was even convinced it was a gator. But this unabashed drunk knew what it was. Gators didn't howl, and this weren't no pack. No, this was a single, big animal. Rumors swirled around the condition the preacher's body had been found in. But even still, this was a big area, and while it wasn't so densely populated as Monticello, say, there were still plenty of places here for it to feed.

When he heard another noise, this time right below his window, he tried to dismiss it first. Skunk maybe. Or a cat. But no, this sounded too big. The rustling was too loud, and something scraped against the siding. And then there was another sound. Not a howl. But nor was it a growl. It was like a chuffing noise. Great blasts of air blown through the nostrils, delivered from deep within the lungs. And then a thud. He followed this trail of sounds until it faded around the corner of the house, faded more, nearly vanished. Then, in the still and quiet of the night, he heard the sound of claws on the porch. More terrifying still, the sound that made him catch his breath in his throat and sobered him instantly, Rayburn heard the rattle of the brass doorknob trying to engage. The lock held.

For now.

Rayburn sat up and looked at his own door as the claws carried whatever it was (*you know what it is, you old drunk*) across the porch. As he was trying to remember if he'd locked his own bedroom door, Rayburn heard the sound of the clicking claws fall silent. When they resumed, he knew the thing was back at the front door. Pacing. Stalking the home. Like a big cat at a zoo might pace its pen, sniffing the prey just on the other side, trying to find a weak point where it could gain egress. Or access. Something was out there, trying to get in.

He pulled the cover off his body slowly, and, knowing every creak of the mattress, eased himself off the bed as gently as possible. Focused as he was on the mattress, he'd forgotten about the old floorboards. One screeched under his weight in a sound that deafened any the mattress could make. When Rayburn would reflect guiltily on this night later, he'd convince himself that it was this sound that alerted the creature and drew it inside.

A great thud resounded from downstairs. In his fear, Rayburn believed the whole house shook. His own steps were unsteady as another and another thud came. From down the hall, he heard a door open. It wasn't Remy Doucet. He was out at his father's tonight. No, it was Vicky Arsenault. This was confirmed when Rayburn heard her call out, "Hold your horses! I'm coming."

Rayburn sprinted for his door and threw it open. "Vicky!" he yelled, spying her through the darkness on the stairs. She turned and glared at him, that combination of sleep and drug-induced high warping her face. This was a place for addicts, after all. He never touched the shit she and Remy shot up, but he recognized the look she wore now from the countless times he'd examined his own reflection.

"Whu...?" she said, as the door below thudded again.

They both looked down. It wouldn't hold much longer. "Vicky, please go back to bed, and lock yo' door."

"Ray—" was all she managed as the next thud exploded the door inward and a sound, something grotesquely triumphant blending a howl with a snarl and growl, erupted from beneath them. The house was still and dark. Rayburn could only make out a massive black shape below. It sniffed and raised what must be its snout to them, then headed for the stairs. Ray was sure Vicky was a goner, but she had some instinct left, some foresight into the danger, for she screamed and ran to her door. What stalked below growled, then ascended the old groaning staircase.

Rayburn ran to his own door and motioned for her to join him. Once they were inside, he slammed the door shut and pressed against it. Vicky paced his room, her eyes wide with fear. She approached the light switch as if she intended to turn it on, but Rayburn told her no. When the door thudded from a heavy knock, she screamed. He raised a single finger in the moonlight to shush her, but the door thudded again, and the fearful look on her face reminded him it did no good to stay quiet.

They waited. Its claws clicked on the wood floor of the hall as it paced the hall. Rayburn knew that this interior door was nothing compared to the exterior one that it had burst through. It was only a matter of time before it realized that, too, and the door would be torn from its hinges, and the thing in the hall would enter. Vicky stood near him, muttering something. He shot a hateful glance at her. Her eyes were shut and she hugged herself with her rail-thin, pale arms, rocking. Tears streamed down her cheeks. The house creaked, a sound nearly louder than the footsteps in the hall, so that when those steps grew fainter (*descending the stairs?*) he nearly missed it. He chanced a shush and poked her shoulder. Had the footsteps stopped? Was the beast now reconsidering the door, studying them? Could it smell them? Hear them? Rayburn gingerly gripped the knob, holding it firm, pressing his shoulder against the wood face.

For several minutes they heard nothing but Vicky's mutterings, and even those eventually stopped, replaced by sniffles and alternately deep and shallow sighs, her nails scratching against her dry, sore-covered arms.

"Open it," she whispered finally, but he didn't respond. His ear was pressed to the door, listening for anything to warn him to stay put or reassure him all was okay. No, such clear signs had never come to him in the normalcy of life, so why would they come now when things were batshit? Uncertainty fed his anxiety, which only muddled the decisions he had to make, and only the bottle had ever broken that cycle. But Miss Louviere's rules were simple. Drink what you want out of the house, but no drugs or alcohol in the house at any time. There was nothing to ease his disquiet. He was at a loss for what to do next.

"Rayburn," Vicky whispered again. Hugging herself, she scratched at the dry flesh of her triceps. He shook his head and muttered another shush.

"I have a cell phone," she said, still whispering.

Rule number two. All technology had to be mediated by Miss Louviere to stay here. A TV in the main room got basic cable. They were allowed something for music in their rooms as long as it only played music. Vicky often blared her stereo during the day. Rayburn had saved some old jazz LP's to play on the Victrola in the corner.

That Vicky admitted this surprised him little. Even a whiff of alcohol, real or imagined, and he'd get the third degree. But he knew Vicky and Remy Doucet were shooting up on the regular and, because Vicky was the granddaughter, neither got reamed as hard as ol' Rayburn. He'd made his peace with this, and he knew it wasn't about race. Bess Louviere loved her granddaughter and because of this, Remy Doucet skated because, by Bess' logic, if Remy were doing drugs, then Vicky would be as well, and since Vicky couldn't be, then Remy couldn't be either. Never mind that acrid smell of burning chemicals, the residue of the meth, that hung in the air thicker than any whiskey or beer or scotch. No, Vicky had been given this second chance. Rayburn knew nothing, but seeing her granddaughter shoot up with her own eyes would change Bess's mind.

Even then, he doubted it. So, when Vicky admitted this bit of contraband existed in her room, he was not surprised, and he knew what she was getting at. If they could get to the cell, they could call the sheriff up in Monticello or perhaps Deputy Bailey.

Deputy Bailey, he thought then. Existing in a drunken stupor blurred the days together, but hadn't he recently been at the doctor's? Maybe up at the hospital there in Monticello? Hadn't he been attacked also when Preacher Larsen was killed? He thought so, and that's when it struck him. This thing might be the very thing that had put that boy in the hospital.

"Where is it?" he asked, whispering.

"Side table drawer," she answered, matching his tone.

"You lock this door behind me, Vicky Arsenault. You hear? And don't open it 'til you know it's me."

He thought he saw her nod. His left hand still gripping the knob, he reached up with the right and unlocked the door, simultaneously turning the knob so the door inched open, slow and steady enough so that it may not creak on its hinges, and just wide enough so he could put an eye to glance down the hall.

It was dark, but his eyes had already been adjusting to the dark, so he could make out the empty hall, the empty stair. His ears scanned for sound and heard nothing. Quiet as it was, he was sure he'd hear something breathing. He'd hear it if it were trying to stay quiet.

He pulled the door open a bit wider and took a more solid glance, then stepped into the hall. He wore his boxers and a tee that had once been white, but was now stained yellow under the arms with streaks down the back from where liquor-soaked sweat leaked from his pores. His feet fell nakedly on the wood floor of the hall, a flat, nearly silent sound that he heard deafeningly because it was so quiet. He took another step into the hall and heard the door slam shut behind him. Muttered a curse. *Stupid girl. Stupid, stupid girl.* Then, from below, a noise he couldn't place or identify, exactly, but nonetheless revealed the crucial fact that he and Vicky were not, in fact, alone in this house. That indescribable noise was followed by a rising growl, something full-throated and gurgling, shaking his chest, the very foundations of this home as its pitch climbed. Claws from below carrying it closer, toward the stairs.

Rayburn ran.

A shadow, hurling itself up three risers at a time, reaching the mid landing before he'd taken two steps. He focused on Vicky's door and prayed she hadn't locked it, reached its knob and his palm slipped. Whatever was in the house with them bounded up the steps and he swore, if you'd have asked him about it later, that he felt its breath on his neck just as he swore that the bitch had locked her door and this was it for ol' Rayburn.

Except his hands found purchase again and the knob turned and the door swung open, and Rayburn was in her bedroom pushing the door shut when such a massive force slammed against him that he thought he was going to sail across the room. The door did tremble in his hands but he held on, and when it had backed off for another chance to ram, he slammed the door closed and locked it. When it thrust against the door again, the door held, and it ricocheted off with a yelp, thudding on the far wall. This sound punctuated by the sound a dog makes when shaking off the rain, and a snapping bark as though it chastised him for daring to lock it out.

Again Rayburn was faced with an impossible decision. Let go of the door and go for the cell, and chance the beast getting back in, or sit here and hope his weight was enough to keep it out. Biting his lip, shaking his head, he realized he'd come this far, so he rose to his feet and hurried to the side table, pulled open the door, and cursed Vicky Arsenault for the second and last time that night. The cell was there, but it was plugged into the charger, and the battery sign was showing red with zero progress. Following the cord to the outlet, he found it hadn't been plugged into the wall, so whatever had been left of the battery had long since drained. *She was probably high when she'd gone to charge it*, he thought.

There was a knock, but not at this bedroom door, though he'd looked to it on instinct. No, next door where Vicky still held fast against that thing, in his room. Through the wall, he heard the exchange.

"Who is it?" Vicky's voice trembled but was clear as day.

"Me, Vick," came the voice all too similar to his own. Similar, but not identical. There was something false in it. Like the words were passing from a mind that couldn't comprehend the words and suffused the vocal cords with an undercurrent of a growl. "Let me in. I got the phone."

It had heard them whispering after all then. From all the way downstairs. And it could speak? Could mimic?

"What's wrong with yo' voice, Ray?" she asked.

"It's coming, Vick. Hurry." It mimicked panic well. Almost convincingly. But he never called her Vick.

"I don't know, Ray," she said. "Can you..."

"Vick, please! I see it, coming up the stairs."

Ray felt like an outsider spectating on the events, forgetting for the moment that if he could hear them, then Vicky would be able to hear him, until he heard the latch to his own bedroom door give and he screamed out: "Vicky! Lock the door. It ain't me!"

But it was too late. The sound of the door exploding inward was so loud he jumped back, stared at the wall. Vicky screamed, and he felt powerless again. His mouth agape, he stared as if he could see through the wall to the horror playing out in his bedroom. As if he could see Vicky screaming, see the flesh being torn from her form and the blood splattering against the floor and ceiling and wall, the bones pulverize to powder as the jaws clamped down with each crunch. He heard, at last, a victorious howl splinter through the house, so deafening he pressed his palms to his ears to shield against it. His head rang and he wondered if one could get tinnitus from a single exposure to such an explosive sound, sat forcefully on her bed and squeezed his eyes shut. Several moments passed before he realized it was safe, probably, to move. The house had grown still and silent.

Ray rose, made his way to the door, listened. *Fool me once*, he thought, but as with before, he heard nothing. With a resolute sigh, he stepped back out into the hall to find it empty and dark and silent.

His bedroom door stood open. Walking to the balcony's banister, he looked down to see the front door was open also. A steady drip, like a leaky faucet, came from his room.

He turned as though trapped in a vivid dream and stepped the short distance to his door. Alien silhouettes that hadn't been there before confused his eyes, so he flicked the light switch to his right. The switch and its plate were tacky, and as the light came on, he saw both why that was so and what those shapes were. The room shined red from the blood splatter, which coated the light switch and now the tips of his fingers. The shapes were the remains of his roommate, a young, strung-out woman who probably would have never gotten clean. Nothing left resembled her, just as her recent state did not resemble the sweet little girl she'd once been. The transformation was complete and Vicky was unidentifiable. The drip, he realized then, was from the shard of a bone jutting out from a chunk of flesh that could have been a forearm or a lower leg, its end dangling off the side of the bed, what blood remained inside pooling below on the floor, drip by drip.

CRSO

Barely an hour had passed since Vicky's demise when Remy Doucet heard the chickens screaming. He hadn't been fond of his uncle's chickens. In fact, over the years, he'd come to hate them. He'd come by this feeling honestly, as it was triggered by an event when he was three. Remy swore to anyone listening to his story that he still remembered the traumatic event to this day. He'd gone out to look for his uncle one day who was out working on the coop, letting the flock free range in the backyard. The rooster saw little Remy not as a small human but as a large intruder stepping into his territory. He hopped from leg to leg in front of Remy, always stepping in front of him any time he tried to go around. The toddler had called out "Unc!" several times, but his uncle either didn't hear him or didn't register the danger. Remy saw the danger. The way the rooster blocked him. The way it stood.

"Unc!" he said again, his voice rising. The rooster stepped forward. Remy took a step back. Jutting its head forward, the rooster opened its beak and cawed. Remy took two more steps back. All of a sudden, he didn't need to see his uncle. He was no longer curious nor did he want to offer to help. He could wait inside. So he turned and headed for the door, and that's when the cawing grew into squawks that blasted his hearing and he felt needle-like claws in his shoulders and on his head. The bird screamed in his ears and was all over him, tearing at his flesh, his scalp. Instinctively, Remy covered his face with his arms, but the bird tore into his wrists and the meat of his forearms. Remy screamed. He tried to get out, "Unc!" but all that emerged was something garbled and terrified.

And then it was done. Sure, he still cried, but the squawking was fading and he no longer felt the claw marks. He slowly uncovered his head and lifted his eyes to see his uncle chasing the rooster across the yard, kicking at it, the bird nearly screaming in pain. Remy smiled. His uncle snatched the bird by the neck and whipped it around, and the bird fell silent and limp in his fist. Remy's uncle spiked the carcass on the ground like a football and rushed back to his nephew. He put an arm around Remy and led him back into the house. The rough hands of a man that built and worked in the dirt were soft as he tended to the child's wounds.

Since that day, Remy completed the chores that related to the chickens begrudgingly, but he minced no words about his love of buffalo wings, nuggets, and KFC. He'd become a connoisseur of all poultry-related dishes. He was as disheartened and distrusting of flightless birds as he was of those that could fly or anything with more than four legs. A regular childhood nightmare included birds swooping from the sky, a land bird chasing him ready to bite, and large spiders waiting with glee for their turn. These horrors may have played a role in him becoming head cook for Duke Livingston, but not in him sinking into drugs.

When his uncle had told him that something had harmed his first batch of chickens, Remy couldn't have cared less. When his uncle begged his nephew to come figure out what was going on with the birds, and had replenished the hen house with a new flock he could barely afford, Remy could think of a million things he'd rather do. But for all his issues, Remy loved his uncle, now a widower, and recognized what the man had done for him. He also knew that this would take him from Vicky Arsenault for at least a night, and he might be able to sleep soberly in a comfortable bed for once, and while he'd never admit it to anyone, Vicky or even himself, he desperately wanted to get sober. He was so tired of the drugs, of the highs. The lows. The need to get high was not as great at his uncle's house, as it had always been a place of refuge. So he accepted and packed a bag and let Bess Louviere know that he'd not be at the halfway house for probably a couple of nights.

Remy listened to them scream in the darkness and to the sound of something big crashing and smashing through the outbuilding. He'd arisen at the first noise and dressed quickly. He did not want his uncle to wake, but a part of him did not mind the sound. The memory of what the rooster had done to him, or more to the point, the fear he remembered, lessened listening to the suffering birds. Still, he loved his uncle and how he'd cared for him, so he grabbed the twelve gauge off the mantle in the living room and step out into the cold night.

He took a moment for his eyes to adjust to the darkness. He hadn't turned on any light in the house for fear of startling whatever or whoever was out there. His uncle was a Black chicken farmer in South Arkansas and had been pretty successful, so both options were open. Plenty of white folk and impoverished Black folk had their feathers ruffled over his uncle. There'd been a time in his teens and early twenties that Remy had bought into that animosity, and for that he was now ashamed.

His boots crunched over the near-frozen dried earth, the smell of gun oil in his nose mingling already with the blood from the coop. The cries were less but not gone, and he could hear whatever stalked the hens still inside. Taking its time.

A few more steps and he pumped the shotgun. Whatever was in the coop stopped. It sniffed the air and let out a grumble. Remy sidestepped, the barrel always trained on the entrance, until he stood in front of the ramp. Whatever walked inside thudded toward the entrance with heavy steps that sounded like boots on a hardwood floor. A looming, man-shaped silhouette appeared in the door. Its very size and familiarity startled Remy. He lowered the shotgun and stepped back a bit. Perhaps coming out here, he suddenly thought, wasn't a good idea. Perhaps he'd be better off inside, watching over his sleeping uncle.

He retreated another step. A dark figure stepped onto the ramp. Reflecting night light, the deputy badge on the dark blue shirt flickered in his eye. The shirt itself was torn in places, with half a shirttail pulled out and dangling, shredded. Through those tears, tuffs of dark brown fur poked out at random. The face, also heavily furred, wore features Remy recognized. The fur on top was lighter, nearly blonde. The eyes were blue, just as human as inhuman. He'd heard the sound of boots because it wore the boots of the policeman's issue, the boots Aaron Bailey wore every day in his duties as town constable, as deputy. But the wolf's feet were too large. Its claws split the leather so that the sole flip-flopped with each step. It settled its eyes on him and its lips curled into a snarl. "Remy," it growled.

Remy dropped the shotgun. *Oh god*, he thought. Even in this state, it still recognized him. It knew his name. His eyes shifted to the claws at the ends of its hands, still dripping with chicken blood. Oh, Jesus, he wanted to call out, but the words wouldn't come. All that he could manage was, "Unc?" "Unc!"

But his uncle wouldn't hear. Remy, of course, would never learn why. He'd missed, walking through the living room, that the front door was ajar. That side of the house, deep in shadow, could hide the details well. He'd missed the broken lock and open door. That wolves, for as bustling and loud and chaotic as they could sound attacking, could also be as quiet as mice, and this thing that looked like both the deputy and a wolf had crept through the shadows and slinked into his uncle's room, and had raked a claw across the flesh of his uncle's neck, piercing not just the skin but arteries and esophagus, so that while his uncle woke for a second and saw, standing over him, this grinning monstrosity of a thing near unrecognizable in the shadow of his room, he hadn't the voice to scream. It pinned his shoulders to the mattress, keeping him from thrashing, and placed a knee over his legs, and watched the blood flow out of his neck and the life flow out of his body while his nephew slept in the next room over.

And now Remy stood, having dropped the gun. He might've had a chance with a weapon. But since dropping it he'd taken another step back, and the Aaron-wolf had taken two steps forward. Its knuckles popped as it flexed its claws.

Before Remy screamed, he muttered, "Unc," once more, and as the Aaron-wolf lunged, his screams fell only to the murdered and the deaf. The wolf bathed in his blood and snapped his fragile bones.

CRSO

Dr. Vance Bellanger awoke to his alarm system chirping much too loudly. He sat up in the somnolent darkness, his eyes—sans readers or prescription no-line bifocals—blurred and hazed. Either the smoke alarm, CO_2 detector, or security system was going off. Did it matter which? None were good options. He sat up and draped his legs over the bedside, padding the soles of his feet with the leather and fluff of his house shoes while his left hand fumbled across the nightstand for his glasses case, two midnight McGuffins he ultimately stumbled upon at the same time. These in hand (or rather on feet and nose bridge), his robe was easily discovered still draped over the bedpost, and he was out the bedroom door to investigate the noise. It never occurred to him that he was in real danger. Just some technical glitch.

Technical glitches had been the tagline for the whole project of renovating the Victorian. The carpenter had come in over budget, forgetting to add in mileage from Northwest Arkansas, a big deal compounded by the fact that this was the only man in the state who could duplicate the intricate millwork found above the shingles. The plumber from Little Rock quoted a base price then quadrupled it when he realized the entire system wasn't up to code. If this beeping were the security alarm, it would be the third such alarm call this month, most likely due to the faulty wiring. The electrician from Monticello had promised that his "workaround" would save the doctor from having to rewire the whole house and serve as just as good a job as if he'd spent that extra ten grand.

Vance padded down the hall, down the front staircase, and froze at the landing where the stairs turned ninety-degrees. The front door stood in full view now. Open. The center window of the door was shattered; bits of stained glass like tiny iridescent stars sparkled in the yellow pool of light that washed in from the outside street lamp. The door itself stood open. The edges of the doorjamb splintered in the faint light, as wooden spears stood cattywampus to the rest of the frame, like trees growing out of a steep riverbank.

He hurried down to the first floor and shut the door, finding it wouldn't even latch. The wall panel device still flashed red, the high-pitched beep echoing from the tiny box. He hit the reset button as a voice came over the intercom. "Everything okay, Dr. Bellanger?"

He hit the same button to respond. "No." He found his voice couldn't break a whisper. From behind him, deeper in the house, deep in the dark, he heard his name. Perhaps that sound, too, was meant to be whispered, but he heard it anyway, carried up to him from and through the darkness, this thick viscous medium that conceals truth and emotion equally, two things Vance Bellanger valued as a doctor and a scholar.

"Do you want us to call the police?" the voice on the other end asked.

"Dr. Bellanger," came the voice again, floating through the darkness of the house, like a whisper on the wind. A crash. More glass shattered. A thump that shook the floor. Vance Bellanger didn't respond because he didn't think it mattered if they called the police. No one they could call would get there in time.

He stepped down the hall slowly, passing the stairs, the sitting room to his left and the kitchen directly in front. The sounds, though, were coming from beneath him, leading him right to the cellar door which also stood open.

Fastidiousness compelled him to a strict nightly routine which meant all lights in the house were off, all interior doors were shut, and all exterior doors and windows were locked. The cellar door should not be open. Such a demanding mind had served him well in med school. Now, in this moment, it reminded him of why he should be afraid. *You would not have left that open. Why isn't it shut? Run, Vance. Run now and run fast.*

His voice cracked the first time he said, "Hello?" and the second was barely a whisper.

Something had been moving down in the cellar. It stopped. He heard breathing.

"Who's there, please?"

"Dr. Bellanger. Help me." The voice, weak, tinged with fear, still rang with familiarity. He knew whoever was down there.

Instinctively, the doctor took a step down, but the man afraid in his own house returned that foot to the top riser. "I... I want to," he managed. "Who are you?"

"Dr. Bellanger," the voice said again after a round of laborious breathing. "I can't control it. I've done bad things, Dr. Bellanger. Starting way back with my family."

Family? "Michael?" Again he thought about taking another step, and again he held back. It had been years since he'd seen Michael

Risten, and it didn't make sense for the kid to be visiting him now. Unless he really was in trouble. Yes, he'd been stuck out at that house and something had happened and he'd come to the only person who could help him.

"I'm in here, Dr. Bellanger. It's full from eating but that won't last long, because it can't stay full. You've been my doctor all my life Dr. Bellanger, so please—"

"Michael!" he called out, the doctor in him taking over. He flicked on the stairwell light and took the risers loudly. "Michael, I'm coming!" he called.

He heard a groan, the sound of true pain, and Michael screamed somewhere down there not illuminated by the stairwell light. "Help me, Doctor," Michael called, and he screamed again. The sound came from his left, so at the base of the stairs Vance Bellanger turned the corner to face the darkness and a deep, subterranean cool with but a faintest hint of moisture.

"Michael?" he said. The smell of pennies hit him. It was sickly sweet, tickling his nose and uvula, not quite as bitter as formaldehyde but just as potent. Only groans greeted him for a time, but when Michael did speak again, the sound ran a chill through his spine.

"Dr. Bellanger," and the voice was already different. Stronger, yes, but more guttural. "It's waking, Dr. Bellanger. It's hungry, Doc—*gah!*" Something like cracking followed by a snort. "No... place... to go. Here or her... *agh*... house. You understand. I couldn't... could—*ngh*... her. Hurt her."

He fumbled for the light switch on the wall to illuminate this corner of the basement.

"I'm coming, Michael. We'll get the help you need."

The light flicked on, and Doctor Vance Bellanger turned and stifled a scream. Michael was not there, perhaps never had been. What stood before him wore the face of a wolf and while its body was covered in fur, it stood like a man. It wore torn rags that might have once been pants. Its hulking form pulsed as it breathed, and it flexed its arms and claws. Saliva dripped from its canines. It growled, and the doctor locked eyes with it. That's when he saw. The tinge of familiarity was there again, just to remind the doctor here in his last moments of his life that he had been right after all. Was still here, in a sense. He was in the eyes of the beast. He recognized the eyes. But of Michael that was all that was left. The beast snarled and lunged, and because they were down in the cellar, no one heard him scream.

CHAPTER TWELVE

The dawn, shocked to silence by the night's events, roused the town from somnolence not as a community, but as a collection of isolated homes as yet unconnected by the deaths. Phillip Cabot found his friend's door wide open, the alarm silent, and Monticello police cars lining the drive. Police tape had already been stretched and an officer prohibited the pharmacist from entering the house. Confusion stood awash over Cabot, until the EMS techs emerged with a stretcher. A white sheet stained with blood covered a form too small to be a human. Cabot grabbed the shoulder of a nearby state trooper. "'Scuse me, officer. My friend lives there. Can you tell me if Dr. Vance—"

The trooper frowned gravely and motioned to the stretcher. "Found him in the cellar," he answered.

No communal spirit of the funerary united the people, leaving those who knew of the various atrocities to huddle alone in mourning. Later that morning, Bess Louviere left the Cabots to their requiems for their friend, and bore her own cross in her own home for her granddaughter and only remaining family member, after Sheriff Charley and Deputy Bailey were done with the three of them. Duke Livingston and his wife Amelia embraced at the loss of their employees, but no one truly grieved for Remy Doucet or his uncle, because ultimately, no one was left to care. Yes, Rayburn Livingston said a prayer and sang a ballad for the two, inventing lyrics as he strummed familiar chord progressions, all of it out of time, which was just as he felt, replaying the night's events under duress from his own fear. And though he was at his room at the halfway house, he was pretty sure no one else heard. All the better, he thought, as the only solid counting he could do were the minutes until the liquor stores opened and he could drown this nightmare.

That was Blue Rock this early, late autumn morning, awaking only to news that would shock and stun the community to mournful numbness. Dew clung to the blades of yellowing grass, and the leaves of all the trees save the evergreens were bleeding out the viridescent signs of life for yellows, purples, reds, oranges, and browns, as nature struggled to carry on. But the timing and rhythm were off.

Everyone felt it. Madeline awoke to a pre-programmed pot of coffee just finishing its brewing and poured herself a cup as the air sizzled around her, the sapphire dawn light seeping in through the windows weak to illuminate, leaving the darkest corners of the home impenetrable still in much the same way Remy's uncle's house had sat. Into these dark corners Madeline could not help but stare and shiver, sensing rather than knowing full well this was where the evil had slunk. Not just in her house, but everywhere. As the day progressed, it hid, masked by the shadows and concealed by the light, until the next time darkness unveiled it. No, she hadn't learned of the deaths yet (that would come in a few more hours as the town itself woke up), but she could feel it. They all could. Creeping upon them. Something vile and evil. Or maybe something that transcended good and evil. Perhaps it was bestial and engorged with stupid power, hellbent on destruction. Whatever it was, it hummed along the wires of the power lines. It tainted the water in the nearby lake that ran through their pipes and gave the air a taste like stale, rotten blood.

The dog plodded out with her. It seemed Dart was growing to appreciate the woman more than his master, so after she snuggled with him on the couch, running her fingers through his soft fur, feeling his warmth pressed against her, sipping her coffee. The love and affection of this animal was all that stood against the unsettled morn. Once the town learned of the night's murderous events, the power of the solidarity of Blue Rock in times of tragedy would ultimately provide it strength to get through. This, at least, is a tenet of all communities, Blue Rock notwithstanding, and this had been true in the past. But that didn't mean it would always be so.

Sheriff Charley called in the state troopers and more deputies, and set about securing the scenes. He ordered blankets to cover the bodies and as much of the blood as possible, putting up barrier tape to keep any onlookers back. Farmers from the area crept in for a look-see at the chicken farm, and a few of the local denizens gawked around the sidewalks in front of Bellanger's Victorian and the halfway house. No one pressed forward. The smell was already too much for most.

Aaron Bailey, doing his part but also a little more as he was in charge of this town, took time to inhale the smell: metallic, warm, sweet with rot. He wasn't cognizant of how differently he reacted to such scenes now. Last death he'd investigated, at least before Larsen and the start of all of this, was that of a local farmer's son who'd drowned in a nearby slough, a boy of four who'd wandered out away from his sibling's supervision and got pulled down by the mud. By the time they found him (this would have been last summer), the smell was something awful, and the bugs were already starting in on him, and Aaron nearly retched his breakfast. Now he could detect familiar hints, just as he'd detected in the earlier murders, but no longer did they churn his stomach. Instead, he heard it growl and rumble, an empty whining begging for satiation.

CR&SO

Michael awoke naked, first aware of that same smell that had appetized the deputy, then of the slickness of his flesh, then of the wetness of the place he'd made a bed. He opened his eyes to a surrounding moat of orange putrescence, in which he nosed elements of blood and flesh and vomit. He'd gorged himself in the night, he realized, rising, until he could eat no more.

"Your appetites are growing," came the voice. Michael saw the old woman leaning on a haystack, and realized they were in the loft in his barn.

From where he rose, the chains and shackles were clear across the room. "Did you let me out?"

Angelique Fontenot frowned and hung her head, her arms folded across her chest. While Michael felt no sense of urgency or alarm, laying exposed as he was, he was embarrassed at his nakedness.

"Not even the potus can calm your other face, boy," she said. "The nightmares will come and the pendant will allow you to change and there is nothing either of us can do anymore."

"How did I get free, then?"

"My grievances run deep and dark with this area, boy. I'm sorry that I've used you as a tool to air those grievances."

"Are you saying you did this to me?"

"I did not. This was how you were brought into this world, I'm afraid."

Michael shook his head, even as the old Creole woman tossed him a towel, one Michael recognized from his own bathroom.

"Brought you a change of clothes, too."

Michael dressed, then led Angelique outside, stopping in the yard between the barn and his house. The sun beat down at a low angle in the sky, more to the south than the days before. The morning was cold, the ground crunched underfoot from the frost. Michael watched his breath cloud and lift to the sky and hugged himself.

"Did you come today, then, to confess your soul? These people I see. The dead. Dead because you let me out! If it were fair, you'd see them too."

"I feel them," she muttered, "but that is not why I came back this morning. There is a man staying with me and my brothers. An older man. Surely you've seen him."

Michael nodded and looked to the tree line beyond his father's field, as if he expected the man to emerge. "At the fall festival," he admitted.

"He is hunting you, Master Risten. I can hold him off for some time, but I can't hold him off forever."

"For his sake, I hope he finds me when I'm like this and not... you know... the wolf."

"Take care to respect, or even fear this man, Michael Risten. For your sake, I hope he doesn't find you in either state."

He watched her shuffle away, cutting a path already well-worn through his family's now overgrown field. Only when she disappeared into the pines did he turn and make his way toward his back door. He reached it, shivering again, his body aching, his eyes heavy, fatigue weighing on him like an anchor. Before he could mount the steps, Byron Calhoun rounded the back corner of his house. Michael was just about to say he wasn't expecting a visitor when from behind Byron, Dart emerged, sniffing the ground. The dog wagged his tail when he saw Michael, the leash hooked to his harness leading to Madeline who could only look at him with sadness.

"Hello, Michael," she said.

He'd failed. He'd never wanted her to see him like this and now, he realized, he'd failed.

⊗

Skeet Davidson rose to a commotion outside in the courtyard, only to stumble into the light, still drunk, to find the residents of the trailer park talking about how two residents of the halfway house down the road, Remy Doucet and Vicky Arsenault, were found murdered, though their conversation hushed as Skeet, blurry eyed from drink and crying, joined them.

Chantal Bailey had been gossiping about what she'd learned from her brother. "Said they was found just like the other'n. Like…"

"Shhh," Chet Kelly said, poking her arm. They turned in their circle, along with Astrid Calhoun and Emily Evans, but it was Astrid who approached Skeet and put her hands up to his shoulders in a kind of embrace.

"How you doin' this morning, Skeet?"

"What's going on?" His words were still slurring, and this embarrassed him, as though his addiction were any kind of secret.

The group exchanged a glance, and then Astrid told him, as gently as if she were telling a child that their favorite pet had died. She left out as many details as she could, but still he could discern the violence, and he was sure that they'd died in a similar fashion as his beloved Casey.

"But they weren't both at the halfway house," Astrid said.

"Vicky was," Chantal cut in.

"But Remy," Astrid continued, not missing a beat, "was at his uncle's farm. Both men were killed."

Skeet stood stoic and listened, thanking them finally, meeting each of their eyes. Then, wordlessly, he turned on a pinpoint and crossed the yard and ascended the creaking, rotting, wooden steps to his single-wide. Inside he shut and locked the thin, hollow aluminum door with the handle and then the chain.

The kitchen light flickered, the fluorescent long since needing replaced. He noticed for the first time the trash lining the kitchen countertops, the side table by his recliner, the coffee table: empty beer bottles, take-out wrappers, coffee-filters, newspapers. Casey had kept this place clean and tidy. But she was gone, and this was what remained.

There was no final shock to it all, no outburst of tears or wailing. In truth, Skeet had known for some time what he should do, but laziness had kept him from going through with it. Now, with the announcement of new deaths and the realization that he'd reached the pinnacle of his existence—other men might have more to aspire to, but those men had more to live for, also—he realized it was lazier to keep existing.

He switched off the fluorescent light as he walked to his bedroom. The curtains over the blinds and the trees outside surrounding the trailers drowned out the morning light, so that the loss of illumination catapulted the trailer back into darkness. In the dimness, he saw easily, long since familiar with the landscape of his home, stepping around his twin mattress to the meager dresser from which he pulled the pill bottle.

Ten, he counted, lid off, feeling them in the palm of his hand. Doc said he could get a refill, and that would give him a lot more, but he didn't want to wait to make it up to Monticello just so Cabot could fill the script. Ten would be enough. They'd at least do their job of numbing the pain so he could carry on with the rest of the task.

He choked them down, dropped the pill bottle soundlessly on the carpet of his room, then returned to the kitchen. He rummaged through the cabinets, hoping the pills would kick in soon, drawing out half bottles of whiskey and moonshine, pulling together as much of the remaining liquor as he could. Then, cleaning off the side table by his recliner, he filled it with as many of those bottles he could. Next, he cleaned off the coffee table, but as it was more centered in front of the old and faded couch, he pulled it within reach, then put the remaining bottles as close as he could. Finally, he drew out the old photograph of Casey at her high school graduation. He'd found it the day of her death and had carried it in his shirt pocket ever since. This was his solace, his grievance, his one source of pleasure, and he looked on it fondly through tear-filled eyes. Some of the bottles had a drop or two, others were partially full. To his surprise, he found a nearly full bottle of Kentucky bourbon, and this he pulled from long and slow as the hydrocodone took effect. How much of the day passed he wasn't sure, but in time his eyes grew heavy and he forced down the drink more and more until his arm wouldn't work anymore. The fingers holding the bottle fell beside the chair, but there wasn't enough of the bourbon to spill onto the carpet. The fingers holding the photograph never let go of his daughter's image, but rested it in his lap. His eyes shut, soon his breath and heart slowed, and Skeet Davidson went to sleep, never to wake again.

CRBSO

Michael sat like one whose addiction had been made public and, faced with the intervention and nowhere to run, must finally confront the truth. This wasn't that far from the truth. Byron stood on the opposite side of the living room staring at the floor and Maddy sat across from him, Dart studying him at her side. Outside the sun had risen but the air was still cool. Later it would warm to above sixty, but for now, a ground-level fog crawled over the Blue Rock earth as the nighttime frost burned in the morning light.

Michael sighed again, unsure of what else to do. His head had hung nearly between his knees, elbows resting on his thighs, hands clasped together, for what felt like forever. Soundless.

"Michael." How many times had she said his name now in these endless minutes? Voice steady, invoking such compassion.

He sniffed and realized he'd been crying, the few tears scarring his cheeks silent rivulets of exhaustion. "I'm so tired," he said, allowing a sigh to escape with the words. "I just want it to be over." This wasn't overdramatized, like a teenager might scream at their parent, but hollow and cold, an afterthought almost, or a solid truth that one may no longer escape.

He knew Maddy didn't know what to say. Knew that she would give anything to be able to say something right now, and that being powerless to help someone she cared about was a feeling she despised.

"I don't want to be this way," he continued. His need to speak was not some great confessional. He was tired of the silence, for that's when the ghosts spoke, and even though Maddy and Dart and Byron were all in his living room, so were the ghosts. To keep them from speaking, he continued. "They know I don't."

"Who, Michael?" Maddy asked, but he looked around, knowing that wouldn't answer her question. Dart looked too, and funnily enough, he thought the dog might see what he was looking at.

"I don't want to be this way!" he screamed before a fresh burst of tears, his face shooting up in defiance, reddening, veins standing on his neck. He could feel this. The color change, the strain of muscle. She couldn't know, but he was yelling at himself while looking at the two newest congregants gathered about him: the mutilated and bloody forms of Vicky Arsenault and his childhood doctor, Vance Bellanger.

"You see them, don't you," Byron said. "Like the ones you kilt. All of them. They ghosts."

Michael nodded, wiped snot and tears from his nose and eyes. "They won't let me rest."

"There has to be help, Michael," Maddy said. "Something we—"

"There isn't," he broke in. "Miss Fontenot had this... potus... she called it. Like a salve, but you drink it. Tasted like muddy stream polluted with shit. But it and this—" Here he paused and reached into his shirt to draw out a medallion, a brass-colored wolf's head over a pentagram all with a circle around it, half the size of his fist, hung around his neck by a leather cord, "—were supposed to keep me from changing and keep them away."

"Them?" Maddy said, but she knew. "Oh. The ghosts you see."

"But it didn't work," he snapped, looking around but refusing to look at any of them, including the dog, in the eye. "That's why I came back here. I ran out of the potus and I thought I had a handle on things, but then them kids were attacked at school, and—"

"Michael," Maddy said. "You didn't do that."

He stopped talking and gawked at her. His mouth hung open stupidly for a moment. "They were murdered. I killed them, I..." his voice trailed off, struggling to remember.

"Do you recall killing them?" she asked. Of course he didn't. Asking him to remember what the wolf did was like asking a drunk to recall the events after his tenth beer or fifth scotch. He shook his head slowly.

"Do you see them?" Byron asked. At this, both Michael and Maddy looked to the boy. "You see the ghosts of the people this thing in you killed, so you must see these college kids Maddy is talking about."

Michael's throat felt dry. "I don't," he said.

"Michael," Maddy said. "The attacks coming from you happen during the fall. Always have. Remember, even when you came to live with us. It was Daddy that would take you away at night, but not during prom our senior year. You were there. We got pictures. But those kids were killed in the springtime."

Michael nodded, but it would be another minute before he made the connection and realized its weight. "Your dad and ma knew. Still decided to take me in. Just wanted to take precautions. I was the one against it. They both insisted. Your dad brought me back here every night to chain me up and was back again every morning to release me. Every morning he'd bring me breakfast and wrap a blanket around me and tell me things like I was a good kid or he was proud of me for not getting out. Hug me."

"Michael," she tried again. The memories of her parents flooded him. The smell of her mother's perfume. The rough blistered hands belonging to her father. How many times had he cried in their arms, mornings or safe, alone moments, when he could hide from Maddy and John Kelly? Her parents had known to hide it from their kids, taking in this terrified boy.

"People think it's easy. Just stop, they say, not knowing the power it has over me."

"I can't understand, Michael," she said, but he could tell she wanted to.

"I tried, you know." He let those four words sink in. When neither Maddy nor Byron spoke, he looked up and saw he had their attention. On Maddy's face was a frozen look of horror, as if she were already able to anticipate what he was about to tell her.

"My father's shotgun is still hanging in the loft."

"Loft?" Byron asked.

"It's where I'm locking myself up at night," he said, nodding. Confessing yet another little secret. "I had tripwires all around, for when I changed. Figured the beast doesn't know what I'm doing just like I don't know what it's doing. So surely it would, I don't know, step in the wrong direction, set the shotgun off. And then…"

"Jesus, Michael," she whispered, then dropped her eyes and fell silent.

He let the finality of that sink in even as he anticipated their next question. "Angelique Fontenot," he said, nodding again. "I thought she was helping me. Turns out, she wanted me out. She did this to me. Says she didn't, but—"

"She didn't, Michael," Maddy said. "At least, I don't think so." He shook his head, ready to lose himself again in his own thoughts, when she knelt in front of him and her soft hand raised his chin so he had to look her in the eye.

"Mad—"

"Michael," she said, and waited for him to pay attention. Of course he would. It was so difficult, wanting so badly to be around her and yet knowing he had to stay away. "Michael, there is someone here coming for you. She told me. Michael, you're in danger, and… listen to me… you did not kill those kids at Ole Miss."

"I…" he stammered, but there were so many things pushing to get out, nothing else emerged. So, she'd been to see Angelique Fontenot who had told her the same thing about the man. He wondered, not for the first time, if he were in danger from more than just the wolf inside of him.

"Michael, I think there is another one like you out there. Michael," she said, reaching for him. He met her gaze. "What if it's also here?"

His mouth opened to respond, then stood silently agape. He stared at her, his mind racing, trying to parcel through the werewolf's memories that were, at best, a fog for him, wondering who'd he passed this curse on to. But what she was saying made sense. He couldn't change in the spring. Had never changed in the spring.

"Dammit," he muttered, clenching his fist. How could he not have pieced this together? How had he not even considered this? And on the heels of that, another fact that dashed his kneejerk reaction. He hadn't passed the curse on, because if he couldn't change in the spring, then surely no one he affected could. He was born with this, after all. Madeline asked him, "What?" and he lined out his thought process.

"Do you have an idea who?" Maddy kept her voice even and low. Michael shook his head. "There's an old man. Do you know him?"

Again Michael shook his head. "Saw him at the carnival."

"He was at Ole Miss too," Maddy said. "A girl who witnessed the attack saw him at the police station."

At this Michael frowned. Worry creased waves in his brow. "You think he's like me?"

Maddy shook her head. "I don't know. I think he's the one after you, though. Maybe he was chasing the other one and it led him here."

"That means the other one could be here too," Michael said.

Maddy nodded, then pursed her lips. He knew the look. This look was one that said the conversation might be shifting, but it wasn't over. "Has anyone ever survived…" Her voice trailed; Michael knew what she was really asking.

"Not to my knowledge. I haven't… made…" but then he stopped, and realized what she was really getting at. "The deputy," he said. "Aaron Bailey."

Maddy nodded again. "Michael, there were more deaths last night."

Michael looked around to the silent ghosts standing vigil in this fucked-up intervention.

"Vicky Arsenault," he said. "Dr. Bellanger."

Maddy glanced to Byron then affirmed with a nod of her head before adding, "And Remy Doucet and his uncle Cletus, out at Cletus' chicken farm."

Michael frowned at this. Like the college kids slaughtered at Ole Miss, he did not see these spirits. "Oh, Jesus," he responded, echoing her early sentiment. Jesus, however, seemed nowhere near these festivities. "I don't see them. Remy or his uncle. Like I don't see the college kids.

"Then you didn't kill them," Maddy said. "So, another one? The one from your school?"

"I need to end this. I do. I need…" *Release* was the word he wanted to say, but that word felt too much like running away.

He knew from how wide her eyes went that she understood what he meant, and she shook her head, wearing such a look of disapproval that he knew from past experiences not to argue.

"No, sir. We will lock you up ourselves, but you are not killing yourself and leaving us to deal with the mess. We'll get John Kelly in on this, and then he and I will go visit Angelique Fontenot and make her give us something that will help you long enough to stop these others."

"And then?"

She realized as she met his gaze that she could not, would not, lie to him. "I don't know, Michael. You've killed people. This thing inside you has killed people. There has to be…"

As her words failed her, he filled in the blank. "Consequences."

That word hung in the air like smoke from a fire, and reverberated through a town hungry for solace and justice.

CHAPTER THIRTEEN

The older man crouched over the campfire, stoking it with a bit of kindling before tossing on another log. The sounds of the forest were few. The brothers could be heard ripping the fur and flesh off the deer they'd killed, but other than that, it was as it had been for a time now: silent.

The witch's hubris would get her killed, thinking she could harness the power that belonged to another. Perhaps she'd been lucky, but luck always went hand in hand with foolishness. He smelled the fire. The tendrils of smoke interwove with the fibers of his mustache and Van Dyke, the facial hair just a bit darker than the white crown of hair atop his head, where the widows peak sat low on the brow as if on a much younger man.

When he stood, his knees did not pop. His thighs were strong and his shoulders were broad, and the lines on his face were fine and barely noticeable even when he squinted or frowned. He did not look or feel his age, which worked to his advantage. *I am dangerous*, he said with his actions, *because I retain my strength and carry with it years of wisdom.*

He decried plenty. Like these brothers. They were older men themselves, who'd lived all these years on the outskirts of society, living off the land. The meat would be rotten if they took any longer to skin the buck. That or the Rougarou would come and snatch it from them. Their sister amused him, thinking she was hiding from him. He'd tracked more duplicitousness and craftiness and killers than the years she'd been alive, so if she thought she was throwing him off her scent, she would be mistaken. He'd come with an eye for reconnaissance. To see what the creature would do, or if it would run, or hunt as if it hadn't a care in the world. He hadn't anticipated the witch woman's revenge or her complicit brothers, and so the carnage was worse than he feared. He'd have to handle them, in time, just like he'd have to handle that deputy who survived his attack. For most Rougarou, this was how they were created, and this was what he hunted. It had been a long time since one had been born, as if the Ristenoff line still existed. He'd been sure, he thought, that the family fire had been extinguished long ago. Yet, here walked one, or so he believed. The cops in Mississippi were close-lipped even as he flashed his stolen Interpol badge, and these outcasts were just as uncultivated as he.

"How's the fire?" Bela Fontenot asked.

Kalos von Slacher nodded. "Ready. Is it dressed?"

"Almost." From behind, Bela's brother Basil let slip a curse. "Bit of tough meat around the hindlegs."

Nonchalantly, Kalos nodded as if he understood, then grabbed the back of Bela's head and slammed it into the ground. The incident happened without warning and with little telegraphing, so the younger man did not call out, and Kalos figured his brother was too far away. They'd been, with no one ever saying as much, his sentries, on the instruction of their sister, always preoccupying him, especially at times when she chose to sneak away. They always deflected his questions and it did not take long for him to realize they would divulge nothing. He'd waited patiently for the opportunity to evade them and follow her. Timing had to be just so, and they were aware. But in the days and weeks since his arrival, he'd earned their trust, and knew that the time would come when they let their guard down. And now, perhaps, it was too late. More people were dying, and more would still, but he could wait no longer.

Without looking back, sure that Bela Fontenot would wake and his headache would indeed be epic, Kalos von Slacher absconded into the forest.

⟡

As night neared, Michael fidgeted. Byron fidgeted also, but because his mother was blowing up his phone, demanding to know where he was. Maddy assured him they would be okay, and Michael assured him he'd make it home safely. Once Byron had left, Maddy sat by Michael and took his hand.

"So what's this plan of yours?" she asked.

He shrugged. Then laughed a little. "Don't really have one. We know what we gotta do, but not how to do it."

He stood and stretched. "So where you goin' now?" she asked.

"The barn," he said simply, as if this were the only logical answer. "To lock myself up."

Maddy stood so they were nose to nose, fury on her face. "And what? Hope Angelique Fontenot don't let you loose? Or what if that other werewolf finds you? Or us? You at least need more security."

His look of incredulity insulted her as he said, "What? You and Dart?"

"Let me call John Kelly," she offered, but he waved her away.

"Just… go home. Lock the doors. The windows. Turn out the lights. I don't know, honestly. But soon, the moon will be up, and I won't be able to control it."

"Michael," she said.

He shook his head and walked away, through the kitchen, and out the back door. Before he pulled the door closed, he said, "Please lock up."

Dart whimpered and pressed against her legs.

⋈

A trained hunter shares a lot of traits with a wolf. His sense of smell is heightened, able to parcel out irrelevant aromas and focus on his target's olfactory signature. His eyes could discern the slightest displacements, recognize the curved arches of partial prints, the faintly bent twigs revealing a path as clear as an ajar door. Sounds echoed differently to the tracker. Siphoning out the camouflaging noise from the relevant movements of whatever he hunted meant attuning his hearing beyond the ability to blindly receive whatever soundwaves existed out there. His ears acted as a directional microphone forever pointed at his target. This was how Kalos von Slacher caught whiff of Angelique Fontenot's path and followed her, as the sun began to set.

⋈

Angelique stood in the shadows as Michael entered the barn and Maddy exited with the dog. She cowered when the dog looked her way and stiffened and growled. Maddy pulled at the leash and Dart obeyed reluctantly, but more importantly, neither human noticed her. Once Michael was inside the barn and the car engine had fired up and pulled away, Angelique stole across the short field and entered the barn. Above in the east, the fat moon rose.

CR80

The barn came into view first, a ground-level loft door squeaking closed on its hinges as the tail of her dress and ankle disappeared inside. The house beyond was, for the time being, inconsequential.

Von Slacher closed the distance as the shadows stretched long across the field. He fell into the barn's shadow quickly, the air shifting colder almost instantly. As he reached the same door she'd entered, he heard the call of the Rougarou, something thunderous and caged bellowing out from the confines of the barn. His moment was at hand.

Unsettling noises drove his attention upward, so he climbed the ladder carefully, listening to the witch's voice grow louder the closer he got. She was saying something in Creole, that bastard language of French. A prayer, he assumed. He gripped the top rung and lifted his gaze above the threshold to see the expanse of the loft. There the woman stood back against the wall, holding an iron key. And there, in its full and wondrous glory, the beast pulled against its chains and snapped its jaws at her until, as he caught full sight of it, its own sharpened senses alerted to him, and it turned and snarled and barked.

"Entêté!" she shrieked, seeing him also.

"How dare you, woman," he replied, climbing on up. The wolf snapped and snarled at him. He sidestepped it, keeping a wary eye but seeing just how much give the chain carried. From his pocket he pulled a gun. "I could have ended this before so many lives were lost."

She grabbed for the gun, shrieking again. "Dis whole town should burn!" she shouted, and in their scuffle, he held the gun tightly, but the key went flying. Both watched with horror as the wolf bent and sniffed the piece of iron, gave them a knowing, snarling glance, then used its all-too-human claw to pick the key up and insert it into the lock.

"No," von Slacher whispered as the lock turned. One chain fell to the floor of the loft, nearly vanishing like a coiled snake under the loose straws of hay.

Von Slacher steadied his gun and stepped closer, squaring the sights between the creature's eyes. It snarled again, bent down, and worked on the second chain, with his aim now centered on the top of its head. Angelique Fontenot pulled at him, begging. He recognized enough of her faux French babble to hear the word 'baby' and turned on her, knocking her against the wall.

"This is not your doing, foolish woman! You did not create this. God did. You cannot hope to control it."

He took aim at the creature again, but the second chain fell into the straw, and the beast sat up, staring at him. Von Slacher lowered his gun as the Rougarou neared. He was fast, but in the moment it was faster. Its snout invaded his crotch, his chest, his neck and ears. Salivating with an unquenchable hunger, it sniffed at him, its nose wrinkling and wriggling, taking in every scent signature that belonged to him. Then, it stepped back, huffed, and turned its gaze toward the woman. Angelique cowered and the beast's muzzle worked, feeling her out, until finally it snapped a growl and leapt out the window, into the night.

CR80

Kalos von Slacher neither wanted to wait for her to catch up, nor risk leaving her behind, so he helped her along, ushering her back into the forest and towards their camp, sure of what they'd find even before they heard her brother's screams. The fire, flickering through the brush, still lit the campground, and Bela still lay near it, though now, they could plainly see, he was wide awake, and he was the one screaming. What looked like a shadow darkened his shoulder and spread across the hand gripping it. Angelique knelt, asking where Basil was, even as von Slacher found the remains of the deer scattered around the fireside and Basil's body, cleaved nearly in two.

Of the rougarou, there was no sign.

Discernable against her wounded brother's wails was the sound of von Slacher drawing his sidearm.

"He needs bandages and salve," Angelique said, looking at the man. "Hurry. They are in my trailer. In the cupboard above the stove."

"Basil is dead," von Slacher said, approaching them. He looked gravely down, then knelt. "I am sorry for hitting your head, my friend. I merely needed to evade you and your brother's watchful eye."

Rapacious, gormandizing, in the firelight, Bela wangled, a violent thrashing and howling from the pain and early draw of the moon.

"He is bitten," von Slacher said. "He will survive the bite, but the curse is on him now, and for that, his diagnosis is terminal, I'm afraid."

He did not allow Angelique Fontenot a moment to process what he'd just said, but stood and leveled his sidearm down and pulled the trigger. Bela Fontenot issued up a great gasp then collapsed against the ground. His eyes went blank and a rivulet of blood trickled from the new hole between his eyes.

"You bastard!" the woman screamed. She rose and slapped at him. "You bastard! What did you do?! Oh, my dear brother!" and she fell on his chest, sobbing, clutching at him, as if her sheer will could restore him. The lamented moans, the song like dirge that issued from her lips, carried with it all her hopes and security and the last of her love. For years it had been just her and her brothers, and in less than ten minutes, she'd lost everything in this world she held dear. The sound of great and irreversible loss fell on the old man, and while he did not show it, he felt it inside. Pitied her, truly, watching her lay prostrate across her brother's cooling corpse. This was, he'd come to know, the way of the wolf. This was what the rougarou brought to each community they visited, and this was why he still worked to stop them. Still, he could guard himself against Angelique's suffering because hers was compounded by her own actions. Had she not helped the wolf, worked to free it to enact her own petty revenge, then perhaps this could have been avoided. Or perhaps not. Perhaps the fates of her brothers were written in stone, and this was always the way it was meant to end, but at least, had she left well enough alone, she could have assuaged herself of her culpability.

"We must," he said at last, and coldly, "accept the consequences of our own actions." She looked up at him, but he could not hide the sorrow on his own face, allowing himself to let slip a simple truth, that this statement was made as much for her as it was for him.

CHAPTER FOURTEEN

*D*eputy Bailey curled his lips every time he saw the trailer park his sister called home. His parents had a nice single-wide on their property, nicer than the rat trap she called home. She could have all the privacy she wanted if she just took it. He had the house anyway and worked the farm himself.

A gray haze blanketed the sky as a stiff wind rattled the trees and fanned their limbs, unmooring the dead leaves from their precarious holds to send them blowing like a torrent across the land. The howling wind stirred something in him. Bailey bit his lip, turned into the drive, thought he tasted blood on his tongue.

Chantal was out smoking on the porch, wearing nothing but a pair of daisy dukes and a shirt too thin and too tight. Always giving them something to ogle. Her feet were dirty, a healthy bruise on the outside of her right thigh. New. Fresh. Shit like this wouldn't happen if she lived at home. Such a nice trailer, going unused. Sure as shit wouldn't wear come-hithers like that.

"What you doin' here, Aaron?" she asked.

He slammed the door and looked around. "Talk like a white woman, Chantal," he said, sniffed, and spit chew. "She home?" he asked, nodding to the old woman's trailer.

"Far as I know," Chantal said. Stubbed out her cigarette, stood and marched over to him, looking around delicately. "Aaron. No one's seen Skeet Davidson for some hours now. We really worried about him."

Aaron looked at the trailer, sniffed the air. Putrescence was setting in. Rot. Microbes were already feasting on the flesh. The temperature in the single-wide was warm, incubating larvae. His ears twitched. Muscles tightening. Rigor would set in soon. Blood was pooling already into his ass, thighs. Sure, he could check it out. Officially he ought to call it in. It's just that he didn't give a shit. Still, Chantal's eyes were wide and pleading, her hands folded together in supplication.

"I'll check him in a bit," Aaron said.

The door to the old woman's house rattled on the hinges. She opened it, a suspicious eye glaring down from on high. "Deputy," she said, and looked up to see Chantal in the distance, fiddling with another smoke as she watched the scene.

"Just doing a quick check," Aaron said. "See who was home, and what time. You was at the rally that other night, weren't you?"

She nodded but didn't provide verbal assent.

"You see anything? Hear anything?"

He scanned her flesh. Forearms scabbed. Dry, flaky skin. Already breaking down. His nostrils flared. Menthol rub, a bit of rot in the stomach. No, intestine. Eating her up. She don't know it yet. Ears wriggled with the creak of her joints, the popping of cartilage. Gristle on bone.

"You used to know that old witch out a ways, didn't you?" he asked. "Her brothers." What made him think of her now? He wasn't sure, but saw an image of her just as clear as day.

"I knew of her, Deputy," Emily said. "What, you think all Black folk should know each other? You wanna lump us in together. Well, to be honest, I never cared for her. She was trouble. Felt she had a mean streak. And she weren't godly. Had nothing to do with her being Black. Could've just as well been white. Fact is, she was Creole, so prob'ly had some white in her. Make her so mean. Why you asking?"

"You ain't asked about your grandson yet," Aaron said.

"Didn't expect to get a straight answer from you."

"You ought to treat me with more respect. I'm the law in these parts. I could take you down. Let you share a cell with that miserable old grandson of your'n."

"You just go ahead and do that if bullying an old woman makes you feel more like a man, Aaron Bailey. But I'm done talking to you."

The door shut in his face. He thought about knocking again, or even kicking it in, then shook it off, turned, and eyed the other homes. Chantal had already gone inside. Place ought to be burned to the ground. Rusted siding. Underskirts missing on most. A tin panel on the roof of the Calhoun place curled up like a peeling onion.

Up the steps to the Davidson place he sniffed, turned away. Skeet wasn't going anywhere.

He knocked at the Calhoun place. Astrid Calhoun's white Corolla was gone, but sure as shit that little faggot was home. He knocked louder.

"Open up, Byron," boomed the deputy's voice.

The door creaked open, slowly. He saw a white sclera pooling around a brown island. Flecks of gold. It smelled like sweet perfumes and sweat.

"We need to talk, boy. Open up."

The door opened and Aaron glanced around. He searched the windows for open blinds. Chet Ludlow's trailer was dark, his space empty. But he'd seen him at Larsen's office a bit ago, so that was to be expected. Nothing at Emily's place. Nothing at his sister's. The boy's shorts were as short as Chantal's. He swung his ass as he returned to the sofa, then curled up at one end, drawing his knees up, arms hugging. Still sporting the remnants of the shiner.

Aaron closed the door and sat in the recliner. The place was clean. It smelled of disinfectants and candles and air fresheners. Maybe a few months ago, this might have smelled nice. To most people it would. But the various chemicals warred with Aaron's nostrils. He sneezed.

"Bless you," Byron squeaked, inaudible to most but not Aaron's ears.

"You clean or yo' mama?"

"I help." Mousy. Weak.

"Where was you last night?"

The boy wouldn't look at him but for some quick glances. He twitched like a piece of roadkill. "Here." Saltine air—a tear? Aaron caught a trickle of urine between his thighs. One more word. *Disrespectful.*

"Some people say they see you carrying groceries. Where you going?"

The boy started rocking to mask his nervousness. His eyes stared forward, not daring to glance around.

"I asked you a question, boy."

"I... I..."

"Spit it out."

"...shouldn't talk to you without my mother here."

Aaron shot out of the seat and landed on the boy, hand at his throat, his weight bearing down on him. He forced Byron's legs apart and planted a knee in his crotch. The urine flowed freely now, not a trickle but a gush. He pushed the boy's head back.

"You listen, you piece of shit," the deputy said. "I ask you a question you better answer. Now you tell me where you're going with them groceries."

Tears streaming as freely as the piss. "Nowhere," the boy choked out.

Mousy, weak, disrespectful. And a liar. A filthy little no good lying nigger. Aaron lifted the boy off the couch by his throat and, recognizing the basic layout of the trailer, carried him back toward one of the bedrooms. Turns out it was the master, the boy's mother's. A queen headboard carved in a French Victorian style. Matching footboard. Just enough room for a matching dresser with a mirror. The furniture dark against black-out windows and a wood paneled room. The pattering of leaves outside, dancing silhouettes against the little backdrop of light that screened the window, nothing near enough to let light in. The wind whipped around the trailer, howling madly.

Aaron threw the boy on the bed. Byron curled fetal, crying, coughing. Aaron grabbed at the boy, came away with those shorts. Flipped him on his stomach. Weak. Liar. Disrespectful. He'd show him to pay respect. Aaron would learn the boy to look at him when he speaks to him.

The belt buckle flopped loose. The zipper came down. The boy wailed. Aaron slapped at the back of his head. Then pulled out his own cock. This was what this faggot wanted, anyway. The screams punctured his ears. Winced but didn't stop. He could smell the sweat, felt the tearing, then the blood. The boy bit into the tiger-striped comforter, fists clenched gobs of it in a struggle to pull away. Aaron grabbed the thighs and pulled him back. Liar. Disrespectful. Blood, more blood. Then semen.

He flipped Byron over on his back. Belly up. The boy's flaccid penis was like a strip of leather laying across his belly, slick with urine. Aaron curled his right hand into a fist and brought it down on the boy's face. Byron's eyes were wonky orbits spinning independently of each other, mouth slack. A bit of spittle. Another strike. He caught a tooth. Byron's lip was bloody like his ass. A small sting alerted Aaron to his knuckle, where the tooth had scraped it clean of the flesh. How dare the kid draw his blood. Two more strikes.

The deputy stood, zipped up, hovered over the boy. He heard shallow breaths, a rapid heartbeat. Eyes closed. Not dead. Not dying. But when he wakes up, he'll wish he was. Bailey wiped at his mouth then spit.

At the front door, open again to the daylight, the distant soft sounds of snapping, the quick motion of blinds closing from the old woman's trailer. Aaron leered in that direction, sauntered to his patrol car, drove away. He was the law in these parts. He was the power. One way or another, they'd all learn it.

ᘓᔟᘐ

It was Maddy who came up with the idea. So clear and simple, Michael chastised himself for not thinking of it beforehand. It hadn't come to him yet because he'd been so concerned with "the moment." In "the moment" he was a prisoner. Dogs, he'd explained, ruffling Dart's fur, live in the moment. Since the death of his parents and siblings, he'd been living in the moment as well. How to silence this thing inside. How to feed it. Quench it. These pervasive questions were never fully satiated, so he could never pry himself from them long enough to explore more intellectual ideas. He never had the time to think about causes or solutions. "The moment" didn't allow for such introspection or philosophy. So when she came up with the idea, and explained her plan, Michael nearly wept. When he awoke in the barn loft unchained, the bloodied and mangled image of one of the Fontenot brothers to greet him, he knew it was time to enact Maddy's plan.

"You were here," he said to the ghosts of the house upon entering the morning sunlit kitchen. "You heard. We have a plan. We have to stop any others, and then I'll..." His voice faded. He knew what needed to be done.

CRLSO

The morning was cold, and the sunlight cut through the frost in a crystalline brightness that portented winter. Deputy Bailey stared livid at the dawn and sipped his coffee. The skies were blue, but he saw only gray clouds, looming and pregnant. He despised winter. It didn't make him sad. Just angry.

He listened to the town using his newfound ears. Chuckles and grunts. Feet scooting. Feet thumping. The wind picked at the trees and tawny grass.

"You hear them," Derek said, not a question but a realization.

Aaron turned toward the voice. "Pris'ner ain't got..."

"Do you smell them also? I do."

"Kindly shut the—"

"I think you do too." Derek smiled and gripped the bars. He bowed his head so that the yellow arches of his eyes seemed more menacing.

Aaron looked at the white scars on his fist where Derek had bit him.

"I tasted you, Deputy."

Aaron took a step forward and chuckled. "So what? Now you know me?"

"I know us," Derek said. "You'n me, we uh lotta like."

Aaron took another step. He expected Derek to retreat. When he didn't, Aaron gulped. That tiny moment of hesitation brought a smile to Derek.

"I ain't nothing like you, boy," Aaron said.

"Oh, you is. I smell it on you. The animal. I hear it in you, like we can hear the people out there walking and talking."

Aaron startled. He'd nearly convinced himself he was imagining things. He shook his head, but Derek kept on.

"You go to them crime scenes—now, be honest—you go, and you get... hungry, don't you? I know you do." Grinning, Derek showed his teeth. "I know you do. I hungry, too, Deputy. I feel it growing in you cause its growing in me. Deep down in the gut. We been restrained, but cages like this," and he looked around the perimeter where the bars met the concrete "ain't meant to hold us forever."

Aaron unclipped his nightstick and smacked the bars. Derek wasn't startled, though the bars rang loudly through the building. Derek cocked his head and stared at Aaron, baring his teeth, his nostrils flaring. The deputy considered opening the door and using the nightstick to wipe the smirk off Derek's face, but if he didn't know better, that's what Derek wanted him to do. Instead, Aaron opened the front door and watched the overcast sky and falling leaves scratching along the sidewalks. The autumn air smelled of burning wood with hints of winter cold.

CRSO

The dry air snapped at the skin, wormed its way into any cracks or knicks, split the skin like thin ice on a pond where something heavy tried to cross. Angelique Fontenot tasted the blood on her bruised and fattening lip and felt the cold sting the cut. She wiped away a stream of blood and spittle from her chin and pulled herself up to her knees, her back arching like a cat.

"Stand, and I will knock you down again," von Slacher said. She looked at him sideways, curling her lip, her stiff arms quaking under her weight. That last blow had nearly taken everything out of her and it would be all she could to stand. She thought she'd had the drop on him. Had thought she'd caught him while he was having his coffee, and brought the hatchet down to cleanly cleave his scalp, but he'd moved too fast. Too fast for an old man. Too fast for anyone.

The audacity, she thought, gripping at the wall in her living room to pull herself to her feet. She hugged it tight and crawled up it like a spider with half its legs working, never taking her eyes off him. The audacity of him still demanding shelter.

"Believe you me, I get another chance, you won't be standing."

"What spell did you conjure, witch woman, to create the Rougarou here? What spell, do you think?" He still held his mug full of coffee in his right hand, the left now holding the chopping hatchet he'd yanked from her after striking her cheek with his knuckles. He sat the mug down on her Formica counter and considered the weapon. "You've no idea how the curse is passed on."

And with a brief smirk, running his thumb along the blade to test the sharpness, he began to tell her.

CRSO

It was afternoon when Michael made it to Maddy's. As excited as he was to see John Kelly open the door, he was still disquieted. He'd stopped by the trailer park on a whim on his walk into town. Had he wanted to say something to Skeet Davidson? There was nothing he could say. Not that it mattered. Skeet didn't answer the door. Nor, for that matter, did Byron Calhoun. Michael thought the boy was always home, and really wanted to place another grocery order, and while he knew he could ask Maddy for help, the silence and stillness of the trailer park had unsettled him. He thought for certain that neither trailer was unoccupied. He caught a whiff of specific odors roiling out from underneath each door. Smells as different from one another as they could be, but each suggesting pain and rot and death and blood. Yes, the wolf in him could smell the smells. It could hear Byron's mewling. Michael's neck grew hot. He wasn't sure why his own anxiety level had risen, but he knew he must leave this pentagram of fabricated homes because the wolf in him was growing… excited. So he did leave, yet he was unable to shake the disquiet.

John patted his back and stepped aside, and Dart sniffed him, wagging his tail, and Michael sat as Maddy walked in with a tray holding a pot of coffee, three mugs, and a saucer with some creamers and packets of sugar.

"I couldn't remember how you took it," she said to Michael.

"She tell you?" Michael asked, and John Kelly, sitting in the easy chair between them, nodded.

"Not saying I believe it, mind you." Michael heard his friend's heart skip. He was lying. Michael could see it in his eyes.

"It's hard to believe," Madeline agreed, pouring them each a cup. Michael wasn't interested in how many creams or sugars they each took. He drank his coffee black and drank it slowly, thankful the roast was thick with nearly a burnt aftertaste.

Maddy pulled out her laptop and opened it. Michael tried tossing her his debit card but she batted it to the coffee table where it lay lifeless, and instead logged herself into a website he recognized as one of those genealogy sites.

"I've been chasing leads all morning," she said.

"It's thirty bucks a month for the world membership," Michael said, to which John Kelly balked.

"I'm not poor!" Maddy snapped.

"We both are," Michael countered. "We're grad students."

"You just feeling chivalrous when you tried to pay?"

John Kelly watched their exchange with a bemused smirk.

"I'm living off my parents' estate. I'm poor. The estate isn't."

She waved him off. "I got the free trial. We won't need two weeks."

"Just don't forget to cancel that shit," John Kelly said.

Michael couldn't help but grin as he took another sip of coffee. The living room furniture, including the love seat he now sat on, was the same. They were the same. Hell, even the coffee tasted the same. And more importantly, there weren't any ghosts here.

"The Ristens have only been known by this shortened form of the name since the early 1800's when they migrated to South Carolina." She looked up from her computer. Michael watched her, but so did John Kelly and even Dart, sitting curled at her feet on the other end of the couch. Michael, glancing back at John Kelly, thought how easy it was for the dog's loyalties to shift.

"From where?" Michael asked. Another sip.

"Immigration forms suggest France, but they traveled from the European interior before that. Your family's old, Michael. From Eastern Europe. Bulgaria. Romania. At least back two hundred years before they came to the United States. In Europe they were the

Ristenoffs, and trace their lineage to a royal line in the Romania and Transylvania regions. You know what a *boyar* is?"

Michael looked at John Kelly who only shrugged. "I think I had one burned off my big toe when I was younger," Michael responded. John Kelly looked into his lap rather than bust up laughing.

Maddy shook her head, ignoring him. "Counts. Dukes. That kind of thing. That's what your ancestors were. They were royalty who served different princes."

"And then they up and left their country to come here and be what, dirt farmers?"

Maddy shook her head. "They didn't just up and leave." Now her eyes never left the screen. Her fingers worked quickly both on the keyboard and on the touch screen of her laptop. She leaned into the computer, hunching her back at what must be an uncomfortably acute angle. "They went all over Europe," she said. Hits from Germany, Belgium, Austria. What's now Serbia, and even France. "Every few years. And then they'd split off. Some Ristenoffs made it into Russia and even Ukraine before they just…"

Michael waited for her to finish. When she didn't, he asked, "What?" but his voice cracked and his throat was dry. He didn't like the look on her face.

"…vanished," she said simply. "Their records stop. Just… stop." She sat the laptop on the coffee table and turned the screen so he and John Kelly could read it. "See," she said. "This branch here. A man and his wife and quite a large family. Eight boys and three daughters. Settled in Ukraine in 1669. But the records stop right after that. Census reports from 1670 show they're there, but by 1675, it's like they all dis—"

"What's this?" Michael asked. He noticed a leafed page with a pine cone and a tag that read: "Historical record." Maddy took the laptop back and turned the screen around, typing again. "Another report tied to the area. Seems there were lots of attacks around then in this village. People dying. A lot of people. They suspected…"

She wasn't one to grow silent, and definitely not twice in two minutes. Michael steeled himself for what was to come next. A part of him already knew what she was going to say.

"…a werewolf," she finished, and looked up at him.

Michael sat trembling, aware of the implications. "This curse," he mumbled, staring back over the long history of his family, had been in his blood for generations. Up until now, he'd been able to divorce himself from the monster on the simple belief that it was separate, an entity he could not control. Even though he could not remember when it first came into his life, he assumed there had been a point when it was introduced to him. Like a kid shopping for a costume at a Halloween store, he had to have picked up this particular visage at some point. It was, after all, a mask.

But this implication meant something more. If it truly had been a part of his family for that long, then it was as much a part of his identity as this character sitting on his friend's couch drinking coffee. It wasn't a mask, something he could take off and put on. It was him.

More than that, it meant that those fleeting moments of depression weren't lapses but glimpses into a darker truth. His reactive embrace of suicide wasn't due to a momentary fear that he couldn't control the monster in him, as he'd previously thought, but a glimpse into what he had to do. It truly was the only way to take off this mask.

"I'm gonna die," he said. He had the presence to set his coffee cup down, but not much else.

"I think we need to take a moment," John Kelly said.

Michael didn't acknowledge him. Instead, it was Maddy who spoke up. "Something's been happening here, John Kelly. Something has been attacking people and animals. Something killed those boys at his college last spring."

"And you said that wasn't his doing."

"It *wasn't* his—"

"You have reports from some scared people trying to make sense of what they seeing, Maddy," John Kelly continued, setting his own cup down. "And maybe it is hard to make sense of, but it don't mean there's a supernatural monster running around."

"What's the alternative?" Michael asked, his unblinking gaze indicating that, for the most part, he was still lost in his own thoughts.

"People kill people and animals every day," John Kelly said. "And maybe you're sick, my guy. You said you seeing your folks and kin when you close your eyes, and seeing these people who've died. But none of that means you a werewolf."

The room quieted. Michael didn't react, but he'd heard every word his friend had said. It would be nice if it were true, or even if he could believe it. John Kelly believed it, and glancing up, Michael was sure Maddy was even partially convinced. A serial killer made more sense than a legendary monster. But without even turning around, Michael knew it wouldn't be long until the sun went down, and he'd spent far too long at his friend's house. Any longer, and he'd be endangering them.

He nodded and stood, stretching. Sitting there for what had been, apparently, a long while, had stiffened his joints and muscles. The release of the tension as the muscles unwound allowed him to loose a content grumble that caught Dart's attention, and the dog jumped off the sofa, caught itself in a stretch, and pressed its side against his shins.

"I was gonna make some chicken and dumplings for dinner," Maddy said.

"Why don't you stay for a bit," John Kelly said. "Hell, even spend the night. We got the room. We can keep an eye on you. You don't need to be alone right now, anyway."

Michael shook his head. He imagined Maddy had inherited the recipe from her mother, whose chicken and dumplings had been legendary, but he could not escape the constraints of time or the rising bright autumn moon.

❧

It would have been easy for Angelique Fontenot to close her eyes and let death take her. Her whole body ached. Not just her muscles and her bones, but her organs and her fibers and every inch of her. It would have been easy. Von Slacher had made it so with every blow, every punch, and every kick. He'd only ever asked one question after making a single statement, as she'd pulled herself up. She lay on the floor, curled, in pain, bleeding. Her eyes watered. Von Slacher knelt over her. When he reached down to caress her cheek, she winced.

"You are protecting it, aren't you?" This had been said as though he were just now willing to believe it. It was more than a tool for her revenge. It was, in its human form, something she cared for. Something she saw as innocent. He was just realizing this when he delivered the brief attack that sent her back to the floor, pain like a fire erupting deep within her. She made no move to acquiesce because she knew no such admission would save her now.

"Who is it?" he asked then, and she thought about how her ma had told them as kids how important it was to name your fears. "Demons got power," her ma had said, "as long as they don't have a name. When you can name 'em, they lose their hold on ya."

"It will go so much better for you to tell me. Tell me about this boy, Michael Risten. It is him, isn't it? Has he... infected anyone else?

He's surely told you. You give him the potus. He must have confided in you."

"If you know his name, then why don' ya go to him?"

He pursed his lips then licked them. "I want to know him first. I want to know who's helping him. I want to know who knows."

She closed her eyes and focused on breathing. She expected another strike to come. When he stood and walked away, she sighed.

CHAPTER FIFTEEN

$\mathcal{T}$he night passed without event. Michael stayed locked up but raged against the chains, creating disquieting sounds. If anyone were nearby, they would have heard the strangest noises coming from the old barn. Scream-like howls erupted into the night, grating enough to elicit chills. Bites and snaps like the jaws of some great beast were ready to shred its shackles and set it loose on the world. Perhaps it would have been better for the town had someone heard the noises from the old Risten barn. But the closest person who might have heard anything wasn't in the habit of warning the town. Even if she wanted to now, Angelique Fontenot faded in and out of consciousness from her injuries. Each time she came to, she knew she was that much closer to death, and that was all she was concerned with.

ᙓᙔᙖ

Kalos von Slacher kept watch, staring up at the nearly full autumn moon. He respected its draw and felt its power. The beast was caged. This he knew because it was so quiet, and he knew where. He sat elevated in a pine, on a metal deck, staring up at the sky, adorned with warm clothes and weapons, fully understanding that he could go to the barn tonight. He could end it. But he hadn't spent these long years hunting and tracking the rougarou across the world, wherever they popped up, to insult the hunt so. It wasn't just about the beast. The rougarou touched lives. The human underneath had connections. One couldn't just remove the beast without disturbing its environment.

"Hey!" The voice startled him out of his reverie. He looked down. A middle-aged man wearing thick plaid flannel and an orange vest toting a shotgun stood on the ground, looking up at him.

"What's going on?" another voice called, and a second man walked into view.

"Some asswipe's up in our blind," the first man said. Kalos von Slacher studied them through the darkness. The man was the self-proclaimed mayor of this little community. The other he recognized as the sheriff.

"You need to come down, sir," the sheriff said with as authoritative voice as he could muster. Von Slacher stood and leaned against the railing.

"It is not safe for you to be out tonight," he said, and with a moment's pause, acquiesced. When he stood on level ground with them, he found he was taller than both men, the mayor by a few inches and the rotund law man, whose stature was not made up for by his cowboy hat, by nearly a full head. "I apologize for interrupting your autumnal festivities, gentleman, but you should know, should you choose to stay out here, that it isn't safe."

"Who are you?" the mayor asked. His voice carried the edge of a knife. This was a man who loved power and was comfortable staking his claim in such a small pond. "You don't have no right to be here, does he, Charley."

"Now, let's not get all rankled," the sheriff said. But he wore a bemused look. He was a puzzler, and puzzled now how this unfamiliar face might tie in with the recent deaths and animal attacks. Von Slacher could read this as clearly on the man's face as he could read a book.

"I assure you, gentlemen, I will not keep you any longer." But as he started to walk away, the mayor reached out and grabbed his shoulder. His hand felt grubby, dirty. How dare he lay his hand in such a manner. He had no idea what big fish had just entered this pond.

"How about you just hang on a minute," Bob Larsen said.

"Bob," Charley responded, his voice like a parent tired of scolding their hyperactive child.

The wind shifted, and Kalos von Slacher's ears perked to the far away sound of the wolf in restraints. Would there be enough time, before the moon set, to unleash the beast and let it track the scent of these two indolent, power-starved little men? He wasn't sure. But that this man laid his paw on the great shoulders of such a fine hunter, von Slacher could not let go unpunished.

"A warning from a friend, Mr. Larsen. A presumptive high-ranking soldier once laid a hand on my *boyar* much in the way you now lay yours on me. That soldier not only lost his hand, but had his throat slit, and what blood of his wasn't used to extinguished the campfire was poured into a toasting cup and savored by my lord."

"You hear that, Charley?" Bob Larsen responded after a moment. He was clearly put off, just the way von Slacher wanted him. "I think he just threaten—"

A growl interrupted Bob. When he realized it came from this stranger, he grew afraid. But it was too late.

CRSO

Aaron Bailey awoke in his bed dripping with sweat and piss and a run of shit that pancaked his ass cheeks together. His sheets had been kicked off and lay in a gnarly pile near the bed. Fine blonde hair matted his thighs and his forearms, and he felt like screaming out at the moon. He could not see it through the window by his bed, but he could feel it. It sang a melodic siren song full of dark blue notes that made his belly rumble. Had he been walking again? *Walking.* That's what he called it, though he wasn't sure how accurate that was. Lately he'd been waking in the morning with his legs sore like he'd been hiking the trails out around Daly Pond or up by Mount Magazine, his thighs and calves burning, a rip-roaring hunger gnashing at him for satiation. His arms quivered as if he'd cut a quarter-mile long ditch of brush with a pair of hedge clippers, and his hands, unable to grip anything with real strength, trembled coldly and indolently against his will for them to remain still. Dreams explained the muscle fatigue as much as a dream could, suggesting he'd exhausted himself in the night, for in his dreams he was running impossibly fast, leaping over deadfalls, cantering by streams, loping lazily through the tree line before he'd rocket into a sprint, smelling something tasty that only grew stronger the more he raced to it, until his sharp teeth punctured the flesh of the rabbit or chicken or (Remy Doucet) whatever he caught, and the buttery meat melted in the gnashing of his teeth and the blood ran down his gullet like a wash of rainwater down a log shoot and his whole body convulsed ferociously with the ecstasy of a kill.

He wasn't sure if he'd been walking, but as he hopped out of bed, he saw no new faces other than those of Remy Doucet and his uncle, staring blankly at him. That was the most recent dream, and seeing them made him think he wasn't just dreaming about "walking." Because they'd died, he'd learned the morning after that particular dream, and they'd died much the same way he'd dreamt. Too bad he hadn't gone walking and found that bitch child Byron Calhoun. He'd drifted off the night before wondering what that child's blood tasted like, but alas, no dream had come.

Crawling out of bed, Aaron stretched away as much of the soreness as he possibly could. He started the shower, thinking about the attack he'd survived and how he felt different. Sheriff Charley had told him they were calling it a bear attack, but it weren't no bear, he knew. For one, it had the head of a wolf, but it wasn't a wolf, either. Wolves don't walk like a person. For another, if it weren't for the head and the body covered in fur, the tattered clothing it had been wearing, he would have thought it was a person in a costume. As the water rushed over him, he focused on the mental image of the thing that had attacked him. It wasn't just a costume. There was a name for it. A familiar name for it, and if the dreams were to be believed, then for him now. But this wasn't just a word on the marquee of a Saturday matinee at the local cineplex advertising some schlock horror movie that could only scare preteens. There was real power here. He could feel it.

CR80

What a strange dream, Maddy thought, caressing the dog's fur as Dart curled next to her in the bed. Her eyes flitted open and stared at the blank ceiling. Michael had not left her mind since he'd left their house the evening before, and so it was no surprise, really, that he was occupying her dreams. John Kelly had been forceful in insisting that Michael stay, but Michael of course had been just as driven to go home. All of this had played out again in the dream.

Maddy had been sitting in some cabin-like interior with a roaring fire. John Kelly asked if she'd seen the dog and she said no, and then Michael had entered, wearing only a pair of shorts, walking on all fours, his arms and legs hinged strangely for a human but appropriate enough for such mode of travel. He was sniffing at the floor, and only noticed Maddy at the last second, where he moved to her, pressed his side against the shins of her legs, then huffed, sat on his haunches, used his left foot to scratch behind his ear, then lay down, curling at her feet much as Dart was curled against her now. But it wasn't his flesh she felt against her bare feet, but a soft down of fur. Once she realized it, she looked down, and saw the largest dog laying there, curled, his face—a wolfish adaptation of Michael's features and wholly his eyes—staring up at her, mouth of the muzzle open, tongue lolled out, the animal panting.

Nothing more happened in the dream, she thought, in this pre-dawn light. Nothing, she repeated to herself, as if to calm herself, only to be answered by a far-off sound. A howl like an echo meandered through the still, dark morning. Maddy's eyes flashed open and Dart sat up, looking in the direction of the sound. Even in this light, the dog looked worried. Or even afraid.

CRER

"What in Christ?" Bob Larsen muttered through blood and dirt caking up beneath his face, threatening to drown him as he laid on the ground. His shoulder sang a dirge to him, a pain so violent it was numb, and he couldn't move that arm. Pity. That was the arm closest to his rifle. He huffed, blowing bits of dirt out of his mouth, and bent his knees up as much as he could in an effort to raise himself off the ground. "Charley!" he called out. But there was no answer save the sniffs of a large animal examining his health through his scent and the cautious footsteps of something bipedal approaching.

⊂⊇⊋⊃

If you asked Deputy Aaron Bailey why he chose to leave his house this early, get in his car, and drive out this particular county road, he might have reflected thoughtfully on it, but his answer would never waver even though it made little sense. Walking up on the scene now, realizing too late he'd not even thought of bringing his sidearm, Bailey wondered himself. The answer—or answers, as it were—came to him completely and easily. 1) He had no idea. 2) He had to.

He'd felt compelled. Perhaps it was something he'd smelled upon exiting the shower, or heard, or felt. Yes, all those senses were involved, and taste as well, but there was nothing rational in his decision. His conscious mind did not direct him. No thought communicated directly through his mind that this was his intent. This didn't mean he felt any less compelled. Nor did any opposing thought push back against his actions. At no time did he question what he was doing or where he was going. He wasn't in a trance, mind you, but alert and aware. He didn't like what was on one radio station, so he flicked the knob to another. The car followed the laws of the road, and behind the wheel, the deputy, dressed warmly in civilian clothes, carefully signaled and piloted the vehicle until he arrived at his destination. Here he parked behind what he recognized as Bob Larsen's pickup on the shoulder of the road. He exited the patrol car and walked into the tree line.

Bailey might have known about the deer blind—he thought he'd heard once that the sheriff and the mayor went to the woods for a weekend every autumn for their annual hunting trip—but he couldn't have told you if you asked what day they went on or if it centered around a particular date. Quite truthfully, he didn't give two shits, so there was no way, other than this preternatural excursion, that he could have known they were here or that he'd find them like this.

Except he did know. The deputy wasn't surprised when he stumbled upon the blind site. The blind itself dangled off the tree, threatening to fall the rest of the way to the ground, some of the black straps caked in blood. Not far away, the sheriff lay in a heap, and something large and fur-covered hovered over his body. Blood was everywhere, and whatever loomed was obviously eating. The sounds of mastication were thick and called deliciously to the deputy. Seeing his former boss lying there, as dead as a slab of barbecue, brought no other emotion to mind.

"Help," Bob Larsen called weakly, lifting his head up, raising the only arm remaining—his left—before dropping his head again to the forest floor. He lay closest to the deputy. Bailey looked at him impassively with no expression crossing his face. The beast feasting on the sheriff raised its yellow eyes and bloodied snout and studied this new intruder.

Deputy Aaron Bailey didn't move when the beast locked eyes with him. He didn't run. The beast stepped over the sheriff's corpse and padded towards him on all fours, a low growl uttering from its throat. Its coat was silver, suggesting age, but the creature didn't look infirm. It didn't hobble or cough or appear in any way to be feeble. In fact, it looked quite fast.

It circled him. Its snout jammed into his crotch, and it studied him with its eyes. Its ears twitched, searching for any sound from him, all while its soft growl vibrated through his chest. Bailey wasn't exactly scared, but he was cautious. This was like the wolf that had attacked him, but it wasn't the same animal. That animal was darker, for one thing. In the end, he didn't think it mattered. Maybe they were part of the same pack, and one could finish the job of the other.

It circled away from him, always keeping at least one eye on him, then sat and regarded him with a cock of its head, as if it were awaiting a command. This was not the case, he knew. He swallowed hard, never letting his eyes leave those of the wolf out of fear it would see that as a sign of weakness or fear, and pounce. He gave very little thought to running. The vehicle was too far and this animal, larger than any wolf he'd ever heard about, would be too fast for him to make it safely. It was powerful. He could see its muscles rippling under the fur. He could hear the timbre of its growl.

After what felt like a long moment, the animal stood to all fours and stretched, sniffed again at the air in his direction, then huffed. Turning its back completely on him, it returned to the corpse of the sheriff and resumed eating. When he didn't run automatically, it turned back, its muzzle caked in fresh blood, and huffed at him, then resumed devouring the soft meat of the sheriff's torso. Bailey backed away, chanced a look over his shoulder, then turned and hurried back to his vehicle.

Once inside, he didn't drive away immediately, but gripped the wheel with both hands and stared at the bumper of the truck in front of him. He thought at first he wanted to vomit, and did his best to prepare for that event, but it never came. Whatever swept over him in that instant passed quietly and coldly. He breathed, knowing and feeling his face was pale, his body was aching, and a deep and unquenchable well of hunger had been tapped at seeing that wolf devouring his former boss. Soon, Bailey realized, he'd get to feast like that himself.

CHAPTER SIXTEEN

Maddy was up and dressed with Dart when John Kelly came stumbling out of his room, giving her the side eye like she'd just betrayed him. The dog, too. He harrumphed and walked past even as Dart trotted up to him, goofy smile plastered on his face, tail wagging.

"Where you off to?" he asked, helping himself to some of the coffee.

"Get dressed," she answered. "We don't have long now."

"I'm gonna sip my coffee and—"

"John Kelly Jeansonne! I swear to Jesus, you don't get dressed this instant I will beat you within an inch of yo' life."

He jumped back, snake-bit, and muttered, "Fine, ma," before padding back into his room. It was too cold outside for the basketball shorts and tee, but he at least threw on a Hornets hoody before they disembarked from the house, Maddy with keys and coffee in one hand and Dart's leash in the other until John felt a modicum of chivalry and took the dog's leash.

The coffee's smell filled the car more than sound that early morning. Maddy had bothered with neither conversation nor the radio in the short drive from their house to the Risten farm, and John Kelly seemed just as eager for the quiet. Her brother had never been a morning person, and she'd only grown into the habit out of necessity at college. Truth was, nothing felt better than sleeping in, but today was not the day for that.

They emerged from the car, Dart tugging at the leash, whimpering and whining. John, never a fan of leashing his dog and never without a harness, realized as he unhooked the collar that they had left the harness at home. As Maddy climbed the front porch steps, Dart tore off around the side of the house. For all the dog's barking and carrying on, it was overpowered by Maddy's forceful knock at the front door. Perhaps, she thought, she had channeled her mom.

"Michael!" she called, banging on the door. "Please, let us in. The sun is up almost. I know you're… just please."

"Maddy." John Kelly's voice from behind her in a tone that was chiding, that was saying enough was enough. But goddammit, *enough* wasn't just *enough*. It had never been enough. She sighed then knocked again, this time harder.

"Maddy," her brother called. She wheeled around, knowing she was angry and frustrated and not caring. John Kelly stood in the yard, but it was obvious he wanted to follow the dog. Suddenly, hearing Dart again, she knew she wanted to follow as well.

Rounding the corner, the sun just on the horizon, the dawn light still a deep blue and the air cold and dry, they found Dart at the front door of the barn, barking, looking back at them, then barking again. Maddy raced to catch up, but John Kelly beat her to the punch and was inside the door and up the ladder just as she was crossing the threshold.

"Nope," he muttered, his feet and calves the only parts of him visible near the top rungs until he scampered on up. Dart growled and yipped, but Maddy scaled the ladder also. As she did, she heard the sounds. Whimpers and wails and kicks, like a dog having a bad dream, growing louder the closer she got to the loft. Her head periscoped up and found John Kelly just inside, staring into the shadows of the upper level of the barn. The smell of rotten hay overcame her and then the smell of sweat and then the smell of blood, in that order, as she pulled herself up. Light was minimal here, the shadows thick like a blanket, but even still her eyes adjusted quickly and she saw what John Kelly was staring at. There, in the loft, with chains around his wrists, the elongated, fur-covered form kicked and whimpered as though it were dreaming. But this was much larger than a dog. Hell, larger than any wolf she'd heard about. Its snout wrinkled and it gave a huffing sound and raised its head, its pointed ears twitching. It saw them but gave no notice of recognition or warning against them, just rested its head and whimpered.

That's when a curious thing happened. The hair fell away in great strands, and the beast began rolling in the hay, as if itching itself, and the hair and loose straw kicked up in a kind of dust cloud that was carried out the window by an early morning breeze. What was left, lying naked and still shackled, was Michael Risten. He was asleep, to be sure, and his appearance as they knew it only returned in degrees, as the ears returned to regular shape and the snout pushed back in and the jaw realigned and the joints popped and snapped back into human form. Michael lay there. A single tear materialized on his cheek to indicate that, even sedated, the transformation was painful.

"Jesus, Michael," she said, rushing past her brother, who could only gape. She cradled Michael's head and brushed his hair from his eyes. A few strands of wolf's hair clung to his slick body. "He's shivering," she said. "Get him a blanket."

Dart was barking again, down below. John Kelly nodded and descended the ladder, returning a moment later with a dusty quilt that probably had nested generations of spiders, but for now that would do. He flapped it open with a pop and helped her spread it over Michael, and partially her, as she didn't rise, but continued to stroke his hair.

"What now?"

"Help me find his clothes. He din't come up here naked."

John Kelly found his jeans and inside the front pocket, a single iron key. This, clearly, fit the lock, and soon Michael's hands were free. Maddy rocked him gently. Michael was mumbling something, starting to stir. She attempted to shush him.

They waited a few more minutes for the somnolence to pass. As awareness returned, Michael quieted and opened his eyes, shocked to find Maddy holding him and then to see John Kelly standing there.

"What...?" he tried, but it was clear he didn't know which question to ask first, so Maddy picked one to answer.

"We got here just before the sunrise," she said. "We saw you change."

Michael sat up and hugged the quilt around him. He did not pull away from her. Even when she chanced an arm around his shoulder, he did not pull away, but rested his head against hers and wept silently.

CR80

It was easy for Deputy Bailey to "discover" the scene. He called the county headquarters with the story that the sheriff said he'd check in with him, and when that old bat said Charley was out with Mayor Larsen hunting, Aaron said he thought he knew where the blind was. Then, he hopped back in the patrol car and rode back out to the spot. Doors securely locked still, he radioed in with as much distraught in his voice as he could muster, begging for help. When he hung up, he sat back and turned on the country station. He thought on some level that the beast, if it were still out there, wouldn't attack him, but he wasn't going to test that by going back out to the blind by himself. He was also reasonably sure the beast was no longer there, just as he was sure that with the sun up, what attracted him to the beast and the blood was no longer pulling as strongly at him. When the other patrol cars and two Monticello ambulances arrived, he shut off the engine and exited, remembering just enough blood and carnage in the daylight to make himself look sick. He led them into the brush and to the blind where the bodies still lay. There, he relished as his coworkers wept and gnashed their teeth and violently reacted to the scene, some vomiting, one tough old deputy fainting dead away, and one guy just bawling uncontrollably. *Power*, Deputy Aaron Bailey thought, and choked down his own smile.

CR80

Byron Calhoun had done well to hide the damage from his mother. He was old enough that she didn't pry on bathroom activities, and the clothes he threw out in the burn barrel out back, so there was little to no evidence. The sheets and comforter he'd sent through the wash cycle twice before she got home that day. The trauma he was processing left him numb and unable to sit still, so he'd busied himself cleaning the rest of the trailer. What his mother took as a nice surprise was merely an attempt to escape what had happened to him.

Lately, her schedule was at odds with his. She was leaving for work before he woke for school and home well after he would get home, given that both Vicky Arsenault's and Remy Doucet's fates left Duke Livingston shorthanded. There was no way she could find out he'd been skipping school; she couldn't afford a cell phone, so their only phone hung on a wall in the kitchen. Of course, had she known, she would have been concerned. Byron was a smart boy, a bit imaginative and sullen at times, but very creative and eager to do his work.

Or, at least, he had been. His mother's schedule blinded her to his current situation. Now, stuck alone in the trailer, Byron curled into the fetal position with thumb in mouth up beside the queen-sized bed in his mother's bedroom, weeping freely because he was sure no one would find him. His mother was powerless to do anything against the deputy, as were most people in town. Telling her, or anyone for that matter, would only bring him more pain, and pain was something he did not want more of. The pain he felt was multilayered already and all consuming. It existed in the deep recesses of his body in the hours and days after the attack, and even now he felt it like a ghost haunting his sex and his identity and his body. It existed in his lungs, keeping his breaths shallow and his chest empty, forcing him to constantly struggle to fill. If he could only take a deep enough breath, he might fill himself with some kind of peace, but that was as illusory as the man in the story he'd heard at school who was forced to spend the afterlife thirsty with the cup of water just out of reach. It existed in his mind, as thoughts as accusatory as they were designed to provide some kind of explanation.

—*If you weren't gay, this wouldn't have happened. My God, you know this man hates Black people, and so you just asked for it being gay too. You drew attention to yourself.*

—*But God, why?! Why can't you answer this one prayer? Just help me, Lord! God?*

—*God doesn't listen to you. What if there is no God?*

—*No, that can't be, there has to be.*

—*Then why would he let you be born like this? What if there is a God but he's cruel?*

—*Oh God, I hurt so much. Oh Jesus.*

—*Jesus don't love faggots. You know this is why you hurt. And you a Black fag. You were born to go to Hell.*

—*I just want to die. I should kill myself. I could take a knife from the drawer in the kitchen, and just draw a bath, and slit my own wrists.*

—*But it hurts, slitting wrists.*

—*What if I fill the bath with ice? What if... what would Mom think?*

—*She loves you.*

—*I should tell her. I should just tell her, and maybe she can... no, there is nothing she can do. He could just kill her too, or kill me, or do... this... to me again. What if I tore something? What if, if this is being gay, maybe I'm not, maybe I'm just too stupid. I'll tell Michael. He'll know what to do! Michael can... What, save me?*

—*No one can save you. You are dirty and weak and pathetic and you deserve this. You brought this pain on and you deserve this.*

These were no-good words, and they failed him. Perhaps a little solace came from voicing them, as this diatribe often spilled from his lips in one form or another. The words changed, but the chaos was always there, a reflection of his traumatized mind. In the end, the words were all he had, and he was both comforted and isolated by them. This was what it meant, he understood, to be imprisoned within your own mind.

The phone rang.

He wiped the fresh tears from his eyes and imagined he felt the rivulets cutting canyons into his cheeks, they'd flowed so much recently. Rising to unsteady feet, Byron made his way to the phone and lifted it from the receiver.

"Hello?" His voice was weak and timid. He knew it wouldn't be his mother. It was the lunch hour, for one, and for another, why would she call if she thought he was at school?

"Byron," came the familiar voice. It was his Pre-Cal teacher. "Byron, dear, we are so worried about you. Why haven't you been at school?"

He sniffed and wiped at an errant tear. "I'm sick," he said. God, it hurt to talk. All this talk of God, to God, and the conversation was so one-sided. He gasped for a breath.

"Byron you can't miss any more school. Tell your momma to call us. We got to get your assignments to you, and we need a note and—" his sniffles interrupted her, or perhaps it was something more. Whatever pain inside him oozed out and through the phone line, because she stopped abruptly. "Byron, are you okay? Byron, has something happened? Tell me, sweetie, and we can send someone."

His lips quivered. More tears. If he could just get his leaden tongue to work, this might be the salvation he found, but all he could do was swallow hard.

"Byron, this is so unlike you. Where are you, sweetie? I can come get you."

She could, he thought. *She could show and pull me out of this hellhole and call the authorities and then they could come and arrest Deputy Aaron Bailey and—*

It was the first time he'd allowed himself to think the deputy's name. Beforehand, it had been *he* or something vague like that, but at the conjuration of the name in his mind came also the conjuration of that face, of that form bent over him, of that voice, that smell of his body. Byron burst into fresh tears and screamed. "Leave me alone! Don't you dare come!"

The phone slammed down on the cradle.

❦

After they had lunch, Michael was a bit more himself. He'd cleaned up and dressed not long after they found him, ravenously ate the breakfast that Maddy had prepared for him and John Kelly in his kitchen, and returned to their home not long after, but it wasn't until they all ate lunch that he felt some semblance of normality. He sat on the couch holding a cup of coffee, alone until the dog made his way to him and curled up beside him, resting his head on Michael's thigh with a huff. Maddy's and John Kelly's conversation was a guise to outline the order of recent events when they were truthfully trying to get their heads around what they saw that morning.

"Other than Aaron Bailey, is there anyone else?" Maddy asked.

"I don't know," Michael said numbly. He met Dart's eyes and realized he would never be as loyal and unflinching as this animal.

"What we do know is that if you were still locked up this morning, then Angelique Fontenot didn't release you last night, so whoever attacked the sheriff and the mayor last night wasn't you." News of the recent attack spread like wildfire when Bailey had called it in.

"So, it was Bailey then," Maddy said.

Michael shook his head. "Could have been." He didn't sound sure.

"What's wrong?" Maddy asked.

Michael shook his head. "I've been afflicted with this longer than he has. I don't remember what happens to me at night."

"So?" John Kelly said.

"So. Even if he would tell you, and I don't think he would, but even if he wanted to, he couldn't. He probably won't remember."

"He woke up all human-like there, right?" John Kelly said.

Michael shook his head. "We don't."

"How do you know?" John Kelly challenged.

"You ever crate-train Dart?" When John Kelly nodded, Michael continued. "Canines are particular. They... we... I have always returned to where I slept. To my shelter. No matter where the hunt took me."

John Kelly nodded. "And since their deer blind isn't his normal shelter, he wouldn't just fall asleep there."

"Too big a risk of being found," Michael said. "I don't know for certain, because I can't remember, but I think... I think the wolf might. Does that make sense? I think it remembers me, remembers the human, and knows not to put it in danger. If he'd have stayed there..."

"There's a risk someone else could have found him," Maddy finished.

"So what?" John Kelly said. "Silver bullets?"

"I don't know," Michael answered. "I imagine regular bullets would work. I don't see why it has to be silver."

"According to the legend of the beast of Gévaudan," Maddy said, "silver was used to dispatch the animal." Both John Kelly and Michael wore the same incredulous look, to which she just shrugged. "What? I do my homework."

"Other than some legends," John Kelly said, "is there any evidence? And don't quote me some Wolfman shit."

"It's all based in legend, I'm afraid," Maddy answered. "From alchemy to a belief that silver came from the moon—which also causes the transformations—"

"It wasn't a full moon last night, though," John Kelly said.

"Doesn't have to be," Michael interjected, sipping his coffee held in one hand while he kneaded the dog's fur with the other. "I only change in the fall, and the moon just has to be bright, not full. I don't change on new moons or when it's a sliver. I get sick. I still lock myself up, but I don't change."

"So where does that leave us?" Maddy asked.

"Tomorrow is Halloween," Michael said. "It's also the full moon. Tomorrow, I'll be at my strongest. So will the deputy and anyone else who's been bitten. Everyone else will be in danger."

Silence settled, broken only by the slurping of coffee and Dart's exasperated huffs. Finally, John Kelly leaned forward, placing his now empty cup on the coffee table, nodding like a bobblehead like he always did when he had an idea.

"So, we train you. Put a harness on you. I can drive you up to Petco in Monticello, get you fitted. We get some dog biscuits and you'll protect us from the others."

"Jesus, John," Maddy said as her brother laughed. Even Michael cracked a smile.

"What?" he said, turning his palms up. "Hey, Mike. Fetch me the remote," John Kelly continued, and not thinking anything of it, Michael picked it up off the other end of the table and tossed it to him. "See," John Kelly said with a laugh. "Already taught him to play fetch." This got them all laughing then. Dart smiled, looking from human to human, and his tail thumped on the couch cushion.

When the laughter died down, Michael said with a sigh, "We need a plan before tomorrow, and I'm afraid I'm not going to be much help. Despite John's suggestions."

"If she's letting you loose," John Kelly said, "then we need to see what that old witch is up to."

"We have to find out who this other wolf is," Michael added. "And how many more have been infected."

"How are we going to do that?" Maddy asked. Michael had no idea. Short of the human walking up to them and introducing him or herself, there was really no way to know who all had been infected. That word, *infected,* made him feel dirty. He was patient zero in this horrible disease, and he shivered when such thoughts loped across his mind.

"Let's say we're sure the deputy is one," John Kelly said. "Cause you attacked him when you killed the preacher. And let's assume there are others. Maybe you shouldn't be chained up tonight and tomorrow night. Maybe you ought to be out, corralling the pack, so to speak."

"He isn't a fucking sheepdog," Maddy said. Michael understood how she felt, wondering if John Kelly was still making light of the situation.

"I'm not saying that," John Kelly snapped. "I'm saying maybe he is more aware than he thinks. He's been out before, right? You never felt threatened. Dart here would have heard something. But look at him, cozying up to Michael like they's best buds. I'm saying, maybe there is a way to bell the cat, so to speak. Make him work for us."

"'Bell the cat' refers to keeping something from creeping up on you," Michael said.

"Don't mansplain to me, Mikey," John Kelly said. "You know what I mean."

"I do," Michael nodded. "But there is something else we've only touched on. You aren't going to reason with these things. Most of them. Probably not any of them. You need to be prepared, and you need to be armed. Even against me. Especially me." He felt like adding something with finality to this, how no matter what happened or how this ended, they needed to be prepared to end this for him.

But, looking at their faces, he wondered if he could add to their burden by asking them to do something like that. How could he put such a weight on them? So ultimately, he let the idea settle there with the inference.

"How I see it, we really have three objectives," Maddy said. "We've got to talk to Angelique Fontenot, gather some weapons, and warn the townsfolk."

"Hold on," John Kelly said. "We go warning people, what if the other'n that are wolves find out? If Mike is right and the wolf remembers, we could be giving away our hand."

"We have to risk it," Maddy said, shaking her head. "We can't know who the other wolves are, but we can't let innocent people suffer."

"I wish we knew better 'bout the silver," John Kelly said. "I..." he looked up to see they were both focused on him. "I did it. Some years back. For Pa's guns. Made some silver slugs. Had this old hillbilly up in the Ozarks do it."

"The antique silver," Maddy said. Ashamed, her brother just nodded.

"I'll have several shots with the rifle and the Glock, but that's it."

"We should work on gathering regular guns and ammo, then," Michael said. "My dad had a big collection. He wanted me and my siblings to all learn to shoot. I'll see what I've got there and get ammo for all of it."

"Our dad had a 12-gauge," John Kelly said. "Pick me up some shells?"

Michael nodded, and John stood and disappeared down the hall.

"We'll go talk to Angelique Fontenot," Maddy said. "It probably won't take as long as it'll take you to go through the guns, so after, we can start warning people."

"We talked about doing this with Byron," Michael said.

Maddy shook her head. "I called a few times. They just got the landline, you know."

"No answer?" Michael asked, then nodded as if he expected this. "Something's wrong. I haven't talked to him either, but I can feel it."

From down the hall, sounds of doors opening and closing and drawers sliding open and closed punctuated their sentences.

"We should go check on him," Maddy suggested.

To this Michael again nodded, but there seemed no conviction. As concerned as they were about the boy, he didn't see them rushing out to the trailer park to check on him.

"Everyone has to know there's something going on here. I think we can warn them without talking about werewolves and risk being committed."

"True," Michael said. He flashed eyes to her that sparkled with tears he couldn't afford to let fall.

John Kelly returned carrying the Glock, a rifle, and the bag of silver shells. Michael, looking at this small gathering of arms, felt his flesh crawl.

CRSO

Sarah Larsen kept her eyes lowered and her movements concise as one of the state troopers spoke. They were in her living room and she'd used her husband's early absence to avoid getting dressed, so she'd greeted them in her robe and a nightgown and her slippers. One leg crossed over the other, her eyes cast down in what some might call demure and others servitude, she pondered the great blue veins crisscrossing her pale feet and how old her legs looked. She had responded little when the troopers entered, and in fact had responded little when they told her.

"Do you understand, Mrs. Larsen?" the other trooper asked. She knew they'd been exchanging looks between them when she hadn't reacted. At least, not in the way they expected her to react. What might they expect such a demure, subservient woman to do with news of her husband's violent, gruesome death? Of course, they spared her of the details, sure she couldn't take it. Never mind that she'd probably dreamed of far worse a fate over the years. Her eyes raised to meet them, aware no tears were following. When they recoiled slightly, all instinct, she realized the reason was because she was smiling.

"Yes," she said evenly. "I understand."

Over their shoulders, she saw the front door stood ajar. A sliver of daylight chanced an entrance and a blue jay's song entered of its own volition. For neither of these things could she recall a precedent.

She rose from her place on the couch and crossed to Bob's recliner, tracing her fingers across its head rest. If she bent and smelled, she was sure his cologne would be trapped in the fabric. Still, she might do the unthinkable and... dare she say it... (the smile broadened but her head was turned away from them)... *sit* in the chair. Crossing the floor, she opened the front door and let her smile reveal itself unencumbered, her back to them completely. The bird's song was accompanied by another and the sun seemed brighter. The warmth on her face didn't reflect the temperature outside.

"Would you like some coffee?" she asked, and realized she'd offered them coffee when they first came, and imagined they found her silly and were exchanging another worried glance and she didn't care. Didn't give two fucks what these men thought, because there was no one left in her life to tell her what she should be thinking and she didn't care what anyone else thought, now. She could think any number of things, and no one would say she was stupid or ridiculous or just wrong. No one was left to tell her what she could or couldn't do, or if she needed to get dressed, or where she could sit or what she could eat. No one could tell her where she could go, but she knew one thing—she wasn't going to stay in this town.

CHAPTER SEVENTEEN

$\mathcal{M}$addy and John Kelly discovered first the rotting and half-eaten corpse of one brother. The other lay dead by the smoldering fire pit, a gunshot hollowing out the space between his eyes. The whole of the encampment was in disarray. The sky hung low with rain clouds and a ground-hugging fog that had partially obscured the carnage until they were directly on it. Until it was too late. Maddy screamed when she saw the bullet-marred skull of a man she'd seen alive not too long before. This was a scream of shock, but in truth, she later confessed, it didn't look much different than what you see on television. Except she'd known this man, and he was not an actor, and he would not get up. No, what disturbed her most was the condition of the other brother. She let loose such an ominous, horrendous groan of terror and sadness, then violently retched any contents remaining in her stomach as she sobbed and screamed simultaneously. John Kelly caught her as she lost her footing. Her brother forced her to bury her face in his chest as she struggled.

This, television and film could not prepare you for. No matter how real it is on the screen, there is an understanding of falsity. But this imitation has been stripped away in the real world, so that all we see is all there is. Not even the best makeup, special effects, or CGI can reproduce the sights, the smells, the taste of the air when in the presence of such carnage. "Jesus," was all her brother could mumble when words escaped her.

From behind them, the smack of aluminum against aluminum made them jump. Leaning against the door frame, Angelique Fontenot, looking ashen pale, holding on to her stomach, stared at them so dully Maddy wondered if the old lady even realized they were there.

"Dey wolf…" she muttered, before her eyes rolled up in her skull and she toppled out of the trailer, falling like a rag doll down the steps.

John Kelly rushed to the aid of the older woman, hoisting her up, carrying her back up the stairs with Maddy in tow, back into the trailer.

Upon entering, he found a chair to set Angelique in. Maddy realized this was her first time inside. It was dark and cluttered. Thick shades were drawn over the windows. John Kelly set up a recently toppled bookshelf but didn't pick the books up that had fallen. From where she stood, Maddy caught glimpses of some of the covers that had titles: all related to magic, folk magic, spell casting, and herb magic, all with different regional names, invoking beliefs from a culmination of cultures that influenced Cajun life: Haitian, African, French. Other books looked more like leather journals without titles, and these Maddy scooped up. On the front of one was scrawled in a thin pen—loup garous / Ristenoff.

The interior of the house smelled like herbs and rot with an underlayer of unkemptness that Maddy chastised herself for judging; casting aspersions was so unlike her. From the way John Kelly recoiled when he entered the kitchen, it was obvious the bulk of the odor originated there and just permeated the rest of the single-wide. He fetched a glass of water and knelt beside the older woman, helping her take small sips. Her tongue like a lizard's flicked out to lap at the water, but her eyes never opened.

"Oh, children," she mumbled. "de rougarou is comin', and it my fault."

Maddy knelt on the other side of her, trying to shush her.

"No, girlie, you got to know." Her breathing was labored. She opened her eyes slowly to reveal pupils of different sizes. The flesh around her left eye had swollen like a mole mound and darkened to the same purplish-black as a half-spoiled eggplant. "I sent the wolf here. When he rejected me so many years ago. I was such a stupid girl."

"Who?" Maddy asked.

"I called for him, I did. You can't trust his name. Name just another mask. People hide behind dere names and hide from dem. Like dat Bob Larsen. Hiding behind his name like it means something. Now what yo' name means?"

"Larsen rejected you?" John Kelly asked. Maddy shot him a look, but she wouldn't explain it to him now.

"I called dem here, because I knew. I could feel de magic, chi'dren. I knew de true name dat even Michael's father didn't know, and den, when Michael learned to change, I sent for another."

"The old man," Maddy said. "Who is he?"

"He says his name is Kalos von Slacher. You won't find dat name anywhere but what he created."

"What does he want?" John Kelly asked.

The older woman rolled her eyes from one to the other without blinking. "Death," she muttered. "He bring death for de wolf."

"Does he know who—?"

Angelique Fontenot grabbed desperately for Maddy's shirt. Her eyes were wide and clear. "He know it Michael, chile, for some time. E'en before Michael come home. What von Slacher want to know was if anyone else knew."

John Kelly frowned. "Why would he…?" A look of realization cut his question short.

Maddy couldn't let it go unsaid. "He knows about us."

The old woman's eyes rolled back in her head and she hitched her breath twice, convulsing. Maddy and John Kelly sat at either side doing their best to support her.

"All us, chile. The whole town. He knows us all. He tole me, when he wadent beaten me, all our stories."

"Oh, God," Maddy said, nearly sick with understanding.

"A wolf done live alone. When de costume come off, it…" The next words trailed off as she struggled for breath.

John Kelly jostled her and tried to open her airway. She blinked and coughed again, her body lurching forward. Nearly doubled over she sat, slowly gaining control of her breath. Because she blinked, he relaxed a little.

"…lives," Maddy said.

Angelique nodded.

Maddy shook her head then turned angrily to the old woman. "He couldn't have wiped out that many people!"

"He couldn't?" John Kelly asked.

"She's suggesting von Slacher kills not just the werewolves, but anyone in his life."

"Dose close to him, yes. He smart, dis one. He like de chess."

John Kelly bobbed his head. "Yeah, and we a small community."

"We think there are others," Maddy said desperately.

Angelique heaved with finality. Her bulging eyes scanned Maddy's face. "He'll get dem all."

John Kelly reclined the chair and helped settle her. Her breathing eased some. Maddy knelt near and touched her cheek. "Miss Fontenot? Is there anything you can tell us about him? Anything at all?"

The old woman swallowed hard. John Kelly braced her, expecting another fit, but she didn't thrash. She lay back and closed her eyes. The next deep breaths rattled.

"Please," Maddy said. "How does he even know about these things?"

"He hunt dem for years. Followed de bloodline." Angelique's breathing was labored and slow. It was obvious to them her strength was fading. She could barely keep her eyes open, and her face had grown ashen and pale, the color of the statue still sitting in the town square.

"How did he know, though?" Maddy wondered aloud, not expecting Angelique to be able to respond much longer.

"Because, chile," she said. Her eyes remained closed. She took another deep breath. It would prove to be her last. "He is one." And with that, Angelique Fontenot slumped back with one final sigh and settled into death.

⊂⊱⊰⊃

In Arkansas, there is no shortage of stores selling ammo. In fact, after federal regulations grew stricter and retailers like Walmart put the kibosh on gun and ammo sales following the numerous shootings, mom-n-pop retailers spread like wildfire in defiance. Controlled by a conservative legislature, there was little pushback against these stores. Michael found one such establishment just on the outskirts of Monticello. He'd removed his car from the barn and driven northward, using Google maps. He had a list of guns and knew that if this dealer didn't have all the ammo he'd need, there would be others.

That Michael didn't look like the clerk's normal clientele didn't matter either. Sure, he felt the clerk's eyes on him. He'd walked into the store, the bell over the door ringing, a handmade sign written in sharpie on the glass reading, "Don't wear no mask in here," greeting him. The clerk was an older gentleman, nearly bald, what hair was left light gray and sheared military-short , dressed in baggy camos. He looked up from behind the desk where he sat, a portable TV on his side of the counter blaring One America News. Michael hadn't shown up in a pickup, wasn't dressed in Carhartt, overalls, camo, or even boots. He didn't have a beard, and when he spoke, he had no discernable dialect. When the clerk asked for his ID, Michael figured it was because he didn't look the part, and the man was more concerned with Michael being a DEA undercover than being underage. Still, the old codger wasn't one to miss a sale, and Michael's money spent like any other.

"Whatchya huntin'?" the man asked as he bagged the ammo boxes into several black plastic liquor bags.

"Wolves," Michael answered.

The man frowned at this. "Didn't think there were any in these parts 'til I heard about the killings. How many you think there are you gotta hunt?"

"More than one," Michael said.

The door's bell dinged again, and Michael and the old clerk turned together. A tall man, older, long white braided hair with a white mustache entered. Michael recognized him as the man who'd been out by the Fontenots, and instantly his blood ran cold. The hairs on his forearms stiffened. The man locked eyes with Michael and his nostrils flared.

"He'p ya?" the clerk said.

The man stepped forward, eyeing Michael up and down. "Yes," he said to the clerk, his eyes never wavering. "I was wondering if you had shells for a .410." He smiled a little, which unnerved Michael and made him take a step back. "I have a .410 over/under .22, sawed off. A riot gun. It can deliver a precise shot and stop nearly any living thing approaching with a peppering of shot. Maybe not enough to penetrate fur, but I'm told it hurts."

Michael mumbled a thank you to the clerk when the latter pushed bags of shells toward him, and, gathering them up in his arms, he cast his gaze outside only a second, but he could feel the stranger's eyes never left him. It felt as if the stranger bore down on him, looming over him. He was a head taller than Michael, but it was more than that, and more than his proximity to Michael, that felt intrusive. It felt as if the stranger had his scent somehow. Like he'd been tracking him and had locked onto him. Michael felt, in that moment, more like prey than he could ever remember.

"Thank you," Michael said again to the clerk, swallowing hard. He stepped around the stranger, who by now was not offering any kind of room. Michael nearly stumbled, rushing out of the store. As he reached his car door, he looked back to see he hadn't been followed, but he didn't breathe easier until he was in his car and driving away. Only then did he sigh and shiver. He turned the AC on high and felt the cold dry the sweat on his brow and upper lip. His hands gripped the steering wheel tightly to keep from trembling. The rearview mirror showed no one.

It was then he realized what the stranger had been driving. Michael had seen it upon leaving, but it hadn't registered with him until he began to cool down and relax. It was the old pickup that belonged to the Fontenots that had been parked in the gravel lot.

∞

For a moment, Maddy and John Kelly stood around her, looking down. The active silence, the willful moment of quiet and peace the siblings offered would probably be the only funeral this old woman would receive.

"We should go," John Kelly said to finally break the silence.

"Miles to go," Maddy quoted.

"No," he responded. "We just live down the road."

She shook her head. "Just pick up a book once while you're out in the forest."

He offered her one of his trademark corner smiles and they stood there another minute, looking over the old woman's dead body before exiting the trailer. The day had warmed some, and they could see a hint of the sun through the canopy of tree limbs above, but this was a false front for a day this late in the season. Halloween was coming, then the cold, short days and long, colder nights of November, and then winter would swoop in to finish off the year. Maddy wondered, as they loaded up in her car and pulled away, if any of them would even see the new year.

∞

Michael hesitated in his car, hands gripping the steering wheel tightly. Whatever sun Maddy and John Kelly glimpsed upon exiting the trailer quickly faded, for Michael only saw a solid ceiling of gray stretching from one horizon to the other. His footfalls crunched on the gravel, carrying him past the empty picnic tables that to an outsider might indicate Duke's was closed, though Michael knew its hours had never changed and probably never would for as long as it was in business.

The glass slid open and Michael was greeted with Amelia Livingston, beaming down on him. "Michael Risten," she exclaimed. "I heard you was in town. Stay there, child, and let me hug your neck."

She disappeared from the window. Somewhere out back, a wooden door slammed open then shut, and she could hear someone walking, and she appeared around the corner, arms outstretched, ready to bring him in. He welcomed her hug, the smell of her perfume and how it mixed with the smell of the kitchen, the way her flesh gave like soft padding as she embraced him. She was short and stocky and hadn't seemed to change in all the years he'd known her.

"What you hungry for?" Miss Amelia asked him.

"I just wanted to stop in and say hi," he said. He suddenly found it difficult to blink, and was pretty sure he had a skeletal look about his face, the way his eyes appeared sunken the last time he caught a glimpse of himself in the mirror, how his cheeks were drawn in.

"You look like death," she said, gripping his shoulders. "Duke, get this boy a burger and fries!"

"Michael!" Duke called from inside the building, then added, "Yes ma'am. Gladly."

Michael wasn't raised to turn down food, so he sat at the picnic table and ate as Amelia and Duke filled him in on the recent goings-on around town, about the Black Lives Matter movement. Michael had been aware of a lot of this, but only the scant details.

"Shit," Astrid Calhoun said. She'd been sitting out with them as well, and had muttered this expletive while looking over Michael's shoulder. Instantly, Duke and Emily's faces soured, and Michael could smell the deputy's cheap cologne and hear the dull thud of his heartbeat before he even spoke.

"What we got here?" Deputy Aaron Bailey asked. "Some kind of powwow going on? Michael Risten. How did I know you'd be sitting here?"

Michael, holding onto his burger and hunched over his plate, didn't turn to face the deputy at his shoulder. *The same way I knew you were walking up,* he thought.

"Well," the deputy began, as though they were all eager to join the conversation he'd been having with himself, "I guess what with Larsen's death, ol' Sarah is skipping town. Can't say as I blame her. Sheriff's death sure got us in a pickle. I can't rightly make up my mind what I should do with Derek in there. Don't know when I can get an escort to help me up with him to Monticello for his arraignment."

Michael had always steered clear of Aaron Bailey. The two never saw a reason to hang out. Bailey had been a bit of a bully back in school, and Michael was sure he'd only skated under the radar due to his family being killed, but he'd also been convinced that this never permanently secured his safety.

"I suppose," the deputy continued, slapping a hand down on Michael's shoulder that made Astrid jump, like he and Michael were old friends, "that whatever any of this means won't matter much, come tomorrow. Can't you all feel it? I know Michael and I can. Right, buddy?" The sound of his chest filling with air, his nostrils flaring, filled the silence. "Yessir, I can smell it. Change is coming.

Coming soon. Coming tomorrow. This town is ripe for a comeuppance."

He removed his hand.

"There ain't nothing wrong with this town," Duke Livingston piped up. "Just with its law."

"You better mind your manners, old man. You just better watch yourself."

"Or what? You'll do me like we all know you did Derek?"

"What happened to Derek?" Michael asked.

"Nothing," the deputy barked.

"Beat him senseless," Duke answered. "Got him all bloodied. Heard he bit you. First that bear attack, then Derek bit you. You won't make it out of this town going like that."

Bailey laughed. "You best not go on talking 'bout things you don't understand."

"Without that badge, you ain't got no bite."

"I got plenty of bite," Bailey said, sniffing the air. "You'll see. Tomorrow. And it weren't no bear, was it, Mikey? Nope. Not a bear at all."

Michael didn't have to turn around to hear him walk off. His senses attuned to the deputy as a carefree whistle drifted through the air.

"What's he talking about?" Amelia asked.

Michael took a deep breath, giving himself a moment to consider what he could tell them. "You need to leave town," he said finally, quietly. "Go to Monticello with your sister. Your kid. Just go."

"Michael…" Amelia said, startled by his insistence.

"All of you," he said, standing. He looked from Astrid to Amelia and then to Duke. To Astrid, he said, "Go and get Byron and just drive. If you need money, I can give you some."

"Michael, what's going on?" Amelia asked.

"This town isn't safe anymore," Michael said. "Just promise me you'll go."

None of them answered him, just stared mute to his plea. They each wore looks of pity mixed with weariness and still their resolute hardness. They all three, not just as Black folk but as citizens of this impoverished town, had toiled for years against insecurity and hardship, and their faces suggested they weren't prepared to give up now. He looked at them sadly, sure he would not be able to help them the next time he encountered them, when the moon would be high and the rest of the wolves would be out.

CR80

It wasn't unusual for Dart to sit up as they neared the house. The dog seemed keenly aware of its surroundings and knew, either by smell or sound or some combination thereof, when they were close to home, so Maddy thought nothing of it when the dog perked up as they turned down the street to their house.

But the dog issued a low growl as she readied to turn into the drive, The Fontenot vehicle parked at the curb. John Kelly pointed to the screen door, swinging on the hinge slowly in the soft breeze.

John Kelly checked that the revolver was loaded.

It was a fact John Kelly could better control the dog, but Maddy wasn't about to take the gun, so she reined in the leash as her brother led the way. Dart was pulling so hard against the leash that he was choking himself, and Maddy let a passing thought through—an admonishment that they should have put on his harness. John Kelly pushed the front door open and yelled, "Hey!" and all Maddy could see was his back. But he didn't fire the gun, and he didn't say anything else. She could hear another voice inside, though what was said was harder to decipher. Dart still pulled against the leash, his own vocalizations a mix of coughing, whimpering, and growl/barks. John stepped aside, looked back, and motioned for her to enter.

She was not happy to see the old man sitting in her father's recliner. Maddy entered to stand next to her brother, who took Dart's leash. *Because he is one*, the old Creole witch had said. Kalos von Slacher smiled up at them as if he hadn't a care in the world.

CHAPTER EIGHTEEN

"As I told your brother," the old man repeated for Maddy, "I'm not here to hurt you. But I do ask that you confess to me if either of you have been bitten or scratched by... a large canid-looking creature, recently."

The door was still open; Maddy could feel the day on her back. She imagined she could run, and John Kelly still held his gun in his hand, though now it was at his side, and this man—von Slacher—his hands were empty. Still, she thought if she tried to run, she would not be successful.

"You mean a werewolf," she said.

The old man's smile broadened. "Miss Fontenot called it the rougarou. I have grown accustomed to rougarou. 'Werewolf' sounds so... cartoonish. So clownish, doesn't it?"

"Sounds like some Lon Chaney bullshit," John Kelly said.

"Sit, children. I've sniffed out the infected before. You are clean. But you know him, don't you? The wolf? He is a friend of yours. Sit, and let me tell you a story that might shake that friendship to its core."

"Why would we believe you?" Maddy said. "We've known him all our lives."

Kalos von Slacher steepled his long fingers and regarded them for some time. In that moment, John Kelly reaffirmed his grip on his gun and cast a sideways glance to Maddy, who retrieved Dart's leash and cinched it around her hand. A disapproving *tsk* redirected their attention to the intruder.

"You'll never make it," he said. "Either of you. You, my boy, as I already told you, will not get one shot off before I slice your throat open. And you, dear sweet girl, will not run far before I am on top of you. I will split your mongrel's hide and entrails and devour the soft meat of your flesh. Oh, do not presume me so old that I could not accomplish these things. See my hands? The claws on my nails? They grow even now, under my sheer will. Something your friend cannot accomplish. Sit and hear me. If I were here to kill you, trust that you'd be dead already."

They exchanged another glance. Maddy wanted to burst into tears and, simultaneously, rip this man's face off with her own hands. He smiled at her as if he could read her thoughts. She remained seated, tugging Dart beside her. John Kelly sat where Michael had sat just a few hours earlier. Maddy could indeed see his claws. The nails had sharpened and darkened on his fingers, looking thick and razor-sharp. Hairs had sprouted on the back of his hands.

"It was you," Maddy said. "You killed those students at his college last spring."

"I could smell him. I've been able to smell him for a long time, in fact, even if I wasn't sure what he looked like. I could smell him there at the university, so I wanted to leave him a little present. Like a rat's head at the back door. A bunny with its neck broken."

"How can you…?" John Kelly began, watching the man's hands, the sheer will in the man's eyes that kept him from changing.

"I have not been tethered to the lunar cycles for quite some time. If Zeus turned Lycaon into a werewolf for serving him the remains of a young boy, what do you think happened to Pilate?"

Maddy couldn't hide her skepticism. "You trying to say you Pontius Pilate?"

This made von Slacher laugh. He laughed hard. He found something so unironically funny about her statement that his response totally disarmed her. Even John Kelly looked at her, and both were infected enough to crack a smile.

"Oh, dear, stupid child," von Slacher said, wiping a tear from his eye. "Not even remotely, though you won't believe my age if I told you. You see, humans and canines have been intertwined for eons. A better symbol for the ouroboros might be a dog chasing his own tail." He punctuated this with a laugh.

"Rougarou appear in many cultures. From the Nordic *Saga of the Volsungs* to France's obsession with the beast. Pierre Burgot and Michel Verdun. Giles Garnier—the werewolf of Dole. Peter Stubbe, of Germany. Even stories from Native American tribes and the middle- and far-east cultures. The Arabian Salu'ah. The wolf of Zhongshan. My children, man and canine have been in a state of symbiosis for as long as they've walked the earth."

"Michael was bitten?" John Kelly said.

Von Slacher waved him off with a chuckle. "No, young sir, he was not bitten. The Ristenoff family has run long with the blood of the canid through our veins. But I am getting ahead of myself. Allow me, children, to tell you how your friend truly came to be."

Maddy realized, as the story began to unfold, that she recognized the path it took, but still the details surprised her and thus held her attention while the older man spoke.

CR&O

The years following the death of Tepes, Voivode of Wallachia, were especially turbulent. Boyars loyal to various factions saw their loyalties questioned and challenged, and anyone who followed Tepes was not trusted. But I was one of his closest advisors and a member of the order, so I stayed loyal to the clan and to the son of the dragon.

It is important to realize what it meant to be a Catholic order in those days. There was not such a strict delineation between cultures and customs of old and the faith the Romans brought us. Magic was still useful on occasion incorporated by the local churches and orders.

Such was the case for the Order of the Dragon. Tepes' father had been knighted by the order years earlier, and well after his reign, their influence reached his son and the *boyars* loyal to the cause. We engaged in numerous ceremonies. Despre de Lupe. We skinned wolves and wore their pelts as our ancestors from the north had done, and we drank the blood of our sacrifices. We prayed to the darkness to grant our revenge. And nearly twenty years after his murder, we were granted it.

The wolf came into us. We no longer wore its pelts, but became it, feeling its power merge with ours. Under the light of an autumn moon, we stole nightly into the homes of the *boyars* that had profited from the death of the son of the dragon, and we slaughtered them in their sleep. We lapped at their blood and we feasted on the muscle and flesh. We howled when they screamed. We devoured them. Their wives. Their children. Until we'd cleansed Wallachia of all the traitors.

But my brethren did not stop there. They butchered those loyal to the *boyars*, and at first this was reasonable. They had aligned themselves with the enemy, after all. They had aligned themselves with those who would back the Turks, and they would suffer. It matters not who gives the order, children. Just the complacency. But as we tasted it more, we savored the taste of blood, and soon not all of us could be satiated. We spread our vengeance, to justify our thirst, to anyone who wronged us in the slightest. But one of my brethren said, finally, enough. We could not do this. At this time, we were unable to control the change; we were slaves to the bright moon. It did not have to be full, just bright, and only during the autumn months when the sun was furthest and weakest, so that little could detract from the lunar light, did we change. We begged for mercy, as we were unable to control our changes, but the truth is, deep down, we didn't want to control it.

It happened then that we were slaughtered. Those of us transforming were hunted down and destroyed. Some of us found amulets and sigils and potions to slow the transformation, to hide in public as we fled the wrath of the great hunter who, once like us, showed us no mercy and gave no quarter. The great hunter chased us out of Wallachia, pursued us across Europe, and eradicated us wherever he found us.

Now surely, you children, you hear me say "we" and think, *he could not mean himself, for how many years have passed since these events? Five hundred and twenty-seven years?* Remember, though, that I told you that wolves and man have lived in symbiosis for eons, and this is especially true for the Rougarou. For as man lives not quite a century, and a wolf only a fraction of that, together they can exponentially increase their longevity. The purer the blood, the truer this is. Those we bite and scratch, while still powerful, aren't nearly as strong as those born into the curse, and this is true the further the blood is passed on. In truth, I stumbled onto such a diluted pack that their pups were mewling, pink, hairless things wallowing in their deformity and weakness. Those I put down with the greatest sympathy, but...

And here, you realize something else, that while I spoke of the great hunter moments ago as though he were an entity plaguing me, it is true, you must have surmised, that I am that hunter. I could not stomach murder for the sake of satiating bloodlust, and I saw what a plague our kind could have been over this globe, so I set about to destroy them. First, I made sure that the rest of the order was extinguished. That their curses were not passed on. Then, one by one, over the course of this long life, I have systematically hunted and extinguished countless rougarou of the clan Ristenoff, and I have exterminated them. This was not as difficult as you could imagine. They ran but kept their name. It was easy tracking the Ristenoff clan from Wallachia to Austria, to Germany then France. Nearly two hundred years after the death of my Voivode, I slaughtered a clan of Ristenoff in a tiny French town. Their daughter had been hunting livestock and then the area children.

I patrolled Europe for years, constantly changing my identity, adopting name after name until I nearly forgot my own. And over time I learned to harness the power. I unyoked from the pull of the moon and found I could channel the Rougarou whenever I desired. This gave me even more strength to face my offspring and their impotent children. I outlived those I knew in the normal span of life, and hunted.

And then I found peace. I had exterminated the Rougarou curse across the entirety of Europe. I had staved off what would have been not just a plague against humanity, but the cause of its eradication. I resolved to live out the rest of my days.

For you see, children, while I have lived a long life, I am not immortal. I am, to be honest, approaching the end of my journey. I am ready to rest. I was tired even then. So imagine my surprise when I learned of the New World. From there, word of more strange deaths and more stories filtered across the ocean, and I realized my work was not yet done.

Oh, I was so at home in Europe. I could navigate the fjords of Iceland and the hills of Austria, scale the peaks of the Alps and swim in the lakes and ponds. I could speak the languages of the people so as to blend in, from Norway to Greenland, from the Baltic Sea to the Pillars of Hercules, but the new world confounded me. Its land was strange, I'd heard, and I would not navigate so easily. My clan had had time to adapt. They changed their name, shortening it to Risten, which I had not been aware of at the time. It wasn't much, but it had been enough to throw me off the scent when I first landed on the shores. I learned that the aboriginal peoples of this world also had their own legends. Tangential stories that were, nevertheless, separate from my own. Did this stop me, however, from exacting justice? No, for regardless of the Rougarou's origins, a plague was a plague. I'd seen whole villages leveled. Entire bloodlines eradicated from this creature's bloodlust. I felt the ghost of every one of my offspring's victims haunt my every hour. They would not let me rest until I'd brought them, each and every one, peace.

Realizing there were so many others, I found myself traveling the world. Our clan, the curse we helped seed and nurture, and the other legends, kept me busy. But I did not actively seek out my justice. If the world were silent, I trusted in its silence to allow me some solace, and even a few times attacks transpired that I let slide, out of fatigue or even, yes, the sheer hope that it wasn't a Rougarou. I knew, too, that I would always catch up with them. It was my destiny.

This, my young friends, is why I am here. Your friend must die, and the curse must die with him. What I do, I do for the sake of you, your children, and this world. We were a plague created for an act of vengeance, and our time has passed. We must be eradicated.

ᏨᎬᎤ

When von Slacher finished speaking, the room fell silent In fact, the whole of the earth seemed too quiet. Maddy was aware of no sounds outside. No birds sang. No traffic moved. No one inside or out spoke. There was no sign of life outside these walls, and inside none of them moved. Not even Dart twitched; he sat with his head on Maddy's thigh.

"The bloodline ends here," von Slacher said, a bit sadly. "And then I may rest."

"How you know?" John Kelly asked. "How can you be sure it'll die with Michael?"

"Michael is a good person," Maddy said, her voice low and just as sad.

"I have killed a great many 'good' people in my travels, my dear. The harm he can do outweighs the purity in his heart."

She kneaded Dart's head, looked down at the dog, who looked up at her.

"You mentioned amulets and potions," John Kelly said. "If they work, we can give him some. Keep him from changing."

"You love him," von Slacher said to Maddy, and when she looked up, she saw that he was looking down at the dog. His gaze might have been meant to look friendly, but Maddy still secured a protective arm around Dart, and the dog didn't pull away. John Kelly glanced at them and sat straighter.

"Yes," she said.

"We do," John Kelly said.

"Yet you would not chain him to the backyard every day all day, would you?"

"No, but he isn't killing people, either," Maddy countered.

"Precisely my point. Even though you love this animal like family, what if he were endangering the lives of others? Even as sweet as he is to you?"

Maddy glanced to the gun in John Kelly's hand, and John Kelly tried instinctively to conceal it on the other side of his lap.

"This is just as true for the Rougarou," von Slacher said, satisfied.

As he stood, Maddy found her voice. "But you slaughtered those college students. You've killed, too. Who made you the judge?"

"My dear girl," he said, smiling, staring down on her. "Who is there, if not me?"

Her flesh crawled and Maddy wished he'd turn that smile away from her. Even when he did, bidding them adieu, walking out of their home and shutting the door behind him, she still felt ill. She allowed herself to watch him from the window. Cross the lawn. Climb into his vehicle.

"He's going to find Michael before tomorrow," she said.

"He's going to kill him," John Kelly said.

☙❧

The camera buzzes. The upper loft of the barn comes into focus. Chains screwed into the wall can be seen in the background. Michael Risten sits on a bale of hay wearing jeans, a flannel, and just some ankle socks on his feet. He holds a remote in his hand.

"I'm Michael Risten," he says to start, then shakes his head. "I'm Michael, Michael Ristenoff. Let me tell you about the first time I changed into a werewolf."

ᏅᎬᎦ

I'm Michael Risten. I'm Michael, Michael Ristenoff. Let me tell you about the first time I changed into a werewolf. It was not, to be fair, expected. Not by me and not by my parents. I had been sick for nearly a week. It started as a pain in my joints, starting with my left wrist, then progressed up my extremities.

By the third day, I was unable to pull myself out of the fetal position, my stomach was cramping so. I'd felt something similar before, though not nearly as severe, whenever I ate anything that disagreed with me. As such food moved through my gut, peristalsis would push the remnants through my colon, causing intense contractions through my abdomen, but as painful as those times had been, nothing compared to this. I couldn't speak. I could barely let out more than a groan.

By the fourth day of that first time, I'd begun exhibiting changes. One of my older brothers walked in to check on me and saw that I'd grown what he thought was a full beard. Mind you, I was only twelve at the time. For me, the change came with puberty. When my parents rushed to my side, they saw my ears were pointier and covered in a fine but darkening mat of hair. I sported the smallest of nubs for a tail, and my jaw was now in severe pain as well, and appeared to be extending. I could hear little outside of the constant cracking and snapping of bones and cartilage. My body awash in pain, I could not tell you (even if I could talk) where the source of the pain was located. My joints felt ripped from their sockets, my muscles felt torn, my bones broken. I could barely utter a sound and was thankful only for the tears I was allowed to shed.

By the morning of the fifth day, it was apparent to anyone who'd watched any kind of horror film what was happening to me. My father left that morning as I lay mewling in my bed, promising to return with help. At the time, I shared a room with two brothers, but both had been relocated to another bedroom so I could wallow in solitude. I watched my fingers and toes elongate and well-defined nails like claws sprouted from my digits. Thick padding was forming on the soles of my feet and the palms of my hands. My mother crossed herself when she saw a canid muzzle for my mouth and nose, and that some of my teeth had fallen out, leaving only the sharpest of canines cutting through my gums.

At the same time, my senses were coming alive. I could hear the blood flow through the veins of anyone in my vicinity. If multiple people crowded about, as was the case with my siblings and parents, then I could hear all of their susurrations or I could focus on one and block the others out. I heard the electricity in the wires and the water in the pipes of the house. I could feel the temperature of everyone near me. I could smell my mother's time of the month, the brother who'd most recently ejaculated in the solitude of his bathroom with one of my father's old adult magazines, the food in the fridge. Over the course of the week, my vision had been shifting as well. While I could still see in daylight, I could also see in the dark better than I usually could. And while shades of red and green faded from my visual palette, I saw more defined features and could detect motion easier. My first kill, in fact, had been a mouse scampering across my floor when I thought I was too weak to move. This had happened on the third night, when I caught the blur of movement out of the corner of my eye, heard the creature's heartbeat, the click of its tiny nails on the hardwood. My hand snatched out lightning-quick and scooped the rodent into my jaws. What was left of it, my mother found that next morning.

My father returned in the afternoon with a local witch. That isn't nice of me, perhaps. She was an older woman who lived with her brothers on the outskirts of town. She was believed to practice some brand of Creole magic, and in fact admitted as much herself to us, not for the first time on that day she saw my transformation.

She recognized my condition immediately and asked my father when I was bit.

"I… was… n't," I managed. She looked at my father for clarification, who only shook his head.

He told her I'd fallen ill the week before, but assured her I had not been attacked.

She asked how many sons my parents had, and my father told her I was the youngest of seven.

This, she explained, was a part of the curse also. It is possible to curse a family, to visit upon them the curse of the Rougarou by infecting their offspring. Not much later, I could hear my father with her outside, by the barn. They were out of range of the rest of the family, but I could hear them. I heard my father ask her if she did this. Heard him shake her and ask if she was responsible because of how he'd rejected her. How she'd been a mistake to visit, that one night. That if she or her brothers told anyone, especially his wife, he would kill her and them. He told her she better fix me, and to this – and perhaps to all his threats – she laughed.

"Dis town gone get what's comin' to dem," she said, laughing. This apparently depowered my father, because I heard next her footsteps leading off into the forest, her laughter growing more faint until her voice carried from far away a warning to my father he would soon heed. "Best lock him up before de full moon 'morrow night!" she said.

After boarding up my windows and bracing my door, my family listened to the final moments of my change the next evening. They heard me thrashing, heard me snarl and growl and yip and bark. They heard me slam the weight of my body against the walls, the boards, the door, in a desperate plea to get out. This, I should tell you, I don't remember. They shared this with me after I... returned. At the time, despite knowing the legends and what the movies said, they weren't sure I'd come back. They also realized they couldn't spare an entire room for my change when we had such a large family, and my temporary prison, once we learned it was temporary, could not be housed in such proximity to the rest of them.

My change lasted nearly as long as the sickness. By day I rested, reverting back somewhat but not fully, but by night my energy had returned and I resumed working my escape. The me that is me dreamed of running through the woods and of longing to get out. I dreamed of what flesh must take like. Raw, living flesh, still encasing a beating heart, still thrumming with life from the blood flowing through the tissue. Would another creature taste different than the mouse? Or would they all taste the same? Like chicken?

I dreamed of my family. I dreamed of hurting them, of the various ways I could kill them. I dreamed graphically of the ways they would eventually die. These things stuck with me, even as the actions of the wolf eluded me. I could not know what it did, what it said (yes, *said*) when it was in control. Not until my parents told me. But I could remember these things. I had yet to take a human life, so I wasn't yet to understand those repercussions, and I think now that my dream experience of their future slaughter was a kind of prognostication of the inevitable made of the same ectoplasm of the spirits of the past. It was the future ghost that haunted me, not unlike how the ghosts of my victims haunt me now.

When I awoke, finally, I remember being thirsty. I was sore from the constant phase-shifting of my body, but not nearly as in pain. What I felt now was more of a dull ache, like I'd spent too much time at the gym. My family told me what happened. For a time, they kept me locked up at night in my room until my father and brothers completed the loft for me. I spent many nights in the barn loft—here—in these chains, during those early months of my first transformations. We didn't realize at first that I would only change in autumn, so by that summer, when I hadn't changed anymore, they trusted me to sleep in my bedroom at night. My brothers even returned to share the room, until, as that first autumn pressed on, I started to get sick again.

In those early days, we were diligent. My mother kept a journal of my changes. We quickly understood the parameters of my transformation. We knew I was safe during the day, reverting back to full normal, and we knew by what hour in the evening I needed to be shut away. My father or one of my brothers would bring me raw meat or chicken to satiate me on those nights, and by the first of the next year, we learned what season would most trigger my altered state. We corroborated as much as we could with the old witch and with internet research. She gave me a potus—a kind of potion—to tamp down the pain and lessen the effects of the transformation. She did these things because my father threatened her, and said he'd go talk to the mayor and get her and her brothers arrested if she didn't. One mention of Bob Larsen and she was ready to assist us. The potus tasted nasty, but it worked, or I thought it did. She confided in me once that she had a medallion made of silver that I could wear. It hung on a rope made of hemp and wolfsbane and it would keep me from changing. She promised me this thing, but I never saw it. Before she could deliver it to me, I would massacre my entire family.

CRSO

Michael pushed pause on the remote, and the red light on the camera began to blink slowly. Double-checking the camera's screen, Michael saw his own visage, frozen, and he walked over to the window and stared out to the forest and field beyond.

How he longed for one more gaze into the sunlight. This, he knew, staring at the clouds above, he would be denied. He wanted to see his friends again. Wanted to feel normal again. Except, he'd forgotten what that felt like. The only road to normalcy led through death, so that must be the next stop. He faced this truth once more with a bit of sad resignation.

Behind him there was a noise. He turned to see the old man standing in his loft, at the ladder. He held a pistol in his hand.

"Hello, Michael Ristenoff," Kalos von Slacher said. "It's nice to finally meet you."

Then he raised the gun, aiming it at Michael, and pulled the trigger five times. Each bullet hit Michael in the chest and sent him careening out the window backwards to the ground below. His vision went black, and he was unaware of hitting his head on the ground. All he thought, before consciousness abandoned him, was that death had finally been delivered.

CHAPTER NINETEEN

October 31st

Consciousness slowly returned to Michael Risten, first as sound and smell and feeling, and lastly as sight. A muddled blur of light and shadow, then lines, growing more distinct. He heard first the clang of metal somethings being dropped in a ceramic bowl. Smelled herbs, and stranger smells like chemicals and seasonings unfamiliar to him, and then the perfume of Maddy Jeansonne. Not just what she wore, but her smell. Her unique identifier. Then he picked up John Kelly's scent, and finally his eyes opened.

John Kelly stood by the door of Angelique's trailer, looking between the blinds of the neighboring window. Maddy sat next to him, holding his hand. He smelled something else: flesh in the early stages of rot, then saw the collapsed and lifeless form of Angelique Fontenot crumpled in the corner. His chest was on fire, each place where the bullets scarred him inflamed and pulsing. But something else, a weight. Michael looked down and saw someone had placed around his neck a kind of necklace.

It was silver, a pentagram, and the corded necklace from which it hung was made of a fibrous material his sense of smell identified as a combination of hemp and wolfsbane.

"How?" he started. Maddy shushed him.

"We got there right when he shot you," she said.

"I put three bullets in him myself," John Kelly said, not taking his eyes off the window. "Third one between the eyes put him down, but I don't think it killed him."

"It didn't," Michael said. "I can feel him."

"You've been sleeping," Maddy said. "We brought you here. Thought it'd be easier, and we could find something to help you."

Michael looked at the amulet around his neck. "She told me about this. Said it would keep me from changing."

"It worked," Maddy said. "Put it on you when we got here last night, and you didn't change at all. I had enough time to pull the casings out of your chest."

"You thrashed a bit," John Kelly said. "We tied you to the chair. But released you when you stopped thrashing. But yeah, you never changed."

"I found a recipe book," Maddy continued, still kneeling beside him. Something nudged his hand, and he looked over and saw Dart demanding to be pet. Michael obliged. "I think I found the recipe for whatever she was making you drink."

"It wasn't working," Michael said.

"She was leaving out an ingredient, I think. She wanted you out, so she made it without the wolfsbane. But if you include it, then it should work. She's got all the ingredients here."

There lay over him a fog so thick, his mind felt cloudy and his tongue and digits numb and fat. "What are you…"

The thoughts formed in his mind and puffed away like campfire smoke. Sounds washed up around his ears like ocean waves at the changing of the tide.

"We can help you not to change while we finish this," Maddy said.

"What day is it?" Michael asked, and when they told him, he sat upright. "Tonight's the full moon!"

Maddy was at his side, trying to ease him back into the chair. "Michael, what's wrong—"

"You have to leave," he said. He pulled himself out of the chair. John Kelly tucked his gun in his belt and grabbed his shoulders. "You have to get out of town. We don't have much time."

"Michael!" Maddy said. "This will help you."

"No! Nothing will. The pull of the moon is too great. I can feel it even now. Please, you don't have much time. You need to leave!"

They heard a car door slam, and all three froze. The first to move, John Kelly returned to the window and muttered a curse. "Someone's here," he said.

CRSO

Deputy Bailey had heard older officers talk of how much freer they were, back in the day, and now, listening to the incessant call of Derek Evans from his cell, he wished he could enjoy such freedom. Who would care, besides Evans's old grandmother, if Bailey walked back to the cell and pulled out his regulation .38 and put one between Derek's eyes?

"You feel it, dontcha?" Derek Evans said from the cell. This wasn't the first time Derek had asked this question. He'd been growing more and more restless all morning.

For his part, all Bailey could feel was annoyance and this aggravated kind of restlessness boiling in the pit of his stomach. He was anxious. His fingers drummed on the air and he couldn't stop pacing about the room, but he always stayed away from Derek's cell. Something made him uneasy, going near those bars. Derek made him uneasy, but he didn't like admitting that. So he stayed away, for as much good as that did seeing as they were in one large room, content to fantasize about clawing Derek's flesh off and gouging out his eyeballs with his fingers.

"Yeah, you feel it. You feel it calling to us. Things are changing, soon. We both know it and we both know we both know it. We can smell it on each other."

Every hour, Derek had gotten a little further into this harangue. This was the first time he'd mentioned smelling each other.

"Smell what?" Bailey asked.

"The violence," he replied, and when the deputy looked at the prisoner, he was surprised to see how still Derek stood and how confidently he wore that toothy smile. "You want to claw my face off. You want to play with my intestines. You want to fuck my eye holes. You dirty, dirty cop. Wanna know what I wanna do to you?"

Bailey turned away and looked out the window. They'd be gathering in the square again soon, at sundown (*moonrise*). If this were any other town, the protest wouldn't occur on a night when kids would be running around, but he could count on one hand the number of children in this town and knew historically they drove to Monticello for trick-or-treating. *They want to tear down the statue of the general. Want to destroy our history. Just erase it like it, and by extension we, never mattered.* He was tired of it, to tell the truth. He'd been tired of it for a while now. Black lives matter. And white lives don't? Cops' lives don't? How many police had been gunned down in Little Rock or Jonesboro or Pine Bluff or West Memphis by Black lives? By thugs and hooligans listening to their shitty rap music and acting like their heroes, the Crips and Bloods? West Coast and East Coast. Goddamn coasts could keep that gangster shit, as far as Bailey was concerned.

All they had to do was obey. Comply when an officer gave them an order. Don't talk back. Respect my badge and I'll respect you. Except, to be honest, Bailey was tired of respecting others. He was tired of playing nice. For as much as it offered him, the badge also leashed him. Kept him from being the officer he wanted to be. The officer he—and Blue Rock—needed him to be.

"Just take it off," Derek Evans said.

Aaron Bailey took a deep breath. "Take what off?"

"The badge. Your mask. I know what you did a few nights ago. I know you found that chicken farm. I lived it with you. Could taste the blood you tasted. All from within here. Just like you and I can taste the other. He out there. Every kill. Every drop of blood he spills. We can taste it."

"Michael Risten," Aaron muttered. He'd heard rumor the boy was back, and then he saw him just yesterday, out without a care in the world, snacking at Duke's place across the way. Derek was right. It was Michael who'd made them. Aaron had known it for a while now. Michael, who had been a pipsqueak back in school, had turned into this thing, and now he'd gone and passed it along to Aaron, and Aaron had passed it along to Derek, apparently. And who...

"Byron," Aaron whispered so that the name was formed more from the shape of his lips than any sound.

"Byron Calhoun," Derek Evans said. "Just how'd you get your blood in him? He a little swisher, ain't he. A faggot. You a faggot too, Deputy? You wanna fuck me, Deputy?"

"Shut up," Bailey said, his voice low. In his fingers, he clinched the tilt wand to the blinds he now stared through, and he twisted it slowly back and forth so that the blinds turned up then down, fanning the light from outside through the room.

"We been caged like dogs for some time now, Deputy, but tonight, we get to break loose. Tonight, when the moon rises, when all the little kids up in Monticello are putting on their Halloween masks, we get to take ours off."

Yes, Bailey realized. It was Halloween. It was also a full moon tonight, the second full moon this month. A blue moon, his grammy used to call it.

"That your plan?" Bailey asked. "Get out and run up to Monticello and torment the people up there?"

"Why not?" Derek said. "After I kill you, of course. Munch yo giblets like chicken liver."

Could Derek get out? The jail was old, but the iron bars were still set firm in concrete. Perhaps, after the change, it wouldn't be enough to hold him. Yes, Aaron thought. He was sure Derek meant to kill him, but this didn't upset the deputy like one might think. He remained calm, collected. How many people had threatened him in the years past? The last one he could think of was this uppity doctor who lived in El Dorado about five years earlier who was passing through on his way to Monticello. Aaron had caught him speeding through this patch of interstate, had pulled him over and run his tags, and issued him a citation. The doctor cursed him and threatened his job, his badge. Aaron had listened, laid his palm on the butt of his gun, and positioned his body at the driver's side window to best stage this for the ranting driver. The doctor, blustering, understood the wordless threat and shut up. Still, to stick the point, Aaron had followed him out of the town limits, turning across the median to head back to Blue Rock just after the last exit leading to town. Had he the right to issue a speeding ticket on the state highway? The way he saw it, if no state trooper was going to park it this stretch (and they never did, having entrusted it to him years ago) then he not only had the right, but it was his obligation.

After that, he went home and drank a six pack and punched the punching bag hanging on his back porch, imagining that doctor's face. He'd run the tag and gotten the man's personal information. Married three times. Three kids, five grandkids.

His patrol car could be found on the highway over the next few days, looking for that BMW with the vanity plate. The extent of it came just a few days after, still thinking about that blowhard's tirade, when he'd driven his personal vehicle to the man's address one balmy evening, parking outside, noting the residential layout, the Beamer in the open garage. He caught sight of the man walking in front of the living room bay window. Bailey had unhooked the holster strap on his personal issue weapon, the magazine full, and imagined walking up to the man's door—*AH-NOLD* style—and putting a bullet in his smug brain. He didn't, of course, but that's how close he'd come.

That wasn't the only time he'd reacted so personally to a citizen not being elated to see him arrive on the scene. There was that time with Chantal and her boss down at the strip club. Aaron had pistol-whipped the man behind his business so badly he had needed stitches. That time, cops from that area came up to have a talk with Aaron. They weren't really threatening (they knew the dude he'd beat up was a scumbag) and Aaron Bailey wasn't threatened by them. He wasn't threatened, in his mind anyway, by anyone, really. He got pissed when people treated him like the kid they'd seen grow up here, or when they dismissed the badge. Aaron knew he had a temper; he'd resolved that with himself a long time ago and had no intention of changing.

So why couldn't he feel that fire in his belly? Derek had made some vulgar threats, and the two had already come to blows. Derek was strong, muscular, but so was Aaron. He wasn't scared of him. If anything, he longed for an excuse. But whatever was in him, clawing to get out and feeling the blue moon couldn't rise soon enough, had in its creation and on the eve of its fully realized birth finally robbed him of that passion. He felt sluggish and empty, turning the heat and fury and emotion over to the wolf birthing inside of him. He had lately only been able to relish in the aftermath of the feeling of the wolf's nightly patrols. He could not remember what it had done to Remy Doucet or his uncle or his uncle's chickens, but he could remember the feeling it felt at the time, and that had sustained him. But it was like receiving lukewarm leftovers after dining on fresh-cooked delicacies. Yes, it was filling him up, but it wasn't as satisfying.

This, then, begged the question: Why was Derek so elevated? Perhaps the wolf takes the persona of the person it infects. Perhaps, because Derek's inner wolf was just emerging, he was at a different stage than Bailey. This idea suited Bailey just fine, because it just reassured him that things would not go the way Derek Evans thought this evening, When the moon rose, when Bailey would start to change, he'd take the key off the ring and unlatch Derek's cell, and then he'd teach that big bad wolf a thing or two. Yessir. Derek Evans would be taught dominance.

CRICO

Amelia Livingston could not tear her eyes away from the police station across the square and watched it through the emptiness of space signaling no one was lining up at Duke's this late morning.

Behind her, Duke washed dishes and pulled double duty, manning the grill to prepare for the day. She had already counted out the till, prepared the deposit from the day before, and updated the books, as was her responsibility. But something felt different today. The clouds above were low and the day was cool and dry. From only god knows where drifted in the smell of burning wood or brush, that definable smell of the season. There was so much of the day that felt normal, she could not pinpoint what was off, but she was sure something was. It gnawed at her from the inside. She'd rubbed the wear off her knuckles, worrying so, the fingers of her hands twisted into some kind of humanoid rat king shape. She could not see into the police station. Bailey's cruiser was out front, but he'd not stepped outside, and the panes of glass were too dark to reveal the interior. Derek Evans was still in there. Those two locked inside a room together was anyone's notion of a powder keg. And that was some of the source of her disquiet, but not all of it.

The phone clicked on the cradle behind her. "What is it?" Duke asked.

"He still ain't answerin'," Astrid said.

"Byron?" Amelia said, a bit dreamily, trailing behind the conversation some.

"Yes'm," Astrid said. An hour earlier, the only patron to Duke's Place was not someone wishing to be served, but the guidance counselor from Byron's school. She'd driven down after not being able to reach or speak to Astrid about Byron. He hadn't been at school for some time, and this wasn't like him, and she was worried. This of course shocked Astrid, who'd not been aware he'd been missing, so she started trying to call home. The guidance counselor had left without ordering so much as a coke.

Since then, there hadn't been any foot traffic or any cars passing. People knew they were open. But this was a sign of season. Every year around this time, they adjusted their winter hours because people didn't just come early in the day and it was too expensive to keep it open. This drop-off of patrons was happening within average parameters. Still, it only enhanced the disquiet, and Amelia couldn't shake the notion that after this particular time, no one would come back to Duke's.

"Maybe you should go check on him," Duke suggested before Amelia could offer the same. It was Amelia that Astrid came to.

"Oh, is that okay, miss? I'd be so grateful. That boy—I just don't know what's going on with him. He's such a good boy, norm—"

"Is fine," Amelia said, not moving from her perch or looking around.

Astrid thanked her, snatched her keys off the table by the cutting board where she'd stored her purse, and bolted out the back of the building, her car sputtering to life not long after.

"Why she double-check with you?" Duke asked. "They always do that." "They" being Astrid, Remy, Vicky. "Damn place got my name on it, ain't it?"

Amelia didn't respond. She was thinking about Astrid and about her own daughter, living up in Monticello full time. Something itched at her. A feeling like she ought to take a drive north and visit her child grew to a desire she did not want to shake.

"This statue," she said then, picking at the errant strands of torn paper on the order pad under her right palm with the fingers of her left hand. "You think it worth it? You think this town'll change?"

From the sound, he'd been back at the grill, using the metal spatula against the griddle's cast-iron top, the sizzle of grease. Hell, the smell was something familiar like a lover's perfume. It clung to them both well after they closed the diner, followed them home, haunted their bedroom like a ghost long after their clothes were washed and their heads had been shampooed.

She heard him set the spatula down. Over the sizzle, she heard him sigh. Out front, still no cars passed. A few leaves blew down the street; she could almost hear them scraping the asphalt. The town was silent, as if consumed by a dirge.

"Don't know," he said. She thought that was it, but he added, "Bob Larsen got a burger last week, before he was kilt. We got to talking."

"Saw y'all talking," she said. They'd shot the shit like old buddies, though she knew Duke couldn't stand the man. The spatula resumed its rhythmic, percussive work on the sizzling grill.

"You know what he told me? Said, 'Duke, I don't understand this protesting. Dr. King didn't protest like this. Why this all being brought up again?' like everything was settled back then with the Reverend. Like we'd 'voiced our concerns'—that's the words he used, *voiced our concerns*—and it was all settled. Said it was uncivilized. What do white folk know about 'uncivilized' anyway. They see anyone living different from how they live and think it's uncivilized. Never mind how they been running shit for years." All the while, during his tirade, the spatula kept pace with his quickening words.

"Something's coming," she said, nearly a mumble. It didn't sound like a response to him at first, she thought, but then she realized it really was. "Bess Louviere used this word once. We was reading this book in our book club by an author named Wilkerson I think, and we'd been talking about race, and Bess Louviere said there was gone be a reckoning. That's the word she used. 'Reckoning.'"

"What an old, rich, white woman know about that anyway?" he asked. He'd never thought much of Bess Louviere. He didn't dislike her, not that Amelia could tell. More like, Duke could take her or leave her. So, she showed up on their side at the protests. So what. He'd told Amelia more times than she could count that if Bess Louviere got that much money writing books, she ought to take that money and really support the causes she said she did. It was easy to talk a good game. Harder to back it up.

"A reckoning is coming," Amelia said. "I can feel it, Duke. Cain't you? Like blood in the water."

From behind, she heard the sound of the metal spatula dropping on the grate and the gas burners clicking off, the flames whooshing away as if blown out. She heard the towel on his flesh, then felt his strong, calloused hands on her shoulders. She knew then he knew what she was saying.

"No one's coming today," he whispered.

"No," she agreed. People were staying in their homes or not venturing down here. Like the town was cursed.

The finality of it sank in, that come the next morning, they may not be in business anymore. But whatever was coming was more dangerous than that. Whatever was coming, if they stayed here, they may not live through the night.

"Go to yo' sister's in Monticello," he said. "Go home and pack what you need, and throw a few things in a suitcase for me too. Then go."

"What're you gone do?"

"I'm gone go find Rayburn," he answered.

She nodded, reached up, and wiped furiously at a tear threatening to streak down her cheek. Lo and behold, there was another behind it, and her other eye was welling up too. Even his strong hands weren't enough to keep her from trembling.

She reached up and closed the window, flipped the sign from open to closed, and realized unceremoniously that this might be the last time she'd ever do that.

"What are we gone do, Duke?" she asked.

His hands rubbed her shoulders. She heard him breathe. Deep, slow sounds as the air passed through his nose. They had a little savings, but it wouldn't last long. However tonight turned out, they might be able to sell the business. Maybe even their home. He'd kept up the maintenance on it, and kept it clean. It was small, but it was paid off, and would probably fetch them a decent price on the market. It wouldn't be enough to retire on, no doubt, but it would get them by until they figured out what else to do. Whatever it would be, it would not involve Blue Rock, Arkansas. She was sure of that.

CR&SO

Emily Evans received two visitors when she was expecting none, and so she'd hurried to brew a pot of coffee and warm up some pound cake for her guests. Bess Louviere, who was near her in age, helped her set up two chairs to join her on her front porch, and Sarah Larsen sat amenably but without touching the cup of coffee poured for her. Bess had been the first to arrive, banging on Emily's door, telling her without so much as a "Good morning" that she'd spoken to an attorney up in Monticello who agreed to look into Derek's charges. That's when preparations began for the coffee and cake, all while Emily Evans juxtaposed "Thank you" with statements questioning if she could afford some big city lawyer. Bess had reassured her, setting herself to help prepare the provisions. When Emily had asked for the third or fourth time just how much such a lawyer might cost, Bess laid a hand on Emily's arm and said it was taken care of.

"He shouldn't have been locked up so long," Bess said. "I'm just sorry I haven't been able to help."

"It weren't yo place," Emily said. She weren't no charity case, and she didn't much appreciate being made to feel like one neither. That being said, she also knew she was no help to her grandson. She didn't own a smartphone, much less a computer, and the few lawyers she'd managed to call didn't want to take the case knowing he had a record, charged more than she could afford, or didn't seem interested in speaking with an old Black woman from a no-name town.

Then someone else knocked on her door, and Bess rushed to open it, and Sarah Larsen walked in. Another woman with trouble, Emily thought. She knew all too well what had been preoccupying both women lately. Bess was mourning the loss of her niece after that vicious attack, and Sarah was probably realizing what life was like after Bob's own death. Lots of death lately, in fact. Too much for a town this size. That was a while ago. Now, sitting on the porch between the two, sipping her coffee, she thought about death and sorrow and imagined that's all life had to give if you lived long enough. Across the way, Astrid's little rusted sedan skidded across the gravel to a stop and she hurried out, not even stopping to wave to them as she ran inside her trailer.

"That boy ain't been gone to school," Emily said.

"What's wrong with him?" Bess asked.

"I think that deputy did something to him," Emily said. "Something... wrong."

The sip of coffee. Sarah still hadn't touched hers. Emily regarded the younger woman, then her car, packed to the brim with all sorts of things. She figured Sarah wouldn't be at the Black Lives Matter march tonight or at their next book club. Something ate at her, said maybe Miss Emily ought to pull up stakes also. But Emily quieted that feeling quickly. As long as her own flesh and blood was locked up, she wasn't going nowhere.

"Got a realtor coming to look at the house," Sarah said then, as if either of them had gone ahead and asked about the car. "Thinks I ought to get enough to pay off what's left of the mortgage and have enough to live on."

Go on then, Emily thought. *I tell you some little Black boy was hurt by the local racist cop and you know my boy is locked up by that same cop and all you care to talk about is how much money you gone make when you sell your house 'cause yo abusive husband been murdered like I should feel sorry for yo' white self.*

The front door to Astrid's trailer flew open and Astrid stepped outside. "Help me, please!" she called to anyone in earshot. "Byron's sick!"

Chet, who'd been working on his old truck, pulled himself from under the hood and raced over. Chantal's own door flew open and she raced outside also. Emily struggled to stand and Bess stood next to her, but Sarah stayed seated, staring at nothing. None of them moved closer.

Chantal Bailey and Chet disappeared inside, and Chet reappeared with Chantal and Astrid trailing him as he carried Byron. The boy was listless and shivering violently, and looked ashy pale. He looked like he was having a seizure.

"In here," Emily commanded, and the two groups joined, Chet carrying the boy up her porch steps and into her living room, laying him on the couch. Emily directed Bess to her closet down the hall, and Bess returned with an afghan that she draped over the boy.

"Baby," Astrid said, kneeling by him.

"Get the boy some water," Emily directed. This time it was Chantal who obliged. When her family situation was a bit larger, Emily had always taken such a role, barking orders like a battlefield general, and everyone around her always listened.

"We need to get him to a doctor," Chet said, but Astrid shook her head.

"We cain't afford that!" Astrid wailed.

"What happened to him?" Chantal asked. Her face looked pinched and she chewed her nails. Emily thought she had the answer somewhere in there and she just didn't want to say it out loud. She directed the girl to her medicine cabinet and dosed the boy with some liquid Tylenol. Once that was done, she made him drink some more water. She told Bess where to find her thermometer and his temperature ran hot, well over one-hundred. Chet reiterated again about getting him to the hospital up in Monticello, but something told Emily that wouldn't help. In some ways, she thought, it could make matters much, much worse.

When he settled some, not long after the Tylenol, she said, "We'll let him rest here. Astrid, if you need to get back to work, go on. He's in good hands here."

"No ma'am," Astrid said. "I'll stay if it's okay with you."

"Suit yourself," Emily said. She'd grown accustomed to her quiet home even as she'd settled back into that role of familial commandant, but something told her the latter was here to stay and she wouldn't be alone anytime soon. "Bess, you put on another pot of coffee. Sarah, if you staying, make yourself useful and help in the kitchen. People need to eat."

"I'm leaving," Sarah said. "And you all should too."

Eyes turned to her. Sarah bit her lip and still would not meet anyone's gaze. "Look at all this death. Tom was mauled by some wild animal. Casey Davidson is murdered, and y'all find her dad dead. Our deputy is attacked. Bess, your niece is killed, and so is Remy Doucet and his uncle, and Doctor Bellanger and then the sheriff and my Bob. People are talking. Saying we're infested by rabid bears or even wolves. People have heard things. Strange things. Chickens slaughtered. We all know it. We all know something is here and it's coming for us. It might've gotten poor Byron here. It'll get all of us one way or another. And this ain't the first time. They say Michael Risten is back, and we all know what happened to his family."

At first, no one said anything.

"You wanna leave, then leave," Emily said. "Same goes for all of you. But it's a damn tragedy what's been happening—"

"It ain't a tragedy!" Sarah said. "People ain't sick. That boy ain't sick. There's something wrong here. You all know it!"

"Now let's settle down," Chet offered, but Sarah turned on him.

"Don't you tell me what to do," she snapped. There was a fire in her eye, something Emily couldn't ever recall seeing. "We all know Michael Risten's to blame."

"So what?" Bess asked. "You think we should take our pitchforks and torches and go burn down his house and run him out of town?"

"He killed my Bob!" Sarah nearly screamed.

"Your Bob deserved it," Emily responded. "If anyone deserved it, your Bob did. Look what he did to you, girl. All those years. Bob, and that damn deputy, they ain't nothing but a plight on this earth."

"Now my brother—" Chantal started to say, like she was going to defend him.

"Your brother did that," Emily said, turning on her, pointing down to the now sleeping Byron. "You know it and I know it too. I can see it in your face. Jesus only knows what he's doing to my poor Derek all locked up there."

"Stones and glass houses," Bess said. "Your Derek may not deserve how he's being treated, but he is a convicted criminal and he certainly isn't a saint."

Emily stopped cold and stared at the old white woman. Her lip quivered and she felt a tear in her eye. "Naw," was all she could manage at first. "You wanna help him, and that's how you feel. Keep your damn lawyers."

"It isn't how I feel," Bess said. "It's the truth."

"You don't know what Derek's been through. What his life been like."

"I don't care," Bess said. "I feel bad for him and what happened to him, Emily, but at some point, he has to be responsible for his choices. We all do. I do, you do, Vicky did. We can't use what happened to us in our past to excuse our current actions."

"It ain't the past," Chet said. "Not for some of us. For some of us, what happened in the past is still happening now. It don't ever get better."

"I'm not talking about race," Bess countered. "I'm not talking about a group of people. Individually, I mean. We are responsible for our own actions."

"But you can't separate the two," Chet said. "For us Black folk, what happens to us as a people impacts what happens to us as a person."

"My baby," Astrid said. She was curled up on the floor next to the sofa, one hand patting the sweaty brow of her son, the other draped across his chest, his shoulder. "He didn't ask for this. Didn't ask for none of this."

Chantal asked, "What is happening to him?" She forced out every word as though she were begging for an answer. Emily felt the word form in her mind, something she hadn't heard in years. She thought then of the Fontenots out on the edge of town. They would know the word.

Byron was sweating now more, crying out some, garbled, muddled sounds no one could make out. His breathing came fast, his chest hitching with each inhale. He made little whimpering sounds.

"Oh, my baby!" Astrid cried, hugging him.

"I know you said you can't afford it, but this boy needs a hospital," Chet said.

"No." It was Sarah. Her voice was calm. She stared at the boy. "No. He's... he's like him, isn't he. He's like Michael Risten."

"What are you talking about?" Chantal asked.

"Loup garou," Emily Evans said. "My pappy used to talk of 'um, way back when. I was a bit of a thing. We was warned, you don't go out by the swamp at night, not when the moon is bright and high up in the sky. Or the Loup garou will get ya."

"What are you talking about?" Chantal said.

"Loup garou," Emily Evans whispered, like a chant. "We could hear them off in the distance some nights. Howling to the moon. Their sounds carried across the peat moss and through the pine to our ears, daring us to come outside."

"Miss Emily. What—" Bess tried.

"Angelique Fontenot knew it," Emily continued. "She knew what that boy was. How Michael Risten was the seventh son born, and what that means. She told me once. I laughed, so convinced it was an old wive's tale. Then, ten years ago, that terrible thing happened to his family. Kilt like they were. Like some wild animal just ripped them all to shreds. And I guess I knew then, but I was minding my own business, out here at the trailers."

"What is it?" Chantal asked. "What is a loup garous?"

Emily looked to the others in the room. Chet knew. She could see it in his eyes. Bess knew too. But Astrid only turned a pleading, desperate look up to the old woman. Sarah wore a bit of a satisfied smile as if she'd won an argument.

"A Loup garou," Bess said, not breaking her gaze from Emily, "is a werewolf."

Chantal let out a sound like a laugh but loaded with derision. She got as far as "You all are—" when Byron shot straight up, eyes opening wide. His eyes were jaundiced and bulging, a cartoonish color, and there was a cracking of bone that filled the little trailer, and his nose and mouth began to slowly pull from his face. Hair began to sprout at his temples and jawline, and razor-sharp teeth lined his mouth when he opened it wide, letting loose an ear-splitting howl.

He fell back. Astrid dumbly lifted one of his hands for the others to see. The fingers were long with dark, mud-colored claws at the end of each digit and a fine layer of hair covered the flesh, having sprouted from out of nowhere.

"Jesus," Chet muttered.

"We have to kill him," Sarah said with a gleam in her eye.

"You ain't killing my baby!" Astrid wailed.

"Hold on," Bess said, but Sarah turned on her.

"Hold on?! Look at him! We don't have time."

"Why is it happening so soon?" Chet asked, then rushed to the door.

"Afternoon's coming along," Emily said, and Chet let out an expletive that she would have normally admonished him for, but he turned to them all and said he could see the moon rising. And it was full.

As if to confirm, shadows shifted slowly as if a cloud passed overhead. They had grown longer in the intervening hours, stretching as best they could away from the sun on its downward arc. Instinctively, as Byron's own shadow started to cross her, Emily stepped away.

"We don't have much time," Emily admitted, her voice low. "He'll grow more alert as the sun goes down. And when he wakes up..." She let the rest hang in the air for them all.

"We gotta warn people," Bess said.

"We have to stop him here," Sarah demanded.

"He ain't the only one," Emily said.

"Michael Risten," Bess said. "We should warn his friends, Madeline and John Kelly."

"And wasn't the deputy hurt?" Chet asked.

"He wouldn't ever tell me," Chantal said. "I'd sit with him in the hospital and ask him what he seen and he'd not speak about it, but he was different."

"We should assume he is too, then," Bess said. "So we go warn people. We warn people and for those who can, they need to get out, and for those who can't or won't, they should arm themselves."

"Go," Emily said to Bess. "Take Sarah with you. Go tell whoever you can. We'll stay here with the boy. Chet, you go on out to the Fontenot place. If anybody knows anything that could help them, it'd be Angelique Fontenot."

"Yes'm," he said and was off, his truck's engine firing up nearly after he exited the trailer. Bess and Sarah left also, and Emily faced the boy, knowing full well what she'd do if Chet didn't get back in time, or wasn't able to get help. Her dear departed husband had a number of interests, including hunting duck and geese. She imagined his old twelve-gauge, tucked into the back of her bedroom closet, would still fire, and she knew there was a box of birdshot up on the shelf in that closet that wasn't yet spent. As she recalled the old legends, she remembered something about silver, but thought that might be a myth too. No, the birdshot ought to be enough, she thought. The boy, sleeping again, was still restless, and it was all his mother could do to hold him.

୧୫୭

Michael realized, as John Kelly opened the door and let his cousin in, a couple of things. One, it was much later than he thought. He thought, when he awoke, that it was still morning, but as his eyes adjusted, he realized the lateness of the day, and that they didn't have much time left. He could feel the moon's pull. It grew stronger the higher it rose in the sky, pulling at the wolf like it pulled at the tides, hoping to draw it up and out. The second thing he realized was just how little time they had.

"What the—" Chet said again, looking from Michael down to the crumpled mass of Angelique Fontenot.

"She was dying when we got here," Maddy said. "Her brothers too."

"You did this?" Chet asked Michael.

Michael shook his head. The room was spinning. His vision blurred; he reached up and pawed at the medallion, then fell back into his chair.

"He don't look good," Chet said. "Looks worse than Byron Calhoun, in fact."

"Byron?" Maddy said, and Chet briefed them on what was happening at the trailer park.

When he was done, Maddy and John Kelly exchanged a glance, then they both looked back at Michael.

"Oh, it's much worse than you think," Maddy said to Chet. Michael knew, if things had gone on uninterrupted, she would have told Chet what they knew, but as it was, she never got the chance. Dart stood and growled as if he were about to attack Chet, who still stood in the doorway. But then an arm tore through Chet's chest as if his torso had birthed a long claw.

The fingers curled and flexed, now painted in blood. Frozen on Chet's face and in his throat were a soundless scream and a look of abject terror. He stood as if he were impersonating a crucifixion for what seemed an eternity, and then his body relaxed and fell to the ground. Kalos von Slacher stood behind him, his arm now withdrawn. Blood speckled his face: his own and Chet's. His left eye was missing, and the wound where John Kelly had shot him was still fresh.

"Now," von Slacher said. "Where were we?"

CHAPTER TWENTY

The blue moon rose.

It did, indeed, wear a bluish hue as it climbed above the horizon, replacing the sinking sun. The hue was a coincidence to the name, but it worked as well, pulling at feral natures.

A werewolf can take several forms. It can look like a large dog or wolf, traipsing about on all fours, but it can also stand like a human. The power of the wolf comes not just from its ability to control its shape, but how primal it can be. The human underneath cannot control the beast consciously, just as they cannot remember directly what the beast has done. But outside of a blue moon, there is still some interference, like a leash connected to a harness. Those bitten, like Aaron Bailey, for example, can barely control their transformations. They can't willfully manage any one particular form, and while they run wild, the beast does not have access to the full capabilities it possesses. For one like Michael, born into it, his control is greater, his strength is greater, and he possesses a bit more cunning, but he cannot recall what happens either.

When the blue moon rises, things change. The wolf taps into the human cunning. It can reason. It understands its actions. When it hunts, it chooses the prey that most pleases its human self. It can control its forms and how it shifts between four legs and two, and it realizes its full potential.

The blue moon is not the final moon of the autumn. There are a few more, before winter takes over and the beast rests for another three seasons. The blue moon doesn't even arrive on a predictable schedule. There isn't a guarantee of one each season. Michael had experienced them before, so he knew at least what was coming, but he was powerless to stop it. But at least he had an inkling. When the moon began its pull on tides and lycanthropes, Deputy Aaron Bailey, feeling the first pangs of the transformation as he inserted the key into the cell to unlock it, thought, ultimately, that this would be like the other nights. Something had been speaking to him throughout the day, true. Like it had been speaking to Derek. But the deputy had thought that this was really just because he'd been changing so much. The wolf was in him and grew stronger with every change. Then he let the key go without fully unlatching the lock and dropped to his knees. The fire shooting through his gut was worse than any he'd felt. The hairs like tiny needles pierced his skin like sprouts from a garden and his jaw broke in several places to make room for the muzzle. Derek slammed against his cell and cried out. Bailey answered this cry with his own, but it came out sounding too much like a howl.

In the minutes prior to this, Amelia Livingston rolled up her sedan behind her husband's truck at the restaurant. As she exited, she heard the commotion. Duke and his brother emerged from behind her, staring across the square, past the statue, to the police station.

"Whattya think's gone on in there?" Rayburn asked.

Sounds like smashing echoed out.

"One or th'other might be in trouble," Duke said, but he made no move toward them.

"Maybe they kill each other," Rayburn said, a bit dismissively.

It was clear where the two brothers stood. The reputations of both the deputy and the criminal he had locked up inclined them towards not wanting to intervene, but Amelia could not ignore her Christian upbringing like that.

"No," she said. "We need to go see. We need to go help."

CR80

Derek was changing faster. Bailey's own transformation had apparently stalled, and Derek was going to be done, and he would kill him. Bailey, crumpled on the floor in the fetal position from the pain, willed himself through it, and willed it to speed up. Derek Evans slammed against the bars. Bailey had been unable to turn the key to actually let Derek out, but he'd left it in the lock, so it wouldn't take long for a rational prisoner to be able to reach through the bars and give it a twist. Derek was preoccupied with his own transformation, but once that was over, and if he could figure that out, he'd be free. The deputy hoped that wouldn't happen.

He felt his ears stretch, the cartilage snap as they extended to something elfish or canine. Derek made it to his feet, his back facing the front of the cage. His body was covered in hair. His shirt fell away in strips of fabric. He flexed his claws. He turned. It turned. The head was lupine, the mane long, the snout snarling and snapping, the eyes yellow and feral. There was a hint of Derek in the eyes. The wolf looked at the writhing deputy with recognition. It raised both hands to the bars and slammed them against its cage. Plaster fell from the ceiling and the jail door shuddered, and while the key jingled and backed out of the lock some, neither the door nor the lock gave. Bailey pulled himself across the floor. He'd left his gun in the belt on his desk when he first felt the change coming, not thinking a werewolf needed or cared for a gun, but now, wondering if he'd even finish changing, he knew he needed something to put the prisoner down should Derek get out. Or, fuck it, just shoot him anyway.

The wolf slammed against the bars again. Again, the key backed out. Bailey pulled himself to sit upright and looked at his right hand. The claws had begun to form, and his hand was nearly covered in dark fur. His tongue flicked over the sharp teeth filling his extended muzzle. But he could still see. He had yet to black out. Dear god, he thought, he wouldn't be changed, and Derek might...

The wolf stopped, looked down at something. Bailey grabbed for purchase on the desktop and lifted himself, struggling to stand. The wolf looked up at him and seemed to be grinning. Then it reached a careful paw through the bars and wrapped its elongated, clawed fingers around the key's stem. It pulled the key back into the lock. Then turned it.

The door swung open.

It wasn't quite a bark or a growl. More a snort, really. A derisive, condescending sound echoing out its jaws at it stepped free of the cell. Bailey, standing now, unsnapped his holster and pulled the gun free. His hands were... claw-like. Had the transformation stalled? He could not recall remembering like this. Could not recall being aware.

He raised the gun as Derek lunged, and fired as Derek reached him, claws outstretched. Those claws raked his chest and face and clutched at what remained of his shirt. Derek hurled him over the desk, crashing into the bookcase beyond, knocking off the clock and the prisoner log and the pencil sharpener. The shelf itself shattered from the impact, raining down its shards on the crumpled body as the deputy fell to the floor. The Derek-wolf let out a triumphant howl, puffing up its chest, stretching back its neck and arms, so as to get the full-throated, earth-shaking effect. Its howl roared with power, meant to cause all-around tremble, to show its strength. And then, two things happened to silence it.

One: The door to the street opened, and the Livingstons stood in the doorway.

Two: The deputy, now finally transformed, stood out of the rubble and let forth his own growl.

CXSO

Chet Kelley's body crumpled to the floor. This happened as the blue moon crested the treetops, and while the sun wasn't completely down, the shadows had grown and night was now inevitable. So were the changes.

Michael felt them coming, and what he felt manifested on the face of von Slacher, who, while obviously in pain, grinned with anticipation. Doubled over, clutching at his gut, he raised his dark eyes and toothy rictus to Michael and his friends as Dart growled, the hackles on his spine rising.

A fire shot through Michael. He'd welcome the change now, even before Maddy and John Kelly had the opportunity to mix any concoction, though he was aware he still wore the amulet Maddy had found. He'd welcome the change because, he knew, that was the only way he'd be able to stand up to this man who meant to kill them all. He'd change and he'd welcome it, because even though this man had shown how he could change at will, it was good to see that even he couldn't control what the blue moon did to him.

The change happened quickly. The wolf sprouted out of Michael like the fur out of his flesh, but with von Slacher, the wolf tore out of the skin much as the old man's fist had torn through Chet Kelly's torso. The explosive transformation painted the trailer in even more blood than had already been shed, and the trailer shook with a mighty growl.

But the growl hadn't come from von Slacher. It had come from Michael, and for a moment, Maddy and John Kelly and Dart found themselves in between both creatures. The moment passed, too quickly, and the wolf that had been Michael Risten lunged. Its eyes were not focused on them, though. They were focused on the thing that had been von Slacher. It snarled and dug its claws into the other wolf's fur and fell into it, knocking it outside the trailer, the two of them rolling in a mass of fur and claws and snapping, snarling, razor-tooth-lined jaws. Spit and blood and fur flew indiscriminately. Yelps and snarls and snaps and barks and growls. Hackles still raised and still growl-snarling, Dart did not leap into the foray, but stayed by his humans, watching as the two large creatures tussled in the yard. They rolled through the ash bed of the Fontenot campfire, snarling. The one on the bottom, still wearing some of the rags of von Slacher's clothing, wriggled out from under the other and leapt out of range three paces, skidded to a stop on all fours, and faced the other wolf. It looked from the wolf to the humans and their dog, standing in front of the entrance to the trailer on the small porch, having followed the action outside. It huffed once, turned and leapt into the underbrush.

Slowly, the Michael-wolf turned and faced them. Dart quit snarling, but his hackles were still raised. Maddy tried to swallow, but her mouth and throat were dry. Sweat, she could see, beaded on her brother's neck.

The wolf stood slowly on its hind legs and took a deep breath. It still wore Michael's pants, but the shirt was gone. Around its neck was the amulet. It wasn't growling. Its eyes softened some, seeing them. It huffed, jerking its head into a nodding motion which looked strangely positive.

"Follow him," Maddy said, her voice shaky.

"Michael?" John Kelly asked, thinking she was addressing him. But she shook her head. She was staring at Michael. He huffed again and dipped his head as if to nod, Then he crouched and leapt into the forest's tree line in the direction von Slacher had ran.

"The Fontenots have some weapons," Maddy said. "More than your handgun."

"I'll go look," John Kelly said.

Maddy stood shivering, Dart pressing his body against her legs. Was the dog trembling also? The potion she read about would take too long to make, she decided. She was sure the Fontenot brothers carried rifles and shotguns to hunt, and she'd heard once about how they made their own ammo. Then, it would be just a matter of finding where they'd run off to.

CRSO

Not like this, Bess Louviere thought as the torchiere floor lamp to her right sparked. She lay in what used to be the dining room, consciousness ebbing like the tide. Her left forearm stung and she could not feel her legs below her thighs. Her eyes failed her. One contact was either curled up under her lid or out completely, and the other was caked in the blood that streamed down her scalp. She was, given the situation, surprisingly numb, which her rational mind understood as her being in shock.

When the tide of consciousness rolled in, she could hear the spark of the lamp, the labor of her own breathing, whimpering that sounded a world away, and something else: a growl or chuffing, something predatory. When the tide rolled in, she saw, through the darkness, the overturned and splintered dining room table, the oak hutch toppled in two, its glass doors shattered with the beads scattered about the hard wood, twinkling in the moonlight from outside. Smoke announced itself not by sight but by smell and danced hand in hand with the blood misting through the air. Her blood. Sarah Larsen's blood. Phil and Lynette Cabot—her neck creaked as she rotated to the right. Half the hutch had fallen on Lynette's torso. Her legs alone were visible from under the wreckage, the back of her calves soaked in the blood pooling still around them, the gory version of what the Wicked Witch of the West should have looked like. The legs were still, like a mannequin's, and that told Bess all she needed to know about Lynette's condition.

When the tide rolled out, she remembered family. Her granddaughter Vicky was little and had blonde curls and wore her Sunday sundress and it was years before she discovered the chemicals that would ease her pain. Bess' brother was still there. In this place where consciousness was not welcome, neither were his predilections, and in this place he would never do to his daughter what he did in life, things that would send him to prison where thieves and murderers in their criminal code would not tolerate a man like him, would send him to an early grave. In this place, her family was normal, and her parents were still young, and everyone was still alive.

"Please." The voice was weak and cut through the smoke and aerosol blood and through the tide to beach her mind. Her eyes popped open. The voice had not been close. Had come from above. Her mind blanked at its owner, and then it came to her. Phil. He'd run. It was answered with something guttural, a sound that shook her weak and nearly collapsed sternum, a sound so far from her, but still too close. It rose like the crescendo of an orchestra, the pulsing bass sounds overtaking the tinny winds and brass, ripping as the conductor waved his wand to draw them out. The tinny scream could barely be heard, the bass growled so loud. The name of Jesus was attempted then cut short, a snare-like snapping noise before the awful sound of flesh ripping.

Unable to react, too weak to move, Bess glanced down at her left forearm, remembering the sound in the moments just after their world turned upside down. The flesh of her own arm had been peeled off in a long strip that, she could see now, lay like a coiled pink worm on the floor. The strip itself still suggested the cold, but other than that, she could no longer feel it.

She had just moved into the dining room at the behest of Lynette, calling her for one thing or another. They were supposed to pack quickly, taking only what they needed, and then the lights flickered and two explosions rocked the house. The first sounded like a transformer failing. The second was the front door exploding inward. Then there came a third sound. The growl like a battle cry that came with the exploding door had been just as loud.

Phil Cabot's scream faded, and now there came sounds of chomping, meat tearing, juices flowing, smacking teeth and bones crunching. It was loud in its feasting and did not care who heard it. It had played with her like a cat plays with a mouse. Once upon a time, she had a calico that did just such a thing, dropping headless presents or bodiless gifts on the steps to her house in the mornings. Upon whose doorstep would her head be delivered, she wondered weakly.

Something heavy rolled down the stairs, and Bess noticed more glints of moonlight off the floor, considerably larger than the beads of broken hutch glass and shards of ceramic dishware. The antique cutlery Lynette had inherited from her grandmother had been scattered about the floor when the hutch had been toppled over. Nearest her bloodied and broken arm were several silver forks and a knife. She stared at the fingers of her left hand, willing them to bend. A disgorged, semi-conscious moan echoed from the front hall, from the base of the stairs. Not Phillip, Bess thought, the desiccating sounds still fresh in her ears. Must be Sarah. Yes. She had run with him when it all went to hell. Now she was trying to escape. Bess' left middle finger twitched. She focused on her shoulder, then sliding her arm just a little, fresh fire roiling up from the skinned forearm. She bit her lip to keep from screaming. From above, its footfalls came slowly, the floorboards creaking under its heavy, plodding steps. Its breath came in snorts. It wasn't trying to conceal its presence. It had no fear of being discovered. Not just that; it had no fear.

Her fingers closed around one of the forks and the knife, drawing the two pieces together under her grasp. Now it was on the steps. It would feast on Sarah, and then it would come for her.

CRSO

Emily Evans was sure Byron was dying. This is what they were watching, of course, the boy in a fetal curl under a heap of blankets, still shivering. Astrid sat next to him, stroking his head, dabbing at the sweat on his brow with a damp washcloth Chantal had fetched for her on Emily's direction. Now Chantal sat by the door, staring out the window, and Emily sat in her recliner, both hands atop her wooden cane, staring at the boy on her sofa.

He was dying, yes, and he'd be reborn, soon enough. The Loup garou was taking over. The boy would die and it would be born, and it would be there, even when it looked like the boy, it would be there just under the surface, and Astrid Calhoun's little boy would be just as gone as if he were buried up in Bluff City's one and only attraction—the cemetery.

"Mama," the boy said weakly.

"I'm here, baby," but she was so lost in caring for her son that she didn't hear it. Emily did. The slight tinge in the voice. The hint of something else poking through from underneath, lulling them in with weakness.

With the foot of her cane she poked at Chantal, then motioned for her to come near with a single, curling finger.

"What?" Chantal said loudly, and Astrid looked over at them. Emily glared at the girl, motioning for her to squat near her. When she did, Emily finally spoke.

"Loup garous change at their own pace. And the moon affects them differently, but even then, it's all the same. What comes when the moon is bright, it ain't who you knew. It's something else."

Chantal did not respond, just looked at her with a kind of dawning horror. Perhaps, while the boy had been sleeping, the idea could be entertained without being believed, but now she must be seeing the truth.

"What do we do?" Chantal asked finally.

"Look at him," Emily Evans said. It was evident now. His nose and jaw crackled like sizzling bacon, producing a grunt-like scream from the boy. His ears were now more elvish (*wolfish*) and when he opened his eyes, they glinted with a yellow feral glow more animal than human.

With great effort she stood then moved down the hall to her bedroom.

"Watch him," Emily shouted. "I'll be right back. I won't be long." She was sure she knew where the shotgun still rested, though it hadn't been fired or cleaned in years. She was less sure about the location of her husband's buckshot. A fear rose up then that there was none left. That she'd given it away to someone years ago. Perhaps Duke Livingston, and that sounded horrifyingly true. If it were true, she knew she didn't have the strength to use the shotgun like a club, so it would be just as effective against the loup garou as the cane in her hand. Still, she made her way down the hall, pushing through the thud of her straining heart, and realized she wouldn't live to see the morning.

જ્ઞ

"She got away, I think," Rayburn said, chancing a glance over the bar and lifting the serving window just enough to peer across the parking lot. Duke, peering over his brother's shoulder, saw no sign of his wife, nor of anything else. The square was empty and quiet. The night hung heavy with a ground fog. Streetlamps barely cut through the soup. The full moon fared just slightly better. Everything in the distance looked blurred and slanted, vague shapes just drunkenly recognizable, their distinct features and details lost to the night.

"What the fuck happened to him?" Rayburn asked.

Them, Duke thought, but didn't answer. Beads of sweat dotted his neck, soaked his shirt to his skin, though the air outside was cool enough. She was in there, and they were in there. His mind produced only an irrational collection of still frames to make sense of what had just happened. They had walked into the police station. There was a commotion, or had that come after Amelia had opened the door? Derek Evans had escaped, but this wasn't Derek. No, something was wrong with Derek. He'd kind of smiled at them, then leapt... *leapt!...* *Jesus, Mary, and Joseph, he leapt...*

But that wasn't all. It wasn't just that he leapt, but how he looked. All covered in hair and his face looked like a dog's face. He had claws, too, it looked like. But the thing was, he wasn't done. It's like, when Duke saw him, he was just in the middle of... *of what, for chrissakes! Just say it...* of changing. He was changing and he smiled at them with this toothy, evil looking smile. But he looked like he was in pain, also. But like he enjoyed it. Christ, he was changing, and he was in pain but he enjoyed it. And he leapt. Cleared the floor by like eight feet before smashing out the window.

Fucking impossible.

"Gas leak," Duke said, nearly to himself. "She still in there and there is a gas leak..."

"What in hell you talkin' 'bout?" Rayburn asked, and when Duke stood to run out, his brother grabbed him by the shoulders, shaking him. "Keep yo' voice down, Duke!" Rayburn snapped.

"Gas leak," Duke muttered to himself, then saw his brother. Rayburn's eyes were wide with fear and there was a pleading look on his face. "Gas leak and that's what made me see Derek Evans..." his voice trailed off. That was the best explanation he could think of.

"Weren't no gas leak," Rayburn said. "I seen him too. We all did. Just like we saw the deputy then. He just like him."

Duke shook his head no. No, Jesus no, it couldn't be. It had to be a gas leak or something messing with their minds, like that time Rayburn brought home some of that canned air back when they were kids and stuck it against his nose and huffed, and he'd offered it to Duke and Duke thought about trying it, but then he saw Rayburn's eyes and how he just kind of fell away into hisself and how he was jabbering about seeing things that weren't there. That's what was happening to them now. Maybe just some sewage or propane or something was leaking. That office looked like it had been hit by a tornado. Mayhaps something got busted and gas was leaking and that's why it looked like Derek had changed and leapt out the window, and that would also explain why the deputy looked the way he did, and that sound that came out of him, and it looked like he'd charged for them and Amelia *godblesser* fell behind another desk and Rayburn was shoving him.

Cause that thing that looked kind of like the deputy was chasing them, only Duke remembered looking back across the street as they ran and he couldn't see nothing. He could hear it, sho 'nuff, but he ain't seen shit, and they ran and he smelled something like piss and it weren't 'til they was safe in the restaurant with it all bolted up did he see it was Rayburn what pissed hisself like when they was kids and went to see that monster movie where Dracula fought the wolfman...

Rayburn was talking, but that's not what snapped him back to the real world. It was the memory of that movie and the howl ripping through the night, sounding dangerously close and just outside the thin walls of the restaurant, this shack that was little more than a food truck. The walls shook at the sound, as if the very breath of the creature could demolish the building and all inside.

Duke, despite himself, began laughing hysterically. *I'll huff and I'll puff...*

Rayburn stood by the door, gripping the knob. When Duke saw this, he snapped out of his cackling fit and straightened. "Where you—?"

"Shut it!" Rayburn snapped, his voice a loud whisper, unlike his brother's—Duke hadn't bothered to be quiet. "I don't think she hurt, Duke. I don't think she hurt at all, and I don't think she dead."

Duke shot a glance to the closed window, as if he could see through it, through the night, across the square to the police station beyond. He wished in that moment he could. Outside, a growl was rising, itself as terminal a force as the howl had been. Whatever the deputy had become, it was ready to pounce.

"When you see her, you get her out of here," Rayburn said. There was something resigned in his countenance, a softening of features that suggested he'd already made his mind up about something, and Duke had no say in the matter.

"Ray—?"

"You get her out of here, and you go get your daughter, and you live, man. Out of this damn town, you go someplace and you live."

"What are you—?"

"I wouldn't've made it this far without you, big brother. So you just let me do this, and you get yo wife, and you two live. You hear?"

"Ray, don't."

The door opened, and Rayburn ducked outside. The door closed just as the growl turned to a snapping like bark, and something heavy smashed against the wall of the building. Rayburn let out the briefest of cries before snarls and sounds of mastication drowned him out. Duke Livingston listened, petrified, as his brother was eaten. He knew he wouldn't have time to run. The thing that used to be the deputy was faster than he, and he was sure that it thrilled not in the feasting but in the hunt. Any sign of fresh meat, of living prey, would outweigh a potential meal. This thing didn't kill to eat; it lived to kill, and it would kill him.

When the sounds stopped, Duke saw the handle of the door turned. Rayburn must have engaged the push button lock before slamming the door shut, but such locks were a distraction at best, and would not keep it out. Indeed, as his back slammed against the stove, his eyes unable to leave the door, the knob itself twisted beyond the hold of the lock and the door peeled with a screech and a splintering of wood off the frame, pulling pieces of door jamb with it. In the doorway stood a twisted form.

The moonlight cast a sheen over the figure in the door. It wore the deputy's uniform, though the sleeves were torn and one shirt tail was untucked, the pants were ripped. From the tears and rips in the fabric, dark fur protruded, and covered most of his face and his hands. The deputy's eyes were there behind a wolfish mask, a snarling snout of a mouth filled with razor sharp canines dripping with pinkish saliva, exhaling a dog's breath of rancidity from its fresh kill. The eyes suggested the deputy, but Duke knew that didn't mean there would be any reasoning with it.

He wanted to back away again, back away more, but there was nowhere to go. His hands groped maddeningly behind him for the door or something to use in defense. A napkin dispenser. A spatula. A plastic barbecue sauce squeeze bottle. Jesus Christ, where were the knives? It took a step into the room, and its lips curled into a snarl. The razor-clawed fingers of its fur-covered hands flexed, the joints cracking and popping.

Outside, something else howled. The deputy's head turned, its pointed ears like radar dishes rotating to source the sound, its nose wrinkling to pick up a scent. Duke thought, sickeningly, that whatever howled was not Derek Evans. There were more out there. Oh, God, Jesus in Heaven, there were more of them.

As the howl died down, it turned its attention back to Duke. Was it grinning? Could it grin? Yes, perhaps it was. He'd heard from dog owners who thought their animals could reflect human emotions. One of Rayburn's old friends from high school had owned a mutt and swore it could communicate with him nonverbally. Remy Doucet's uncle had owned a dog to keep the foxes and coyotes away from his chickens. Remy swore the dog understood English and could smile just as bright when you rubbed his belly. Duke had never owned a dog, had never believed such stories, but now…

What if it's the man underneath the wolf? he thought. *What if it's the deputy that smiled now.* That still didn't mean he could reason with it. In fact, it meant just the opposite. Aaron Bailey was not a reasonable man in the sunlight. Especially not with the Black folk, and not with anyone who challenged him, and he saw anyone who didn't kowtow to him as a challenge. No, if Aaron was still even in the slightest bit of control or held any sway over the animal in front of him, Duke knew that only solidified his fate.

The deputy took another step into the room. It was toying with him. Daring him to run. It wanted the chase. It wanted the game. It parted its stinking, rancid maw and bared its bloodstained arrow-tipped teeth and exhaled a growl, and Duke forced his eyes to stay open. He would not run, nor give it the satisfaction of cowering. *Come on, you damn dog,* he thought.

A gunshot echoed through the tiny building. The growling stopped, though the mouth stayed open. A dark spot spread over the deputy's chest. Another shot, and it closed its mouth. As it fell forward, smoke wafting off its back, Duke saw Amelia standing behind it, holding a handgun. Even in the low, shadow-laden light of the moon and the fog crawling over the ground, he could see she was trembling. He looked down at the deputy, but the thing wearing his uniform was unmoving. Not wanting to take his gaze away from it for even a second, Duke skirted the perimeter of the room, his back against the wall, until he had only one move to make. He had to step over it to get out the door. Amelia, still trembling, trained the barrel of the handgun on the back of the fallen creature, where what had started as two puddles pooling underneath had now coalesced into one. Duke made to step over the beast and plant one foot between the splayed legs of the deputy, then stopped. He'd looked away for a second to check on his wife, and when he looked back, the beast, even in this heavy shadow, was gone. Aaron Bailey, blond and clean cut, pale faced, lay in front of him. The yellow eyes that had glowed were dim and staring, unblinking. The hands, resting easy on the floor, clawless fingers slightly bent. The fur was gone, as if it had retreated back under the flesh, for there was none on the floor. It was as though the wolf was a mirage and now that he was dead, the mirage was ended, like a magician's poor trick, and all that remained was the corpse of a bullet-ridden racist.

Duke stepped into the night and grabbed his wife, pulling her to him. Out of the corner of his eye, he saw the crumpled mass of flesh that had been his brother, and shut his eyes tight, pulling her closer. In that quick glance, he did not recognize anything about the mass that had been Rayburn. The body had been ravaged unrecognizable. Teeth had shredded flesh and muscle and organ and soft tissue and sprayed the remains in blood.

From the darkness came again the howl, and it was answered. When Duke pulled away, he turned his wife so that her back was to the building and the remains of his brother. Perhaps she'd already seen it, but he wasn't counting on that and he wasn't going to stop and ask her. Not if there were others out there.

"We gotta go," he said, and she nodded. He led her to the car, sat her in the passenger seat, and climbed in behind the wheel. Arching his back against the seat, he fumbled in his pockets for his keys. First the right, then the left. Another howl, this time closer.

"Maybe you left them in the office," she said.

"Where's yorn?" he asked. She always kept hers in her purse, and she didn't have it on...

Her eyes brightened, and she popped the glove compartment, drawing out her purse which she unzipped quickly and produced the ring of keys like a parlor trick. He snatched them away and jammed the silver key into the steering column. The next howl to split night sounded as close as their bumper. Thankfully, there was no drama with the car. It started immediately, and Duke shifted into reverse, peeling out of the spot, cutting a J-turn so that he was facing the right way on the street. Amelia slid into him, desperately grabbing for her seatbelt. To be sure, as he shifted to drive, his left hand smashed the door lock button. Had he heard a frustrated growl just then, and something tugging at the door handle? He couldn't be sure, and the night was so dark it gave nothing away, and he wasn't about to look around and see. He twisted the headlight knob until two beams illuminated the street in front of him. The fog hanging over was thick and the headlights barely cut through. Visibility might be twenty feet, but in this moment, twenty feet was all he needed. He stomped on the gas pedal and the car lurched forward, tires spinning, then caught the pavement with an iron grip and rocketed forward. Duke's right hand found Amelia's left and he steered them out of Blue Rock, Arkansas, for the last time. They would never return.

CRSO

Maddy knew, when the howls came. She'd been waiting on John Kelly to gather the remaining ingredients. She'd loaded some ammunition and guns into the vehicle, and now stood hunched, petting on Dart who pressed against her protectively, feeling the night air sizzle around her. From the direction of the howls, the report of two gunshots.

John Kelly soon emerged from the trailer, carrying the potion, his back sweaty and his shirt dirty. She knew her brother well enough to know he could not have let the siblings rest like that. He had put them to rest in the backyard as best he could, buried them in the marshy ground even though there was little time for it. Not deep enough to deter scavengers, just deep enough for respect.

"We have to go," she said.

"We don't know where."

"I do. He wants to destroy this town. He's gone to the town square to call the others there, and Michael has followed him."

They climbed into the car, John Kelly behind the wheel. "Why?"

"They're a pack," Madeline said. "Right now, because Michael turned them, they're his pack. This man wants to kill them all. What if he thinks Michael can call them all to one place?"

"Easy pickin'," John Kelly admitted.

"And what would be easier than luring them to the town square?" she asked.

Dart whimpered from the back seat. John Kelly sped on.

⚭

When the howls came, the footsteps near the bottom of the stairs stopped. Bess Louviere lifted her head to the sound and swallowed hard. The saliva in her throat was as acrid as blood, a sweet, tangy taste, clotted in thick globules. The footsteps resumed. Sarah Larsen could only let out a whisper, and when the tearing sound came, like a swatch of thin denim fabric being ripped, that whisper died. There was only the horrible sound of chewing and in the air, fresh blood, followed by more footsteps.

Why had she thought it was on all fours? What walked into the dining room walked on two legs. The orange prisoner jumpsuit pants were ragged and torn at the bottom. The legs dark with fur, and the feet no better than canid paws, the nails clicking on the hardwood with each step. The remainder of the matching shirt dangled around the waist like a kilt, exposing the torso, dark and fur covered. The arms and hands might have been human if not for the undercoat and claws. The neck was massive, and the head decidedly wolfish.

It sniffed the air and looked around the room before settling its gaze on her. Its ears twitched in the shadows, searching for sound. My god, the magnificence of the beast, she thought. Such a thought was safe now, for her fate was known. Not pleasant, and not what she wanted, but known. And it wasn't the one that killed her niece and severed her final tie to this world. It couldn't be. She recognized this one. She thought she knew it. Underneath the mask, she thought she spied the trembling boy who played in the streets years earlier, the grandson of the woman who ran the local trailer park and who Bess called, "friend." He'd grown into a bully. Into someone who craved power and ran roughshod over anyone who stood in his way, but beneath even that exterior, he was a scared little boy who'd been given a raw deal in life.

Bess Louviere swallowed hard. "I know you, Derek. You don't want to do this."

The wolf's head turned this way and that, much as a dog might if it doesn't understand the command or why you're angry it pissed on the carpet. Unlike a dog, this thing wasn't interested in commands or pleasing a master. It squatted, far too human an action, placing its forearms on its knees. Its snout was open, the tongue out, pink and moist, the sharp teeth also pink from stain. It panted. If she reached up and scratched it behind its ears, would it roll over? This thought came maddeningly, and she bit her lip to keep from laughing.

"We fought for you, Derek. I'm sorry. Sorry we weren't enough."

The muzzle snapped shut, and the beast studied her. Then it spoke. "I am enough."

Did the literature suggest they could speak? If it did, she wasn't aware, and the very words unsettled her. In the fairy tales and fables she imagined they could. Such things spoke to the three little pigs and to Little Red Riding Hood. She thought about Guy Endore's novel, the werewolf born from the sacrilegious predilections of a randy priest.

"Why should you be shut up for your crimes," she asked, the words from the novel rising like a shadow in her mind, "when larger crimes go unpunished? When society can churn out animals that storm and celebrate their monstrosity, and imprison the innocent and threaten our very humanity with jingoistic racist ideology? As their own flags unfurl in the winds, why can't this dog have its day as well?"

It bent its black snout and brushed the flesh of her neck, drawing the air around her in, drawing in her scent. Was that its tongue flicking out reptilian-like, tasting her? Tasting the face wash and soothing creams and the perfume she'd applied a lifetime ago?

From outside came another howl. She saw, terrified as she was to move, one of its ears twitch again. Its weight was nearly on her so she dared not move, barely breathed, but could not help but swallow again and gain some semblance of all she had left: her voice.

"They're calling. You want to go. You... *need* to go."

"Yes," it said. The snout worked with the tongue to produce the word. "But first, I must eat."

"You've eaten," she said. She thought of Sundays on the back porch with the Cabots and cribbage and iced tea and egg salad sandwiches, and how they tried tirelessly to fix her up with Dr. Bellanger. She could smell, just briefly, the mayonnaise, sweetener, lemon, the boiled egg, and the honeysuckle from the overgrown bush that Lynette always threatened to trim but never did.

It parted its snout and laid either side of its maw across her neck, the tongue tickling her throat, the canines needling like a thousand pinpricks, like an acupuncturist ready to begin the session. She closed her eyes. What she hoped it didn't know, hadn't noticed, was the subtle shift of the utensils, dividing the silver cutlery pieces from one hand to both. Now, the beast over her, she raised both arms.

Thankfully it did not bite down at once. If it had, it would have ripped her throat out and she would have died instantly. Instead, she felt pinpricks all across the flesh of her throat, and felt the beads of blood well up at once and coalesce together, and that allowed her enough time to thrust her hands down. The fork pierced its haunches just behind its ribs, and the knife penetrated its neck. Blood spurted out like a fountain and the wolf thing lifted its head, howling in pain. It had released its grip momentarily, and for that she was thankful, but then it turned its awful, yellow eyes back on her with such hate. She had just enough time to wonder what she'd done, and then its jaws locked on her again. Its teeth tore and shredded the flesh of her neck, simultaneously shredding and unthreading her jugular like it was a rope toy, denying her the opportunity to scream.

Bess gasped for breath and felt the air catch in her throat, her own blood damming the flow. Her body flailed, and the wolf pinned her down. Then it tore into her throat again as its own blood fountained out. It felt pain and wanted its victim to feel that pain. When it rose, it lifted a claw to stem the blood loss, and Bess Louviere lay still beneath it. It grasped the knife and pulled it out, never taking its yellow eyes off her. *Bitch*, it thought, the word rolling off its mental tongue easily enough. The word made a kind of sense now that it hadn't before. It had used the word before, back before the bite. It had looked at the opposite sex as a kind of plaything, and had used the word condescendingly, but now… Now in this new state, the word meant something simpler. The bitch had one of but two purposes: breed or eat. This one was too old to breed, so it ate. But on the air it smelled another, approaching the howls, and thought that one might be there to breed.

⚮

Blood papered the walls, and Astrid lay crumpled in the corner like a lifeless lump, her slit neck allowing her chin to touch her breast, nearly doubled over so her head was almost in her lap, her legs splayed out straight-kneed and slightly parted in front of her. Chantal wasn't sure how it had happened, save that the old woman had just hobbled to the back of the trailer, when Chantal heard two howls and the reverberation of gunshots in the distance, all from the same place. Byron's eyes had snapped open and he changed all at once.

Chantal pushed the small, circular breakfast table off her crazily ruined left knee, feeling it throb and pulse and stiffen. It felt like someone had tightened a blood pressure cuff around her thigh and pumped it up as high as they could. It felt like that time she had a cavity in the tenth grade and her molar had pounded in her jaw like a bass drum. She was sure she couldn't stand on it. The table felt like a lead weight chained down on her to a concrete base, and for a moment, as Byron—*or whatever he'd become*—focused on his own mother after knocking Chantal across the room and into the table, Chantal knew she was pinned under it. But the table gave just enough, and while she couldn't stand, she could slide across the linoleum, then pulled herself up slowly using the cabinet peninsula for support. Whatever Byron had become hunkered over his mother's form, studying her. That part of the room was dark from the shadows of the creeping night and from the blood that cast a deep velvet shadow over the walls. Astrid Calhoun was dead, no doubt about it, and Chantal knew if she didn't move her ass, she'd be dead too.

The thing that had been Byron—*but my, didn't he look like a dog now, like a Husky or a German Shepherd*—turned to face her as she clamored to her feet. She chanced a bit of weight on her left foot then realized it was no good. That leg was dead to her now, so she shifted her weight back to her right and used it for support, her hands gripping at the walls for balance in the narrow hallway and retreated back down the hallway the way the old lady had gone. She'd been after something, Chantal was sure. At the very least, there was a bedroom at that end of the trailer, and she could shut its door and lock it and that might buy her some time.

Her right hand fumbled for the wall and found the accordion doors, barely thicker than wallpaper, that sectioned off the washer and dryer, and she nearly toppled over, but as the Byron thing made for her, she caught her footing as flimsy as it was and skidded backward. Chancing a glance over her shoulder, she caught just a glimpse of Emily Evans. The hem of her skirt, really, and a whisper of her calf, and called out for her. Byron stepped into the kitchen then doubled over, wincing at some unknown pain. From afar another howl came, and his ears (*my word, those look like the ears of an elf*) twitched to pick up the sound. Chantal took advantage of this distraction and hurled herself backward, her spine smacking on the footboard and her shoulders slamming on the mattress of the bed. Byron saw her and growled, and rushed forward, the claws of his feet clicking on the linoleum. Chantal thought crazily, *we've belled the cat,* and stifled a laugh, even as a fire ripped through her midsection from her spine and she was sure she was crippled. But fear and danger do peculiar things, and she found she could bend, and she found her left knee didn't even hurt that badly, and she snapped up as if on a spring and slammed the door closed, forcing the lock in place just before Byron slammed into it. Still, her whole body rocked as if she were on the Tilt-a-Whirl at the county fair. This hollow, cheap, plyboard thing trailer homes referred to as a door would not hold the beast out for long.

"Miss Evans," she said, turning, then froze. Emily Evans lay on her bed, eyes wide open. Her arms cradled a shotgun and a box of buckshot lay scattered over the quilted bedspread. Chantal could hear Byron outside, but he was breathing hard and he wasn't ramming into the door. Instead, he was speaking. His words sounded rough like barking to her, or snarling.

"Open up. It'll be so much easier if you open up."

She knelt by the old woman. There was no blood, but why would there be? Already her face was an ashy pale, her features locked. Chantal thought her lucky. Retreating to this room, Miss Emily had found the only hint of egress were two high placed, six-inch cranked windows not nearly wide enough to escape from. Chantal saw them now and wondered what hope was there for survival.

"Open up, Chantal," Byron called. "You know, that's what he said to me, or at least what I think he said to me, before he took me on my mother's bed. Your brother. Do you know what he did to me?"

Her face was slick with sweat. She fumbled at the buckshot and the shotgun. Though he'd shown her numerous times, Aaron was more comfortable with guns. Prying the 12-gauge from the old woman's cold, dead hands, she broke the barrels and slammed a round into each chamber, slapped the shotgun closed and cocked both hammers.

"Come on in and tell me," she said.

The door handle turned. The lock wanted to hold, much as she was sure the boy had wanted to fight back against her brother. Neither were strong enough. With an explosion of manufactured wood the door exploded off the door frame, and Byron entered. He flew through the air, and he was on her in a second, his teeth sinking into her shoulder, jamming the gun between them. The pull of the trigger was something secondary. Accidental, even. An afterthought. She'd just wanted him off. Instead, the barrels turned up between them, the shot blasted up and exploded her left breast and shoulder and half her face and took his snout and most of his chest and his right arm. What remained of them lay like embracing lovers one on top of the other on the queen-sized mattress of Emily Evan's double wide.

CRSO

The night settled over Blue Rock. The air, tinged with blood, wafted through the town, and in this moment, the heart and soul of the community was finally laid to rest. In the coming weeks, the state police would investigate and marvel at the scattered horror. They'd wonder about how to clean up and what to tell the public. All they could agree upon was that this town had died, and it had died on this night. In the end, bureaucracy would take hold, and claim that this town was merely an incorporation, as if that solved all the problems. The governor would wave his hand and erase Blue Rock from the record books, and no one but the few stragglers who survived would be the wiser, and a big enough settlement would guarantee they kept their mouths shut. Official word would blame it on the pandemic. Mass casualties. Politicize it to antivaxxers if they must, but don't let anyone know the truth. The pandemic that struck this town was not a coronavirus deterred by a filtered cloth face covering and a shot.

CRSO

They drove slowly from the campsite, reaching the square in a matter of minutes just as they penetrated the embankment of fog that had, surreptitiously, rolled in. The delay they experienced with John Kelly in the trailer, pilfering for items to concoct something dark green in a syringe he carried out to the car, had to be worth it, Maddy told herself. Behind the wheel, her hands trembled. Sweat stained the back of her shirt down her spine. John Kelly had handed her the pistol and in the passenger seat, cradled the rifle, butt on the floor and barrel at the ceiling. The syringe he'd capped, she was sure, but couldn't see it now, and imagined it was in the front pouch of his hoodie.

"We going?" he asked, but there was a nervous twitch in his voice, something antsy and on edge.

They could drive, she thought. Drive away and never look back. She willed that thought away, realizing that even if that had ever been a possibility, it was no longer one now. That von Slacher would find them. He would kill Michael first, and he *would* kill Michael, she was sure, and then he would pursue them. Hunt them. He would not stop.

"Yes," Maddy said, as much to resolve herself to a decision as to respond to her brother.

The car lurched forward into the autumn evening, into the fog rolling across the South Arkansas plain, but toward what end she could not know.

The square was deserted. There came the distant rumble of a car fading fast, which Maddy recognized after shutting the engine off by the Confederate soldier's statue and exiting, drawing the pistol to her side. She opened the back door and removed the leash from Dart's harness. The dog didn't need any kind of restraint, she was confident he'd listen to her or John, and she didn't want to hinder his movements at all. Dart leapt to the pavement and looked around, huffing quickly before focusing on something she could not see and issuing a low growl.

"Easy," Maddy tried, but the Lab only turned an indignant eye up to his adoptive mother.

John Kelly clicked a button. The sound felt distant across the hood of her vehicle from the passenger side.

The mad barks and spit-snapped saliva-laden snarls from iron jaws, yapping, howling, bare-toothed growls slithered through the fog like an almost-forgotten melody, fading here and there with chords or chorus, beats thinned then roaring back to tinnitus-deafening decibels. When the two bodies stumbled through the glow of the headlights and slapped against the base of the statue, Maddy jumped and Dart positioned himself in front of her, stiff-spined against her legs. The wolves rolled and tumbled, fur flying through the fog, and blood splattered like autumn rain drops, fat and thick. A yelp. One wolf rolled away and stopped, just a heap. The other took a few steps on all fours before turning its gaze on Maddy and Dart. John Kelly rounded the corner, rifle aimed. The wolf stood.

Its face, still very much like a canine, took on softer, human features. The fur on its body whitened as the arms and legs looked a bit more human, though claws still extended from the digits. It looked to each of them, a low growl erupting from its slightly parted lips, the tips of canines protruding pink-stained. Its tongue flickered.

"Are you fast enough?" it asked, its eyes settling on John Kelly. "Can you pull the trigger before I reach you, you think?"

"Michael!" Maddy called to the heap, but it still didn't move.

"He can't help you, miss. He isn't quite dead yet, but he will be soon."

"And then what?" she asked. "You kill us?"

Von Slacher stretched a grin across his lips and bared his teeth. The claws on his hands flexed and he coiled the muscles in his thighs and calves with a slight bend of his knees. The growl rose out of his throat and gushed out, matched only by Dart's snarls. It was because of this that von Slacher didn't see the attack coming. Michael tackled him back against the statue, smashing him into the base, slashing and snarling at him. Von Slacher threw him up and over, slamming Michael into the granite horse, and Maddy heard a great crack like the world's largest melon had split open. The statue crumbled over the wolves, raining on them in splinters and shards and fragments, burying them. Maddy took a step forward instinctively, scanning the rubble for signs of movement. What she heard came from behind and made her blood run cold.

"Hello, Maddy."

She turned and screamed.

CRSO

What stood before her might have once answered to the name Derek Evans, but not anymore, she thought. He'd been stuck mid-transformation, one arm comically longer than the other, both ending in claws, but the left closer to the leg of a wolf looked shriveled and withered in comparison. Blood pumped as if from an underground spring from a gash in his jagged neck, from where the handle of a silver knife jutted out. Blood soaked his chest and body and he wobbled on his feet unsteadily, his eyes half open. It must have taken all his effort to draw him here.

He hadn't said, "Hello, Maddy" clearly, but in a jumble of sounds that sounded similar, so her brain had filled in the rest.

"Loosk ath'em. Tho... thompleeth," he said now, staring past her to the crumpled forms under the pile of crumpled stone. The voice was jagged and broken, strained. He staggered toward her. His jaw was a grotesque mishmash of human and dog, the teeth uneven, his tongue lolling out to the side. One eye was a bright yellow and one, the human one, the *Derek* eye, was still dark brown but clouding over fast, the sclera bloodshot and the eye itself wandering aimlessly between the two wolves.

"Jesus, Derek," John Kelly said, turning to steady the rifle on him.

Derek coughed, the tongue a thin strap of lifeless leather flopping wildly. "Heeth noth hee-uh, I donth'ink."

He focused his gaze on Madeline and his smile, more closely resembling a jack o' lantern than man or canine, widened. "Hetho, bootheeful."

His non-wolf arm uncoiled fast like a snake, the claws flexing to snatch her up, but Dart jumped up, sinking his teeth into Derek's arms. Derek howled in pain and tried desperately to shake the dog off. A blast exploded from beside her, a bright flash in her periphery, and Dart leapt free as Derek fell backward. He lay on his back just behind the fog bank, his body partially obscured. His left foot twitched reflexively twice then lay still. Maddy approached and looked down. His Derek eye was open but stared at nothing. His lips worked soundlessly. Blood trickled from a new hole in his chest, and Maddy thought perhaps he'd already spilt all the blood he had left. She knelt. The way his face was turned, the profile showed only the human mask. His breath hitched in great hiccups that shocked his chest. Then his good eye closed, and his chest stilled, and he was silent. For the first time in his existence, she thought, remembering the anxious, trembling, wiry, angry young life of Derek Evans, he was still and silent.

"Rest in peace," she said.

⚬

Movement from behind. Maddy jumped, her senses on fire again, but saw only one wolf emerging from the rubble. From the fur she could tell it was Michael. Blood poured from one of his ears and from his left nostril, and there stood a long gash on his side that darkened the fur. He limped toward them, eyes cast solely on Derek. Still, Dart growled as he approached, until the wolf stepped past them and sniffed at the body. Only then did it look back and regard them.

Maddy thought its eyes lingered on her, and then it huffed much the same as Dart had done at times.

"What do you want?" Maddy asked under her breath. The wolf wagged its tail then turned back to the body, sniffed again, then bit into the neck. Nerve endings that had yet to lose their charge allowed the body to twitch briefly, but soon the only movement was the feasting animal, scavenging the carcass for any nourishment, digging through the muscle and cartilage, teeth scraping against bone.

John Kelly turned away, gun at ease against his shoulder, and dry heaved with a gagging sound. Dart pressed his side against Maddy's shins. As much as she wanted to, Maddy could not look away. For as it ate, Maddy stood fascinated that its fur dried and the gash in its side narrowed and vanished. The blood on its muzzle and down the side of its head crusted and flaked away, and the wolf appeared stronger, more whole. It turned on steadier legs and regarded them again once it was done. Then its lips curled into a snarl and its ears, already perked, stiffened more. The hackles on its back stood on end and, with no time for Maddy to move, the wolf leapt—

ॐ

—vaulting between her and John Kelly, its claws out. She turned to see von Slacher, mostly human now, pulling himself to his feet, only for Michael to tackle him back into the rubble. This time, though, Michael seemed to be winning. Von Slacher was pinned against the stone, Michael on top snarling and snapping at him. John Kelly, also entranced by the fight, absently pulled the syringe from his hoodie pouch and uncapped the needle.

"What is it?" she asked him.

"Wolfsbane," he answered. "Concentrated. Depending on when it's given to the werewolf, it can either change them or kill them."

He jammed the rifle into her hands and moved closer to the melee. She saw at once what he was waiting for. A clear shot, just one clear opportunity to jab that needle into von Slacher, and this whole thing could be over.

Michael reared up with a triumphant howl, claws like daggers angled at von Slacher's face. John Kelly leapt, aiming the syringe's needle at the old man's face or neck. Maddy allowed herself a momentary grasp for hope, for a happy ending.

But von Slacher saw him, grabbed Michael by the torso, and pulled him over. The needle sank into Michael's back and, as John Kelly's thumb had been positioned over the plunger already, forced the poison into his muscle. Michael howled and snapped as the wolfsbane coursed through his blood stream. Von Slacher easily tossed him off and Michael fell at Maddy's feet, writhing and whimpering. The wolfsbane traced silver scars across his flesh, his body a living roadmap showing the poison spreading. His howls quieted first, and then he changed, the fur shuffling off him like dead autumn leaves fluttering from tree limbs, his claws retracting. He lay silent and still and human, naked save for the medallion around his neck.

Naked also save for the blood and stone dust, von Slacher stood and made like he was brushing himself off. He glanced at the siblings and their dog, then down to Michael when he groaned.

"Well, this has been exciting," von Slacher said. "Certainly the most fun I've had in a long time."

Michael sat up, leaning against Maddy's legs and Dart.

"And thank you for that assist, Mr. Jeansonne. Very kind of you."

"I was aiming for yo' ass," John Kelly said, taking the rifle back from his sister.

"Are we ready then, Master Risten, to finish our little dance? I think we are."

But before he could lunge, before Michael could even stand, John Kelly shouldered the rifle and pulled the trigger, and von Slacher fell backwards. They paused only long enough to see him lay motionless before Maddy helped Michael to his feet, knowing full well he was more likely stunned than dead.

Michael was pale, growing paler, and coughed as though that would expel the poison. He was weak and she put an arm around him to steady him. He opened his mouth to speak, but she led him toward the car and shushed him.

"Don't. Whatever it is can wait," she said, helping him lean on the roof of her sedan, hoping the blood he smeared across the white paint could be washed off.

A noise alerted them to the direction von Slacher had fallen. The old man was rising again, and changing, a snarl on his lips. "Fucking silver," he growled, his change slow and methodical. "You fucking shot me with silver." Blood dumped from his open maw. "I will kill you." He stumbled a bit, caught himself, then lurched toward them. With every step, the wolf seemed surer.

"We better run," Michael managed, and just like that, they were in the car. As he was closest, John Kelly got behind the wheel, and Maddy and Dart climbed in the backseat as Michael fell into the passenger side. Maddy handed her brother the key and he turned it, grinding the engine then shifting roughly to drive. The car lurched forward just as von Slacher lunged, barely missing the bumper. John Kelly cut the wheel and stomped on the gas, and the car skidded out of position and sped down the road, tires crunching over the remnants of the statue. Madeline watched out the back window. Von Slacher galloped on all fours. The motor whirred and the car jolted, John Kelly mumbling a curse. Dart scrambled for purchase as the car shifted to one side and Von Slacher flew past them into the side of the mercantile store. Brick shattered and a cloud of dust rose from the collision, but even as John Kelly righted the car, Von Slacher was shaking off the impact and galloping toward them again. He was gaining on them.

"Where are we going to go?" Michael asked.

"I got a place," John Kelly said, and they sped on.

⚭

Despite the night swallowing von Slacher, they knew he was still out there, chasing them.

"Where is he?" John Kelly asked.

Maddy searched for any sign of movement outside. "I don't—"

"I can smell him," Michael said.

They could feel him. They had no real plan to stop him, and the only plan they'd half-concocted had failed spectacularly. This retreat—Maddy had no illusions as to where they were headed—only solidified this belief. Not only was he still out there, but he would catch them, and he would kill them.

Designated parking for the lumberyard existed as a gravel- and woodchip-covered clearing amidst a coppice of pine. The lumberyard itself could then be reached by traversing a short path slightly uphill through those trees, positioned in another clearing. If John Kelly could have, he would have driven them right to his cabin's door on the other side of the lumber mill, but the car—compact as it was— was too wide to navigate the grove, and the pine would not yield to it.

Parking, he said, "We'll have to walk from here."

"What's the plan?" Maddy asked.

"We hoof it to the cabin," John Kelly said, looking around. To drive, he'd handed the rifle to Michael to hold, but took it back now as he examined the surroundings. Maddy wasn't sure what he was looking at. Outside the windows, it was dark and still. Maddy looked down to the door lock. Dart turned in seat nervously, whimpering a little.

"We can't…" her voice faltered.

"We can't stay in here," Michael managed. "He'll kill us."

"He'll kill us out there," she said.

"We got options," John Kelly said. "Out there. I can shoot him. We can run. We can blockade the cabin—"

"—if we make it," Maddy added.

"If I try and shoot the rifle in here," her brother continued, "I'll probably hit one of you."

Without ceremony, without pause for more discussion, her brother's mind made up, Maddy heard the click of the door locks and watched John Kelly and Michael open their doors, and so after a quick consolatory rub between Dart's ears, she and the dog exited also.

The air was cold. Maddy felt the wind prickle her arms, and for a split second she wished she'd dressed a little warmer. Dart sprinted around, sniffing the air and staring into the darkness. Very little moonlight or starlight made their way through the trees even though the fog had lifted. The curtain of blackness revealed only the nearest pines, the nearest objects, and gave the illusion of desolation surrounding them. But this forest was far from empty.

Her ears strained for any sound other than those they produced. Each footfall on the dry pine needles screamed their location, but the night would not reveal to them anything else. Perhaps, she started to allow herself to think, but no, von Slacher was here. Couldn't she smell him also? It was probably just fear or her imagination, but she thought she could. Her eyes scanned the darkness continuously, dry from staring and her will not to blink out of fear of missing something important or crucial. Lifesaving. They moved through the pine,

John in the lead with a flashlight he'd drawn out of the glovebox to illuminate their path, then Michael, barely clothed save for an old blanket she'd had in the trunk of the car, and finally her, staying close enough in formation to keep even her brother in sight. Dart, unleashed, walked beside them, then sprinted into the darkness with a huff, then returned to walk beside another of their troupe for a short while before sprinting off again.

When they were kids, their parents always took them to Little Rock for back-to-school shopping. Back then it had always been John Kelly, bored with the car ride, who asked how much further. But she found herself thinking this, fearing with each step that they were being drawn more out into the open and they were becoming more exposed for the kill.

The hill they ascended had been so gradual Maddy had barely noticed, not until the car alarm fired off behind her and she and the others spun to see, down below and through the pines, the flashing of headlights and the whomping of the horn, then the lights jostling in the night as something heavy smashed into the vehicle. Metal ripped like thin paper, a screeching sound in the dead of night. Michael didn't need to say what he said next, and Maddy could have done without it, because she already knew it.

"He's here."

They broke into a run.

From behind, the soft pad of paws on the dead dry needles were cracking and crackling, growing ever closer. They heard the sound of breathing, of huffs of breath firing in asthmatic spurts through the nostrils, the low growl issuing like a death whistle between the jagged teeth. Just a hint of blood on the tongue flying out as loose spittle to give the air she breathed something electric and deadly. Dart stayed with her, but looked back, and Maddy barked, "No," several times to keep the dog's attention on her. He would, in all his canine bravado, turn to protect his human family, but he would not stand a chance against that creature.

Cresting the hill, she nearly ran smack dab into the lumbermill's main shed. Or, more specifically, one of the poles holding up the tin roof. The mill itself had no walls, just the roof to cover the gigantic saw that, with the angle of the moon and the elevation of the mill, glinted in the soft white light. She could make out the feeder belt, the stacks of processed and uncut lumber, smaller saws all around. John Kelly had stopped at the other side, looking down another slight slope to another clearing and a collection of cabins. Michael unabashedly dropped the blanket, grabbed at his own elbows, and shivered. Now he only wore the medallion around his neck. His body, pale in the moonlight and stringy-skinny, nearly glowed against the pitch silhouette of the necklace.

"We won't make it to the cabin," Maddy said, her eyes darting around for any sign of the wolf.

"I know," John Kelly said.

"You might," Michael said. His hands raised to the charm hanging around his neck. Splotches of red tattooed his pale, moonlit flesh, but all his wounds were healed. There was nothing sexual in the way he stood, revealed and opened, under the moonlight. His penis hung small and limp, a piece of flaccid flesh between his legs shriveled in the cold night. "I can buy you time."

"You can't take him," John Kelly said.

"I think I can," Michael replied. "And if I'm right, and he doesn't kill me, then I want you to."

"Michael!" Maddy protested, but he was shaking his head.

"This has to stop. I can't go on like this, afraid I'm going to hurt more people. People I love. I need to know you'll do it."

"I'll do it," John Kelly said.

Maddy bit her lip, pet Dart who looked between the humans with bright, glowing eyes, then finally nodded.

"Go," Michael said then. "Get in the cabin. And stay there."

And he took off the charm.

CR80

The moon called to him. The charm, with what was left of the wolfsbane coursing through his system, had kept him human, but casting off these trinkets and potions like detritus, he changed, and changed quickly. His form grew more muscular. His jawbone popped and snapped as the muzzle grew out of his face. Hair sprouted like weedy creeping moss to overtake his body. He howled triumphantly, rearing back on his legs, arms splayed and claws glinting the moonlight, head tilted up to the sky to the chorus of night. Dart's hackles raised, but he did not growl. Nor did he disobey when Maddy tugged his collar but ran along with his master and mistress as they bolted down the hill. The wolf that had been Michael Risten did not give chase. Rather, it peered through the dark, scanning for the other one. It could smell the other. The old one. It smelled of age and earth and rancidness. It should have died a long time ago, but it had persisted. It would die tonight. Movement to the left, from the direction they'd run, and the wolf that had been Michael Risten turned its gaze as a massive form leapt under the roof of the lumber mill. Its claws were bared and its teeth shined pink and white and a growl hummed off its tongue, but this time, Michael Risten was ready.

CR80

The cabin door wouldn't budge. John Kelly tried the key again, but the knob would barely turn. Maddy was right as his shoulder, pushing in, smothering him, restricting his movements. "Hurry," she said, but he could tell she was looking back up the hill, and he refused to.

"Give me some room," he snapped. Dart was now pressed against his calves, his body shivering in contrast to the growl rising out of him, trilling through his tongue.

He heard the lock give, turned the knob, and pushed. The door gave way to darkness and the three fell inside. The lights came on as John slammed the door closed and refastened not just the key lock but also the deadbolt. When he turned, he saw Maddy had found the light switch, and he saw the terror on his sister's face.

The cabin seemed strangely silent, oblivious to the sounds from outside and up the hill, a sanctuary that refused to allow the violence.

Maddy whispered something and John, after a quick glance out the window (*We should barricade that*, he thought), crossed the room to his sister and knelt. "What?" he asked. It came out gruffer than he intended.

"We could have just gone home."

Her head had been lowered, her long curly hair obscuring her face, but when she said this she raised her wide, red-rimmed eyes to him, showing him all the fear she held inside.

"He knows where we live, remember. I didn't think I could protect us there."

"So you brought us here?" She stood, pushing her way past him, punching his shoulder with a fist then began to pace. "Here!?" she turned, flashing only anger at him. "The middle of nowhere. He's going to kill Michael and he's going to kill us next, and no one will find us, and…" Her voice trailed and her shoulders slumped and she relaxed her fists, releasing it all, and she was crying, so he stood and wrapped his arms around her and pulled her to him.

"We're going to make it," he said between shushes like their mother used to offer them when they woke from nightmares. A strange sound issued up then. Laughter. John Kelly pulled away and held his sister by her shoulders. "What?"

"I accused you of being indecisive, and now look at us."

"Yeah," he agreed. "I ain't e-quit-vacatin' now, am I?"

This made her laugh harder. "Equivocate, you illiterate shit."

He laughed too. A glance down at the dog showed only a bemused face. Dart looked at them, undoubtedly wondering what was so funny.

"Listen," he said once the brief moment passed, "I got an idea. You and Dart stay here. Barricade the window. I'm gone take the rifle and head up the hill and turn on the saws. I think I can distract them, and maybe even that von Slacher cat just long enough to hit him with another silver bullet. Get his ass caught in one of those saws, it'll suck him in. Won't matter if it's silver or not. Those blades will chop him into kibble."

Maddy wiped at the tears at the corners of her eyes and uttered another little laugh. "That is the worst fucking idea I think I've ever heard," she said.

He smiled. "Would you expect anything else from me?"

She shook her head. "You can't, John."

He pulled away, turned and snatched up the rifle from where he'd placed it, propped on the wall against the door. "Ain't got no choice," he said, though that wasn't necessarily true. He unlocked the door and returned to the night.

Behind him the door latched and the locks clicked home. John Kelly cradled his rifle and looked up the hill to the tin-roofed mill. The wolves were still up there. It was too dark to see them, but he could hear them. Their snarls and growls, hear them as they smashed into things. How the mill was still standing he wasn't sure. One post giving way would send the whole thing down and bury them in the saws and wood and rubble. Both of them. Gripping the rifle tightly, he crept off the cabin porch and started up the hill.

CRX80

She still thought they should have just gone home. Her brother's choice seemed less logical and more driven by a need to prove himself. *See*, he was telling her, he could make a decision. And now, she thought dismally, his incessant need to prove himself right, or more importantly to prove her wrong, was going to get them both killed.

Dart was pacing, the metal tags on his collar rattling like chains with each step. This made him sound tough, but there was the slightest whimper, and the unsettled look in his eye. Kneeling, she called him over, then ran her fingers through his fur and wrapped her arms around him. The dog panted but didn't pull away, and while this seemed to calm them both in the past—she'd come to understand how people could rely on these animals for emotional support—their embrace did little to comfort each other now. She closed her eyes and breathed in the dog's smell, praying silently for all the violence outside to go away.

And that was when the window exploded inwardly, raining glass shards and beads all over them, and something heavy and dark thudded against the far wall.

CRX80

The wolves had been alerted to John Kelly's presence before he was even halfway up the hill. He caught the gleam of one of their eyes, glowing much the same way a dog's do in the night light, then heard a snarl. He drew a bead with the rifle but hadn't secured the butt against his shoulder when he pulled the trigger. The gun kicked, knocking him to his ass, sure to leave a large purple bruise from his right shoulder, down across his armpit and around his ribs, as that side of his body exploded with pain. From above he heard a whimper and then he saw them, a tumbling mass of dark fur rolling and snarling and snapping and growling, falling like a tumbleweed down the hill toward him. He grabbed the rifle and rolled out of the way as the beasts tumbled past him. His head struck a half buried rock as he landed on his side. John Kelly saw silver flashes before his vision went dark and his eyes closed. The fall overcame them and whatever hold they had on each other loosened, and they rolled apart, one crumbling into a heap while the other, breathing so hard its whole body rocked, stood shakily.

It steadied itself as the other struggled to gain its footing, and it approached the other wolf like a triumphant warrior, standing upright. It reached down with its massive arms and hoisted the other above its head, and let loose a victorious growl, then hurled the body through the cabin's window. Cutting short its cry for another breath that nearly doubled it over, the wolf regained itself, lifted its eyes and muzzle to the sky, and opened its yawning maw in a victorious dirge.

CRESO

The howl that crashed over them froze Madeline and Dart. Dart, transfixed by the sound, stiffened, staring over her shoulder into the darkness. The sound vibrated into her skull. It was awful in its volume, its joy in victory, its fullness. She feared only when the sound would stop, and the triumphant beast would leap through the window and finish her off.

The crumpled dark mass straightened, stretched, and lifted its head. Did its eyes recognize her, or was she just imagining it? She knew almost instantly that it was Michael. She felt pity for him then, in this cabin, more than fear. The way he looked at her seemed jealous, as if he longed to be stroked and held the way she stroked and held Dart. As if just her caress would exorcize his ghosts. Those ghosts she now imagined she saw, gathered around them, as from behind, the other wolf climbed across the sill and entered the cabin.

"Come on then," Maddy whispered, holding Dart, needing Dart to stay with her. "Why don't you just attack me. Get it over with." She looked over her shoulder. Von Slacher was changing back, and already looked more human. "You see them, don't you? The ghosts of the victims. The ghosts of Michael's victims."

"My dear lady, I see the ghost of each victim killed by every wolf over the years. They outnumber the pines in this forest."

"They won't stop until it's all over," Maddy said.

"At some point, they'll stop," he said, and sounded almost as if he believed this.

"They'll never stop," she cried. Around them, more shapes, more shadows. They were legion in their darkness, and they were all here for von Slacher. "They'll never stop until you're dead, and if there is a God above, not even then. They'll follow you to hell."

"My dear, this *is* hell. I have become the mask I wear, and they will not let me forget it."

"Good," she said, and closed her eyes, squeezing the dog tight with one hand while   reaching the other, weak and trembling, up in defiance.

She heard it then. The growl rising like ground fog up her spine, the nape of her neck, and swore she could feel its hot canine breath on her neck.

The shadows pressed in as if to protect her, but it was Michael who rose, lunging from his perch, an arm extended and claws glinting in the light, slicing first through flesh, then vein and muscle, and finally, yes, even through bone. A spray of blood arced through the air as von Slacher reached with both hands to try and dam the blood loss, as it spilled through his fingers and down his chest, permitting only impotent gurgling from his frothy mouth, his eyes staring but blank. Maddy saw it all in slow motion, just as she saw Michael's ears perk and shift, and his eyes widen. He stretched both hands and pushed her and Dart. From behind von Slacher, an explosion ripped open the old man's chest. Flesh and blood spraying out, organs instantly liquified and spewing tissue and shards of bone over the cabin. Von Slacher fell forward, his face smashing into the floor. The blood pooled underneath him. Michael was knocked back against the wall, and the cabin shook from the collision.

C≈ED

Around them, the shadows faded until nothing but the cabin remained. She'd rolled out of the way at the sound of the explosion, a desperate attempt to fly from the danger, dragging Dart with her. He had pulled away but still stood near, surveying the scene and alert even as she got her bearings. The handgun lay halfway between her and Michael, just a finger's breadth away from von Slacher's outstretched hand.

Oh God, she thought. *Let him be dead.* She stood. Michael lay sprawled, keeping his eyes on her. He watched her, much as an animal sedate and curious what its master's next move would be. Two steps. Maybe three to the gun. She crossed the floor and picked it up, jumping back as she did so in case von Slacher was still alive, and when he didn't move, she admonished herself. There was too much blood for him to still be alive.

She retreated a few steps and unlocked the door. John Kelly didn't take long to enter, cradling the rifle. Dart approached and stood between them, and all three looked at Michael. His eyes on them, he was silent for a moment longer, still also until he forced himself to rise to four legs. He huffed and shook as if he were drying off after a bath, then turned his gaze up to them again. She could not be certain if he recognized them now, but she remembered her promise, reluctant as it had been. Even as she raised the handgun and leveled the sight, the wolf, watching her, did not growl. It made neither an attempt to retreat nor to attack.

Her hand shook, and Madeline swallowed hard. There were many things she could say in the moment, but her words failed her, so she simply pulled the trigger. Her aim was true, and Michael collapsed, his eyes closing, and soon what lay before them was not a beast, but the scrawny white kid they'd grown up with and loved.

CHAPTER TWENTY-ONE

For a long time after, the nothingness when she slept was jolted by any one of a variety of nightmares that involved the idea that not all of them had died. Maddy awoke on those nightmare nights just as sweaty and shivering as on the nights when there was nothing, and the silence and peace of her house unsettled her. Something like several months bled together, and peace seemed elusive, extinct in fact. Madeline, resigned to this, would wake and fix herself some tea, or some hot chocolate, or even some coffee, and force a reminder that all of it was done. Her days were spent conversing with graduate programs, preparing for the possibility that she'd be accepted into one, knowing the workload that would come with it, never allowing herself to think she wouldn't get in. She did get accepted, in fact, to a school in Chicago the following fall. The winter she spent in their house, talking with state police who looked at her and her brother with suspicion, given that nearly everyone else in the town was dead.

Never mind she herself had called the police, after they'd carted Michael's body back to his family farm, burying him in the garden with the amulet around his neck and wolfsbane crammed down his throat. When she really needed a reminder, she drove out to the farm and watched as the dirt settled by degrees until his grave stood truly unmarked, and what remained of him existed rotting somewhere deep in the earth.

The official story was an easy one to accept. A contagion not unlike the coronavirus sweeping the country had contaminated the people of this town, driving some insane and killing everyone with nearly one-hundred percent fatality. Not as quick to explain was how John Kelly and Madeline (or the Livingstons, who were interrogated several times up in their new residence in Monticello), weren't infected. John Kelly attributed his social distancing to his job at the logging camp, and Madeline said she'd fallen out of touch with the town since being away. This seemed to be enough. One of the state investigators, a broad-shouldered young guy out of Cabot with jet black hair and big green eyes, seemed a bit sweet on her, and she played that to her advantage to make sure they didn't try and pin anything on her or her brother. He went away and they were left alone, just as Madeline liked it.

That spring, she visited the farm regularly. Both lost in the reverie of remembrance and drowning in grief, the solace the farm brought her was as warm and tangible as a ghost, but those visits grew more and more painful, until she told John Kelly she could no longer step foot on that property.

Her brother had proved more diligent. They'd buried, before the arrival of the cops, not only Michael's body, but also the body of

Kalos von Slacher. No one needed to bother raising questions about their departed friend, so they said Michael had vanished, and they knew it would be better for everyone if von Slacher was not even known. John Kelly regularly loaded up the shotgun or rifle or a handgun and toured their gravesites, and at first this confused Madeline, not sure of what he expected to find. It was on Christmas Eve when, sitting in their living room, John Kelly provided his reasoning.

He'd taken to drinking some. Not enough to concern her, and not enough to cost his job, and in fact it was tapering off by the time he confessed to her that Yule night, but it was still more than she could remember in the past. The wind howled around the house's corners. Neither had felt like setting up a Christmas tree, but John Kelly had hung their stockings and one for Dart on the fireplace mantle, and three wrapped gifts sat on the coffee table, one for each of them. Dart's gift was shaped suspiciously like a bone, and he was already needling at it with his nose, eager to open his gift. When John Kelly let him, Dart, to his surprise, carried the bone off tucked between his teeth as if it were a secret, prized thing he would share with no one, and eyed them both suspiciously as he lay with it between his forepaws, chewing and licking at the periosteum.

"All the old werewolf movies say the same thing," John Kelly said between swigs of Old Turkey whiskey. "Larry Talbot always comes back from the dead. The curse, they say, transcends death."

He'd cited this as if it were scripture, but Maddy could think of a number of movies where the creatures stayed dead. Still, he seemed to take comfort in this mission, to find some purpose for himself, so she let him wax on this like a scholar and did not offer debate.

That night, she dreamt there was a Santa, but as he piloted his sleigh over the remains of Blue Rock, Arkansas, he looked down like

God on creation and decided what lay there was not worth stopping for.

CRSO

Not long after her last visit to the farm, before the weather truly warmed and the spring had been suffuse with enough rainstorms to soak the land, Maddy and Dart and John Kelly ventured to Monticello on a rare clear day where the temperature barely hit seventy and ate at an outdoor café with Duke and Amelia Livingston. The mood was reflective; the group sat about, saying little at first but the superficial: what insurance covered, what the state was paying out, what the next plans were. This all felt perfunctory to Maddy. Even Dart seemed bored. His muzzle on Maddy's shoe, he thumped his tail on the wrought-iron table legs sporadically once he learned they made a hollow, booming sound. When that didn't get them moving, he added huffs that managed to sound derisive.

"I killed the deputy," Amelia said at once, breaking one of the silences that had, for Maddy, nearly allowed them to segue into goodbyes.

Duke glanced around to see if anyone at the nearby tables reacted, but no one seemed to. Still, to be safe, he leaned back and boomed, singing the reverse of the lyric, "but I did not shoot the sheriff! I shot the deputy, but I did not shoot the sheriff-ey."

Amelia slapped at him, more playful than angry. Maddy smiled at that small act of love. John Kelly found Duke's reaction amusing and guffawed unabashedly, even standing and dancing in place, raising his voice. When Maddy glanced down at Dart, she found the dog looking back up at her, and she honestly wasn't sure which of them was more embarrassed. Still, John Kelly did force a smile to her lips, and she laughed at herself for laughing at him.

"What happened?" Maddy asked. Her thumb on the glass of her iced tea smeared slug tracks across the condensation.

Amelia took her husband's hand in both her own and scrunched her face to dam the tears, took a deep breath and held it for a second, before exhaling coolly, pursing her ruby-red and waxy lips. Her eyelids fluttered, the last sentry against those predatory thoughts.

"I thank Jesus he di'nt see me, is all I can say," she said finally. "Lord Jesus, yessuh. I don't know why he took after you and yo' brother," she said, looking at Duke and kissing his hand.

"I love you, baby," he said, getting a bit teary-eyed. Damn them, Maddy thought, wiping at her own eyes. Now it appeared John Kelly and Dart exchanged a glance. *Dumb dog is a real Benedict Arnold.*

"Anyway," Amelia went on, using a handkerchief from her purse to dot the tears away from her eyes. "He'd had this recent scuffle, we think, with Emily Evan's grandson—"

"Oh, we know it," Duke interrupted, wide-eyed, leaning across the table. "We saw him leap thirty feet across the room and nearly ten feet high! Brotha' flew out that muthafuckin' window all up with claws and hairy and shit."

"Things were overturned," Amelia continued. "Including the weapon's closet. All broken open. I saw that gun and I found the shells and I thought that it oughtta work. So I took it and I followed them all out. I knew just where Duke and Rayburn would go, so I followed."

Now she began to cry, and couldn't stop the tears, and wiped furiously at her eyes so that her makeup smeared. Duke wrapped his arms around his wife and pulled her near. The empathetic Dart raised his head and whined.

"Oh, Duke, if I hadn't been so scared. I would've walked faster. I could've, for sho'. But I was so scared I could barely hold that gun.

But if I had've walked just a bit faster, perhaps Rayburn... oh dear Lord..."

She raised her fingertips to her lips and choked back the rest.

"Oh..." Duke said, understanding washing over his face. "Oh no. My dear, oh no. Don't think like that. This weren't on you."

"Oh, Duke, I'm so sorry."

"Oh, my sweet baby," he said, pulling her in. Together they calmed each other, and then looked at Madeline as if challenging her to top that.

"I have dreams," she said. "Some nights. Not all of them. Nightmares, really. Realistic, if you can call them that. Alternative versions of reality."

All eyes were on her, and all mouths were silent. "Michael is alive in them. Last night he was just sitting on our loveseat, in the dream. I walked in from walking Dart and there he was, naked and covered in dirt and wearing that goddamn medallion and he just smiled at me and said, 'I know dogs have to get their shots but that was ridiculous,' as blood is pouring out of the hole in his forehead from where I shot him. He is, of course, partly covered in fur and his jaw has somewhat stretched to a muzzle and he has more prominent canines, but I know it's Michael because it has his eyes and I was the last thing those eyes saw before I planted that bullet between them."

"Sis?"

Madeline shook her head. "He's alive in every fucking dream I have. And that's why I've been going out to that farm. To make sure it's just in the dreams."

"I scared ya with that, din't I?" John Kelly said. "When I talked about the OG werewolf movie."

Again she shook her head. "You didn't do this. In the dreams, it's so real. I can't..."

"We understand," Duke Livingston said, reaching across the table. Amelia followed suit, and Maddy held both their hands. "You don't need to blame yourself no more than Amelia was just doing."

"It's just that, it is what *he* wanted. He begged me to do it. He wanted it."

"And if he did?" Duke asked. "Tell me how that's a bad thing? He wanted it? Good."

"How can you say that?" Amelia asked him, pulling away.

"Wasn't he the cause of all this? I mean, we all know what happened with his family way back when."

"It goes back further," Madeline said, and John Kelly cleared his throat as if that were inconspicuous.

"What?" Duke asked.

Maddy shot a glance to her brother. "It goes back generations. The original family name was Ristenoff." She steepled her hands with elbows propped on the table and considered her interlaced fingers. "We learned this through research. Michael was as much a victim of circumstance as any of us."

To this they all hung their heads in a moment of silence, and now the segue to closure and an exit seemed more natural. Maddy stood. Then Amelia. Then Duke. And then, because he liked to make a production, John Kelly, scooting the chair back so loudly that Dart jumped and banged his head on the glass tabletop.

They shook and smiled and agreed to keep up, never intending to fulfill that agreement. As they walked away, Maddy sighed heavily. In the car, she listened to the engine rev. The rain moved in then, fat drops splatting over the car's windshield and smacking lackadaisically at its sides. John Kelly's Spotify was set on a jazz list. He pulled into traffic and steered them south.

CRUID

The morning she was to leave for Chicago, Maddy awoke nervous, unable to shake this feeling that she'd been watched in the night. She asked John Kelly to check on the burial sites. He did so dutifully as she packed and returned to say all was as they'd left it. Maddy hugged her brother and loved on Dart, accepting kisses, promising to text or call when she made it to her friend's apartment in the city. John Kelly offered bits of advice on finding the right apartment and told her he could come up and haggle if she didn't feel able, and she told him to quit mansplaining and they shared a laugh.

Time passed quickly once she was settled in the Windy City. Her responsibilities kept her mind occupied so she didn't dwell on the recent past, but it was still there, lingering like a ghost in the closet. Relegated to nightmares and isolated moments, the past whispered to her. People who knew her in Chicago said she was a bit sad, sometimes seemed like she was off in another world. Competitors thought her cold and distant. Friends wondered at the tragedy that had befallen her, as she remained tight-lipped with her newest relationships. She never talked about where she was from (although they all knew Arkansas), never talked about family or old friends or her life BC (Before Chicago). She focused on work and school, on the wellbeing of her friends and their concerns, always taking on their drama but never providing her own, something that her roommate told her once, as nicely as possible, seemed in some ways selfish.

John Kelly visited that following winter, bringing Dart to live with her, once the roommate was on board (luckily she was a dog person and fell in love with Dart upon meeting him). Maddy didn't mind, but thought Dart might enjoy the travel even though John Kelly thought the displacement would be too much for the dog. Two things struck her immediately. That her brother wouldn't look her in the eye meant he was cagey about something, and historically that meant he had news he didn't want to share. That first night, when her roommate went to spend time with her boyfriend, the siblings talked openly while drinking wine and eating pizza.

"People are moving back in, Maddy," John Kelly said. "We got a pretty penny for our place." They had, more than it was worth, she thought, but it was just a sign that people rallied against death in all its forms only as long as such rallying served them. By rights, Blue Rock should die, but gentrifiers and fools who hung on to the past would not let it. A logging camp was renovating the downtown to secure their offices and make room for their trucking operation, and the houses were bought up not just for the executives, but also for the loggers. Blue Rock's name had even survived as the name for this newly formed organization, born out of ArkMo Lumber Associates and B&J Trucking—the new conglomeration was called Blue Rock Lumber and Shipping.

"They offered a honey of a deal," she agreed.

John Kelly shook his head. "That check should do you for a time," he said, and she thanked him again for splitting the sale of the home with her. "I can't stay down there," he said after a moment of silence, as if she'd suggested he do just that.

"Where you gone go?" she asked. She hadn't used the Southern accent in a while, but found she slipped back into it comfortably enough with John Kelly around and no one from Chicago to hear.

He shrugged, slurped up his slice of pizza. "Canada, maybe." She tried to catch his eyes with her gaze, but he refused to play tag.

"What is it?" she asked finally. "You been cagey since you been here. What's going on?"

"I just… things don't feel finished," he said finally, but when she tried to press him for an explanation, he just shook his head and said he didn't know what he meant. The rest of their visit went smoothly if not a bit coolly.

∞

The spring evening was cool, bringing a pelting rain and light thunder rumbling across the area. The bay window in her apartment shook as she unhooked the leash from Dart's collar, and the dog gave a shake before jumping up to his spot on the couch.

"Water," she commanded, but he just panted at her, then rolled on his back a little, huffing at her. It was his way of saying, *Pet my belly and come snuggle, now that we got my walk in*, and Maddy laughed.

In the bathroom, as she undressed for the shower, she could hear him lapping at the bowl of water eagerly. She hurried under the faucet, ready for some quiet time with the dog. Her roommate had been spending more and more time with her boyfriend (now fiancé) and less time at home, so Maddy was positive she'd have a peaceful evening. Dressed only in her robe, she padded out to the living room and hugged Dart again before snatching her laptop off its charger and plopping down on the couch.

Several emails filled her inbox, but none from John Kelly. It had been over a week since he'd last reached out to her. Even then it was a brief update on his job at the logging camp and asking how she and Dart were doing.

Maddy opened the recent draft of a paper due in a week when her cell rang, and seeing it was her brother, she closed the laptop and answered.

"I was right," he said, before she barely got out her hello. "Shit ain't…" but he broke off, as if he'd lost his train of thought.

"John!" She heard the panic between the words. The way his breath hitched. The way the words were clipped. He was on edge.

"I been checking them," he said. "You know, making sure all is still okay. And all is. Byron is buried and so is Derek and Aaron goddamn Bailey, and of course that old dude, von Slacher, but…"

"What is it?" she asked. Her heartbeat was increasing and her palms felt sweaty.

Dart had been sleeping beside her on his side, but as she stood and began to pace, the dog woke and glared at her. Outside, just above the Willis Tower in the distance, she could see the nearly full moon hanging over the city and the hint of just a couple of stars as the clouds retreated.

"His grave," John Kelly spit out finally. "It's empty."

"What do you mean?" This question was more a reaction than a curiosity. She knew what he meant. Her darkest nightmares had been about this very thing.

"The curse won't let him stay dead. Goddamn charm was there, but there was a big hole where we buried him."

Dart growled, his ears flattening to his head, staring not at her but at the door, just as there came a knock.

Maddy turned to the door, fear washing over. "Who?" she muttered. She knew who. She needed her brother to say it. At the door there came another knock, more deliberate, forceful.

"Michael," he said.

The knock at the door persisted.

The End

ACKNOWLEDGMENTS

When I was in fifth grade, we lived in Nacogdoches, Texas. My dad was going back to school for his Psychology degree at Stephen F. Austin State University after the briefest stints in the Army as a medic. The year was 1987 and, at ten years old, I was falling in love with comic books and horror.

I didn't get to see *Ghostbusters* when it first came out, but I'd seen it on TV and rented it numerous times by this point. I'd caught *Fright Night* and *American Werewolf in London* on TV too. In the theaters, I'd gone to see Return to Oz and Transylvania 6-5000 at 8 years old, Labyrinth at 9, and I'd watched the *Dark Crystal* on television along with the *Secret of NIMH*. I'd been a fan of *Star Wars* from the earliest of ages and comedies as well. *Young Frankenstein, Gremlins* – I can still remember the local theater showing the old Universal Classics on Halloween.

I bought all the standard bearers for comics: Batman, Spider-man, Superman, Captain America, X-Men. There was a really cool used comic shop in town and I nabbed first appearances of the Scorpion, the Brotherhood of Mutants, and the first time Venom appeared and Spidey had the black suit. But they also had Tales from the Crypt, The Witch's Cauldron, and the Vault of Fear. Not the originals, mind you, (though I spent countless hours drooling over their copy of Amazing Fantasy #15 in its cellophane sleeve), but EC reprints. A few years later, when the HBO show came out based on those horror comics, I watched it religiously. I also got into Spawn, as well as the darker comics brought to you by Marvel and DC: Constantine, Dr. Strange, Man-Thing, Swamp Thing, Blade. I was introduced to Elfquest and Lone Wolf and Cub and this became my artistic zeitgeist.

The earliest iterations of what would become RISTENOFF began then. I imagined a man sitting in jail, waiting for the next full moon. I set the story in East Texas and in South Arkansas pine lands and in the North Central Ozarks. Characters like Michael, John, Madeline, Angelique, Byron Calhoun, Casey Davidson, Aaron Bailey, and Derek Evans began to form in my mind, with their names attached (though Michael wouldn't get the surname Risten until years later), but I always knew he'd be the werewolf. I imagined names like Basil and Bela Motos, and Kalos Von Slacher. Perhaps some cinephile or media-savvy historian can tell me the origins of those names. As far as I know, they popped in my head fully formed. The name RISTENOFF came to me then as well, though I attributed it to a vampire story I wanted to tell, for I'd just gone with either an uncle, a cousin, or my dad, to see The Lost Boys. The original werewolf story I scribed out putting pen to a yellow legal pad.

It's funny what you remember. Some of this I haven't thought about in years, and yet as I trigger the memories, scents and smells return. The heavily-buttered popcorn at the one-screen theater that showed movies just out of main cinemas but not yet available for rent for a buck a ticket. And while I associate these movies and these comics with that time period, including Tim Burton's BATMAN (which would come two years later, but while we still lived in Nacogdoches), I know logically that it didn't all happen at once. Comics were purchased with allowance money earned on different weeks, and movies were seen at or shortly after their release in the main theater. Except, now, almost forty years later, it is easy to say it did happen at once. Or, at least it's okay that it felt like it did.

The amount of time we live from fifth to eighth grade feels greater than the seasons and months and weeks and days and hours that pass in our forties. The world is no longer new in our forties, but it is still new to us as kids. As kids, still trying to figure out what this place is about, trying to figure out how to make friends when you're the new kid in school and how not to be weird and how not to be an asshole to kids less fortunate or more picked on than you, every day that passes in those few short years that make up kiddom both run together once we're older and seem to last forever when we're living them. Even looking back on it, knowing that those ages between 8-18 are only a decade, and I've lived four times as long, no other decade is as pronounced, as informative, as impactful as those years. It is here where Ristenoff was born. Here where the characters took shape and grew. And for years, here where they slept.

Or *percolated*. As a coffee enthusiast (black with creamer, nothing fancy, because I had fancy coffee in Italy once and nothing Starbucks has to offer comes close to what Italian baristas can conjure up), I love that word. It reminds me of the test tubes and chemistry sets in Dr. Frankenstein's laboratory. That's what the characters were doing all that time. Percolating. Waiting for me to give them life.

As I entered college and started working on short stories and reading literature, the characters were there. I read *Frankenstein* and *Dracula*, and Shakespeare and William Goldman and Thomas Pynchon and James Joyce and the Brontë sisters and everything you are supposed to read. Through all of this, the characters were there. When I started my MFA program, I chose a different subject for my creative thesis. One might argue magnanimously that Michael and the werewolves and the gang just weren't ready yet. One would be wrong, of course. Either I had grown tired of them, or thought myself too *old* for them, or perhaps I thought their time had passed.

Another decade or so passed. I worked on short stories and taught creative writing. The characters were still there, but now they were in the back of my mind. Not gone, just old friends I'd not checked in on for a while. Michael and the gang kept waving, kept saying, we're here. "Hey, Jeremy, we're right here. Hey, old buddy."

I revisited them several times, of course. But nothing kickstarted me to want to tell their story. Instead, I thought about a guy who entered a cave that led directly to Hell and how the celts thought Samhain meant the line between the physical and spiritual worlds thinned at its start for several months. Instead, I thought about a schizophrenic who might actually see and hear the dead and an homage to my favorite show: The X-Files. I thought about a twisted fairy tale where a princess must rescue her prince from a monster (a ghoul) in a cursed town. I thought about a million half short stories and published only a fraction of that. I thought about grading policies and senate obligations and semester meetings.

Then one day we were told not to go to work. A pandemic swept across the globe. Bodies in major cities were being crammed into freezer trucks because the morgues ran out of room. Hospitals overflowed. Gas prices rose because no one was venturing out. Civil unrest exploded. People were wearing their masks to protest injustices and corruption. Racism and hate stood full and strong ready to push them down. The world felt like it was burning and, in some cities, it was. I'd spent years trying to walk two disparate ideologies in my own writing, not realizing that horror and the Southern gothic were the same sides of two different coins. I worked through Under the Churchyard in the Chamber of Bone as solace for recent losses in my life, I grew Sley House, and I heard the call of the wolf. Now it was time for the werewolf story. Now it was time for Michael (his last name should be Risten, a derivation of his ancient Eastern European surname) and the werewolves to come out. Under the bright autumn moon over South Arkansas, amidst a pandemic and global unrest, it was time. For Ristenoff...

So I guess if I'm going to acknowledge anyone for this story, I have to first revisit my wife and son and dog, as they are more a true pack to me than any of the werewolves turned by Michael in the course of this story. But I can't forget my childhood and those five or six years in Nacogdoches, Texas, where I explored my love of horror and comics, either. And I should also thank Sley House's own Lillian Ehrhart for her editing skills, and for KA Hough for giving it another read through. Asra, for bringing the image of the werewolf to life with his cover and interior illustrations. You know, from the Wolfman to Jack Nicholson's Wolf to the American werewolf that terrorized London, to every version in between, there have been so many types of werewolves out there, but I've always known what Michael's werewolf looked like. Wolf's head, fur-covered human form, a creature looming over us on two legs with great sharp claws at the end of its human-like hands.

I guess I should thank Michael and Madeline, John Kelly, and the rest of the cast, for not letting me give up on them. This has been the story I've wanted to tell all my life, or, more to the point, this has been the story they have wanted me to tell all my life. I am so thankful to this cast of characters for hounding me until I got it told.

ABOUT THE AUTHOR

J.R. BILLINGSLEY has been publishing short fiction for nearly two decades. His MFA allows him to teach, but he considers himself a writer first and foremost. When the two publishers who picked up his first novel both closed their doors, he had the bright (and somewhat naïve) idea of starting his own publishing house. Since then, Sley House has put out anthologies, novels, radio dramas, collections, and continues to grow. He lives with his wife, son, and their yellow Lab, Shadow in Northwest Arkansas.

ALSO FROM SLEY HOUSE

NOVELS

A Mind Full of Scorpions
(Eyes Only, Book One)
JR Billingsley

Ground Control
K.A. Hough

Bad Form
Joe Taylor

Persephone's Escalator
Joe Taylor

The Cartography Door
Sean Edward

Black Echoes
JB McLaurin

Under the Churchyard in
the Chamber of Bone
JR Billingsley

ANTHOLOGIES

 *Tales of Sley House 2021*

Tales of Sley House 2022

 *Tales of Sley House 2023*

Tales of the Sley Siblings

STORY COLLECTIONS

 *Melpomene's Garden*
Curtis Harrell

Observations and Nightmares:
The Short Fiction of JR Billingsley
JR Billingsley

See more at https://www.sleyhouse.com

CONTENT WARNINGS

Acts of bigotry and racism

Sexual violence/abuse

Depictions of grief and loss

Blood and Gore

Depictions of self-harm and suicide